Simply Irresistible . . .

A pang of yearning, deep and primeval, pierced his heart. Nigel had no defense but his own self-derision. The enchanting Miss Woodard was very plainly English: the hair of deep honey, dusted with gold; the skin far whiter than his own; the furious eyes, though outlined in dark lashes, stunningly blue. But she was more than beautiful, she was exquisite—with something entirely exotic in her grooming, in the fine arching curve of her lightly oiled eyebrows, in the neat plait curving down from her nape, in the flaunting of form. Like the naked curve of her waist, everything about her spoke of a profound sensuality.

And in the fine curl of her nostril she wore a small gold stud.

The delightful shock of it flooded along his bones.

He had told her to stay away tonight, to avoid the unholy contamination of his presence. And now he saw in her eyes, beneath the rage and the courage, an overwhelming uncertainty and fear—like a virgin facing rapine. It left him uncomfortably disoriented for a moment. Dear God, had he started something that would crush her in its path?

Illusion

JEAN ROSS EWING

BERKLEY BOOKS, NEW YORK

ILLUSION

A Berkley Book / published by arrangement with
the author

PRINTING HISTORY
Berkley edition / September 1998

All rights reserved.
Copyright © 1998 by Jean Ross Ewing.
This book may not be reproduced in whole or in part,
by mimeograph or any other means, without permission.
For information address: The Berkley Publishing Group,
a member of Penguin Putnam Inc.,
375 Hudson Street, New York, New York 10014.

The Penguin Putnam World Wide Web site address is
http://www.penguinputnam.com

ISBN: 0-425-16447-0

BERKLEY®
Berkley Books are published by The Berkley Publishing Group,
a member of Penguin Putnam Inc.,
375 Hudson Street, New York, New York 10014.
BERKLEY and the "B" design
are trademarks belonging to Berkley Publishing Corporation.

PRINTED IN THE UNITED STATES OF AMERICA

10 9 8 7 6 5 4 3 2 1

Acknowledgments

THERE ARE MANY generous people to whom I owe heartfelt thanks for their help in the creation of this book. Most especially: Al, Anne, Catherine, Diana, Doug, Gemma, Isabelle, Jennifer, Jim, Laura, Laurel, Margot, Mary, and all the wonderful ladies at the library. Thank you.

My sincere gratitude is also due to my editor, Gail Fortune, and my agent, Nancy Yost, without whose wise help and encouragement it couldn't have been written.

Passionate actions cannot be defined and are as irregular as dreams.

— The Kama Sutra of Vatsyayana

Illusion

Prologue

∽

"DISCREET," SAID NIGEL, glancing around the dim hall-way. "And very definitely depraved. My favorite type of establishment."

The hefty proprietor had come up behind him, scowling. Nigel watched, amused, as the man's expression changed from belligerence to stunned recognition. "Devil take me! If it ain't your lordship!"

"The same, sir."

"Nigel Arundham, as ever was! Ain't you Lord Rivaulx now?" George wrapped his Cockney tongue around the name, flattening it into a caricature of the French vowels—*Ree-voh*.

"Such has been my misfortune, sir, in the eighteen months since my father died." Nigel smiled at him. "Marquess of Rivaulx, Earl of Derwent and Felldale, and lord of a string of smaller properties scattered from the once-debatable land of the borders to the white cliffs of the south coast: Nigel Frederick Beaumont Arundham, at your service. So when did pugilism lose its charms?"

"Damn me!" George grinned widely and spat. "So you do remember the old days! But where have you been these last four years, my lord? I'm retired now, but I'll give you a bout anytime you name it. At one time you were a handy enough lad with your fives."

Nigel handed George his hat and cane and peeled off a pair

of fine kidskin gloves. "But you don't want to try me now,"
he said dryly. "I fight dirty."

∞

Nigel walked softly into George's gaming hell. The raucous
atmosphere assaulted his senses like a battery of guns, bringing a sudden, fierce longing for the sweet air of the northern
moors. He crushed it. Dear God, surely he had long ago destroyed any desire for rustic simplicity? He pushed ruthlessly
through the crowd toward the hazard table in the corner. Several men looked up at his approach.

"Do you give us a game, Rivaulx?" asked one of them,
obviously surprised.

Nigel gave him a wink and glanced absently at a broad-
shouldered man with a cluster of red-brown curls who sat at
the table. An elaborate burst of starched linen engulfed his
chin. Donnington knew he was handsome, in a bluff, very
English way, and enjoyed showing it off. At the look of faint
derision on Nigel's face, he laid down the dice.

"Lord Rivaulx does not play," he said mockingly.

Nigel gave his quarry one of his most amiable smiles. Did
Donnington realize he had just been caught, like a fish? "Ah,
Donnington! I had no idea you were such a close observer of
my habits."

"It would be hard to ignore them, Marquess." Lord Donnington leaned back and smiled. "So elegant, yet with that
deliciously feral edge! You have a notorious enough reputation."

"Do I?" Nigel made a slight adjustment to his cuff and saw
his reflection move in the dark glass of the window. The flickering candlelight cast sinister shadows across the bones of his
cheek where they met his black hair. "Of what kind?"

"Well, I hear tales."

"Really? That I gamble, perhaps?"

Donnington colored slightly. "Hardly! You are never to be
seen at the tables. Perhaps you don't have the nerve for deep
play?"

The men around the table drew in a collective breath at the insult. "By God!" someone muttered.

Nigel deliberately let the uneasy tension build before he replied, his voice pitched to be light and humorous. "Alas, I prefer wine and women. They take a great deal of fortitude, but very little nerve." A shout of laughter rose from the other men. Nigel didn't allow his voice to change, but he gave his quarry no mercy. "Do you invite me to summon my courage and risk my purse, sir? How deep will you wager? If I am to change my habits, it had better be worth the game."

Donnington's flush deepened. "Take a seat, Rivaulx. We'll try your courage and your pockets, won't we, gentlemen?"

Nigel signaled to the waiter and ordered more wine for the table. "Then by all means, let us play hazard."

The air was thick and hot with the smoke from the candles. Burly waiters, all ex-fighters, thrust their way back and forth through the haze. The glasses that littered the table were soon refilled with an excellent claret. George understood his gentlemen. The man had once been a rare teacher of the honest English art of fisticuffs. Nigel reflected briefly on those other deadly arts, less honest and less gentlemanly, that he had learned later. Ruthlessly he buried the thoughts somewhere far out of reach and concentrated on the dice. Almost casually he began to keep track of the numbers as he assessed the table, his adversary, and the odds.

"I have lately heard talk of a new house of gloriously ill repute," he said after a moment.

"Have you, by God?" With satisfaction Donnington downed the contents of his glass. "Damned fine claret! There's no place like George's for wine and hazard."

"I am thinking rather of lechery, dissipation, and wickedness—of deep play, contraband wine, and willing women of unmentionable habits at a very private house. They say it boasts a rather unusual and tempting new mistress, shadowed in mystery and the scent of frankincense. The alluring aura of sin clings about her." Nigel paused briefly. "The place is in Sussex."

Delight surged around the table. Donnington turned puce. "What the hell is another man's mistress to you!"

The dice rolled up and gave Nigel a small loss. "As easy a conquest, to be sure, as another man's wife—and a great deal cheaper if discovered."

The men laughed openly. Donnington made an outrageously high wager on the next throw. "I thought you spoke of a brothel, sir, not a gentleman's private residence!"

"But anyone may have a party, Donnington. And with such a hostess, think of the carousal! She has been trained, they say, in the harem. No doubt she will oversee an entertainment of exotic and forbidden delight."

An onlooker leaned forward and grinned. "And how do you propose to get us all an invitation, Rivaulx?"

"I shall win one," said Nigel, "at hazard."

He collected an unseemly amount of winnings as Donnington tossed back another glass. And wished, as he wished every day of his life, that every action were not shadowed by such intense self-awareness. He did not want to be here. He did not want to get drunk. He had nothing to rely on but his wits, and he detested deliberately blurring them. But he would do it anyway. Once he was foxed, no doubt such scruples would conveniently disappear. If he was to keep his adversary's trust, he would have to match him glass for glass, and Donnington was reputed to be a six-bottle man. Thank God the wine was of decent quality, at least. Nigel signaled the waiter again and mercilessly prepared himself to drink more than he wanted.

Three hours later only he and Lord Donnington remained in the game. The dice rolled between a clutter of empty bottles, and Donnington was belligerent and glazed. The crowd of spectators watched breathlessly as the stakes climbed ever higher.

"Dear me," Nigel said at last as the dice spun on the baize and rolled to a halt. "That's twenty thousand pounds, I believe? I would be happy to accept your vowel, Lord Donnington."

Donnington lurched to his feet and stood swaying against the table. "Twenty thousand? I'm done for!" His voice was slurred and his face ashen. "For God's sake, the devil must like you tonight!"

Nigel leaned back in his chair. His head buzzed like dry

wheat stalks in a high wind. "Is it more dangerous to accept Lucifer's good graces than to spurn them, do you suppose? Shall we try one more game, sir? If I lose, I'll leave empty-handed."

"But if you win?" Donnington dropped back to his seat. A sheen of sweat lay over his features.

"Then your home shall witness some revels. I'll exchange my winnings for a note to your butler allowing me to hold a party at Farnhurst Hall to commemorate the occasion." He gave a broad wink to the crowd. "I shall be happy to provide the ladies."

"Are you mad, Rivaulx?" asked one of the spectators as a delighted rustle ran through the watching dandies. "You'll trade twenty thousand for an orgy in Sussex?"

"It will have to be a particularly memorable frolic." Nigel idly fingered the dice. "For I fear I shan't lose." He looked up and smiled with great charm at his adversary. "And of course you will allow me to pick any one item at Farnhurst which takes my fancy." He gave Donnington time to wipe the moisture from his face. The man looked ill. "Are you prepared to part with something precious and exquisite, Lord Donnington? What do you value most?"

The dizzying effects of the wine thrummed in Nigel's ears. Every undertone of the evening seemed to have run together into a deafening crescendo. Had he judged correctly? Would Donnington throw open his house, believing the ruse? *A rather unusual and tempting new mistress, shadowed in mystery and the scent of frankincense.* For no reason he could fathom, a verse he had read somewhere ran unbidden through his mind: *If she be a wall, we will build upon her a palace of silver; and if she be a door, we will enclose her with boards of cedar.* The effects of the wine, no doubt. It didn't matter. All he needed was access to Farnhurst and an excuse to be there. He concentrated on Donnington's white face.

"I'll take the wager," Donnington said into his handker-chief. "If you win the next game, take what you like and be damned to you!"

With a strange distaste, Nigel picked up the dice.

"Have paper and quill brought for Lord Donnington," he

said quietly some minutes later. "He has a letter to write to
his butler."

∽

There was a sudden scream. Miss Frances Woodard woke with
a start, her heart hammering. There had been such a cry once
in the *zenana,* when an intruder had met sudden death among
the fragrant oleander and night-blooming vines.

Shaking, Frances slipped from the heavy four-poster, caught
up a robe, and crossed to the window, where she leaned her
head against the cool, damp glass. The silent spaces of the
night stretched around her. There was no endless ripple of
water falling on tile; no sultry perfume permeated the air. She
was no longer in India. She was in England, at Farnhurst, the
unexpected sanctuary that Lord Donnington had provided, apparently free of charge.

Bright moonlight bathed the landscape in shades of ivory
and silver. There was no oleander—only dark oaks and sleeping fields, the landscape of her childhood.

Who had screamed? A mouse caught in the talons of an
owl? Or had she cried out in her sleep and woken herself?

Images crowded, jostling in her memory—brilliant, hard,
scintillating with jeweled colors. In the bright splashing fountains the goldfish had been fitted with gold rings in their noses
to amuse the ladies. Her mouth went dry.

*What connection can I possibly have to these soft, innocent
pastures and a horizon broken only by church spires? Dear
God, how naive were those long-ago schoolgirl dreams of a
Season in London and a splendid marriage!* If only she could
reach back to that time before India and hold it tight! But she
might as well try to grasp a butterfly that left nothing but a
scattering of glistening, iridescent scales dusted over her fingers.

Frances closed her eyes for a moment, horrified to find them
damp with unshed tears.

*A public woman, endowed with a good disposition, beauty,
and other winning qualities, and also versed in the arts, ob-
tains the name of a* Ganika.

In English eyes, she was ruined. India had ruined her.

It was a bitter pill, but Frances swallowed it as she had faced the day when the women of the palace had changed her forever. It wasn't so great a thing. She could cope. There was nothing to be gained by palpitations or senseless fears. Life took courage. What could not be changed must be endured. It was the first lesson of India.

One

∞

THE DOOR OF George's gaming hell closed behind him. Nigel stepped into the street and stared up at the moon for a moment. Cold and white, it sailed high above the London chimneys, faintly veiled by their trailing banners of smoke. The moon: symbol of purity, grace, and virginity. Attributes which—if he had ever known them—he had heedlessly wasted. How could there have been cause noble enough to justify it? The last four years tasted like ashes in his mouth. There would never be purity or grace in his life again, and certainly not virginity.

Recognizing the absurdity of his thoughts, Nigel laughed aloud. Here he was gazing at the moon like a lovesick youth, when he was about to go into Sussex and ravish Donnington's whore, for God's sake, with half of the ton as witness. Given what was said about her, no doubt the experience would be desolate and rapacious. But why must fate's requirements be so ludicrous? He suppressed any deeper misgivings that stirred beneath his laughter. No regrets, no regrets! He had made his bed; he would lie on it.

The horses standing next to him in the street stirred and shifted a little, blowing nervously. Nigel grinned up at his coachman. The man was looking down from his perch with barely concealed curiosity. His stolid features wavered in the glow of the gaslights. *Dear God! I must be more foxed than I thought!*

The coachman coughed into a curled fist. "Home, my lord?"

"Home? If you mean Rivaulx House, the answer is no. Take me to Betty's!"

"Very good, my lord."

The rampant griffin of Rivaulx—a creature half eagle, half lion—glared balefully from the crest on the door panel, its bared claws promising destruction to all enemies of the marquess. Nigel mockingly tipped his hat to the griffin and swung himself into his carriage.

∽

Betty's house sat modestly back from the street. A prim butler answered the front door. Yet as soon as the inner door opened, indecorous light and music flooded into the hall. The contrast always gave Nigel a moment's amusement. But he did not follow the sound of the harpsichord into the parlor where the girls waited. Instead the butler showed him down a side hall into a private wing. A dark-haired woman instantly held out her arms to him.

"Dear Lord! Nigel? It's four in the morning!"

Nigel kissed her lightly on the cheek. She was dressed in a charming maroon evening gown accented with black jet, and a massive single diamond hung from a chain around her neck. "Betty, my sweet angel, how's business?"

She pulled down his head with both hands and kissed him thoroughly on the mouth before thrusting him away and holding him at arm's length. Her shrewd gaze swept over his features. "Business is very well, you wicked child, no thanks to you. I hear dreadful things of you—they say you've been gaming for infamous stakes. The talk's been of nothing else all evening. Do they hound you to death, my dear?"

Nigel hated to see the distress in her eyes, but he smiled. "The dog has a bad name, but he's not hanged yet." Gently he disengaged her hands. "Unfortunately, however, this time the tale is true."

Betty sat down suddenly. "What on earth made you wager for a woman over dice? Why don't you visit my girls? They are desolate for a glimpse of you. You haven't spent one night here since you came back from France. It's not natural.''

"Your girls were the light of my life when I was young, foolish, and learning, my sweet. I've outgrown them. But I shall never outgrow you. You become more beautiful every year.''

"Oh, stuff! I am forty-five and a harlot. What do you want from me, my pretty boy?''

Nigel grinned. "I want to hire you, Betty, and every girl here. I will make it worth your while.''

"If you like, I'll make it worth yours.'' Betty gave him a wide smile, deliberately allowing her clever, heavily ringed fingers to stray.

"Oh, no, you don't!'' Nigel caught her hand and kissed her knuckles. "Though you're a lovely creature, my sweet, and it breaks my heart to refuse you.''

Betty blushed like a virgin. "Ah, but you know I can refuse you nothing, my dear. Whatever you want from me you shall have, even if it's to turn my bawdy house into a nunnery and myself into the mother superior. So what do you really plan in Sussex?''

Nigel bit gently at her index finger until she laughed and pulled away. He felt an honest, uncomplicated fondness for Betty, entirely devoid of desire. It was many years since they had been lovers—a professional relationship that had burned briefly into something bright and deep before fading into the warmth of genuine friendship. When he came back from Paris brittle and wary and empty of love, she had offered him a haven of comfort and affection. Nigel was perceptive enough to know how much that generosity had cost her. For what could he offer in exchange?

"You have surely heard about the lady that Donnington discovered in Dover when he returned from Paris? Like a transport of exotic spices, she has just arrived from India— mysterious mistress of the erotic arts. Yet she languishes alone at Farnhurst, a regrettably dull house of brick, while Donnington loses wagers in town. How on earth can the most depraved rake in London allow such a dreadful state of affairs to continue?''

Betty reached for his hand with an intimacy that asked for a serious response. "You are looking for something new, my dear? Some fresh sensation?"

It was a test of their friendship he knew he must fail. He did not shake her off, but he let his fingers lie in hers, relaxed and open, returning nothing. It was a subtle enough reproof, and Nigel hated to give it.

"Oh, dear God," he said with deliberate humor. "After Moscow and Paris? I am sated with sensation! You find me jaded and wrung out by experience, Betty."

Betty released his fingers, her lovely dark eyes locked on his face. "Which is why for all this time—in spite of everything whispered about the libertine marquess—you have lived like a monk. But now you have won a harlot at hazard, and you want my help to create your night of debauchery. Should I give it?"

He reached forward, touching the pendant jewel at her neck. "You will have another diamond as lovely as this one, Betty, from my own hands. Besides, hasn't all London been expecting me to steal this Indian voluptuary from Donnington? Surely you would not deprive me of a lady with a reputation almost as illustrious as mine?"

The diamond leaped, sparkling in the light, as Betty made an exasperated gesture. "Do you think to pull the wool over my eyes, Nigel? I know what you have been through, and how you have suffered. You won't fool me, my dear, with all your bravado."

Nigel walked to the fireplace. The candles flickered. He watched dark shadows move over the fine veining of his hand where it rested, relaxed, on the chimneypiece. He felt blurred, as if he were fabric stretched too thin, the patterns of warp and weft distorted. "Oh, dear," he said with a wry smile. "I suppose I deserved that."

"Few of us get what we deserve."

He lifted his head and turned to face her. "But I cannot afford to be so transparent, Betty."

"Fiddlesticks! You are very foxed and you are worn to the bone. You can let down your guard just a little, for heaven's sake. You know you are safe here. But isn't it over now, my dear? Can't you rest?''

Nigel began to pace. ''It sometimes seems as if it will never be over! After Napoleon retired to Elba last spring, important papers lay in a trunk at our headquarters in Paris along with routine reports, plans for remodeling, and bills for wine— whether because of incompetence, bungling, or plain bloody-mindedness, I don't know yet. They had lain there almost a year when they were shipped back to the Foreign Office, and it was noticed that some were in code. Now that Boney has escaped and is in power again, it was thought that I might find it amusing to decipher them, just in case.''

Betty closed her eyes. ''Amusing? My dear Nigel! After all this time? Good God!''

Hiding his real emotion, Nigel winked at her. ''Yes, fate has a way of casting our laughter back in our faces, does it not?''

''So what has Donnington done?''

Nigel didn't want Betty to feel the dark depths of his anger, so he kept his voice light and mocking. ''Lord Donnington was in charge of the office where the papers lay lost. For that inefficiency, he is about to be the recipient of my most iniquitous fancy. Nothing lethal, merely extravagant, wicked, and suitably humiliating. I shall seize his mistress before the eyes of his cronies, and it will be an orgy to be marked in the annals of the ton. But only you can make it so.''

In spite of herself, Betty laughed. ''But now, my naughty man, what if the lady is a vixen, ready to devour the pursuing hound?''

Well aware how little he had really told her, Nigel grinned and on a sudden impulse leaned forward and kissed her. ''Sweet Betty, don't you trust that I myself have the cunning of the dog fox?''

∽

As the candles guttered in Betty's parlor the tale of the wager with Donnington flew briskly through town. It might have reached Prinny drinking with his cronies at Carlton House, or even mad King George snoring fretfully in his lonely bed. Winks and knowing laughter followed the story through taverns and town houses, into the clubs and the gaming hells, and at last into the printing shops, rapacious for any hint of scandal.

The sky was paling in the east when the news brought two figures hurrying into a dark, disused stable yard where some rabbit hutches were stacked haphazardly against an empty carriage house. The cages sprang into strong relief in the sudden glare of an open lantern. In each wicker cage a single rabbit, pink nose quivering, chewed rapidly at its meal of leftover lettuce leaves and vegetable trimmings.

"Are the rabbits doing well?" asked a man's voice. There was the trace of an accent there: French, perhaps.

"Oh, blooming, sir! Was you wanting some butchered? I've fed them just as you said."

The man glanced at the boy: a nameless, barefoot urchin. The light outlined the pinched face and scrawny hands. Thousands of similar guttersnipes swarmed the backstreets of London. No one would miss this one if he disappeared. "And the gray one. You have fed him as I directed?"

"Yes, sir," said the boy. "He's been fed special. But ain't it an odd thing that the rabbit don't die. I mean, one bite of that dwale and it'd be toes up for me or you, wouldn't it?"

The man peered thoughtfully into the cage holding the gray rabbit. The animal's wide, nervous black eyes stared back. The rabbit was chewing at the leaves and dried berries of a tall weed; it was common enough in the waste places and old quarries that surrounded London.

"Yet the rabbit enjoys his food without ill effect while the poison gathers in his flesh. So it will be toes up for someone else, won't it?"

The rabbit stopped chewing for a moment and crouched, black eyes unwavering.

"*Tiens!* Eat up, little fellow," the man added calmly. "Fill your veins. For you'll have your last meal soon enough." He leaned down and put his face close to the bars. "They say there's to be an orgy in Sussex, and the Marquess of Rivaulx will need rabbits for the pot.''

Nigel had sent his coachman home. He walked back through the empty streets to his town house and felt a poignant regret for the warmth and welcome left behind in Betty's parlor. It was almost morning. He ought to feel more satisfaction for a night's work well done, yet the whole business left a familiar enough bitter taste. He felt sour with wine and tobacco smoke, and he hated his nagging guilt about Betty. She always gave him more than he could possibly return.

Tossing aside his coat, he entered his study, then crossed to the fireplace and stared at the ashes. Nothing remained of the documents he had destroyed that afternoon. A broken glass lay shattered in the grate, mute witness to his momentary loss of control when he had first discovered what Donnington was doing. The rage still burned, and with it memories bitter enough to gall. Had Catherine gone to the guillotine because of someone like Donnington?

He turned and tried to take comfort in the paintings that hung on the opposite side of the room: an overly romantic view of Rivaulx Castle, perched on its crag above the waters of the Rye; his first Thoroughbred horse, Randal, staring wide-eyed, head high, in the hand of a diminutive groom; a portrait of himself as a child, with Georgina, his little sister who had died, and their wolfhound, Hazard. He loved Rivaulx with a passionate longing, but he had not been back there in four years.

Nigel sat down at his desk and buried his face in his palms. He remained perfectly still and silent for perhaps twenty minutes, then he dropped his hands to the table and stared at them. They were elegant, smooth, revealing nothing of what they had done. The third finger of his left hand was graced with a heavy ring bearing the family crest. With its rancorous grimace, the griffin glared back. The thick gold made an odd contrast to his slim, strong fingers. A dark hair was caught in the ring and he pulled it out. The same fine, lustrous hair that had been his mother's pride.

And now, of course, he must face her.

Her portrait hung above the fireplace. The late Marchioness of Rivaulx, painted when she was twenty and dressed as a gauzy Aphrodite with white flowers scattered like stars in her unbound tresses, smiled gently down at her son. Born in Paris, she had never entirely lost her French accent. In his memory, she seemed always to be surrounded by that Gallic grace and some sweet, potent scent.

He had inherited her fine bones and good looks. He had the same compelling, dark brown eyes under startlingly straight brows; a masculine version of the same cleanly carved cheek and chin; and the same smile, designed to break hearts. A damaged nose—so that the bridge was slightly crooked—was all that saved Nigel Arundham from being beautiful. *La beauté du diable,* the marchioness had called it.

Not unaware of the comparison, Nigel met the sardonic dark gaze that was so like his own. What would the lovely Marchioness of Rivaulx have thought if she had known what her only son would become?

"Vous me pardonnerez, madame, ma mère?" he asked dryly. "I intend to wallow in the pigsty with the nice little hogs."

And then because he couldn't bear the empty spaces of his great bedchamber, and because he felt no desire at all for sleep, Nigel began to pace while dawn light filtered through the cracks between the shutters.

It was a clear morning when the footman announced a visitor. The gentleman stepped into the room and closed the door behind him. Dressed in a brown cutaway coat and cream-colored pantaloons, his manner portrayed a carefully cultivated elegance. Yet the face under the fall of blond hair was almost angelically innocent.

"Dear God," said Nigel with deliberate sarcasm. "What a

night, blessed throughout by events of portent and magnificence! I am wanting breakfast. Instead I get Lancelot Spencer, the anxious friend, come to hover like a seraph in a triptych—six wings spread with sacred ardor, full of beatitude, and dispensing holy wisdom. What if I prefer to sit here, like Orpheus, playing the lyre alone?"

"Lord Rivaulx," said Lancelot Spencer, taking a pinch of snuff. "You are a damned bastard."

"Very likely," replied Nigel. "My mother was of weak morals and easily tempted, as I am." He glanced back up at her portrait and winked at her. "You have heard what happened at George's, I suppose? Let me get you a drink."

"Have you seen this?" Lance held out a paper.

Nigel strode to the side table, where he poured out a measure of brandy. "The latest scandal sheet? With the usual assumption that the dishonorable Marquess of Rivaulx is tumbling in a haze of wine fumes to Hades? I make it a point never to read them. Surely you can find something more edifying to enlighten your idle hours?" He held out the glass. "Now we're no longer employed in Europe, sir, you need to develop new interests. Napoleon is back in Paris, Wellington gathers armies, diplomacy collapses, and the specter of renewed warfare raises its nasty head. However, there is nothing for us to do until someone decides to act. It's time to lose ourselves in more lighthearted pursuits."

Taking the brandy, Lance walked to the fireplace. Shards of shattered glass glimmered at his feet. He began to push them aside with the toe of his boot. "As you have? You know, I wonder if it is quite honorable for someone of your mathematical talents to play very deep. Didn't you once tell me that you had sworn an oath never to do again what you just did to Donnington?"

Nigel felt his self-awareness turning into mockery. It often did. He clearly remembered the results of that arrival back at Rivaulx when he was eighteen, falling drunk from his carriage with a chest full of money and no idea where it had come from. The marchioness had reduced his wild young pride in his skill with numbers into a shame that burned to this day.

How could Lance know that in order to abandon that promise to his mother, Nigel had wrestled—like Jacob—with a demon?

"And tonight I broke it." Nigel poured a brandy for himself and retreated into sarcasm. If Lance didn't like it, he could damned well leave. "As earlier I broke one of my best glasses. Do you come to save me from the devil?" The gold ring of Rivaulx flashed brightly for a moment as he raised his brandy in a salute that was close to an insult.

"Then it's true?" Lance crushed the scandal sheet with its crude woodcut of two copulating figures, and tossed it into the grate. His face was pale and a damp sheen lay over his features, as if a Botticelli angel wept. "For God's sake, Rivaulx! Don't do this! I lived there. I saw you together. When you looked at each other, the house ignited!"

"Our little house on the Rue des Arbres?" Anger and bitterness clamored in his brain. Nigel heard the rage in his own voice. "The house of secrets! Why on earth did you bother to get me out alive?"

"Because however much you may want to die, a man of your talents is a rare thing. You cannot be nasty enough to stop men from idolizing you, nor charming enough to prevent their petty jealousy. Why the devil do you waste yourself in dissipation?"

"Dear God!" Nigel laughed aloud. "May I not have a little fun? There will be a delightful orgy. I am going to a deuced amount of trouble and it's going to cost me a fortune. It will be noisy and rancorous, but very amusing. Why don't you come to Farnhurst and lose your precious virtue to a nice, plump whore?"

A faint flush stained Lance's fair skin. His blue eyes narrowed. "For God's sake," he said with considerable heat. "One of these days someone is going to kill you, and it'll probably be one of your long-suffering friends! After Moscow and what we went through together in Paris, do you expect me to applaud your intention to ravish another man's mistress?"

Nigel considered this very carefully for a moment. He

walked to the window and threw wide the shutters. Sunshine poured into the room and washed over his face. He closed his eyes against the brightness.

"If she is pretty enough," he said.

Two

FRANCES SAT CROSS-LEGGED in her comfortable robes in a small marble folly shaped like a miniature Greek temple. It had been three days since she had woken shaking in the night. Over her blue *angya-kurti*—her fitted top with its short sleeves and silk vest—she wore a diaphanous *peshwaz*. The long muslin gown was the color known as "the white of the August moon." Open at the front, it framed the long, embroidered ends of her silk belt and the narrow band of naked skin above her loose trousers. There was an odd comfort in the familiar caress of the gauzy fabric.

She watched silently as a little bird hopped into the marble ruin. It pecked at a scattering of grass clippings and seed that had blown across the floor. English birds lacked the brilliant color of the birds of the East. There was an honest plainness to them, as there was to the staff in the house—the fresh-faced country girls who made up the beds and scrubbed the floors without prostrating themselves if she walked by. Instead the girls nudged each other when they saw her, and suppressed nervous giggles behind reddened, work-worn hands.

The bird hopped closer, then stopped and boldly surveyed her for a moment. She allowed herself to slip into the deep, slow breathing that she had been taught, the breath that calms. The bird relaxed and pecked at a grass seed near her folded knee. Frances concentrated on the frozen breath, feeling her muscles slip into deep relaxation, so that she became still, like a bush. The bird launched itself in a flurry of wings to perch on the veil over her hair. The neat little claws tickled her scalp and her concentration broke. She laughed, and the bird, offended, flew away.

Thank God for these cool woodlands and kindly skies! Yet surely Donnington's generosity could not last forever? And then how long before the inescapable future arrived? *I will accept it. More. I will embrace the inevitable.*

Frances folded her hands, breathing away that fluttering of fear and anger at the cruel turn of destiny that had made her a harlot.

Donnington had found her as she stood stunned in the lobby of the Green Man in Dover. Frances had just discovered that her Aunt Jane, her father's sister and her sole surviving relative in England, had died while the ship had creaked and groaned around the Cape of Good Hope. Except for the tiny amount of gold she always wore, the passage had cost her the last of her jewelry. She'd been almost penniless. She'd had nowhere to go. And as she had learned on the ship, her notoriety had already traveled with the trade winds from the gossips of Calcutta to the dowagers of London.

So at the Green Man, alone and afraid, she had been forced to wonder which man held her future and how much careless cruelty she would have to endure. For in spite of her English childhood with its innocent diversions and sunny days, there was no possibility of marriage or respectable employment. Miss Frances Woodard had spent four years in the harem of a maharaja in India, and been trained in the notorious ways of the *Ganika,* the professional courtesan.

"Madam," Lord Donnington had said politely, his expression only a little nervous beneath the red-brown curls. "Are you lost?"

She had been convinced he would want her as his mistress. But he had offered her a sanctuary here at Farnhurst. Good to his word, he had left for London and made no demands on her. All he required in exchange was her reputation for him to use as he desired, and what could that possibly matter? It gave her a little time, and then she would ask him to help her find a permanent protector, some elderly lord, perhaps.

Frances allowed herself to imagine it: a gentle, scholarly man, demanding little, smiling up at her from an open book in the sanctuary of his library. In return she would fill his days with graciousness and pleasure, and the gifts of her training.

She had suffered enough of change, and intrigue, and secret, hidden designs.

There was nothing to be gained by palpitations or senseless fears.

She lifted her lids and blinked a little against the spring sunshine of England. It was lovely here, almost as lovely in its way as India. Yet there had been a price, and Frances acknowledged it with poignant sorrow. A second lesson: India had taught her to mistrust beauty.

There was a rattling somewhere in the distance and a flock of rooks rose clamoring into the sky. The calm shattered. Frances stood up and shaded her eyes. A cavalcade of carriages was trotting up the drive, and across the park, a lone horseman drove his mount—a metallic sheen of gold and silver dapples—white mane and tail streaming behind. Her breath caught as the rider set the powerful animal at the high stone wall bordering the garden. She had a sudden impression of fierce, lithe strength before they soared into the air as if the gilt horse might unfurl wings and challenge the sun in the heavens. Bright light fired the mane and tail with an edge of flame. Landing in a spray of dust, horse and rider disappeared into the stable yard. Frances ran rapidly back to Farnhurst.

The carriages had stopped at the front of the house. From doors emblazoned with an intricate crest they were disgorging menservants in leather or linen aprons; burly footmen in an unfamiliar blue-and-silver livery and white powdered wigs; and several men in evening wear who carried cases for musical instruments. Behind them came a procession of carts and wagons, laden with food. Farnhurst was being invaded!

The butler was standing on the step. Thrusting a note into her hands, he stalked into the house.

There was no personal word. Just a simple direction to the staff: *The Most Honorable the Marquess of Rivaulx is to have full use of the house in order to host an entertainment tonight. I will expect the complete cooperation of every member of the household—Donnington.*

Why? Who was this marquess? In the next hour Frances watched her quiet home erupt into chaos. A French chef and twenty minions took over the kitchens, ordering the dispersal of great baskets of bread and barrels of fruit. Whole sides of beef and mutton, strings of chickens and rabbits, two whole swans, and an entire flock of tiny ortolans followed like an edible bestiary. Incongruous among the birds lay a spare rabbit with dark gray fur, its ears lolling among the feathers. Perhaps it had fallen from the wagon and been tossed back among strangers? Frances turned away. She had not eaten meat in five years.

Menservants swarmed over the house, moving furniture and rolling up carpets; bedrooms were turned out and the beds aired; musicians began to tune up in a dreadful disharmony. The name of Rivaulx ran about the house—*my Lord Rivaulx would wish it thus; the marquess has given strict instructions.* Soon all the regular staff of Farnhurst, including the butler, piled into the carriages and disappeared, leaving Frances surrounded by strangers. *An entertainment tonight.* Of what kind? With dread tugging at her heart, Frances walked into the library and closed the door behind her.

"It is a day of great promise," said a cultured voice thick with irony. "The sky seems as moody as treacle. Do you think we shall have thunder by tonight?"

On a sudden instinct, Frances veiled her face before turning. A man stood at the window gazing out into the garden. Sunlight outlined his strong profile and sparkled on his dark hair.

"Good Lord, I am surrounded by madness," she said. "Treacle cannot have moods." And then she realized how completely the stranger had taken the advantage, for she had been effectively arrested by the absurdity of his comment. Now she could not leave the room; it would look altogether too much like flight. So instead she crossed to the sofa and sat cross-legged in her *peshwaz* on the cushions. "I assume you are another minion of this almighty Lord Rivaulx?''

"I know him quite well, certainly." The man turned from the window. "A gentleman of uncertain fancy and odd inclinations." He seemed a little derisive. "Perhaps even sugar syrup will summon feelings just to please him."

"What kind of inclinations?" she asked immediately.

The man leaned carelessly with one shoulder against the bookcase. How beautifully he moved—with a lithe grace that belied his tall, powerful frame—like a Bengal tiger! She knew without question that he had been the rider of the silver-gold horse.

"He likes mathematics," he said with mock gravity, "among other things."

"Then since you know him so well, perhaps you would tell me why Lord Donnington has agreed to let this marquess have use of Farnhurst."

His face was entirely shadowed by the glare of light behind him, but Frances could feel his intensity. "Rivaulx won a game of hazard. As a result he may host a party here."

"How very charming." She felt suddenly vulnerable, as if he could read her uneasiness. "A wager. I assume this marquess takes pleasure in such profligate diversions?"

"Of course." His voice filled with lazy humor. "He is commonly thought to be a lost soul—a man of depraved habits and iniquitous tendencies, a friend to dissipation and licentiousness, who won't scruple to ruin innocent maidens and set a bad example to youth."

"Why does the wicked marquess choose Farnhurst for a party?"

As if reluctant to answer, he pulled a volume from the case and began leafing through it. "Donnington has a very complete library," he said absently. "Has he read any of it?"

Frances stared at him, disconcerted for a moment by the change of subject. "I don't know. I suppose so. But surely the marquess has a library of his own?"

"Indeed. And finer, no doubt, than this one. But then Lord Rivaulx, for all his other faults, likes to read."

His fingers rested for a moment on the spines of the books, drawing her attention to his hands, strong and supple. The third finger of his left hand was graced with a heavy ring bearing a deeply engraved crest—the griffin rampant that had adorned the carriages. She felt a rush of indignation. So the marquess would play games!

Frances allowed some bite to hone her voice. "A man of both words and numbers, but also a rake? What a paragon of versatility! I pray you will enlighten me further and answer my question: Why does he come here tonight?"

He smiled. Even in the shadow she could see that it was a smile of immense charm. "Because of you, of course." He dropped the words like a challenge. "Miss Frances Woodard. Lord Donnington claims that you have a perfume about you, of cinnamon and oleander, of sultry nights under a foreign moon whispering of the arts that drive men wild with longing. You are beautiful, are you not?"

Frances folded her hands. *Oh, dear God, it had happened!* The inevitable future had arrived too soon. But it didn't matter, of course. If she could cope with the *praudha* who ran the *zenana,* she could manage this. Surely she was resigned to her fate? There was no escape. And if she must play out her life as a courtesan, she would do it with every ounce of courage she possessed. "Lord Donnington may say anything he likes. He is my protector. He gives me a home here."

She was glad of the veil. The fine gauze would not entirely hide her face; he would be able to get a hint of her coloring and her carefully arched brows, but it must make it impossible for him to read her expression. It gave her a moment to collect her thoughts and control her feelings.

But instead he was watching her hands.

Memory almost submerged her. She could hear the unrelenting battering of the monsoon on the roofs and courtyards, the deluge flooding the fountains and drowning the little goldfish. Against the backdrop of the downpour, she had learned to play *shatranj,* the Indian chess. She had moved the pieces, heavy with semiprecious stones, across a board with squares of ebony and ivory. There had been a cruel rap on the knuckles if she did not do so with becoming grace and elegance. Her hands had learned to move like the wind on grass, or like the soft folding of a bird's wing at sunset, and the nails that she had bitten as a girl were now as smooth and round as burnished almonds.

Frances pulled herself back to the present and looked down at her fingers, lying relaxed and curved in eloquent, unconscious invitation in her lap. With his casualness and his careless, arrogant humor, did this man think he was immune to the effects of that hard-won training?

He replaced the book and turned to face her. The whole mood changed. She had learned to sense danger, and the atmosphere screamed with it.

"Do you have a room of your own with a lock?" he said with sudden intensity.

Frances found her breath coming too fast. Carefully she slowed it. "Why?"

He moved restlessly across the room. Frances saw his face clearly for the first time as the light fell over his features. Ah, how unfair! Lord Rivaulx was beautiful: dark, fine-boned, beautiful! With perfect clarity she recognized her response and with the control she had labored so hard to learn she tried to suppress it. But how strange that the face of a man could be so enticing! She wanted to smooth her hands over his eyelids and the olive skin of his cheekbones, and let her palms feast on the sensation. Confusion knifed through her.

He had come up to her and was standing so close that if she reached out she could touch him. "Retreat into it tonight and lock the door."

"I am not afraid," Frances said.

"No?" His voice held nothing but light humor, but deep undercurrents ran well guarded beneath it. "Nevertheless, do not be out of your room at midnight."

"What happens at midnight?" she scoffed. "Does the marquess turn into a werewolf, or devour the guests like a Rajasthan lion?"

"Not at all." He took her hand and turned it palm up in his long fingers. They were the smooth hands of a gentleman, but the touch was firm, full of competence. It sent a shock through her blood, like a tidal wave. "The wager allows Lord Rivaulx to take any item here at Farnhurst that pleases him—otherwise Lord Donnington loses twenty thousand pounds. As the clock strikes twelve, to the amusement of the company and the chagrin of your protector, the wicked marquess will choose his prize.'' He was tracing small circles on her palm. She caught her breath as his thumb slid sensuously up to her wrist, so that her hand was encompassed, trapped by his insolent strength. ''It is commonly expected, Miss Woodard, that he will choose you.''

Bending from the waist, he kissed her hand once in the center of the palm, then dropped it.

Frances covered her fingers instantly with a fold of her robe. The flush spread all over her body, leaving her shaking. She took three long, deep breaths and was relieved to find her odd mood dissipating to be replaced with a clear, passionate fury. She had been traded! Her fate had been snatched from her own hands. As if she had neither mind nor will of her own, this man had wagered for—and won—her favors over dice.

''I am amazed!'' she said. ''Not even the Padshah Begum with her peacock feather fan is worth twenty thousand pounds. Yet this is my home. I shall not retreat behind a curtain like a *punkah wallah*.'' Hot with rage and humiliation, she rose from the couch and bowed to him. ''Aren't you curious, Lord Rivaulx, to see what you have won?''

As she had been trained, Frances pulled back her veil.

A pang of yearning, deep and primeval, pierced his heart. Nigel had no defense but his own self-derision. The enchanting Miss Woodard was very plainly English: the hair of deep honey, dusted with gold; the skin far whiter than his own; the furious eyes, though outlined in dark lashes, stunningly blue. But she was more than beautiful, she was exquisite—with something entirely exotic in her grooming, in the fine arching curve of her lightly oiled eyebrows, in the neat plait curving down from her nape, in the flaunting of form. Like the naked curve of her waist, everything about her spoke of a profound sensuality.

And in the fine curl of her nostril she wore a small gold stud.

The delightful shock of it flooded along his bones.

He had told her to stay away tonight, to avoid the unholy contamination of his presence. And now he saw in her eyes, beneath the rage and the courage, an overwhelming uncertainty and fear—like a virgin facing rapine. It left him uncomfortably disoriented for a moment. Dear God, had he started something that would crush her in its path? Or something that would drag him, willy-nilly, into a place he had sworn never to visit again?

Nigel swallowed. The grim reality of his own emptiness stared back at him like a wavering candlelit face seen reflected unexpectedly in a mirror.

The moment was gone, and she gazed steadily into his face with an infuriating calm beneath that flashing, gallant fury. Had he imagined the vulnerability? *She is just a courtesan. Devil take it, none of this will matter a damn to her!* He had to get through just this one night and he would never see her again. In the meantime she was offering herself and the gift was exquisite.

With the mocking, hard-won detachment learned from those harsh years in Russia and France, Nigel tried to suppress his doubts. It was too late to back out now; the game must go on. " 'Thou hast ravished my heart, my sister,' " he quoted lightly. "You guessed who I am? A lady of keen observation."

She faced him, still with that defiant courage. "One learns to be observant in the harem, Lord Rivaulx."

"And what else did you learn?" he asked dryly.

With a grace that left him breathless she walked up to him. Arching her back a little, she slid off her long veil. "Would you like to find out, my lord?"

The white muslin ran through her hands like a fall of water, sinuous and graceful. It trailed lightly over her body, forcing his attention back to her round breasts. Her Oriental robe was designed to tease—revealing, then concealing, alluring glimpses of shadow and softness as she moved. He burned to touch the pliant depression of her navel and feel the curve of her hip under his palm. Without surprise Nigel felt the familiar, presumptuous tightening of desire.

"Madam, I am entirely at your disposal," he heard himself say. "By all means, do with me what you will."

Her glance as she looked up at him under her thick lashes spoke of shimmering fields of opium poppies, deep purple under a blazing sun, an enchantment of the senses. Would she lay aside those layers of muslin, one by one, and offer herself for him to drown in? For one moment he wanted it, wanted—just once more—to take that ingenuous plunge into pure lust, to bury himself in a woman's softness and heat, and take her with him until she cried out with passion. Ruthlessly Nigel reined in his vision. She was only a pawn temporarily caught between the king and checkmate. She might be beautiful, but he had known many lovely women, and he knew now that lust was never simple or without price. This was only a game, entirely without meaning—a game where he must dictate the rules and guarantee the winner.

"Give me your left hand," she said.

Her voice held sultry, provocative promise.

He offered his hand. The cool touch of her skin as she took his fingers seemed to throb into his very soul.

"*Sinister*. The hand which is closest to the heart." She looked up at him as she closed her fingers around his palm and held them there. "Are you sure you are wise, my lord, to surrender it?"

Her pulse throbbed against his hand, mingling in a crazy melody with his. He felt restraint sliding through his fingers like dry sand on a beach.

" 'Even a fool when he holdeth his peace is counted wise,' " he quoted.

She released his palm and wrapped the end of her veil about his wrist, then walked behind, pulling his hand with her. Curious, Nigel obligingly stood still for her. He felt the muslin catch hard over the fine bones of his other hand, then bite into his wrists as she jerked it tight to tie them together behind his back. He glanced over his shoulder. She had looped the other end of the veil about the leg of the massive oak desk and knotted it in place. Reflexively he tried to move his arms, and failed. For God's sake, he was tethered!

He was disconcerted to feel his body react with a flush of heat.

Nigel looked down on the smooth honey-gold hair as Frances walked back to face him. Her eyes calmly assessed the neat white cravat, tailored cutaway jacket, breeches tightly outlining his thighs. She must be able to clearly see his arousal. Her gaze momentarily lingered there, apparently without curiosity, then flickered to his face. The slow burn in his body seemed to follow her gaze. How could she stay so unmoved?

Frances moved closer to him, her eyes pools of cobalt. "So, like a mare, or a brace of hounds, I am won at hazard and must submit willingly to the halter. Who am I to object?"

"Dear God! I am the one harnessed now!"

He saw her swallow, the slight movement rippling up and down the column of her throat. A tendril of hair curled enticingly beneath her jaw. Nigel became harder, taut and swelling with anticipated pleasures, his body mocking his attempt at detachment.

Deft and certain, she unbuttoned his jacket, then his waistcoat. Nigel stood still, quiet, waiting, drawn as tight as a bowstring. Awareness of her flooded his senses. He could smell her scent, a clear jasmine, and hear the sensuous rustle of her clothes as she moved. And somewhere outside, maddening in its claim on him, he heard a bird begin its song, a waterfall of liquid sound.

Sunlight gleamed golden on her hair as she opened his outer garments wide and ran her hands over the soft fabric of his shirt. Her palms rested flat on the front of his breeches for a moment, directly over his navel. Another inch lower and she would touch him where he both yearned and feared for her touch. His mouth went dry. Nigel drew in a breath, fighting for calm.

The tip of her tongue slid from her lips, as a child's does when lost in concentration. The gesture was intensely female and oddly vulnerable. "But if I am to be your concubine, Lord Rivaulx, I must make my mark on you, don't you think?" Her fingers moved down to the buttons of his breeches.

His detachment shattered.

"Shall we start with *Ardhachandra*, the half-moon?" she

asked with a lift of her perfectly plucked eyebrows.

With every ounce of his considerable control, Nigel suppressed his reaction as she undid the top buttons at his waistband. She pulled out his shirt and rolled it up, so that the cool air of the room caressed his skin. The firm touch of her hands trailed fire over the muscles curving up from his waist and across his ribs. It was almost more than he could bear. His pulse beat loudly in his ears as she knotted the shirt over his chest. From breastbone to navel, his skin lay naked to her touch.

His thoughts clamored with wild, unfocused speculation. Excitement, hot and urgent, fused in his loins.

"Seven areas of the body are receptive to scratching," she said calmly.

The barely perceptible touch of her nails trailed up from his waist to pass, as insubstantial as thistledown, over his right breast. It concentrated his attention instantly. Nigel felt goose bumps rise all over his body, and his cock leaped hard against the confines of his breeches. He wanted to caress her, feel those sweet curves under his own fingers, tear away that provocative silk and muslin, bare her breasts, and explore her warmth and softness with his hands and mouth until she softened to him, moaning. Unconsciously he tried to move. The muslin cut sharply into his wrists. He was entirely vulnerable to her whim.

Nigel took a deep breath and looked down at her. Her fingers lay lightly on his body, shaking slightly. Her blue eyes were wide and dark, like the ocean. Was she unsure—even afraid?

In an act of pure bravado, Nigel half closed his eyes and gave himself up entirely to the sensations she was creating in his body. She pressed her nails a little deeper, cutting a track of exquisite sensation over his skin.

"*Achchuritaka*. The knife," she said softly.

Her touch became a blade, peeling back restraint, exposing the core of his desire—the intense pulse of longing, a great well of need. Nigel dropped his head back, the sinew and muscles of his neck stretched into steel wire, his shoulders stiff with tension. He wanted to howl. Her caress ran down again as if to trace the center line of his body, touching his navel, igniting wildfire into the groin.

"Dear God!" He felt ready to burst.

Slowly she ran the nails of her right hand back up to his chest, stopping just beneath his nipple, and gathered a small pinch of his tantalized flesh in her fingers. Nigel drew in a breath and held it. In the loud silence a flutter of wings beat thundering against the window as the songbird flew away. Her nails bit suddenly into his skin.

"Damnation!" The word burst out on a rapid exhalation. He looked down. A small moon-shaped bruise on his chest throbbed with a delicious sensation, leaving a vast empty ache.

And like an echo in the roaring silence he heard his own words come back to mock him: *Thou hast ravished my heart, my sister. Until the day break, and the shadows flee away, I will get me to the mountain of myrrh, and to the hill of frankincense. Thou art all fair, my love; there is no spot in thee.* It was from the Song of Solomon.

"*Nakharadanajati*, the art of scratching. For remembrance." Beneath her infuriating calm ran a deeper note, but he could not fathom it.

"I promise you I won't forget," said Nigel raggedly.

He closed his eyes in a vain attempt to ignore the clamoring in his brain. For God's sake, he was the notorious Marquess of Rivaulx. He had tasted every depth of depravity. He knew how to manipulate the most sophisticated of women. What was she, Miss Frances Woodard, but another harlot? Nigel concentrated on her stinging mark—*Ardhachandra*, the half-moon—until he felt his erection die slowly away. And at last he found his armor of detachment, still undamaged, as his pulse returned to normal.

She has done nothing but touch me! For God's sake!

A shaft of sunlight from the window fired her hair with gold and caressed the intoxicating lines of nose and cheek and jaw. Her eyes were fixed on his face and dilated into blackness. She was trembling with a high, fine energy. And then he saw it: the slightest dilation of her nostrils, a small flush stealing into her cheeks like the glow of a fire banked for the night. As their eyes met, the flush deepened until her skin was stained with carmine, a helpless reflex, infinitely female, revealing the woman, fragile and vulnerable beneath her rage. So she was not—in spite of her infuriatingly cool manner—so indifferent.

"For when love becomes intense. It is also used by an angry lover or an intoxicated woman. Take your pick, Lord Rivaulx."

In a susurration of robes Frances left the room.

Nigel allowed himself to savor a single dark blossom of rage, then let it go. He had challenged, and she had replied in full measure. There was no fault he could in honor attach to Miss Frances Woodard. So because there was nothing else left to him, he found release in laughter. The muslin veil bound him no tighter than the exacting demands of duty. He could not walk away, for the game was not yet played out, and he could not abandon that fragile, brave beauty to the monster he had created: a mob, drunk with excess, that would soon be let loose in this house.

But, dear God!

" 'Take us the foxes, the little foxes, that spoil the vines,' " he quoted to himself. " 'For our vines have tender grapes.' "

He was committed. He must spend this one evening with her. One evening out of a lifetime. The prospect unfolded like a bolt of spun silk, unfurling in rich splendor.

I do not want intensity, or intimacy. But I shall take my revenge on her for this! Just a little. Just enough to let her know who the devil she is playing with.

And then he laughed at his own absurdity. Amidst the splendid ruin of his preconceptions, he knew now that the evening was not going to be carnal and rapacious. It was going to be delightful.

Nigel dropped neatly to the floor and rolled. Within seconds he had the knife out of his boot and had cut his bonds. He looked at the weapon for a moment—gleaming, deadly, sunlight flashing brightly from the blade—before he thrust it away, tucked in his shirt, and buttoned his waistcoat and jacket over it. Briefly he touched the place over his heart where she had marked him—*Ardhachandra*, the half-moon. *For when love becomes intense.*

Nigel left the ruined white muslin, slashed into three pieces and still deformed by its knots, limply trailing across the sofa where she had been sitting. No doubt a servant would clear it away.

Three

@

"SO YOU LOST face, but saved twenty thousand pounds," said Frances, gazing at the flushed face under the red-brown curls.

They were alone together in her bedroom. Lord Donnington was breathing heavily. "Just a wager, Frances."

Her protector had returned and come straight up to her, but he seemed strained to the breaking point. How little she knew him! Had he noticed how completely his house had been taken over—that every item had been assessed and valued, every room searched?

"A very wise choice, my lord, but I might have been consulted before I was traded away like a horse." She turned and walked restlessly to the window. A dark-haired woman was climbing from a curricle that had stopped in the driveway below. She had a lovely face, but it was the face of a man that Frances couldn't get out of her mind.

What could have possessed her to confront Lord Rivaulx as she had done? She felt shaken to the soul, bereft of all sense of direction or purpose. She had known since Dover that Donnington would not last forever, that there would be another protector, and then, very probably, another. That she would trade her body for gifts and trinkets until each man tired of her. She knew what it would mean and that it was her only possible fate. Though he was far from the elderly man of her fantasy, she had hoped to choose some rich lord, and Rivaulx was a marquess. Yet uncertainty trembled in her breast like a caged bird. What did it matter if she had been traded for a gaming debt? And to a man as lovely as a god and as mysteriously enticing. Why should she be angry and afraid? But when the moment had come, from fear, from shock, she had lost her temper!

She had been sold, like a vase or a painting! And he had told her so with that arrogant, patronizing humor.

Damn him! In her sudden rush of rage, she had wanted to humiliate him, so how could she have found herself trembling with the force of her own reaction? As she touched him she had thought for a moment she would melt, deep in her womb. The treacherous heat had spread through her body and made her breasts ache. It had taken all of her training to hide it. Something had happened to her! Something she had not been prepared for, had not been trained for. Something she could never allow to happen again. Yet his chest had felt delectable, a marvel to her touch. She had wanted to kiss him there, and through her moaning breath dissolve her entire being into his, where the small nubs of his nipples had risen hard under her palms.

He had wanted her. He had not shown any shame at his obvious arousal. Instead, insolently, he had flaunted it. And in that appalling indifference he had shown her something terrifying—a callousness, a capacity perhaps for cruelty? Frances didn't know. Why had he allowed her to mark him? He had not been humiliated. He had been amused, then a little angry, perhaps, but not humbled. Lord Rivaulx had allowed her to lead—though hardly to win.

And she had left him tied to a table in the study! What would he do now? Would he take revenge?

Oh, damnation! Why was she afraid? At the very worst she would become his mistress. It would take only a little courage to face it. Meanwhile it was very plain that Donnington, for all she was indebted to him, owed her an explanation.

Before Frances could turn from the window, she saw the dark-haired woman hold out her arms. A tall man came out of the house, caught her by both hands, and kissed her. The sun glanced off his hair and cast shadows across the planes of his face as he affectionately escorted the woman into the house. So Lord Rivaulx was entirely profligate with his charm and his attentions!

Frances turned from the window with contempt. "Perhaps it was bound to happen. I accept that you wanted everyone to know you had a mistress, and I am grateful for your care and generosity in exchange." She made herself smile. "In fact, I hear you have been boasting of me all over London."

"That was our bargain," said Donnington stubbornly. "And a pretty one-sided one, too! You have had a roof and food, haven't you? You were no use to me if I kept you a secret. How was I to know what Rivaulx would do? The man's a very devil."

"Yes," said Frances. "I have had the pleasure of meeting the marquess. He made his intentions plain."

Donnington was trying to bluff it out. "I've asked nothing of you before, but I gave my word—he can take anything he wants. When he chooses you, you must go with him and do whatever he demands. Do you understand?"

"Of course I understand. Yet even though I owe you a great deal for taking me in, I never said I would whore for you."

Lord Donnington colored. "You will do it, though, won't you?"

Frances saw the rigidity of his face and knew there was no way out. "I suppose I should consider myself fortunate to have attracted so powerful a peer."

"What other future is there for you?" He collapsed into a chair and dropped his head in his hands. "Why does he want to persecute me? What the hell have I ever done to him?"

She went to the door and opened it. Lord Donnington would never protect her. Why should he? His real reasons for rescuing her in Dover were still a mystery to Frances. What had he gained? The ability to tell his London friends that he had an exotic mistress, when he had never touched her? It made no sense, and now it was over, as suddenly as it had begun. "It seems more likely that I am the one to be persecuted, my lord. If I am to entertain your friends at Lord Rivaulx's party,

I must take my bath. Should I not make sure that he gets his money's worth?''

"But you don't know what he is!'' Donnington's face was ashen. His next words hit Frances with the force of a blow. "Lord Rivaulx betrayed his last mistress to her death to save his own skin.''

With great care Frances began to prepare for the evening. She spent at least an hour in her copper tub, scenting the water with a light fragrance of jasmine. Her hair was very fine and dried quickly. She braided it, then took a length of the finest white muslin, fine enough for an Indian princess—*shabnam,* the muslin of the morning dew—and draped it over her shoulders and about her head. Removing her small stud, she picked up a ring of the finest gold wire. If she was to be known only as the exotic courtesan, she would dress the part. Perhaps her jewelry would help her feel defended against him. She had learned her lessons well. She would not show fear.

Frances stepped back and caught sight of her reflection in the mirror.

The memory burned. They had done it during the Hot Month, when India baked under a relentless sun. Outside the *zenana* the countryside lay prostrate, breathlessly awaiting the onset of monsoon. When the heat became so oppressive that even the monkeys sat listless, hidden servants rolled a great iron ball along a secret track so that it made a noise like thunder, mingling with the relentless tinkle of fountains and the swish of cloth fans in the palace. It did not bring the longed-for monsoon. There was no rain, only the maharaja's ladies applauding its paltry imitation. But one day, as the goldfish gasped in the fountains, they had rolled the thunder ball to hide her cries in case she struggled. Frances had not made a sound as the needle pierced her nostril.

She had hardly been afraid of the pain. That had been momentary and minor. She had been afraid because it was final. It could not be changed or undone. She gazed steadily at the woman in the mirror. Frances had no idea who she was any longer. Did she have any real identity? Any essential core inside herself? Was that the real cause of her panic? That she must act out her life as if it were a play?

From the glass, a stranger looked back, a freak. English ladies wore their hair in curls, not smoothed into a long plait. They knew how to flirt and simper, not offer a blatant sensuality. Yet she no longer knew any other way to be. How absurd to think that even if Aunt Jane had lived, Miss Frances Woodard could have become a respectable English lady, with a right to security and a life free from fear. She could never claim that title now as long as she lived. In India she was *Chandni,* light of the moon, but in her homeland she was a common Cyprian, a member of the demimonde, and marked as such forever by the gold wire ring she wore now in her nose, curving over her lip like a symbol of bondage.

Yet if she did not have a protector, she would starve.

The noise of the party assaulted Frances as she stepped out of her room half an hour later. Everything seemed to have been moved: carpets, furniture, even tapestries. The house had been subtly rearranged, then covered with flowers and great swathes of fabric—enough flowers to have emptied every garden and hothouse for miles about, and a wealth of exquisite, shimmering silk. The effect was to hide its English innocence behind something exotic and wild. Incense was burning somewhere, scenting the air with the sensuous fragrances of the East. It was as if Farnhurst had become some scornful caricature of the *zenana.* Hot rage took her entirely by surprise. *How dare he!*

Music swelled and faded as doors opened and closed. More guests had begun to arrive. Frances could hear a steady procession of carriages pulling up before the front door, disgorging gaggles of squealing women and half-drunk dandies. Lifting her chin, she went down the stairs to face them.

The dark-haired woman intercepted her. "My dear child, you are exquisite! Perhaps you would like to work for me instead? Come, I must talk with you." The woman laughed

with infectious gaiety, took Frances by the arm, and led her
into the study where she had left Lord Rivaulx tied to the table.
The room was empty. Even when the woman began to pace,
it seemed empty. "What a silly question, when you are getting
Nigel on a platter. You are fortunate, my dear. There is no
one else like Rivaulx."

Frances sat down. She felt lost. "You are a friend of his?"

"Friend? That is a title I would be honored to claim, but
I'm only a whore, my dear. My name is Betty Palmer. Yet
I've known him for a long time."

Only a whore! Frances allowed herself a purely defensive
sarcasm. "Then if you know him so well, perhaps you can
tell me: does the marquess make a habit of winning new mistresses at dice?"

"You think him a villain, don't you?" The older woman
looked keenly at Frances. "He really isn't, you know. There
is something else which brings him to Farnhurst, my dear.
Something important. You are just a convenient ruse. He
would not force you!"

"Since Lord Donnington collaborates in my transfer, I am
being very competently forced."

Betty dismissed this with a shrug. "Even one night with
Nigel would be a precious gift to women in our profession.
No, he has something on his mind. He would skin me alive
to think that I'm telling you this, but I know he's very deeply
upset about something."

"So his lordship plans to solace his wounded feelings by
outraging mine?"

"Oh, Lord! Even coerced, you can give him something of
kindness, can't you?"

An angry recoil jarred her. "*Kindness?* The *Ganika,* the
professional courtesan, is treated with respect even by kings.
She is the guardian of *Kama,* one of the three aims of life.
Now that I'm in England, I am prepared to be some man's
mistress, but only of my own choosing. Yet Rivaulx has wagered for my favors over dice. Should I repay his barbarism
with *kindness*?"

"I would give him my soul fried with onion for his breakfast if I thought it could save him," said Betty seriously.

"I am not in the business of saving souls. Find him another mistress. I am not interested in the position."

"Ah, my dear child." Betty's dark eyes were filled with genuine compassion. "You have already been given the position. But it's not just a mistress he needs. Why does no one believe that a man can have experienced so much that he has had enough of sensation?"

Frances stood up in the single smooth motion she had learned in the harem, and went to the door. She didn't want to hear any more. But Betty's next words were said so wistfully they seemed to burn into her heart.

"You cannot give him what he needs, can you?" Betty continued. "There's too much passion and despair there of your own."

Frances turned to her, unable to tell why her voice was shaking. "So Lord Rivaulx needs a more skilled lover?"

"Not really," Betty said. "What he needs is a friend."

He betrayed his last mistress to her death to save his own skin.

"A *friend*?" asked Frances, fighting back her panic. "I am a courtesan, committed only to myself and my survival. I'm damned if I know anything about friendship."

Crushing her reaction, Frances left the room and walked toward the ballroom. Devil take Donnington, the marquess, and the world of all men! Frances felt as if she were about to be slaughtered.

Nigel stood with Donnington in an anteroom. He had changed from the plain riding clothes he had worn in the library. White silk breeches and stockings now tightly encased his long legs. His velvet evening jacket was exquisitely cut to follow the strong line of his shoulders. The deep collar rolled back to reveal a white silk waistcoat, subtly shaped over an even whiter shirtfront. It exploded at the neck into elaborate ruffles. A large diamond shone in his cravat pin. The dark hair curled in careless abandon over his forehead, as if in deliberate contrast to the precise tailoring of his clothes. Nigel knew perfectly well that the overall effect was flawless, and that his valet would boast of his master's incomparability—in spite of the fact that the man had been left in London.

To the chagrin of Lord Donnington, Nigel was examining the furnishings with exaggerated care. He was relaxed, at least on the surface, and deliberately displaying the entire dazzling, diabolical edge of his wit. Lord Donnington, in contrast, was extremely red in the face. He had been drinking. A small group of young men, some with ladies hanging affectionately onto their arms, were watching the proceedings with open glee. For the sake of all of those who had died in the cold snows of Russia, Nigel was determined to make Donnington sweat, just a little, before claiming his prize.

The crowd fell into a rustling silence. Nigel glanced over his shoulder. Frances had walked into the room. His reaction was visceral. She was draped in a length of gossamer-fine blue silk. Like moonlight on midsummer water it shimmered about her body as she moved. The sari was modest, graceful, and intensely alluring; the color turned her eyes to cobalt. A veil as fine as cobweb drifted over the honey-gold hair. In place of her small stud, she now wore a loop of gold wire in her nostril, enhancing the exquisite bones of her face.

She met his gaze with a seemingly absolute indifference.

Nigel felt a wrench of dislocation. He knew he had been left with his plans exploded and his hands filled with dust. Nothing else could be allowed to matter tonight but the exposure of a traitor, and she was his excuse for this entire masquerade. There was no backing down now. But did she think she could offer him that infuriating, cool challenge as if she were the only one who could play this game? It was his turn now. Like a lazy, sunning cat, the knowledge curled among his thoughts. A small revenge. *It is going to be delightful.*

He watched as Frances walked up to Donnington. A ripple of appreciative comment ran among the dandies. Nigel laid his hand over his heart, over her hidden half-moon mark, and bowed.

"Ah, Miss Woodard! To fulfill the terms of the wager, I must select something in the house. I am trying to decide whether I prefer the Vulliamy temple clock or the Storr silver urn: white marble and gilt versus precious metal on the grand scale. Having spent the afternoon studying everything here, I admit that I am tempted to claim one of them. What do you think?''

It was impossible to watch her mouth without wanting to kiss her. The sari flowed and shimmered, emphasizing her softness and grace.

"Since they are both graced with classical scenes, my lord, perhaps you should pick whichever allegory seems most appropriate."

Nigel saw the disdain in her glance and felt his body respond to her in spite of it. He forced himself to smile. "But the carving on the clock shows poor Paris about to hand the apple to Aphrodite, thereby displeasing two more powerful goddesses, and the urn seems to display the abduction of Persephone. In both cases, ladies given cause to be angry at a man. Either seems appropriate to me."

She met his eyes without hesitation. "Do you mean to imply that feminine anger is just pique? The result of Paris's foolhardy self-confidence was the Trojan War, and we are cursed with winter because of the theft of Persephone. Destruction or barrenness, Lord Rivaulx, the choice is yours."

"The depth of your analysis has quite destroyed my interest in either, ma'am, for the only thing which appeals to my depraved tastes is the unrestrained portrayal of the beauties of the opposite sex."

Nigel waited for her reaction with deep self-derision. Even Betty would probably be at least a little discomposed if confronted so directly. But Frances studied the three goddesses displaying their marble charms on the clock and glanced at Persephone, whose silver drapes revealed far more than they hid. Then she looked into his face with an eloquently casual acceptance of the erotic.

"How very clumsy they are," she said calmly. "Merely a kind of coy, hypocritical titillation."

How could she? His curiosity flared, and with it an urgent heat.

A wit in the crowd decided to interject. "If it is representations of females that interest you, my lord, you should see the portraits of Lord Donnington's ancestors on the walls of the dining room.''

Another man responded instantly. ''But are they worth twenty thousand, dear sir? Though I have wondered if Donnington's grandam mightn't answer, I'm afraid Rivaulx wouldn't have given a shilling for her even in her prime. I hear he likes his women with a bit more salt and a lot less vinegar.''

Donnington blushed scarlet. ''My grandmother was a lady!'' he blurted.

''Was she?'' asked the wit. ''Then what on earth happened to you?''

The crowd burst into hilarity. Nigel ignored them and turned back to Frances. ''Yet without your wise guidance, Miss Woodard, my shameful desires may lead me into an unwise decision. What else does Donnington have in this house? I have looked at a very fine Riesener desk, some Aubusson tapestries with optimistically bucolic scenes, a charming upright pianoforte by Stodart with brass inlay in the modern style, and the most exquisite Sèvres porcelain, yet nothing stirs my cupidity so far. Surely something here outshines all else—something enticing enough for the jaded tastes of a rake—something perhaps with an unusual edge to it?'' He took her hand and bent over her fingers.

The crowd applauded.

Frances could feel the tension in him as he touched his lips briefly to her knuckles. His salute was subtle, correct, and made her heart leap unwittingly in her breast.

''Be careful, my lord. If the edge is sharp enough, you might get cut.''

''No, I am only bruised.'' He glanced up at her through his outrageous lashes before releasing her hand. Then he turned to Donnington. ''Come, sir. What else do you have that might tempt me? Let us admire your grandmother!''

As they walked to the dining room the marquess continued to offer judgment on each valuable item they passed. Lord Donnington was wilting, comment by comment, under his biting wit, and their following of dandies shouted with unrestrained laughter. Frances found herself filled with indignation.

What could possibly justify this public humiliation of Donnington? What did Lord Rivaulx really want at Farnhurst?

The dining room was packed with people, and decorated with flowers—not reticent English roses but exotic lilies, which shamelessly offered themselves to the air. Mingling with the scent of the blooms, a heady perfume danced in the atmosphere like a counterpoint to the music of the string quartet. Beneath the regiments of family portraits, the table was groaning under a masterpiece of culinary art—fragrant meats in sweet sauces, vegetables carved into whimsical fantasies, pastries so delicate it seemed that a breath would blow them away.

Her mouth watered.

As she looked closer Frances noticed that the whimsy had produced shapes that were endlessly suggestive, though never crude or obvious. Platters of pastries, oozing cream, lay side by side with dishes of oysters in beds of seaweed. The smiling, open shells of mussels floated in their sauce of garlic and wine beside long loaves of crusty bread packed into a basket. A fountain of wine in the shape of a delicate gilt nymph with a jug in her arms kept everyone's glasses filled.

It all expressed exquisite taste, but that dark humor lay under it, as if the nymph might suddenly wink and abandon herself to lasciviousness, or the oysters open themselves to embrace the bread. Frances glanced up at Rivaulx, at that perfection of bone and muscle: clean brow, hawk nose, carved cheekbone. No doubt the marquess had arranged orgies before, and cared nothing if the scents of the East should fill her with disquiet.

A footman stopped and held out a platter. Lord Rivaulx took a small confection of sugar and almond paste curled in the shape of a flower bud. It lay for a moment in his palm, like an offering. Frances saw the amusement in his dark eyes as he spoke. "Now, this is very appealing, don't you think?"

Very deliberately he bit into the edge of it.

His teeth were white and even, and he curled his lip a little to make a clean bite. The pastry crumbled and broke into two. He swallowed. Fascinated, Frances watched his mouth as his eyes smiled into hers. It was as if the taste of almonds flooded her own mouth with sweetness.

She could almost hear the words of the ancient text in the zenana: *The lovers can then eat sweetmeats, according to their liking, and may drink fresh juice—the juice of mango fruits, the juice of the citron tree mixed with sugar, or anything known to be sweet, soft, and pure.*

Frances felt a confused upsurge of strange sensations. *Sweet, soft, and pure?* These feelings were urgent, hot, and uncomfortable. "Do you always go straight to the sweets, Lord Rivaulx? Without subtlety or restraint? Hardly a way to provide nourishment!"

"Restraint can be overrated, Miss Woodard. Tonight is not designed for nourishment, only for caprice and the indulgence of fancy." He turned to Donnington. "My lord, you don't eat? The feast is rapidly being devoured. For God's sake, indulge yourself while you can."

Lord Donnington flushed. He had been watching Nigel eat the pastry with an odd longing. Instantly he abandoned Frances's arm, took up a plate, and began to fill it with food. Frances looked after him as he moved away, every once in a while gulping down some rich delicacy. Of course she hadn't expected that he would defend her, or even make any serious objection to losing her. She looked back at Rivaulx.

"Do you find English cooking bland after the spices of India, Miss Woodard?" he asked, almost casually. "Indian food is hot, isn't it?"

"Hot food is suitable to a hot climate, my lord," she replied. "It cleans the blood and purifies the humors."

"So if such spicy fare were to be served in cold England, would the consumer be burned?"

"Not all spices burn, my lord; some are more subtle than that."

"Too subtle, no doubt, for our English talent. We like everything boiled, with plenty of salt. I knew I could not tempt you with our restrained British cuisine, Miss Woodard, which is why I have hired a French chef." He handed her a dish of candied cherries. "I have always marveled that sickly sweet is such a popular taste with the ladies, and these cherries are a perennial—however many are offered, more always remain. Aren't some Indian spices sweet?''

She felt out of her depth. His beautiful, wanton laugh left her shaking and helpless. ''Of course: *ardraka, bhringa, dhanyaka.*'' He raised a questioning brow. ''Ginger, cinnamon, coriander,'' she explained. ''But it is an Indian specialty to blend the sweet with the savory.''

''We have our own ways of blending tastes in England. Fortunately the French have taught us.'' He offered her a finger of thin toast topped with mushroom pâté. ''As they taught us to kiss. They say Anne Boleyn brought the sin of kissing with the tongue back with her from the French court, and so bewitched King Henry—to the destruction of the monasteries.''

''Do you think Englishmen did not know how to kiss until then, my lord?''

''I don't know that Englishmen know how to kiss now.'' He glanced around the room, where several of the ladies were being fondled by their escorts. The dark eyes looked back at her, alight with laughter. Frances realized with disquiet that in other circumstances, and with other knowledge of him, she might have been charmed by his company.

He took a handful of strawberries from a great bowl of fruit. ''Come, Miss Woodard. Let us eat a strawberry without sugar, as nature intended.'' He dipped the ripest berry into a pot of clotted cream and held it out to her. ''A strawberry should let us know that sweetness is most satisfying with undertones of tartness. Cream alone is enough to display that.''

They should then carry on an amusing conversation, and also may talk suggestively of things. Such is the beginning. The ancient words had seemed so simple when Frances had learned them in the harem. The verses had offered a certain security, a set of expectations that she could easily fulfill. Nothing seemed simple now.

Frances took the berry by the stem and bit into the fruit. Juice and cream ran over her forefinger. She would have wiped it away, but he caught her by the wrist.

''You would no doubt have received a rap on the knuckles

for such carelessness in the harem," he said. "Let me have your hand."

Frances looked up at him, desperately trying to calm her thundering pulse. She could not guess anything of what he was thinking. What could he know of the *zenana*—of that exotic world of intrigue, peril, and hidden violence? "Why?"

"I let you have mine in the library," he said with a devastating smile. "And more: I let you have your way with me." He hesitated, and she saw something else in his expression, something dangerous, as his voice cooled. "Do you think, Miss Woodard, that I could not have stopped you, had I wished? Should we not deal fairly together? I gave you my hand and you bound it with muslin. Now let me have yours."

Four

೧೦

BOLDLY MEETING HIS eyes, she surrendered her hand. Delicately he kissed away the juice. Heat and moisture and softness enveloped the sensitive pad of her fingertip. His tongue lingered. His lips caressed. A confusing heat and heaviness flared in her belly. His dark gaze locked on hers, he drew her forefinger completely into his mouth and suckled. Expert. Ruthless. Sensation roared, like oil tossed on fire. Frances smothered a gasp. She was burning; his fingers burned her wrist; his mouth burned her hand. Her courage wavered. Letting his tongue stroke sensuously from palm to nail, slowly he drew her finger out of his mouth. With a mocking smile, he curled her hand into a loose fist and returned it to her.

"There," he said. "Now we are even. To complement all that sweetness and cleanse the palate, after the strawberry should come wine—something heady and light, like champagne."

Surely she could not lose her way now? *They may then talk about the arts, and persuade each other to drink. At last, when the woman is overcome with love and desire, the citizen should dismiss the people, giving them flowers, ointments, and betel leaves. Then the two are alone.*

She had thought she could cope; she had been prepared to trade the gifts of her body for security. But she could not handle this! Nothing could have prepared her for the power of a beautiful man as he looked down at her through those thick lashes, for the way he had taken command, for his cynical mastery of the game. For it was no longer a lesson learned from the texts, a cool, cerebral exercise in sensuality. This conflagration of her senses threatened to consume her. She must regain control!

She challenged him deliberately. "In India also, food is prepared to best complement its attributes. After all, culinary art is the twenty-third of the sixty-four arts—the accomplishments of amatory technique. I have learned them all, my lord. Name any one you would like me to demonstrate."

His recoil was immediate. In a voice like ice he asked, "Then you don't see any difference in preparing a meal and going to bed with a man?"

"Of course not," she replied with conviction. "Love is only an art, after all, like dancing or chess."

"Oh, dear God." Frances could not be sure if it was contempt or compassion that flooded his voice. "What a brave philosophy!"

"What other philosophy should a woman have, when her access to her food may depend on her skills with her body? At least Anne Boleyn sold herself for a crown."

His voice barely concealed a sudden flare of anguish. "Too high a price. She paid with her head. What will happen tonight will bear little resemblance to art of any kind. Will you retreat to your room before midnight, as I asked?"

Frances glanced about. It was all exquisite: the music, the refreshments, the tailored jackets of the men, and the lovely dresses of the ladies. There was a merriment and a wanton sensuality decorating the air. Yet running beneath it all, like the hidden track for the thunder ball in the harem, rolled that distinct undercurrent of danger, and this man was the hub of it. "There is more going on here tonight than your idle whim, isn't there, my lord?"

"My whim is never idle. When I am determined upon something, I get it."

She looked into his eyes and saw it there: a deeper emotion than flirtation and a purpose far more serious than the humbling of a rival. Once, in India, Frances had come face-to-face

with a tiger and, frozen with fear, stood her ground. Her father
had shot it, then explained that her courage had saved her. For
had she run and the tiger charged, he could never have aimed
with enough accuracy to kill it. She knew that her stubbornness hadn't been bravery, but it was still a lesson she valued:
the tiger was safer where you could see it.

"I refuse to retreat, Lord Rivaulx," she said.

"Yet perhaps I will not choose you after all, Miss Woodard.
I find there is too much spice in the food for my tastes. Go,
rejoin your poor protector. It would soothe his troubled soul
to take care of you." Frances looked around to see Donnington pushing his way through the crowd. Lord Rivaulx took
her hand and held it out to him. "Here, sir, escort Miss Woodard. Regrettably I am about to disgrace myself with unbecom-
ing raillery—not something suitable for a lady."

The marquess turned and walked away. It was a powerful
walk, full of confidence. Frances saw him take Betty Palmer
by the elbow and say something in her ear. The dandies within
earshot gave a great shout of laughter. As Donnington helped
himself to more wine a footman came up to Rivaulx with a
dish. The marquess absently helped himself to the piece of
herbed rabbit that lay in solitary splendor in its bed of parsley
and mint.

"Let us go to the ballroom, Lord Donnington." Frances
watched Rivaulx cleanly bite the meat from the rabbit's bones.
"Don't you think I should dance at my own wedding?"

Donnington frowned at her. "For God's sake, there won't
be anything as civilized as a wedding." Thrusting her aside,
he charged through the crowd after Lord Rivaulx's retreating
back.

Frances let out one long, shuddering breath.

∞

Nigel easily lost his pursuer and slipped outside. He walked
rapidly to a field behind the stables where a rider was just
checking the girths on a fast horse. A small troop of mounted
soldiers waited to provide escort. Another man stepped from
the shadows. In the moonlight his yellow hair shone like a

silver coin against velvet: Major Dominic Wyndham, an old friend and comrade.

Nigel stopped. "Alas, did I blunder about like a hen in a basket? Or is this just the trained acumen of another infernal spy?"

Wyndham laughed. "That outrageous wager with Donnington? I know you better than that, you damned rogue. Obviously something underhand was afoot." He nodded at the rider. "Lord Trent's man? It's treachery, and you found proof."

Nigel gave him a keen glance. "Was I so bloody obvious? After all my trouble! Yes, Donnington had hidden papers, but he was far too busy flinching at my assessment of his hideous taste to notice my search."

Wyndham grinned again, widely. He looked like a phantom. "So you'll play the game out until midnight. And at midnight, the woman? You're a damned dark horse, Rivaulx."

The rider swung up onto his mount and rode up to the two men. "Lord Rivaulx, Major, I'll have the papers in Whitehall by morning." He tipped his hat to Nigel. "Devil of a fine ruse if I may say so, my lord: a house full of whores, the lads dressed as footmen, and the rest ex-prizefighters!"

Nigel patted the horse on the neck. "Provided by an old friend of mine. In case there is that kind of trouble."

The rider turned his horse and signaled to the soldiers. "Damn Donnington! He deserves to swing for this. There are good men dead because of his nasty little game."

The horses bounded away.

Major Wyndham gazed at Nigel thoughtfully. "You will watch your back, won't you? If Donnington discovers what you've done, he might try revenge."

Nigel raised a brow. "In a house filled with guests, including peers of the realm? With every servant in my pay and my debt? No, the revenge is all mine. I can manage our poor traitor, Major."

The yellow-haired man laughed. "Then I hope you can manage his mistress as easily!" He bowed and strode away, back to the house.

Nigel stood for a moment looking up at the stars. Ah, yes.

The beautiful, intoxicating Miss Frances Woodard. What the devil was he going to do about her? It had all seemed so damnably simple in London. With his reputation, the shameless pursuit of an exotic woman had made a perfect excuse for him to come here like this. He had started this damnable wager thinking he could simply use her—or more likely, let her use him—and then abandon her. Now, instead, he found that he didn't want her hurt.

How could he have predicted that disturbing mixture of challenging provocation and unexpected vulnerability? He understood nothing about her, except that she disturbed him too deeply for comfort. She was not a merry wanton like one of Betty's girls, nor a coarse harlot, nor even simply a voluptuary. That defiant, dignified courage! If he did not protect her, the revelers he had let loose in her house would tear her apart like a pack of wolves. Yet she was obviously afraid of him.

Nigel faced the irony of his feelings with sour amusement, but as he stared across the shadowed pastures he didn't laugh. It made no difference. His purpose was fulfilled. Afterward, it would hardly be difficult to find her some other protector. Perhaps Major Wyndham, his friend of the yellow hair, who had instantly surmised what he was about. Nigel grinned. Dominic Wyndham might have guessed the serious purpose of this orgy, but the major wouldn't hesitate to avail himself of the wine and women before slipping back to London.

Nigel turned to go back to the house, but the stars swung wildly about in the night sky, and a wave of dizziness struck him dumb. He thrust out a hand and found the supporting bark of a tree. Dear God, what the devil was the matter with him? Surely he couldn't be this foxed? Trying to remember how much wine he had taken, Nigel looked back at the lights of Farnhurst. They glimmered innocently through the trees, then shattered into myriad bright points. Shadows raced about in the dark field as he lost focus for a moment.

A second wave of dizziness surged over him. The bark crawled under his hand, and leaves rustled in a shattering cacophony, like a thousand shaken cymbals, over his head. Then Nigel gasped at the pain and the sudden rush of nausea. He

staggered, reeling into the tree trunk, grasped his head in both
hands, and was violently sick.

Above the sound of the music there was a great deal of laughter. Frances walked through the house, senses alert. The envious glances of women and the covetous stares of men
followed her, but she ignored them. Something was going to
happen; she knew it with a dreadful certainty. As she had
known during the Hot Month among the innocent, tinkling
fountains.

Farnhurst did not boast a large ballroom, but two of the
reception rooms had been joined together by folding back a
partition so there was enough space for dancing. In other
rooms tables had been set up for dice and cards. The stakes
were already outrageously high. The atmosphere slowly, inexorably, was changing. Wine and spirits flowed more freely,
the merriment was louder and less controlled. From somewhere came the sickly-sweet smell of opium burning, and the
higher, sharper note of hashish. More than spices came to England from the Orient.

Couples began to slip from the room, and one pair of lovers
simply dropped where they were, to writhe on the floor behind
a great tub of greenery. Of Donnington and Rivaulx there was
no sign. No doubt the outrageous tour of the house continued.
At least she could be grateful that she was being spared the
marquess's unsettling company.

She was standing at the end of the ballroom when there was
a disturbance near the big double doors. Breaking away from
it, the revelers ran shrieking and laughing to the opposite side
of the room. In the confused rush, Frances found herself
whirled almost to the front of the crowd. There was a great
deal of shocked whispering and pointing, and a masked lady
suddenly tumbled to the floor in a faint. Frances slipped between the dancers until she could see what was going on.

The Marquess of Rivaulx stood in the doorway.

He had an empty wineglass in one hand and a stool in the
other. It was carved with lotus buds in the Egyptian style. He

had shed his cravat. High color burned on his cheekbones, making his dark eyes glitter with a strange brilliance. He looked absurdly handsome. Yet with the air of a man threatened with disaster, Rivaulx held the stool before him like a shield. Frances could only assume that he was completely drunk.

Ahead of him trotted a black-and-white cow with a leather halter on her head. The cow lowered her horns at the crowd of excited faces, then charged into the empty space in the center of the room. Laughing with drunken glee, Lord Donnington stumbled after her, dragged by the halter rope he clutched in one hand.

"It is time," said the marquess with a sardonic smile as he came into the room behind Donnington, "to try the livestock."

With Donnington at the halter, Rivaulx put his stool down beside the cow. He rubbed at her ears and spoke softly to her, so that the cow looked around at him with her soft brown eyes and relaxed. He sat down and leaned his head into her flank, as if fighting for control, but he proceeded to milk her very competently into his wineglass. Tossing back the foaming white liquid, he laughed at the sea of fascinated faces. A ripple of appreciation for the sheer audacity of it swept through the crowd. Frances heard their comments: how splendid, how delicious, the most scandalously outrageous *on dit* of the year!

"Milk," he said with a grin, "the universal antidote to all life's troubles. And in a Beilby wineglass, what could be more elegant? Should I take the cow for our wager, Donnington? No lady ever had such lovely lashes, and she is placid, patient, and generous to a fault." Rivaulx took another glassful and swallowed it. Then he made an exaggerated face. "Oh, devil take it," he said. "Bossy has dined on onion! You will please excuse me?"

Rivaulx stood and bowed a little unsteadily, then left the room. Apprehension moved in the back of her mind, like an echo of the hidden intentions that had corrupted the very air of the harem. Lord Donnington let go of the cow, and the animal bolted for the exit. There was a roar of laughter, and as if contaminated with their host's wild mood, a sweep of madness ran through the crowd. Frances tried to escape. It was almost impossible to get through the excited mob. She managed finally to reach the dining room.

It was already too late. The remains of the fruit pastries, the ortolans roasted on spits, the elegant fish mousse, had been pushed aside. A woman was being lifted onto the table by three men. It was Betty Palmer. Frances watched as she took one of the men by the shoulders, pulled him down, and kissed him. Another man pushed up her skirts. Around her naked thigh someone had pinned a cravat with a diamond pin. With a small shock Frances recognized that it was Rivaulx's. She glanced at the clock that sat between the silver candlesticks on the mantel. It would soon be midnight.

A hand closed on her shoulder and a young man began to swing her into his arms. He was seized from behind by one of his cronies. "By God, Jones, let her go! She belongs to the marquess."

"Ah, Mr. Jones!" cried a woman's voice. "Come this way, my dear. You'll not have the Indian lady, and I'll not have Rivaulx, more's the pity. Let us console each other."

The man released her, and Frances escaped into the hallway. She was spoken for, purchased already by private treaty. As if he walked at her side, simply by the strength of his reputation, Lord Rivaulx had created an aura of protection around her. It was almost more disturbing than comforting. In passing, she saw Donnington. He had his arm around the shoulders of a fresh-faced youth with a halo of fair curls, and they were sharing a bottle of wine. The marquess was nowhere to be seen. There was a sudden swell of song and the excited giggle of a woman. A bedroom door banged somewhere upstairs. Was Lord Rivaulx behind one of those doors, donating further pieces of clothing?

Frances slipped into the garden through a side door that led to a patio. It was surrounded by a marble balustrade, and a vine trailed up to an overhanging balcony. She breathed in great gulps of the clean night air. Far above, the summer constellations rode high.

A faint crash echoed behind her. Someone in the house had broken something.

"If there is any damage, I will pay for it," said a voice from the shadows. The words seemed to take some great effort. "At least I will if I am able to do so."

Frances forgot the sky. A man seemed to materialize from the darkness in front of her. As he moved into the beam of light that streamed from the window, deep shadows outlined his nose and jaw. She looked up at his face, the face with the devil's own beauty. He seemed to be fighting for breath. "Is nothing but crockery damaged by wantonness, Lord Rivaulx?" she asked.

He looked at her without moving.

"Are you incapable of answering a direct question, my lord? Farnhurst was a place of innocence until you came here. How could you bring your cronies and your whores to this house?"

He smiled. She could see the gleam of white teeth, yet he seemed to be shaking. He rubbed a hand over his forehead. "I hired carriages, of course. What is it that disturbs you? The loan of the house for a saturnalia?"

"Hardly. How could Lord Donnington's mistress be so nice that she cannot entertain other doxies?"

"Indeed. What could either of us know of the innocent?" The tone of the question was almost wistful.

Frances had begun to shiver. Why had she thought Farnhurst safe? She could never know innocence, could she? The night air was cool after the heat of the house and her sari was thin silk. Goose bumps had risen on her bare arms. Rivaulx shrugged out of his jacket and flung it about her shoulders, using the sleeves to pull her against him. She put up her hands to ward him off. He was far too strong.

"Why do you stay, Miss Woodard?" He seemed remote, even faintly amused. "I am glazed with intoxication, and you cannot trust me. My most idle gesture might be a dire threat. I can't tell the difference myself any longer."

Under her fingers his waistcoat was sensuously smooth, but beneath it his skin seemed to be burning, as if with fever.

"What do you want with me?" Frances asked.

"What do you think? An immense incandescent blaze of lust, or a little patience? A glimpse of heaven, or tales of tigers and the wild beauties of the Himalayas? A single night of ecstasy, or a lifetime of slavery? Perhaps all of them or none of them. We meet each other as equals now, don't we? Your hand for mine. I shall not force you to become my mistress."

"Lord Donnington has given me up, my lord."

"But if I offered you freedom, would you take it?"

Freedom! To a penniless woman in England with a ring in her nostril? The question seemed cruel. Scorn colored her voice. "I am a ruined woman. What earthly use would freedom be to me?"

"Then we are both trapped by public expectation. And a man would be a fool to refuse paradise, freely offered, and delivered on a platter. Shall I demand your surrender at midnight, and let you demand mine? And like Anne Boleyn risk the damnation of our souls? Shall we seal the bargain with a kiss?"

She must face it: Rivaulx was her future! She braced herself to be assaulted by his lips.

Instead she felt the shock of their hot, dry touch, as if his veins ran molten copper. His mouth gently touched hers until her lips trembled, then he began to tease her, moving his mouth over hers with an odd restraint. It was a waiting kiss, not as a man would give a harlot, but as a very experienced lover might give a young girl. It asked for trust and forgiveness, perhaps, and delivered a tormenting concentration of sweetness. Why, why was he doing this? Frances felt ravaged to the heart.

He pulled away and dropped his dark head against her shoulder for a moment, as if to drink in her scent. She ran one hand up to his naked throat, then over his neck to the curve of his ear. The carved lines of his jaw were entrancing, as enticing to her touch as his chest had been in the library. But the pulse under the burning skin beat madly under her fingers. What was the matter with him?

Rivaulx stepped back and, catching both of her hands in his, turned them over and raised them to his lips.

"Thank God it is almost midnight. 'For he on honey-dew hath fed, And drunk the milk of Paradise.' " He dropped a searing kiss on each palm.

In a daze of longing that confused all her senses and left
her thoughts incoherent, Frances stood transfixed. Was this the
beguiling claim of desire, mixed as it was with fear and with
fascination? Did Rivaulx really want a way out? What on earth
would become of her if he did? Would Donnington take her
back? For if the marquess claimed her as his mistress, the bluff
she had worked on with such bravado would be revealed.

The great clock in the hallway sounded out the strokes of
midnight.

"It is time, Miss Woodard," he said.

In spite of the cool night air, he stripped off his silk waistcoat as if it burned him. Then he caught her again by the hand
and turned to go back inside, tugging her behind him. His
jacket fell from her shoulders. Frances tried to match his long
strides as he dragged her through the house.

Most of the guests had packed into the ballroom. With
knowing whispers, they moved aside to let Rivaulx and Frances pass. She was the concubine from India. No one saw beyond that, least of all Rivaulx. Yet what did they all think it
meant? She had been groomed and trained and stripped of any
vestige of modesty, but she had spent those years imprisoned
in a world inhabited only by women. How the devil did they
think she had ever known a man? Yet it didn't matter, did it?
Her virginity was meaningless. There was nothing any man
could demand that she would not understand and expect. She
was not afraid of a man's body or the mysteries of his desire.
As for the rest, she could control her fears and her emotions.
So why did she feel so desolate?

With her heart in her mouth Frances watched Donnington
stumble in through the double doors. Disheveled and unkempt,
he was puce, laughing unsteadily, his cravat undone. His coat
appeared to have lost its fit. Frances realized vaguely that he
must be wearing another man's jacket.

Rivaulx towed her to the very front of the ballroom.

"Wait here," he said, his voice husky. "Don't move. You
will be safe."

Dropping her hand, Rivaulx stepped onto the dais that held
the musicians. Lord Donnington followed. Then a great noise
battered at her ears as the crowd stamped and cheered. Frances

closed her eyes for a moment and tried to take a calming
breath, but her heart hammered too loudly for her to concentrate. The crowd fell silent.

She heard the marquess's words fall softly into the hush.
"It is time, my lords, ladies and gentlemen, for me to claim
my prize from Lord Donnington."

Is it all a jest to him? Wild applause broke out again. Frances opened her eyes.

In the brilliant glare of the chandeliers his intense gaze
seemed to swallow the room. Dark hair fell wildly over his
burning forehead. Fire glittered in his eyes. His white shirt
gaped open at the neck to reveal the strong curve of his throat.
His earlier elegance was gone, as was any trace of tenderness,
or civility, or restraint. Lord Rivaulx looked like a pirate. And,
like a pirate, he was about to plunder whatever he desired.

He held up one hand and silence descended.

"He can take anything he likes to satisfy our wager." Donnington was bleary-eyed. "Anything at all!"

The marquess turned to Donnington and gave him a bow.
His ease seemed forced, as if his movements took some great
effort to control. "Should it be you, my lord? Perhaps not.
After all, I am considered a connoisseur. But I am lost in
indecision." His gaze sought the room for Frances and his
dark eyes met hers. She fought for a calm that had wantonly
deserted her as the marquess turned back to Donnington.
"What I am in need of is linen."

Betty jumped onto a chair and pulled up her skirts to show
his cravat and the diamond pin sparkling on her thigh. Lord
Rivaulx winked at her. "Since I seem to have abandoned my
cravat, Donnington, would you do me the honor to endow me
with yours?"

The room broke into a cacophony of noise: laughter, jeers,
cheers, and the clapping of hands. Donnington's face crumpled
into tears, but he pulled off his own neckwear and handed it
to his tormentor. "Then honor is satisfied, Marquess?"

Relief fought with fear. Waiting for Rivaulx's answer, Frances thought she might suffocate.

Lord Rivaulx began to fold the cravat, but it dropped to the
floor as if his supple, long fingers were unable to tie it. Tension

throbbed violently at the corner of his jaw. "Good God, Donnington, it would prove to be a damned expensive cravat! Twenty thousand was the amount, was it not? Only one item here at Farnhurst could possibly be precious enough to satisfy our wager." He turned and gestured with supreme arrogance to Frances. " 'Who can find a virtuous woman? For her price is far above rubies.' "

But his pupils are huge, glazed with confusion! What is happening? Frances knew pure terror as Rivaulx moved too quickly and seemed to lose his bearing. The chandeliers echoed as the crowd roared, but the marquess subsided—with a great deal of grace—to lie on the floor at the feet of the first violinist.

Dear Lord, was he sodden with drink, or was he ill? Without thinking, Frances ran quickly up the steps and bent over him. Rivaulx looked up at her and laughed. It was the wild, uncontrolled laughter of deep intoxication. Then his wide, unfocused gaze was instantly shuttered behind closed lids.

"Am I wandering in the purple fields of the lotus-eater or the wild forests of Dionysus?" He rolled over onto his back and shook with secret hilarity. "Alas, Miss Woodard. Let us retire from this ribald crew!"

"For God's sake," said someone. "He's completely foxed!"

Rivaulx laughed again. "Not too foxed to know what to do with a beautiful woman, sir!"

He took her head in both hands and pulled her face down to his. Although she struggled to pull away, he pressed his lips to her mouth. The crowd roared their approval, and he released her.

Burning with humiliation, Frances took him by the collar and slapped his cheek, his hard jaw bruising her fingers. "You are completely dissolute," she hissed, "indecent, lost to all honor!"

The eyelashes fluttered open again to reveal that fevered, unfocused gaze, and he laughed uproariously. Dear God, but he was dangerous, with his beautiful face and his evil humor, yet there was more than that behind this wildness, and it was deeper than Frances could fathom. Those dark eyes did not

show the pinprick pupils of an opium addict. But neither was
Lord Rivaulx drunk.

He reached up a hand and grasped her by the wrist. His
grip burned into her skin. "Then shall we prove it, dear
heart?" he asked. "Come, let us to bed!"

In a movement of decadent power, he pushed himself to his
feet and caught her against his heart. The crowd seemed to
have reached some kind of frenzy. Abandon throbbed like a
drumbeat. Bodies surged against them as they were swept
from the ballroom and half carried up the stairs. Rivaulx kept
that death grip on her, his arm about her waist, using his body
to shield her as they were bustled down the hallway and finally
thrust through the doorway into his room.

"Thank you, friends," he said, his voice trembling, yet
shadowed by an immovable determination. "Enough! I don't
need an audience. Go away, like the wicked wantons that you
are, and make whatever mayhem of your own that you please!
The night belongs now to the pagan gods."

For a moment the crowd wavered, so that Frances feared
she would be stripped and raped before a jeering audience, but
Rivaulx's confidence was a wall of steel. The door slammed
shut behind them, and the sounds of the revelers faded away
down the hall. He released his grip on Frances and turned the
key in the lock.

"You are safe now." His voice shook with intense emotion.

Frances stalked away across the room. What now? And
what, what was the matter with him?

He leaned his head back against the door and put his palms
over his face for a moment. Then the griffin on his ring grimaced at her as he held out a hand in a gesture she couldn't
understand. Was it imperiousness or supplication? Lord Rivaulx smiled at her, a long, slow smile of pure seduction.

"Or at least, you would be if you were not locked in a
bedroom with a madman."

Five

❧

SEVERAL CANDLES BURNED on the mantelpiece, leaving the rest of the room in shadow. Frances took a single candlestick and crossed to the bed. She threw back the covers and exposed the sheets. Now that the moment had come, all her certainty and calm had deserted her. What use her education with a man like this? She had been prepared for sensuality, not violence. Trembling with the high, courageous anger she hoped would sustain her when she was raped, she looked up at him.

"Come, then, my lord!" she said. "Come here and ravish me!"

Lord Rivaulx stood very still, leaning back against the door in his shirtsleeves. In their rush up the stairs his shirt had torn; it gaped open, exposing the hard curve of his throat and the dark bruise she had given him, a soft brand on his chest. The candlelight flung moving shadows in the hollows at the base of his throat and under his jaw. The bones of his face were stark against his dark hair; his eyes burned like black coals. He was, quite simply, devastating.

"Damnation!" He was looking at her through narrowed lashes. "I am hardly in a fit state for company."

"What do you mean?"

"I mean, dear Miss Woodard, that I shall not, as you so quaintly put it, ravish you."

"Then why did you claim me and bring me up here?"

"Do you think I could have left you down there with that mob? Every woman in this house is a harlot. What the hell do you think would have happened to you? Dear God, if you balk at rape by one man, would you have liked it better from twenty?"

He had closed his eyes. Both hands were spread and pressed into the paneling behind him. He was shaking. As Frances watched him an appalling realization began to blossom in her mind. *Milk,* he had said as he leaned his head into the dappled flank of the cow, *the universal antidote.* She could still feel the burning of his hot, dry lips on hers.

She was seized with a conviction so impossible that she tried to dismiss it. But there had been menace in the air all evening. She could see it clearly now, and Rivaulx had expected danger. *Do you think we shall have thunder by tonight?* Yet he could never have expected this. Gathering her courage, she walked up to him and set the candle on the table next to the door.

"What is the matter? Are you ill? Or damned? Did you trade your soul for me, my lord?"

The dark eyes opened and bored into hers. "Damned? No doubt I am. 'Confin'd to waste in fires, till the foul crimes done in my days of nature art burnt and purged away.'"

He reached out one hand to the candle. The smooth skin glowed as he deliberately began to lower his palm onto the flame. Frances snatched the candle away, but his lean fingers closed over hers, taking command. Wax spilled and the flame went out. She relaxed into his grip and concentrated on the energy she could feel flowing from his palm. There was a frantic strength in it, far too uncontrolled, and her appalling suspicion coalesced into certainty.

It was just as she had seen it in India: the huge pupils, the fight for control. There had been a demonstration on some slaves in the *zenana,* and then once in a village, an accident to a child. That time it had taken only fifteen minutes to bring about death, but the slaves had raved in their fever, shaking their fists at imaginary demons. There was no certain outcome, no usual progression of the symptoms, only a torment that drove men to insanity and made death welcome.

"My lord," she said, forcing her voice to stay calm. "I know what the matter is."

He released her hand and leaned back against the door. Frantically, he watched the flames on the mantel. "Tell me: do houris like you welcome souls into paradise?"

Frances set down the candlestick and reached up to touch his forehead. His skin was as hot and dry as the desert in the Hot Month. Fever consumed him. And she had slapped him! "Would the pain of a burn be enough atonement to win you heaven instead of hell?" she asked gently.

He grinned down at her, running one hand over her cheek in a gesture of pure flirtation. How could he? She could see the illness running in him like a sandstorm. "I thought you might be heaven."

Frances looked directly into his eyes. "Stop it! Think less now about dalliance, Lord Rivaulx, than about dying."

The dark eyes were shining with self-derision. Grasping her fingers, he walked across the room to the four-poster. It took a visible effort. Frances was dragged behind him. "A ludicrous end. It's no doubt what I deserve for my depraved habits."

"You already have fever. After fever comes coma. From coma, death. You may be depraved, my lord, but I don't believe you are stupid."

He released her hand, dropped to the bed, and leaned back against the headboard. "But I do have a very wicked sense of humor."

"This is someone's idea of a joke?"

His grin carried a dreadful bravado. "Not mine, believe me. In spite of my naughty manners, I wanted my wits about me tonight. Instead I seem to have been thoroughly trumped."

"You play a game? Why?"

"For amusement, of course. Do you never play games? I thought we had shared some already."

Dangerous shoals eddied about her. "I know some, but not this one. You have been poisoned. How long have you known?"

His eyes were unfocused, the pupils swallowing each iris. "For a few hours, perhaps. When my vision began to swim after I had taken only one bottle of wine, and little demons began to claw at my spine. Yet the effects seem to come in waves. A moment ago the room was clear, now I'm seeing monsters in the corner. If I had a sword, I'd be slashing at the curtains. I drank the milk as soon as I could—isn't it the cure?''

"You have taken nightshade or henbane. And henbane would have killed you by now. Milk is not really a universal antidote. It's no use for either.''

He grinned. "So I realized, once I tried it. But I hate milk. In addition, I ate salt and chewed my own temper. Thus, between my admiration of Lord Donnington's furnishings and the claiming of his cravat, I made more than one visit outside. Each time I cast up my accounts it seemed to help, but there is nothing left now of my supper. Will I live, do you suppose?''

How could he be so casual about it? "If you deserve to,'' she said.

Nigel laughed as if this were hilarious. "Oh, God! Not you, too? It is enough that someone in this house has administered poison without adding your condemnation of my disgraceful behavior. Dear Lord, but I wish I hadn't had my reasons.'' He lay back on the pillows and flung out his arms. "Deadly nightshade?''

"Atropo belladonna.''

"Ah. Named for Atropos, the oldest of the three Fates, the one who cuts the thread of life. English country people call it dwale.'' She could sense his frustration as he fought for control. "How the devil was it administered? For no one else seems to be fevered and stripped of their senses.'' His lids closed.

With both hands she shook him by the shoulders. "You mustn't sleep!''

" 'By a sleep to say we end the heart-ache and the thousand natural shocks that flesh is heir to.' You should have let me burn myself.''

"So the pain would keep you awake? There will be enough pain. Let me fetch help. Betty Palmer is your friend.''

He made a wild gesture. "No! No one must know about

this! Not even Betty. If I die, it won't matter, and if I live, I'd like to see who is surprised by my survival.''

"Then talk to me," she said. "Tell me anything you like, but keep talking."

"What about?"

"You could begin with telling me why you have searched this house. For love letters? Accounts of wagers lost or won?"

His eyes narrowed to slits. "How very perceptive of you."

"The *zenana* is a hotbed of intrigue, my lord. There are many ways to hide a secret message, but none that cannot be discovered, and your search was obvious enough to alert even a *punkah wallah*."

He looked confused. "Who?"

"The boy who sits behind a screen to pull the cords of the fans in the palace."

"Then thank goodness for your powers of observation, for here you sit like Baucis at the bedside, ministering. At least there will be one witness of my last descent into Hades."

Frances heard the frustration in her own voice. "I have watched you all evening. Don't you think I had cause enough? You have some deeper rivalry with Lord Donnington than an idle wager, don't you?"

"You think I can tell you? Oh, dear God, I can't lie here like this!"

He pushed himself violently from the bed and began to stalk about the room, like a caged cat, lithe, graceful, frantic. Suddenly he pressed his back against the wall. There was nothing but the sound of his disordered breathing for a moment. He closed his eyes.

"Tell me about India!" It was almost a command.

"You would like to know how an English girl became the concubine of a maharaja? It is quite simple. I was taken and sold when my father was killed. I was fortunate. I was bought by a potentate of enormous wealth and kept in luxury."

"And then escaped?"

"Yes," said Frances. "But long before that I went to school in Essex. It was very ordinary and dull."

Rivaulx gave no indication that he noticed how smoothly she had changed the subject. "Yet you know about henbane and the effects of deadly nightshade. You know the Latin names of plants.''

"I am a lady of rare accomplishments,'' she replied.

Once again, as if from somewhere deep inside, he found the strength to smile. Frances felt stunned by the sheer courage of it. Whatever else he might be, Lord Rivaulx was dauntless.

"Some of which you learned from your father when you joined him in Bengal. He was a botanist. He wanted to explore, and after your mother died, he took you with him. When you traveled into hill country infested with bandits, he was killed during an attack. You joined the household of the local maharaja. Your return to Calcutta four years later caused a sensation which sent ripples all the way home to London. When you arrived penniless in England, it was to find the lurid stories waiting for you.''

Frances began to feel a rising panic, and spun away. "How do you know so much about me?''

"Oh, dear God,'' he said. "It's my damned profession—information, gossip, the blossoming of a rumor. Such filthy knowledge is my stock-in-trade. Were you very afraid at the inn in Dover when you discovered that the aunt you had hoped to join in England had died, and that there was nowhere for you to go?''

"How could I have been?'' Damn him! Damn him! He had spied on her? Had he planned this entrapment? Her voice was heavy with sarcasm. "I met Lord Donnington as he returned from France. It didn't take very long to secure his protection. With my training, how could it have been otherwise? Men can be ensnared like rabbits.''

His next words were almost a whisper. "I'm sorry,'' he said.

The candlelight danced over his ravaged face. His pupils seemed fathomless. Oh, dear Lord! When he milked the cow, during that burning kiss, when he took Donnington's cravat—all evening he had been fighting the devastating effects of this drug. She was angry with a sick man. Yet he had not abandoned her to the mob. And whatever he might be, Lord Rivaulx faced death. He had no one but her to offer comfort. Did he know the degradation the next hours were likely to bring? Closing her lids for a moment, Frances took a calming breath, and opened her heart to compassion.

∞

Nigel saw her hazily. The room had become a swirling blur. His own voice was dim to him, as if someone else spoke. She was lying. It had not been easy for her to accept Donnington's protection. But there wasn't time to explore that further now, for if he survived the poison, his task had just become all the more urgent. "I have a question to ask you, Miss Woodard. Do you hold Lord Donnington in affection?"

"Why, my lord?"

"Oh, damnation!" The edges of his vision had gone dark as if he peered through a tunnel filled with rushing projectiles. The floor seemed to boil up at him, nails exploding from the oak boards. He flinched and put his hands over his eyes. "Please. Can you help me to the bed? If I don't lie down, I shall fall, and I seem to be going blind."

He heard her footsteps as she came to him and put her hand about his waist. The generosity of it stunned him.

"Come." Her voice seemed ineffably gentle. "You won't die. The devil rarely takes his own."

With the entire strength of his will, Nigel tried to make his muscles obey. To his shame he knew he shook like a sail in the wind. He leaned one arm on her shoulders and put his head against her hair. She smelled so enticing, sweet and clean and feminine. Hating his dependence on her fragile strength, Nigel allowed her to help him across the room. He collapsed to the bed and knew he had unwittingly pulled her down beside him. His fingers had somehow become entangled in her plait. With infinite care he tried and failed to extricate them.

Her hair felt like sunshine, like strands of silk glowing warm in the sun. It seemed a marvel of beauty. He wanted to let it loose and cover her breast with the honey-gold strands. A man could swim there—in the floating sanctuary of her hair.

Gently she freed her plait, but she kept his fingers firmly in hers. The griffin flamed on his ring, burning into the bone. Would this consuming fire in his body burn her, too? Nigel tried to pull away, but her cool fingers held on steadily. They seemed to spread balm into his disordered blood. Her breath came in a deep, calming rhythm. Nigel tried to let his racing mind follow her regular, slow pulse, but his heart was thundering loudly enough now for her to hear it, and the sound of his own blood was deafening in his ears.

"Aren't you afraid of me, Miss Woodard?" Nigel whispered. "The beautiful lady, Belladonna, she makes men mad."

"Stay calm," she said. "Let me help you."

Ruthlessly calling on what was left of his sanity, Nigel opened his eyes. His vision slowly returned, but it was shattered and dazed as if he had stared too long at the sun. He tried to focus on the beautiful face with its golden ring in the nostril. It was as if she had traveled to another world—some place he could never reach, could never join her. Frances seemed like something from a dream, a vision of desire and exotic allure. *A damsel with a dulcimer in a vision once I saw; it was an Abyssinian maid, and on her dulcimer she played, singing of Mount Abora.* Before he died, would he go insane? Would he gibber and rave in front of her? God grant him simply coma and death! Nigel returned her steady grip on his hand and concentrated on it.

How sweet the pliant touch of her mouth had been beneath his burning lips—his houri, his damsel of the dulcimer. He wanted to pull her down to him, fasten his lips to hers, drown in her. Desire, ardent and demanding, filled his whirling mind. *God knows, I don't want another entanglement with a woman. Not now, not ever! How can I repay her generosity and compassion with lust?* Yet his erection mocked him. Then his head was filled with a clamoring of voices, commanding his attention. *You want her, Nigel. She's only a harlot. Take her!* Was that another effect of the belladonna? He laughed.

"Stop it!" she said sharply. "Do not give way to it! Talk to me."

If he died, he didn't want her to think him a wastrel or a lunatic. But his judgment felt suspended. She could be anyone, she might even be the hand behind the poison. Because she was living in Donnington's house, he had discovered what he could about her, but it was not enough. Nigel didn't care. He heard himself speak. To his relief the words sounded calm and sane.

"I didn't come here for personal revenge. All this—the wager, the women, the carousal—was just cover for my mission. I'm sorry, but Lord Donnington has been sending information to France, and today I obtained proof of it. He is a traitor. He will be arrested in the morning and Farnhurst will be seized by the government."

He could feel the leap in her pulse as her small world fractured. The fever shook him again. He smiled with bitter self-derision. For mixed with his importunate lust was a painful tenderness for her—for her aloneness, her beauty, her stalwart courage—and an odd regret that he had nothing to offer her except ashes.

The last shreds of control were slipping away. Nigel knew himself wild, unfocused, lost in complete abandon. *Take her!* said the small, wanton voice. *You won her fairly. She's yours.*

The posts of the bed began to writhe like dancing girls. In spite of the sudden panic and fear he saw in her eyes, with irresistible strength Nigel pulled Frances down onto the covers beside him.

Silk tore.

∽

Lord Donnington stared at the embossed leaves in the ceiling plaster and laughed weakly. He was very drunk.

"Damn his bloody eyes!" he said aloud, then laughed again.

His house was being demolished around him, randomly and without malice, a mere side effect of the revelry. This orgy would never be forgotten. The name of Farnhurst would echo down the ages. And wasn't there a certain glory in that?

The man next to him touched his hand. "Do you think he is having pleasure in her, *mon cher?*" The word *pleasure* seemed to have a life of its own, the last syllable drawn out, sinuous and full of promise, yet still mocking.

Donnington sprawled against the table leg. There was spilled food on the floor next to him. "Damn her bloody eyes,

as well." He glanced down at the fingers stroking his own.
"You were in France—" With a weak laugh he began to sing.
" 'A frog he would a-wooing go . . .' "

"A frog is a small amphibian, *mon cher*. I am but a man,
like yourself."

"Like me, eh?" Donnington looked him in the face, and
winked.

The man leaned forward like a conspirator. "Let us be private. It is a very fine night. Won't you come outside? When
Rivaulx is finished with the little Indian whore, he will hunt
for you."

"For me?" Donnington felt the betraying tears, but he
didn't care. "No, not him! He'll not look for me. Yet, by God,
I want him. I've always wanted him. It's what makes it all so
bloody unfair."

"I am his friend. I can deliver him to you . . ."
The man's face seemed to swim in the wavering light, yet
he was smiling with unmistakable meaning. Donnington
grinned back. Leaning his weight on the other man's arm, he
stumbled to his feet and grasped a bottle and two glasses. He
thrust the glasses into his pocket. Waving the wine bottle in
his other hand, Donnington allowed his guest to lead him from
the room.

Thyme crushed under their feet as the two men followed
the stone path through the sunken herb garden. Beyond the
formal lawn the shrubbery was dark and dry, rustling with the
secret sounds of the night. Donnington followed his guide past
the statue of Hermes and up a long meandering track to the
ornamental fishpond. Moonlight rippled across the dark water.

"There are things I could tell you about him." Everything
was blurred out here in the dark. His cheeks felt wet. Donnington rubbed at them with his fist. "And about Paris. Paris,
that's where he was, with the Russian woman, Catherine."

Donnington sat down heavily on the small stone wall
around the pond and attempted to fill the two glasses. Wine
spilled and ran into the water like blood.

His guest took one of the glasses and raised it in salute. "*À
plaisir, monsieur*. You want him, but you hate him, don't you?
Which is why you have never told him anything. Never mind.

Lord Rivaulx will not come to you now. But I am here.''

The man leaned closer. Donnington felt maudlin and a little resentful. French? Who was French? His tears ran freely as the wineglasses dropped to the ground.

Silk tore. Her sari gave way as Rivaulx pulled Frances into his arms. At that moment she knew nothing but fear. He was strong, and dangerous, as the drug took its stranglehold on his senses. She could hear his heart hammering, drumming against her, loud like storm waves pounding a shore. With inexorable power he rolled her onto her back and pinned her beneath him.

''Dulcimer damsel,'' he said, his breath hot against her hair. ''Don't. Don't. Don't fight me.''

The lines of his face were cut clear and pure in the flickering candlelight. His pupils seemed huge, like the eyes of a cat in the dark, fathomless and without soul. In one fierce movement, he pulled away her veil and discarded it over the side of the bed. *Shabnam,* the muslin of the morning dew.

She heard herself speak, breathless, possessed by a strange calm, though the fear flickered beneath like a banked fire. ''It is all right. I shan't fight you.'' Donnington was a traitor. He would be arrested. She had nowhere to go. *I am a courtesan, committed only to myself and my survival.*

He reared back on his heels and violently stripped off the remains of his shirt. The white fabric landed in a heap over her veil. He was naked, corded arms and broad chest, above the flat waistband of his breeches. The bruise she had given him leaped with his heartbeat.

He took her hand and laid it over the bruise. ''I am burning, dulcimer damsel. Here, feel.''

The smooth skin flamed beneath her fingers. She felt her courage strain, stretched taught over panic, like a flimsy barrier trying to keep out a mob. His pulse melted into hers, pounding, leaping. The griffin blurred as he moved her palm to his lips and kissed it. Frances lay still. His mouth was hot and soft, his tongue flicking lightly. She felt a treacherous melting, and tears pricked at her eyelids. *It is unfair. Unfair!*

His fingers moved to her sari. Very deliberately he began to tear it. Cool air touched her skin. He exposed her throat. Her collarbone. Now the valley between her breasts. The brush of his knuckles against her bare flesh feathered lower. Her ribs. Her waist. Her navel. The touch of his fingers. And the sound of silk ripping.

It stopped. Pinned beneath him in her ruined clothes, she could feel her heartbeat racing to match his.

"Your hair. I want . . . Let me . . ."

His words were gone. The huge black pupils devoured her like a dumb beast's. He slid her plait through his palms and tried to unfasten it. His fingers fumbled in the ribbon. Shaking, he began to curse.

Quickly and neatly, Frances untied her hair. *I shall not be afraid. There is nothing he can do that need make me afraid.* He took the ribbon from her and, watching it intently, let it slide to the floor. Then his long fingers moved to her arms, as if to lift her toward him. Frances sat up, offering herself. Her hair fell free, and the remains of her sari slipped from her shoulders. The short blouse that she wore underneath—torn in two—fell away, baring her breasts beneath the curtain of hair.

"Ah." It was nothing more than an escaping breath, as he reached out one hand to trace the fall of her hair and let it slide beneath his fingers. His knuckles grazed her nipple, and Frances swallowed hard, looking up at him, as the shock of sensation sank into her body.

Blindly he took her by both shoulders and pulled her against him. The hot trail of his fingers burned along her spine, past her waist, pushing away fabric, stripping her. She was trapped, captive, crushed, her skin ablaze with his, her nipples aching. His mouth closed over hers. His kiss sought and demanded, and a strong, masculine hand caught one of her breasts and caressed it.

His mouth trailed lower, over her arched neck and the little hollow at the base of her throat, nuzzling, nipping, suckling. Frances gasped for a breath, then another.

Even one night with Nigel would be a precious gift to women in our profession.

And she wanted, fiercely, to give back. She knew how. She

had been trained. He was only a man, with a man's needs. He should have what he had won, but embellished and graced with the ancient wisdom of the East, where nothing was forbidden and nothing unknown. He should have his pleasure and she could heighten it to ecstasy. Lost in her own desire, Frances moved against him and ran her nails over his back, around his ribs, and into the waistband of his breeches.

Six

HE PULLED AWAY. Violently.

As Frances sat, naked, abandoned, he turned and dropped his head into his hands.

Tentatively she reached out and touched his shoulder. "What is it?"

The face that glanced into hers was devastated, the eyes haunted. "Oh, God. Oh, God. I am mad."

Though his arousal still thrust against the front of his breeches, he tried clumsily to pull the shreds of silk together over her body. Her robes were beyond repair. With a terrifying concentration he lifted his own torn shirt from the floor and draped it around her shoulders.

He reached down for her veil, and fell forward from the bed.

Frances slid her feet to the floor, but he was already up. Hitting with one shoulder, he had rolled and leaped upright. Candlelight flashing over his skin, he strode away across the room. He jerked out a knife and threw it hard, so that it struck quivering in the molding high above their heads. Then with one wild gesture he sent the washbasin and pitcher crashing from their stand. With another he demolished a spindle chair, smashing the wood and the embroidered seat into a mess of splinters and threads. In a concentration of destruction he stalked around the room, breaking furniture and ornaments.

China hit the oak boards in blossoming shards, the wire sprang, twisting, from a cloisonné enamel clock.

Clutching his shirt over her breasts, Frances shrank back against the pillows as he rampaged. After that moment of unexpected tenderness, this rage was shattering. *Locked in a bedroom with a madman.*

At last he stopped, shaking, leaning his head into the curtains, burying his face. There was a long silence, broken only by the breath rasping in his throat. His shoulders shuddered, as if he kept his arms still by some enormous effort of will. At last he looked up.

"They aren't really there, are they?"

Frances had closed her eyes, seeking calm, slowing her breathing, escaping into that hidden place where she could be removed and safe. His words dragged her back, startling her into speech. "What? What isn't there?"

He turned to face her then, clinging with both hands to the heavy velvet at his back. "Frenchmen."

"You are having visions. They cannot hurt you. Don't be afraid." She didn't know if she was trying to reassure him or herself.

"It is not the French that I fear." A spasm passed over his face. He dropped his head back, exposing his throat. "I don't want . . ."

She said nothing, fighting for understanding, though her heart hammered.

He looked at her, his hair tumbled onto his forehead and agony in his dark, heated gaze. His voice resonated with intensity. "What just happened . . . *almost* happened. I don't want it."

Frances folded her hands. "It is what I have been trained for."

He thrust the side of his fist into the wall. "I don't *want* it."

She leaned forward, hugging his torn shirt in both arms, letting her hair drift over her face as she turned her head away. There were tears in her eyes, painful and hot. "You came to Farnhurst to claim me. I thought I was to be your mistress. I have agreed to it."

His fingers clutched desperately at the curtains. "I don't want a mistress. Can't you understand that? God help me, I want you, but I won't . . ."

She made herself look directly at him. "Lord Rivaulx. I am a courtesan."

"Oh, for God's sake!" With both hands he took the curtains and in one violent wrench tore them to the floor. "Do you think I don't know that? That I don't crave what you can do? I despise it! I don't want a mistress, *any* mistress. And I don't want this—" He swept his arm about the room, the mitered muscles leaping into definition. "I don't want any of it. Dear God. Dear God, help me."

He dropped, wrapping his arms about his head.

Frances could feel herself shaking. The drug was running in him again, like wildfire racing through dry grass. She knew he was in pain, but he did not move. He crouched in the ruin of the curtains, white breeches stark against crimson velvet, his body tawny in contrast, sculptured and shadowed with bronze in the flickering light. At the base of his spine, the white fabric curved over his loins and stretched down the powerful length of his thighs, a mockery of elegance. He looked like a hunting cat, ablaze with hunger in the jungle, and quivering.

"You must restrain me," he whispered at last. "I cannot do it for myself much longer."

Frances was shocked into speech. "Restrain you?"

She saw him swallow, the ripple passing down his strong throat.

"Will you make me beg?" He knelt, holding up the heavy braided curtain cord in both hands. "I beg you."

"What do you want?"

"I cannot fight it anymore—*Atropo belladonna,* the mistress I cannot refuse—and what else? What else have they given me?" His black eyes bored into hers. "I beg of you, dulcimer damsel. Tie me down."

Frances shook her head.

He lurched to his feet, his grace gone, control and strength robbed by the poison in his veins. "You did it in the library, but you won't do it here? I am going *mad*. It is coming afresh, and worse this time. God knows what I might do! Tie me to the bed, then leave." He walked slowly, carefully, to her, holding the cord bunched in one hand as he felt for the bed with the other. His fingers touched her arm. He dropped to both knees in front of her. "I beg you."

The tears ran openly now. She knew he could not see them. "You don't need to beg. Lie down."

Frances took the cord from his hands and helped him onto the bed. His muscles bunched convulsively. For the second time that day she bound his wrists, this time to two of the uprights of the four-poster. She did the same to his feet, so that he was spread-eagled.

"I shan't leave you," she said. "Whatever pain you feel, they are only illusions. You are going to live."

His body arched. He gritted his teeth and strained against his bonds.

"Damnation! I want—" He broke off again.

"Do not want anything. Just let yourself be." She knew she was shaking, too, with a fear she could no longer hide. Using every skill she possessed, Frances kept her voice steady and calm. "There is a tale they tell in India. Once it was told in twenty-four thousand verses. Now, they say, there are one hundred thousand, beyond counting. There is one verse that goes like this: 'The man who denies his desires is tormented by them. The enlightened man pulls his senses into himself. Desire cannot enter.' " His eyes were fixed on her face though she knew he was sightless. "Desire nothing. Do not be afraid. What is happening is not real."

He closed his lids. "There is a tale they tell in England." Each word was deliberate, carefully enunciated, and excruciatingly slow. Frances could not imagine the effort of will it took for him to speak rationally now. "A man met a maiden once by a fountain. She rode away with his horse and his hound. He was a knight. He did not want to leave desire behind."

Frances laid her hand lightly on his chest, over the bruise she had given him. "What was her name?"

"Catherine."

"And does she still have his horse and his hound?"

He turned his head away. "She is dead. Now, for God's sake, leave."

∞

Frances did not leave. While he raved on the bed, straining against the cords, she walked around the ruined chamber. He thrashed and called out more than once, but much of it was a language she didn't know. There was water caught in the bottom of the broken pitcher. Whenever he was quiet, she used it to sponge his face, neck, and chest, and dribbled a little between his parched lips, but she knew he was no longer aware of her.

At last he lay still.

She crossed back to the bed and looked down at him. He was deathly pale, but his breathing was normal and his skin was cool to the touch. He appeared to be sleeping in deep exhaustion, but it was not coma. Nigel Arundham would survive. Frances walked to the window and stared out into the night, cocooned in silence. That profound hush just before dawn. The background of music and revelry had faded away hours ago. Was she the only person still awake? Who else knew that the Marquess of Rivaulx had lain here fighting for life and sanity while the guests indulged—then slept off—their debauchery?

She dropped her head against the window frame. Oh, Lord. So this shattering day had come to an end. She was abandoned again, as she had been at the Green Man. Unless Donnington could somehow find a way to provide for her—in spite of the charge of treason? Or might he be proved innocent, and still find her that safe, elderly protector she had imagined? It was a weak hope, but it was the only one Frances had left.

Rivaulx stirred and groaned. Frances took the damp cloth and sponged his forehead as she cursed him silently. What a hideously unequal bargain this had been! He had destroyed more than the room. He had destroyed her life here at Farnhurst and her dream of a secure future. Yet this man filled with desires did not want her. She was left with nothing, while he would survive and undoubtedly triumph.

Frances dropped the cloth, part of the ruin of her sari, and curled up on the huge bed between his outstretched arm and leg. She faced her own despair, underlain as it still was by anger, knowing that she, too, was trapped on the wheel of worldly desire—and that nothing could be more dangerous. Eventually she slept.

∞

Someone was hammering. Against a blue-black, thunder-filled sky, white cranes soared toward the distant Himalayas, their wings bright against her eyelids. Frances blinked. Immediately it all came back to her. Farnhurst. The marquess. The poison. She blinked again and opened her eyes. Sunlight flooded in through the window where Rivaulx had torn down the curtains. It was morning.

The hammering was replaced with a loud thudding. Someone was battering at the door with something heavy.

"For God's sake," said a familiar voice, full of irony. "I am coming."

It was Rivaulx, striding to the door. As she sat up he turned and smiled at her.

"Your knots were excellent, Miss Woodard. Except that my wiles were even better. Curtain cord makes a damnable rope for fetters, and I have had some practice at escape."

He was pale, exhaustion clear on his features, but she had not misjudged. He looked sane and undefeated, and he was no longer blind.

The door was shaking in its frame. Rivaulx turned the key in the lock and opened it.

∞

When he had first heard the thunder of noise, he thought it was cannon. He was stretched between the butchering rings in a Russian barn while French guns pounded in the distance. His clothing was Cossack. Beneath the fur cap, long hair hung to his shoulders, his face obscured by his beard, filthy and ragged. They must not discover he was a British officer, but dear God, these Frenchmen were filled with hatred for Cossacks! How much pain would they inflict to gain information, or would they damage him just for the fun of it? Light flashed on a knife. He opened his eyes.

A bedroom and brilliant sunlight. Nigel wondered briefly why he was surprised he could see. This was England, Farnhurst. His hands weren't held by French rope. It was heavy silk cord, and he was spread out like a starfish, bare from the waist up. The cord was too soft and round to make tight knots. In a matter of moments he had his left hand free, then the right, and had slipped from the bed.

Miss Frances Woodard lay curled in sleep, her hair a drift of gold. Under his discarded shirt she was almost naked. He felt shaken by a profound tenderness, yet beneath it lay a dreadful apprehension. What the devil had happened between them? Nigel pulled the bedclothes over her.

The sound heightened to that of wood splintering. She woke and he tried to reassure her. Then he crossed the room, turned the key, and flung wide the door.

"Good Lord," he said. "It's the importunate messenger Gabriel, determined to disturb my dawns. Lance, I really don't want to see you."

A sheepish footman was looking at Nigel behind the head of a large and threatening ax. He dropped it and stepped back. Lancelot Spencer leaned against the wall in the corridor, his arms folded across his chest. Nigel waved away the footman. The fellow bobbed his head and left.

Lance stepped forward into the doorway. "Something important has . . . Dear God! What the devil went on in here?"

"I really don't know." Nigel yawned deliberately behind one hand. "It would appear to be a bedchamber. I believe I slept in it."

Lance's blue gaze swept over the room, at the devastation of broken furniture and crockery, at the ruined curtains and the spilled water. And at last, as if it pained him, at the bed. From his immaculate neckcloth to his blond hair, Lance flushed scarlet. Frances was sitting up, watching the two men. She had pulled the cover around her shoulders. The skin beneath her eyes looked bruised, and her hair was tangled.

Shreds of blue silk lay scattered, and each of the four posts still trailed its length of cord, the ends eloquent on the rumpled sheets. It was an ugly enough picture.

"I heard about it." The flush faded, leaving Lance's skin very white. "The party, how you claimed the woman. I knew you were wedded to dissipation, but I had no idea you would sink—" He looked sick. "Oh, dear God. How could you?"

"It's a mess, I admit. I must have been very foxed."

"You well know that is not what I mean!" Lance started toward Frances, his voice unsteady. "Madam, if there is anything I can do?"

"No," said Frances flatly.

Nigel thrust out one arm, stopping Lance in his tracks, and suppressed his small flare of anger. Why the hell couldn't he remember exactly what had happened? "Would you pray refrain from leaping to conclusions? Surely what I do with a woman in a bedroom is my own affair? Now, why the devil were you breaking down my door?"

Lance turned to him, the fine nostrils flared with distaste. "There has been some kind of accident. I decided to come down from town, and was given the news as I arrived. Since you are in charge here, it seemed important to wake you."

"Important enough to take an ax to my bedroom lock?"

Nigel dropped his arm. Leaving Lance standing awkwardly in the wrecked room, he strode to a door that was disguised as part of the paneling and pushed it open. A dressing room lay beyond. His clothes were hanging on the rack, his razor and brushes neatly arrayed on the washstand. His traveling case, with the griffin crest stamped into the leather, sat on the floor beside it. He felt a moment of dislocation at the normalcy of it all. It was as if a storm had flattened a village, yet left some delicate toy untouched. Nigel splashed cold water on his face, pulled a clean shirt over his head, and thrust his feet into boots. Then he took a long dressing gown from the back of the door and carried it to Frances.

She glanced into his face, her expression blank, and took the gown. "Thank you, my lord."

Whatever had happened, how could she seem so unmoved

by it? With a certain amount of acerbity, Nigel spoke to Lance. "What news?"

"I don't know if it's what you wanted—if it was part of some damned diabolical plan of yours—but your host drowned himself in the fishpond last night. I thought you ought to know: Lord Donnington is dead."

Nigel turned immediately to Frances. Like a doe facing a man with a spear—wild with thoughts of flight, yet mesmerized by imminent, inevitable death—her eyes had darkened to cobalt.

"Miss Woodard. I am very deeply sorry." It was only as the words came out that he realized how deep was his own shock. Had he driven a man to take his own life? May God forgive him! "May I get you . . ."

She shook her head, her hair a golden veil over her shoulders. "Nothing!"

Nigel wanted very badly to offer comfort. The emptiness of the thought was derisive. He was presumably the last person in the world who could offer her anything. There lay the bed, the crumpled sheets, and the curtain cord. Her blue sari lay in shreds, her short blouse was torn in two. She looked infinitely beautiful, but in his distress he felt no desire. What games had he played here last night? Had he driven a man to suicide by raping his mistress? Lance moved impatiently.

Nigel had never in his life felt so powerless. "I am sorry, Miss Woodard, I must go and see to this. Will you be all right?"

She nodded.

"The body has not been moved," Lance said stiffly from the doorway.

Nigel turned to him. "Very well. I am coming."

He followed Lance through the house. Everywhere lay the evidence of the previous night's debauch: spilled wine, tumbled furnishings, and a scattering of revelers, still sleeping off their liquor. The morning air washed over Nigel's face like water. Dew lay heavily on the ground. On the path to the sunken herb garden, it had been trampled into dark moisture, but on the lavender and rosemary it still sparkled untouched, nature's diamonds.

A similar dark path had been furrowed across the lawn. Nigel's boots soaked in moisture as he strode toward the statue of Hermes. The winged stone shoes were poised, ready to run. Stone hair blew back in an imaginary wind. Beneath the wild curls, the statue's face was stern and uncompromising, focused forever on the heavens and its latest message to the gods.

Nigel watched Lance brush away a strand of cobweb, beaded with water, that trailed from the Hermes to the shrubbery. His elegant back was rigid.

"If I believed about you what you are thinking about me," said Nigel quietly, "I would offer to kill you for it."

Lance stopped and turned to him, eyes wide. "What?"

"You think that I raped her, don't you?"

"What else am I to think? The room was just about destroyed. Good God, she must have fought you hard enough!" His face convulsed. "Yet you forced her!"

"And thinking that, you will say no more about it?"

"I suppose you must have had good reason. It's none of my business, is it? You made that clear enough."

Anger burned in his voice. "By God, if you raped a woman, I would damned well make it mine. In fact, I should call you out for it and do my best to avenge her, even if it meant facing an old comrade on the dueling field."

Lance leaned against the base of the statue. It was veined with lichen, the stone weathered and damp. "Easy enough for you to say! No one would ever call you out. It would be a death sentence. Yet I will fight you if you insist on it."

"Lance, your faith in my prowess is touching beyond belief, and your moral fiber shines like the armor of God. But I wish you had equal faith in my character. I like to think I am not capable of rape. I would have hoped for your support in that belief!"

Lance stared at his reflection in the silver lid of his snuffbox. "But you tied her to the bed."

"As it happens, I woke with my breeches on, and I was the

one tied down. Which makes me sound a little absurd, now I come to think of it.''

"*You* were tied down?" There was silence, then the angel's face paled to alabaster. "I know you have a reputation for vice, but for God's sake, Nigel."

He laughed. It came from some deep place that delighted in absurdity, though he felt no mirth. "Let your imagination run wild with prurient speculation, if you like. After all, that is what I am doing."

"Nigel, don't." The sun broke suddenly between the trees, firing Lance's hair to gold. "By God, you are worth so much more! Why the devil do you insist on wasting your gifts like this?"

Nigel looked up at the statue. What secrets had Hermes witnessed out here in the garden last night? Had the messenger of the gods watched Donnington stumble alone down this path in the dark, or had he had company? "I may owe you my life, but I'm damned if I owe you any more mercy than I have just received."

Lance seemed genuinely surprised. "Mercy?"

"Why the hell should I answer your concern for my morals? I do my level best to refrain from commenting on yours."

"I don't know what you mean."

"Then let us start with one small act of bad manners, and leave it there. In spite of your admirable concern for Miss Woodard and the tortures you believe I may have inflicted on her last night, you felt no compunction about announcing the death of her lover without warning. How the devil do you justify that? It wasn't necessary. A million excuses could have been used to get me away from her first."

Lance flushed. "Unfortunately, I was only thinking of you. Hold that against me if you will."

"And with such exquisite logic, we shall always find grace. Lance, I believe I spent a bloody hard night. Shall we agree to let this drop? We have a job to do. Now, where the hell is Donnington?"

☙

The body floated facedown in the fishpond. Several of
George's prizefighter friends stood guard.

"Morning, guv!" said one, doffing his cap. "His lordship
had a bit too much to drink, I reckon. Gardener found him
about half an hour ago. Nothing's been touched."

Like an odd glass fish, an empty wine bottle bobbed in the
water, a trapped bubble of air keeping it half-afloat. At the
foot of the small stone wall around the pool, a wineglass had
shattered, as if dropped there. Donnington's body swam lazily,
the red-brown curls darkened to mahogany and matted to the
head.

Nigel stood silent for a moment, looking at his lifeless adversary. Donnington couldn't answer any questions now, nor
could he plead his case if it warranted mercy. *Nothing lethal,
merely extravagant, wicked, and suitably humiliating?* Even
though he knew everything he had done had been justified, it
had proved lethal, after all. Nigel felt a sharp regret, both personal and professional. He signaled to the men. "Take him
out, lads. He will rest easier on the grass."

As the men waded into the pool Nigel bent and took up the
shards of glass. They fitted neatly together. It was only one
glass.

"He was alone, then," said Lance, watching him do it.
"Did you foresee he would do this?"

Nigel glanced up at the bright blond head. "No, I did not.
When I left him he was enjoying himself. He was the center
of attention and he had begun to find it flattering. Of course,
he was drinking heavily."

The men heaved the corpse ashore and laid it down on the
grassy verge. One of the footmen rolled it over so that the
face stared vacantly at the sky. Nigel bent and closed the eyelids. Donnington had obviously been dead for hours.

While I destroyed his house and terrorized his mistress?

He couldn't afford the luxury of the emotion. Nigel concentrated on the task at hand, as he had learned to concentrate
through all those hard years fighting Napoleon. Had Donnington found out that his papers were missing and killed himself
in despair? It was a rather extreme measure, and meant that
Nigel had not only seriously misjudged Donnington's char-

acter, but also betrayed his own hand to more than just Wyndham, an uncomfortable thought. After all, competence was
about all he had left. Yet he felt along Donnington's lapels
and in his pockets, anywhere he might have hidden a note,
then ran his forefinger around the sodden folds of his cravat.

His cravat.

It came back quite clearly and as suddenly as thunder. He
had claimed Donnington's cravat. After he had discovered he
was poisoned. When he had determined at any cost to get
Frances Woodard away from the revels. So why the devil was
Donnington wearing a cravat? Nigel pulled out the knot and
let the strip of linen fall aside. His surge of anger was barely
controllable.

"What are you doing?" asked Lance.

"It seems cruel, don't you think," replied Nigel caustically,
"not to let him breathe easier. Lads, take him up to the house.
And quietly. We are witness to a tragedy."

There was a soft rustle, a sinuous whisper behind him. Nigel
looked up.

Frances stood watching. She was dressed in a long cotton
robe over loose trousers. She had combed and braided her hair.
Beneath a light veil it curved neatly over her skull. Nigel
caught himself holding his breath, remembering that hair drifting free, and his anger dissipated, leaving him empty. She was
pale, but composed. Betty stood beside her, wrapped in a long
cloak.

"She would come," Betty said to Nigel, her face clouded
with anxiety. "I'm sorry."

"It is all right," said Frances. "I have already faced it. Do
not try to protect me."

In respect for her, Nigel stepped aside as she walked up to
the body. She looked down at it. He could not safeguard her
from this, nor soften it, and he knew quite clearly that she
needed to see for herself what he had discovered. She had
expected it when Lance had first broken the news, hadn't she?
Which is why Frances Woodard had seemed pierced, stricken
by the discovery. He wanted to reach out to her, to offer apology, condolences, but there was nothing he could say.

"Madam!" Lance moved forward, as if expecting her to faint.

Frances turned to Lance. "Sir, you are very kind, but I do not fear the dead."

In an odd parody of good manners, Nigel formally introduced them, the woman with whom he had spent the night and his old comrade, as the footmen lifted the body. He was amazed that he could go through the motions, for his energy seemed to be fading like dew. Frances bowed to Lance, but without looking at Nigel, she walked away.

"My dear, you look barely more alive than poor Donnington." Betty came up and took him by the arm. "What happened to you last night? You weren't drunk, were you?"

"No." Nigel sat down on the low stone wall. Dear God, it would be splendidly humiliating to be the one to faint! "Why don't you sit down, Betty?" He indicated a curved stone bench that stood opposite. "I was not drunk."

"Then what?" Lance asked sharply.

Nigel looked up at him, straight into the blue gaze. "I was poisoned."

Betty dropped immediately to the bench. "Poisoned! Then Donnington found out why you were here?"

"By God!" Lance ran both hands back through his blond hair. "Nigel, if all this is part of some scheme connected to our work, why the devil didn't you tell me?"

"Because, whatever my personal certainty, if my suspicions had been wrong, I'd have spread calumny against a merely incompetent man. But as it turns out, I was right. Donnington was a traitor."

"We fought together for years." Lance paced away. "I should think I have earned your professional confidence by now."

Nigel was watching Frances. She had picked something from the bottom of the hedge and was gazing away across the cold water. She did not move as he outlined to Lance and Betty what he had discovered. Lord Donnington, a key official in Paris during the peace negotiations the previous summer, had worked steadily against British interests. He had sold secrets. And now that Napoleon was back in the French capital, gathering armies again, Donnington had continued his dirty trade, sending information from London.

"It wasn't a matter of confidence, Lance," he finished. "Papers came to light recently which proved he had fouled things up, but in spite of my nasty suspicions, I had to have proof of more before I told you, or anyone. Last night I found it. Our men have died because of what he was doing; a little humiliation seemed mild in comparison."

Betty's dark gaze seemed turned inward, as if she searched for sense somewhere in herself. "Good God. Donnington poisoned you for revenge, then took his own life?"

"This scene would make it seem so."

Lance indicated the shards of glass that Nigel had laid out on the wall, the single stem, foot, and bowl. "He was drinking by himself. Perhaps it was an accident."

Nigel leaned his head on his hands, supporting an elbow on each knee. The nausea he had felt earlier was returning. Was he to be ill again, after surviving that wretched night? It was too absurd! "It was not an accident. He drowned wearing a very nice new cravat: French, I believe."

"A new cravat?" Lance was frowning. "Why does that matter?"

The headache exploded behind his eyes like a rocket, as his sense of absurdity threatened to undo him. "Because I claimed his last night."

Lance looked vaguely uncomfortable. "I heard about it. Look, I suppose I owe you an apology. You had to have an excuse to come down here, I see that now. I'm glad that I was misled about the orgy—"

"Oh, no, you were not misled." Nigel grinned up at Lance. "It was a very, very naughty orgy, wasn't it, Betty?"

Lance flushed scarlet.

Betty threw back her lovely head and laughed aloud. "Lance, surely you have learned by now: any attempt to cast a halo around Nigel's wicked head only makes him all the more bloody-minded!"

Nigel stood up, feeling as if his blood had drained completely, to seep away into the fishpond. His head continued to pound. Presumably one did not eat nightshade without some inconvenient physical reminders the next day.

"Go back to the house, Lancelot, there's a good fellow. I need someone competent to oversee a final search, in case anything was missed last night. Sadly I have a headache like the Black Knight being pounded on the pate by your Arthurian namesake." He grinned. "Such is the price of dissipation, of course."

"Why do you need my help?" asked Lance. "You seem to have wrapped up the whole episode neatly enough by yourself."

"Oh, no, this is not the end of things. It is only the beginning. Go look for yourself." Nigel indicated the retreating men, carrying the body back to the house. "There are bruises around Donnington's neck, left by a wire. Someone went to a certain amount of trouble to cover them up."

Lance stepped back, as if struck. "What?"

Nigel was still watching Frances. In her hands she held wildflowers she had found by the hedge. She began pulling away the petals and casting them onto the water. He found his anger returning, as profound as his sorrow.

"For God's sake, don't be so bloody obtuse, Lance. Miss Woodard knew it as soon as you announced his death: Lord Donnington was murdered."

Seven

LANCE BOWED AND left, stiffly, without a word.

Betty frowned. "Really, my dear, you might be a little easier on the man. After all, you went to hell and back together. He worships the very mud where your boot has landed."

"God knows why," Nigel replied absently. "He's a unique character, a spy full of cant, yet there's no one I'd rather have behind me in a fight."

"Then you trust him?"

"Professionally? Of course. He's a rabid patriot. Though I'm damned if I trust his execrable morals."

Nigel had already forgotten Lance, and he was barely aware of Betty. His attention was concentrated only on Frances. She stood with her head tilted a little to the sun. She had closed her eyes. The morning light caressed her lids and glinted on her small nose stud. The exquisite gold ring she had worn the night before had been replaced. Had she so casually laid aside everything that had happened between them? To his shame he could still feel the fine silk of her robe tearing, inch by inch, under his fingers. Her skin had been even softer underneath.

The scattering of petals drifted and spun on the flat water. It seemed inconceivable that only twenty-four hours ago he had never seen her, and in that short time he had met and through sheer carelessness almost destroyed such a woman.

He forced himself to look away. A man had been strangled.

Professionally, brutally, and without compunction, as he sat here with a bottle of wine. Even a traitor deserved a fair trial, and a chance to defend himself.

Betty stood up and walked over to Nigel. She laid her ringed fingers on his arm. "You are too hard on Lance, my dear. Why? Can't you tolerate his friendship? Is any spy full of honesty? Are you?"

Ignoring the hammering headache, Nigel took her hand and kissed it. Absurdity seemed to be the order of the day. The thought left a trace of genuine humor in his voice. "I try to be, Betty. But sometimes life presents me with damnable choices. Being devious is the very marrow of my work."

"As is holding orgies?" There was no archness in her tone. "Nigel, the murder is your affair. If Donnington was a traitor, it was a merciful enough way out for him. Meanwhile Frances has asked for a home with me. Is it for the best?" She smiled. "I will expect you to pay me for her upkeep, for I don't intend her to earn a living like the other girls."

He thought she was too far away to hear, but Frances spoke close behind him. Her words were soft and apparently calm. "That isn't what we agreed, Betty. I will earn my keep."

She had walked silently up to them, or perhaps the noise in his head had drowned out her footsteps. How the devil had he allowed himself to so let down his defenses?

"My dear child." Betty's voice was light, but compassion lay beneath it. "Last night you saved Nigel, didn't you? It is enough. If he won't pay, then I will. You may stay as my guest."

Nigel could not look at Frances. This was hardly the time for sentiment. He knew what he must do, though it seemed like a form of madness to insist on it. But, surely, surely, he had the strength to resist the temptation she would offer him daily? And what alternative was left?

"I would wish," he said deliberately, "that my friends would refrain from ordering my affairs. Your offer is generous, Betty, but Miss Woodard is my responsibility. I won her at hazard. Yesterday she publicly agreed to be my mistress, and in the eyes of the world that agreement stands. No one will question it. She will live in my house."

"*Your* affairs! I thought it was my future at issue!" Frances moved, forcing him to face her. "Last night you told me you did not want a mistress."

He smiled at her, keeping his voice light, yet knowing that events of enormous importance might depend on the outcome of this. "I meant it. But I think I must offer you my protection, don't you?" In spite of his pain, his mirth was genuine. "I have a certain reputation to uphold. What will the world think if I don't?"

He almost held his breath, waiting for her reply. He had not known until that moment how very much he wanted her assent, but he was not to get it.

Calm disinterest seemed to drop over her like a veil. "I'm sorry, Lord Rivaulx. I will not live in your house."

Nigel sat down on the wall and stretched his legs in front of him. The damp had stained his boots. As if in deliberate contrast, she was wearing embroidered slippers with a design of intertwined leaves and flowers. As he looked at them, fascinated, the hammers in his brain became a bedlam. The very idea of laughing aloud was torment, but that's what he wanted to do.

"She has chosen to stay with me, Nigel." Betty's voice held real distress.

He put both hands over his face, and the truth surfaced, though he hadn't wanted to have to use it. "None of us has choices any longer. A man has been murdered, for God's sake, and I have no idea why or by whom. Frances may be a vital link in this puzzle with Donnington. In your pretty house, Betty, where everyone is welcome, she would be an easy target. I have enough on my conscience without adding her death to the list. She will stay with me."

"And if I still refuse?"

It is only a headache, he told himself, it will go away. "I will have you arrested and jailed as Donnington's accomplice."

"So I am to be coerced again!" She could no longer disguise the bitterness.

The slippers moved away, leaving him sitting alone. The pain was excruciating. He was afraid he might pitch his voice too loud and shout, but perhaps his words were only a whisper against the deafening scream in his head.

"When the danger is over, I will find you a new protector. Until then, I don't intend to let you out of my sight. I'm sorry, but I insist. In return you may tell me every detail you can remember about Donnington. Do we have a bargain?"

The agony threatened to overwhelm his control. Damnation to all of her certainty and calm! Must she be the rock against which he would break himself? Nigel could not look up. If he opened his eyes, he knew he would shatter, and then his humiliation before her would be complete. He heard her soft slippers, and the rap of Betty's shoes on the flagstones, moving away. She had not said yes. Perhaps she would prefer a jail cell to another day in his company?

Huddled in his cloak, the man watched the ship for Calais prepare to take on passengers. He had left Farnhurst six hours ago. His voice made a low murmur beneath the creak of sails and the hubbub of seabirds wheeling over the Channel.

The woman glanced up at him as he finished speaking, her dark eyes faintly derisive. She also spoke French, rapidly. "Well done. Donnington will tell no secrets now. It was not difficult, surely?"

"As simple as the guttersnipe."

"Ah! The boy with the rabbits? He is nothing. It is Rivaulx who matters."

Seagulls whirled and dived, shrieking. "The marquess is a professional. He won't have missed the signs."

She smiled. "What ill effects will he suffer, do you think, from his little debauch?"

"He will shrug it off soon enough, though I added enough other sauce to the meat to let him think he would not. But I cannot speak to the state of his . . . soul?"

The hood of the woman's cloak fell back, the ocean breeze ruffling her black hair. "His *soul*! Before I am done, he will wish himself in hell, and his soul carved up and served to the devil. The marquess is a man enamored of sin and beset with demons. What is a night with a little belladonna?''

It was interesting, certainly, to serve someone more ruthless than oneself. ''You will feed him more?''

''No, no. I have fed him a whore from India instead. She will be an exotic enough toxin for a while. Rivaulx is a man who believes he knows how to manage pain, but none of us do. None of us do. And the pain has barely begun.''

They stood quietly for a moment watching the whirl of seabirds about the French ship.

She pulled her hood over her dark head. ''Rivaulx has all Donnington's papers?'' He nodded. ''Then the stage is set. It will not be long before those papers send him to Paris, where the trap will close.''

Betty had persuaded her, though everything in her rebelled at the thought. Yet at least this prison would probably be more comfortable than that of His Majesty. Frances stepped from the great carriage with the griffin crest, and allowed the footmen to usher her into the town house. Lord Rivaulx's town house. She was in London. Frances had her small silk bag with her, containing all of her clothes. The lightweight fabrics folded away into a tiny bundle. It was all she had. That and her training.

Rivaulx had not ridden in the chaise with her. Instead he had encircled her with silent, burly footmen and surrounded the carriage with armed outriders. As the horses trotted away from Farnhurst she had looked back once. Rivaulx was standing before the red-brick facade, deep in conversation with Lancelot Spencer. The rest of the guests had left hours before, including Betty and her girls. It had all been arranged with the same absolute efficiency with which he had organized the bacchanal.

Frances followed a maidservant up the stairs to her new bedchamber.

''What room is this?'' she asked, startled.

''His lordship's orders, ma'am.'' The maid curtsied. ''It's

not a room we use in the regular way of things. It used to be the nursery.''

Frances walked across to the windows and touched the bars. A jail, indeed. The iron grille would no doubt keep out intruders, but it also kept her enclosed, like a nightingale in the *zenana*, forced to sing in a cage.

"We have changed the furniture, ma'am, to be suitable to your needs." The maid indicated a tall bed, washstand, desk, chairs, books—the furnishings of any English guest room. "His lordship sent particular orders ahead. Do you like it? I'd have brought flowers, but he said no flowers. Is that right?''

The girl was bursting at the seams with curiosity. Frances smiled at her. "I am English, like you," she said. "Although I have lived in India. I have had enough of flowers.''

And suddenly she knew it was true. She did not want a scented chamber, or one hung with silks and brilliant paintings, This austere cell suited her better. Had Rivaulx guessed that? As the thought came Frances dismissed it. How could he understand, and why should he care?

"But you like the painting?" persisted the maid.

Frances crossed the room to look at it. It was a wild landscape, thunder black in the air. Yellowing trees clustered in the foreground, framing the long rise of open moor and distant mountains. A river tumbled white-foamed down its valley. And startling against the gathering storm, a white horse challenged the peaks, mane and tail flying in the wind: defiant, beautiful, and free.

"Oh, ma'am! Lord Rivaulx ordered it brought from his bedchamber—it's the moors, ma'am, at Rivaulx Castle—but if you don't like it, we'll have it changed.''

Frances brushed away bitter tears. "No," she said fiercely. "Leave it. I like it very well.''

∞

He returned about six hours later. Although she did not hear the front door, it was as if a ripple went through the house: of scurrying maids and bowing footmen, a new alertness. The day was drawing in. Long shadows fell from the window bars across the floor. Frances laid down the book she was reading. A polite message was sent up to her, requesting her company. To refuse would be merely childish.

She followed the footman down the stairs. The hallway was lit with wax candles in a brass sconce on the wall. It was very like the one in the entry of the home where Frances had grown up. She was vaguely surprised that Rivaulx did not make a display of more up-to-date fashions. Presumably he had the wealth.

He was standing in his study, below a portrait so like him that Frances felt oddly disoriented. With a flash of anger she realized he must know that and had planned it.

"My mother," he said dryly. "She died several years ago, before—"

Frances sat cross-legged on the sofa at the side of the room, her hands resting on her folded knees, and interrupted him. "Before what?"

"Nothing. There are times I miss her."

Candlelight caressed his face—the slightly hooked line of his nose, his carved nostrils—above the fresh white linen and dark blue coat. He seemed stretched by tension, as if in pain, though the words seemed simple enough. Yet this man said or did nothing without design. Did he want her sympathy? How could he be so manipulative?

"She was very lovely. Am I to be disarmed by her portrait, my lord, or by your loss? I am sorry for it."

"And so I am put thoroughly in my place. Miss Woodard— Frances—I offer a truce between us. I regret that I had to force you to come here. I am entirely culpable for what happened at Farnhurst. There is no adequate apology. Nevertheless, you have one, now: I am sorry."

She kept her breath steady. "And so we have exchanged regrets. What next?"

He sat down at his desk and ran both hands over his hair, as if weary to the bone. "I know you do not want to be in my house. I do not want you here either. I regret the entire damnable farce you were forced into last night. I will not make this any more distasteful than necessary, but Europe hangs on the brink of destruction, and my work is vital. Our personal wishes are entirely irrelevant.''

"Obviously, my lord," she answered with deliberate sarcasm. "I have already learned that mine are."

To her surprise he did not respond with anger. Instead he seemed faintly amused, as if he recognized something absurd in himself and met it with irony. "Since we have shared a certain intimacy already, I think you might call me Nigel. It is my given name."

It was disarming, as he knew it would be. She despised him for it, and herself for reacting as he planned. Deliberately she forced disdain into her voice. "Very well, Nigel. The interrogator may dictate what conditions he pleases. This is to be an interrogation, is it not?"

The line beside his mouth deepened as the humor disappeared. "Very well. Let there be no further attempt at civility between us. When Lancelot Spencer announced Donnington's death, how did you immediately know he'd been killed?"

She willed her hands to stay still and relaxed. "Why do you think that I did?"

"Because—like a hare that looks up into the talons of an eagle—your immediate reaction was fear, not sorrow."

It was true, of course. Frances glanced down, concentrating on her next breath. The talons felt far too close for comfort. He said nothing as the moment stretched into minutes, until she looked back at him.

The skin beside his mouth was blanched, the creases set. "I will not force you, Frances, but I must know. Donnington was not likely to take his own life. His type never does. He was boundlessly confident, and in spite of everything, he was having a good time. You knew it wasn't suicide. It could have been an accident, but when Lance announced Donnington was dead, that thought never occurred to you. I believe I know why, but I must be certain."

"And if you are not?"

"There are other interrogators. If that sounds like a threat, it is, but I am only trying to give you the courtesy of the truth. My opinion has a certain weight, but I do not run the government, nor make the final decisions." He stood up and crossed to the mantel. "Your fear was not because of anything specific to Donnington, but because in the harem a sudden death usually meant a killing. Am I right?"

She closed her eyes, her carefully regulated breathing scattered as if a strap had suddenly tightened around her lungs. "You are a brutal man, aren't you?"

There was silence for a moment, as if he was thinking about it. "I try not to be," he said quietly. "A suspicion of your complicity in Donnington's death would be far more brutal under the circumstances, believe me. If you will let me, I can at least clear you of that."

Beyond the courtyard of the *zenana*, there were acres of exquisite gardens. One day she had walked there among flowers so dazzling they could have none better in paradise. The next morning the hot wind blew off the desert, shriveling the flowers until petals spun like white paper across the dying garden.

She tried to keep her voice steady and tell him calmly, as if it didn't matter. "You are right. When you have lived in a place where either intrusion or escape means instant death, you don't think first of accident. So what else do you wish to know?"

He should have looked triumphant, shouldn't he? After all, he had just won. Instead it seemed as if he loathed himself. He turned away.

"Tomorrow is soon enough. I will find you when I need you. Don't hesitate to ask the servants for anything you need. You may have the run of the house. Apart from this room, I rarely use any of it."

"Not even to sleep?"

As if dismissing her, he went to his desk and began sorting papers. "I don't sleep that much, and never in my bedroom."

She could not help herself. He had exposed her fears so ruthlessly! "No. I imagine there are other bedchambers always available to you in London. Or do you mean to share mine, after all?"

"Do not try to goad me, Frances—" He cut it off, the sharp tone and the warning.

So she could break through his armor! Frances slipped from

the couch and crossed the room to leave, but his voice arrested her.

"You have seen my vulnerability—dear God, you saw me raving. Was that not humiliation enough? Must I beg for your forbearance?"

She turned. "I was also humbled."

His hands stilled on the papers. "I know what is between us. Lust is a powerful vice. I don't deny it." He stared down at the desk as if blind. "But we have both been through a hard school. We well know how to control our desires. I did not bring you here to share my bed."

It was torn from her, though she didn't want to say it. "Then what future do I have?"

His back stiffened. "Do you ask that seriously? What you did to me at Farnhurst, you will do to every man who meets you. It is your gift and your curse, so do not worry for one moment about a secure future. Give me just a little of your time—until I can discover why Donnington was killed—then I swear I will find you a duke who will treat you as you deserve."

Candlelight danced over his elegant, square-ended fingers. The hands that had taken her silk robe and torn it in two while she shook beneath him with a new awareness. "And how is that, Nigel?"

To her immense surprise, he laughed and turned to face her. "Like a palace of silver."

She didn't understand the reference and said so.

"It's in the Bible." He moved to the sofa where she had been sitting. "Shall I offer you more of the truth? I sleep, when I can, on this couch. I don't like bedrooms. Good night, Frances."

Nigel watched her leave, though some more primitive part of him wanted to invite her to stay. It would be easy enough, wouldn't it? He was about to maintain to the world that she was his mistress. How bloody tempting to let it become the truth! He had never seen a woman move with such grace, like a gazelle. Only last night he had seen her, eyes dilated, offering herself with her hair unbound. It was an image he would take to his grave.

He walked to the fireplace and stared into the flames. After the disaster at Farnhurst, nothing could happen between them now that was not a manipulation. Even when he gave her the small truths about himself, it was only to deceive her, to get behind her guard. Quite desperately he wanted escape, dissolution.

With wry derision he realized he was tempted for the first time in years to get drunk. For God's sake! He needed all his faculties and he couldn't let the presence of Miss Frances Woodard disrupt his work. Yet Donnington had been only a petty spy. As far as Nigel knew, he hadn't been involved in grand designs of assassination or coup d'état. So why the hell had Donnington been killed? And why at Farnhurst, on that particular night? Presumably the same unknown hand was behind the poison and Donnington's death. The implications were terrifying.

Frances discovered the music room the next morning. She had already examined the formal dining room, the drawing rooms, the guest bedrooms. They all seemed cold and unused, as if frozen in time—even the great master bedroom. The four-poster dominated the chamber, its canopy topped with coronets at each corner, each boasting the gilt strawberry leaves and alternating silver balls of the marquessate. A pale rectangle of wallpaper showed where the painting of the horse had once hung. But, of course, he would not miss it. He never slept there.

The music room was at the back of the house. Tall windows, Georgian archways, with grace in every line of plaster: a room made for civility and refinement. It was filled with instruments and music stands. As if set down for only a moment, a violin lay on a spiral-legged table, the bow beside it. Yet the strings of the violin were broken, the hairs of the bow dried and fraying.

The lid of the harpsichord was up, with music open on the carved stand above the keyboard. The pages were yellowed and curled at the corners. Frances sat down on the stool and tried a few keys. She heard his step only a fraction of a second before she heard his voice.

"It is shamefully out of tune, like an organ grinder's box in a rainstorm. I will have it tuned, if you like. Music is no doubt one of the sixty-four arts? I trust you slept well?"

Nigel had come into the room behind her. Frances tensed. If not for this man, she would still be at Farnhurst, or she would have found a protector, someone safe and easy to understand. Instead she was imprisoned. The cell was luxurious, the jailer dangerous, like all the prisons of her life. Was she to be restricted forever? Was she never to walk free, or ride unafraid under an open sky, or order her own life? She took two deep breaths and let the tension dissolve.

"In my cell near the roof? Well enough," she replied, not looking at him. "Did you?"

His voice was light, softly humorous. "I don't believe I deserved it, but I slept as soundly as Abou Hassan in the *Arabian Nights*. A charming result of my close brush with death, I suppose. Perhaps Lazarus, too, went singing into his new life. You see, I no longer have a headache."

She turned to look at him then, impeccably dressed, freshly shaved, and despicably confident. Yet he seemed taut and untamed, with the faint scent of horse and the outdoors about him. Infinitely civilized, he made her think only of pirates. What was he, really? Why did he admit to any weakness? It seemed oddly out of character.

"You had a headache?"

"All day yesterday. A churning carriage wheel inside my skull: iron-shod, rattling on cobbles, and driven by a madcap youth who had just lost his entire estate in a wager. It was a suicide run, I believe. No doubt it was well deserved for my unwise experiments in lotus-eating. Yet the interesting thing about physical pain is that the body holds no memory of it . . ."

"Only the mind?"

". . . which can usually be convinced to think of something else."

He walked across to the violin bow and picked it up, running a finger along the ruined horsehair. Frances thought she saw genuine sorrow on his face.

She closed the harpsichord lid over the yellowed keys. "Like music?"

"If you like."

"Whose room was this? Did your mother play the violin?"

"No, the harpsichord."

Restlessly she left the stool and moved across the room. On the wall between the windows hung something that resembled a long-necked guitar with a triangular body. It was richly inlaid, almost Oriental. Frances touched the strings.

"What is this?"

He set down the bow and looked up. "A balalaika. It's Russian." He was letting his fingers follow the scrolls on the violin. "I lived there." He smiled at her. "I brought it back. It's strangely alien among these more civilized instruments."

"You play it?"

"No. This violin was mine. Napoleon Bonaparte interrupted me." His long fingers stroked the curved body, the neck and elegant waist, caressing the shining wood. "Servants tend to be so damned literal."

She was groping to follow his meaning. "How?"

"Four years ago I gave instructions to clean this room without touching anything in it. My violin should have been put in its case, but I don't believe it is damaged."

"You have not been in here for four years?"

"No. Should I have been?" He left the violin and moved to the harp that stood before the window. "I was out of the country—Moscow, Paris, Vienna for the conference. I have barely been back in this house two months."

"What do you do now?"

He answered without looking up. "For amusement? Every morning I go to an establishment run by friends of a retired pugilist named George. I fence with a rapier and a saber, and practice my marksmanship with several different pistols. Then

I allow a prizefighter to batter me into daily submission. Men like such things.''

"And in the evenings?"

"To Betty's." She had the feeling there was another, deeper answer that he did not give her, that he gave her the truth, but not the whole truth.

"How wonderful to have the freedom to come and go as you please!" she said acerbically. "You will allow me a little covetousness? Is it impossible that I be allowed out? Can't you sometimes take me with you?"

He glanced up, raising a brow in comic dismay. "To *Betty's*?"

Frances wanted to slap him. "Betty no doubt provides the other things that men like! But you no longer welcome music to your house?"

He smoothed his palm over the arch of the harp. "While you lived in India, French armies burned and hacked their way across Europe. In places Napoleon swept away an old order that was admittedly rotten to the core. In others he created a frenzy of destruction. The result was unprecedented chaos and suffering. No one had much time for violins."

"You were a soldier?"

"Of a kind."

"But Napoleon was exiled last year, wasn't he? Even in India we heard the news."

He sat on the stool by the harp and ran his fingers over the slack strings. The response was a wail of disharmony. "He escaped Elba in March, just after I left Vienna. Napoleon is now back in Paris and raising armies again. We shall have renewed war by July at the latest."

"And you think to stop him?"

He replied quite seriously. "Frances, we must win this time. Finally and irrevocably. Or Napoleon will plunge France into blood to her knees once again. She doesn't deserve it."

Frances kept her voice level and open. There seemed to be a high-strung fragility to this moment. She was afraid that if she spoke carelessly, she would break it. "I thought France was the enemy?"

Almost unconsciously he had begun tightening the harp

strings, listening intently as he brought them into tune. "My mother taught me to speak French in my cradle and hired fencing masters for me from Paris. Unbridled ambition is the enemy. I fight Napoleon because his defeat is the only hope for peace in Europe. At one time I might have supported his ideas of reform, but he has tried to play God and has spread his enlightenment in blood. For that alone he must be stopped."

"Be careful whom you pick for your enemy, they say, for you may become like him."

A rotten string snapped under his fingers. "You think I am a petty Napoleon?"

"I think you are no stranger to ambition, or to presumption. What else happened at Farnhurst?"

"A bloody mess, of course." He walked to the window, the morning sun dazzling on his dark hair. "It doesn't matter what you think of me. What matters is that I was outwitted. Which means that more is at stake than I imagined, and that it is vital to discover the players."

"I do not imagine Lord Donnington was amused by the play."

"Lay Donnington's death at the door of my vanity if you wish. But someone is more ruthless than I am, Frances. Though I offered Donnington a little punishment, I did not take his life. It is imperative to discover who did." He turned to face her, apparently without guile, the sunlight throwing him into sharp silhouette. "Will you help me?"

This was a side to him she had never imagined. "As simply as that? I am astonished. I had thought you incapable of plain speech."

He moved back to the harp and plucked the strings one at a time. "I am only trying to offer you fair dealing. You don't like me, for good reason. To try to use charm or guile would only be an insult. But with what I have just told you, I have tried to give you a higher cause."

"Patriotism?"

He ran one hand rapidly over a few high notes. The sounds soared like birds set free. "If you like. Or an end to suffering for thousands of ordinary people in Europe. I ask you to ignore your dislike for my person, and tell me everything you know about Donnington.''

Frances felt stunned. This was a whole new level of play, marked by the naked intensity of the truth. ''You don't fight fair, do you?''

''A concept for schoolboys. I must know, Frances. Every nuance, every last detail. Whom he knew, where he went. Anything you can remember.''

''There is not much to tell. I barely knew him.''

''No, I guessed not. Let us start at the beginning. How did you meet him?''

The questions came, rapid-fire. He displayed a terrifying concentration and an intellect like a machine. She was not allowed to gloss over anything, no detail was left unexplored, no nuance left unchallenged. Without allowing either of them rest or mercy, Nigel stripped the last month to its bone.

''That is all there is,'' she said at last, dropping her head forward onto her hand. ''He approached me at the Green Man. He took me back to Farnhurst. He left for London. I don't know why. I was too grateful to care. He was not my lover. How did you guess that?''

He stood up and stretched. ''I wasn't sure. Sometimes men with his tastes will bed women as well.''

She was too exhausted not to respond with the simple truth. ''It was my surmise, also: Lord Donnington preferred boys.''

''No doubt he hoped your reputation would hide that, which is why he told all London of his exotic new mistress. To be a man with his preferences in England is dangerous.''

''Dangerous? Why? It is harmless, surely?''

''It's illegal. A hanging offense.'' He gave a wry smile. ''As is betrayal of one's country, of course. Thank you for what you have told me. It was generous of you.''

She felt drained, shattered, and furious that he had achieved his desire so easily. ''No! Generosity had nothing to do with it. As Napoleon is a brilliant general, you are a master manipulator. I had no real choice. You are a man of many talents, aren't you? But they are all used to gain ascendancy over others. I find it repulsive. What other nasty gifts do you have?''

His lip curled. "I am expert with thumbscrews and an afi-cionado of the rack, of course."

"Can you not give me the courtesy of the truth, after wring-ing it out of me without mercy?"

He sat down, resting his long fingers on each side of the harp strings. "Don't think you can shame me, Frances. I forgot the niceties of saving others' feelings a long time ago. Down-stairs I have several trunks of papers, sent from Donnington's office in Paris when Napoleon landed, as well as those brought back from the search of Farnhurst. They are mostly in code. It is my job to decipher them. That is what I do between my mornings and nights. It is one of my talents. As I told you, I like mathematics."

With a last run across the strings, he stood up to leave.

"No," said Frances, "that is not enough. If we are not to spare each other's feelings, now it is my turn. After what you have just done to me, you cannot leave so complacently. So I have a question for you."

He turned at the door and smiled, as if sure of his own invulnerability. "Certainly," he said. "Name it."

Frances wanted to hurt him. As she asked the question she knew that nothing else could have succeeded so well. So why did she regret the impulse as soon as it was spoken?

"Who was Catherine?"

Eight

TENSION BUILT IN his face, white in the flare of his nostril and the corner of his jaw. "So it is war," he said at last. "I did not want to do what I just did, but I thought you understood my reasons. Is this to be the price?"

"It is always wise," said Frances, "for the prisoner to know the jailer's secrets. The power is all yours."

His knuckles shone white on the doorknob. He was staring at his hand as if seeing it for the first time. "I thought I had already offered you what I could in trade for your information. But I see that it wasn't enough. Very well. I am happy to tell you." He wrenched open the door. "But not here, in this room, where my mother used to play the harpsichord."

He strode away down the hall, leaving her sitting alone among the instruments in the light of the arched-top windows.

And if thy hand offend thee, cut it off. Nigel watched his fingers move across the paper, the feather of the quill an oddly frivolous counterpoint to the messages that were being revealed. He was getting a permanent ink stain. He laughed a little grimly to himself. His entire being offended him, which didn't leave many options for amputation of the erring parts. It was three days since he had interrogated Frances in the music room. Three days in which to avoid her, and despise himself.

Even that was an indulgence he couldn't afford. He concentrated on the work in front of him.

Donnington had not used a very sophisticated code, nor had he been leaking very sophisticated information. A few memos about armaments, supplies—just enough over the years to cost British armies the lives of a few extra men. And then, during the occupation of Paris the previous summer, a note here and there about Allied plans. Nothing, surely, that had changed the course of the war, or the temporary peace, in the end. So why had Donnington been important enough to kill?

It was obvious, too, that Frances knew nothing. So why did he have this nagging sense of danger where she was concerned? Instincts that had kept him alive before screamed for his attention now. Was it simply a combination of deeper fears, or was the unknown enemy likely to attack her next? Nigel had no idea, but if there was any risk at all, he must keep her here, at whatever cost to himself.

The power is all yours, she had said. He had forced her to come here and forced her to talk to him. She could not know how abhorrent he found that. So because she had asked, he would tell her what she wanted to know. Not to do so was rank cowardice. She had seen him stripped of reason and begging for aid. How could a little more degradation matter? There was no reason for him not to tell her about Catherine, and here, in his study, he believed he could safely do so. Yet Miss Frances Woodard had plenty of power of her own, and of a kind that left Nigel feeling dangerously defenseless.

He glanced at his watch and rang the bell on his desk.

The impassive face of one of his footmen appeared at the door. "My lord?"

"Where is Miss Woodard? I invited her to join me at least an hour ago. Mary took the message. Did she send no reply?"

He had spent some time composing the note. A carefully worded apology and an invitation, not an order, that she come to his study.

The footman coughed uncomfortably into his hand. "I believe Miss Woodard has not been found, my lord. The maids are searching.''

Ink splattered across the lines of careful symbols as Nigel leaped to his feet. ''What the devil do you mean? Not been found?''

''Miss Woodard does not appear to be on the premises, my lord. We have hunted everywhere, but—''

The footman's words were cut off as Nigel strode from the room. He rapidly interrogated the maid, Mary.

The girl's eyes filled with tears. ''I don't know, my lord, truly! Miss Woodard was in the music room not an hour ago, but now she's disappeared without a trace!'' Mary threw her apron over her face and wailed. ''Oh, Lord Rivaulx! The lady must have left the house without us knowing.''

Nigel gave the maid his handkerchief. ''Don't cry. It's not your fault. She cannot have left the house.''

Rivaulx House was a detached building in its own grounds off Piccadilly, not one of the town houses recently built in the fashionable squares and crescents nearby. In style it was a neat Georgian manor, with no Gothic or whimsical features where anyone could get lost. He had hired enough guards to keep out the French army—and to keep in one woman. Yet a large establishment like this needed a constant stream of deliveries, and the maids couldn't be imprisoned forever, so there were still people coming and going. But each maid had to have his personal permission to go out. No tradesman was allowed in past the gate. Even though it had been three days since he had questioned her, three days since he had seen her, she could not have left.

Nevertheless Nigel went to all the outside doors and into the kitchens. Even the coal hatch was watched over by one of George's prizefighters. The man looked at him oddly and spat over his shoulder. No one had come or gone, not even a rat. He was certain of it. Nigel put each of the guards through a similar cross-examination. Whether they met it with respect or resentment, the result was the same: each man would swear on his grandmother's soul that the lady had not left the house, and that no stranger could possibly have entered.

So how the devil could she have disappeared?

Nigel organized the household staff and left them to make a systematic search from cellars to attics.

As the servants scattered to obey he went to the music room. It looked cold and deserted. His violin lay silently on the table. Absentmindedly he put the instrument inside its case, where it should have lain protected these last four years. She could not have left the house without being seen. She was hardly likely to be hiding in a closet or under a bed. No one could have entered without George's fellows seeing him. She must still be here somewhere. It was a perfectly logical analysis.

Yet like a riptide tearing underneath his thoughts, Nigel had a clear vision of Frances in the hands of a villain, a man with no face, his hand clamped over her mouth. She struggled silently, her veils tearing, her hair coming loose in a golden net as the faceless creature dragged her from the room. In her eyes was the panic she had revealed when Lance announced Donnington was dead. The thought of it filled Nigel with a kind of madness.

As the vision faded it came to him. No other possibility was left. When all other explanations have failed, the one that remains, however unlikely, must be the answer. With a grim smile he left the room and ran rapidly up the servants' staircase.

At the top of the house, the attic rooms were arranged in two rows. Some of them were used as bedrooms for the maids, some for storage. The maids had the better rooms, with windows. The storage rooms were locked. He and the housekeeper had the only keys. At the end of the hallway was a plank door, heavily bolted, and painted white. The paint was chipped in places. Nigel never came up here. As he strode to the end he noticed the dingy corridor. With vague surprise he realized that it had not changed since he was a boy. As soon as all this was over and he could safely allow workmen into the house, he would have this hallway and the maids' rooms repainted.

As he had guessed, the bolts were drawn back on the white planks. Someone had just been through the door. He opened it silently. An unknown hand had kept the hinges oiled. An efficient servant's? Any other possibility was unthinkable. Behind the door a steep ladder led upward. Nigel climbed up rapidly, pushed open the second door at the top, and emerged onto the roof with every instinct urging stealth and caution.

Four great chimneys thrust up through the center of the house. Between them was a small flat space, roofed in lead. The ladder and the doors were access for maintenance, never normally used. But they had been used now.

Nigel caught his breath and pressed himself against the nearest chimney, but caution wasn't necessary. She hadn't seen him. At the edge of the flat space, her face upraised to the sun, Frances sat cross-legged, apparently asleep. Her breathing was deep and regular, her eyes closed. But her back remained upright and her hands lay on her knees with the fingers curled like petals. She could not be sleeping.

The sun was dropping in the west, firing the edge of her veil to gilt. The air was hazy with moisture and the smoke of thousands of fireplaces, wreathing about the chimneys. The clamor of the city filtered up past the roof—a faraway rattle of carriages and the clatter of horses, iron-shod pattens and shrill street cries—yet it all seemed remote, like sounds in a dream. The tops of the elms made a tracery of lace where new leaves were unfolding. By midsummer they would be as dense as waves on the ocean, a seascape of greenery. Almost as if it were ghostly music, Nigel heard an echo of his boyhood, those long-ago days of viridian freedom. But in place of that boy with his devouring curiosity for life stood a man who could never be innocent again.

Like Miss Frances Woodard, he was corrupted by knowledge.

She was beautiful, her face carved like alabaster. Her robes caressed the curves of her body. In the very palms of his hands, he remembered the swell of her breasts as her blue silk tore. He could still feel the satin of her skin. With a ferocity that took away his breath, desire surged. Yet it was not only a desire of the flesh. It was a desire of the soul. For that peace. That stillness. That seemingly absolute serenity. Something he could never, never know.

As if he witnessed miracles Nigel noticed a house sparrow, calmly perched on her shoulder, preening itself.

How say ye to my soul, flee like a bird to your mountain?

He made a small movement. In a flash of brown wings the bird sprang into the air. Frances turned to look at him.

"What is it?" she asked calmly. "You look alarmed."

His anguish was instantly under control. "For God's sake, Frances! The house is in uproar. I thought you had been abducted. I had a vision of you being carried away, like a Sabine."

She lowered her lids. "No. Only one man has ever done anything close to that."

Nigel leaned his back against a chimney. "Yes, me, of course. I seem to have a remarkable facility for making a fool of myself where you are concerned. However, although I may have dragged you publicly from the ballroom at Farnhurst, we did not go on to found the Roman empire. Meanwhile the situation stinks of danger, I am responsible for your safety, and I would have appreciated your not disappearing without warning."

"I am in danger up here?"

"No, of course not. But when you couldn't be found—"

"You leaped to unwarranted conclusions." She leaned forward, pressing her fingers to her temples. "I spent four years in a jail of flowers and over half a year on a ship. I was trapped at Farnhurst. I am imprisoned again here. I have accepted it. Isn't it enough? You interrogated me as if I were vermin, then ignored me for three days. Am I to answer to you now for every waking moment?"

"I was busy," he said lamely.

A bewigged head thrust out of the doorway. "My lord?"

"Oh, damnation." Nigel went to the door. "Miss Woodard is here with me. She is safe. Tell the staff to go back to their duties."

The head disappeared.

He turned back to Frances. "I had sent you an invitation to join me in my study. It created an uncomfortable household disturbance when the note couldn't be delivered. However, the invitation still stands. You asked about Catherine. I am quite prepared to tell you whatever you want to know."

"No!" She folded her hands in her lap, but her voice was

dark with intensity. "I do not need to know anything about you. I am very sorry I asked."

He dropped to sit on the roof. "Frances, if we are to share the house for some weeks, there has to be simple cooperation, at least."

The warm, limpid air stirred tendrils of hair at her cheek and brow. "Does there? You do not own my soul."

"I must know that you are safe."

Her lip curled. "When the maharaja died there was . . . chaos. I was in fear for my life. I managed to steal a horse and ride away. Once I was clear of the palace, I traded a bracelet for a man's robe and wrapped my head in a turban. I smeared dirt on my face and tried never to meet anyone's eyes, in case they noticed that mine were blue. I thought I had escaped. Yet when I reached Calcutta, another prison awaited: that of English propriety. One of my father's old friends offered to help me retire to a nunnery. I sold my jewelry and took a ship instead. You know the rest. You do not need to set the servants to spy on me. I know how to be a model prisoner. I am not impulsive or naive about danger, but I owe you nothing. You pledged to find me a protector. Will you keep that promise, at least?"

It was a courage that left him stunned. At that moment she could have asked for the moon on a platter and he would have sailed the far reaches of the Milky Way to bring it back for her. Though afterward, of course, he would make sure that she and the moon found a home of their own, even if it left him in the dark.

He did not know what to offer her, except an excuse to thrust aside whatever dark memories had just stirred. "I will invite my friends here. I'm sure we can find a likely candidate amongst them. The thought occurs to me—though arriving a little late, like Sir Simon de Montfort's eldest son at the Battle of Evesham—that you might like a dress."

Her frown intensified the blue of her eyes. "A dress, why?"

"An English dress. I owe you one for the sari I destroyed at Farnhurst."

"What on earth would I do with an English dress?"

"I imagined you would wear it—to entertain the beaux

about to fall at your feet. Though if you prefer, you may make
dusters out of it, or an umbrella, or even a saddle pad—but
then you might ride away.''

"Wear an English dress?'' She laughed as if the thought
were absurd, and stood up. "You think I won't meet approval
dressed as I am? Who was Simon de Montfort's eldest son?''

It took him a moment to adjust, to remember what he had
said. "A man who hesitated when his father needed troops,
and arrived too late to win the day. Thus Simon lost the battle
and his life. He was defeated by Edward the First, so perhaps
the tardiness of his son made no difference, except to him.''

"Edward the First? You are talking about the Middle
Ages!''

It had worked. She was distracted, and the moment was
gone when he might have asked: *Chaos? You were in fear for
your life—why?* He smiled. "I like history. Those who ignore
it are doomed to repeat it, they say. Sir Simon de Montfort
taught Edward everything he knew. These two men were the
greatest of friends, until one killed the other.''

She walked to the door. "An odd kind of friendship!''

Red sunlight danced like fire on her veil. Flickering at the
edge of his vision, it sent a stab of desire, like a knife, through
his veins. "It will be difficult to hold a dinner party if we are
at daggers drawn.''

"Will it? You are always armed. My daggers are all I
have.''

"You are wrong,'' he said deliberately. The hard edge of
the chimney bit into his back. Bricks sanded his cheek as he
turned to look up at her. "With you I have no weapons at
all.''

But she had already gone.

That night Nigel walked to Betty's, striding through the dark
streets with cane in hand, as if he drove an invisible chariot.
He had discovered something in Donnington's papers, something so disturbing he was unsure how to handle it. A hint
here, a slip there, but the implications were plain, and left a

disturbingly limited circle of suspects—each of whom Nigel expected to see tonight.

He was shown into Betty's private parlor. This time, in addition to Betty, three men awaited him there. They all looked up as he came in. A tall, powerful man dominated the others. He had an untidy air, yet the green eyes were filled with intelligence. Nigel studied him briefly, hating the necessity to look at an old friend with suspicion. In the bright candlelight his red-blond hair no longer looked like a silver coin. Surely Dominic Wyndham could not be the one?

"*Bonsoir,* Rivaulx." Major Wyndham spoke French entirely for his own amusement, since he came from Hertfordshire. "You don't mind, I hope, that we invade what is usually a haunt of pleasure to discuss such foul business?"

"Why should Rivaulx mind?" asked Lancelot Spencer dryly. "It was his idea."

Nigel bowed and took a seat. "As you say, Lance. Good evening, Wyndham." He could surely dismiss Lance? If he was certain of anyone's loyalty, it was his. Lance was susceptible to romantic imaginings, but not on behalf of Napoleon. Nigel turned to the third man in the room. "And I particularly appreciate your accommodating my wishes, Lord Trent. It seemed that this was a little more discreet than to meet in the back room of someone's house during a ball."

"And more in keeping with your reputation." Trent smiled. The light from the candles sparkled on his white hair and on his deceptively pink, round face—the face of an innocent boy, hiding one of the most penetrating intellects in the Foreign Office. Lord Trent had been in Russia, although as far as Nigel knew he had never left St. Petersburg, and later, of course, he had been in Paris. But Trent was a peer of impeccable reputation. It was impossible to imagine him personally involved in anything underhanded, even for the sake of England, though he had coordinated much of the work that the younger men had done. Nigel would stake his life—indeed he had staked his life—on Lord Trent's loyalty. So who the devil was the traitor?

"No one will suspect our purposes in attending a brothel," Trent continued. "Except possibly my wife. It is certainly what everyone expects of you, Rivaulx." He tossed a handful of papers onto the table—the familiar scandal sheets with their lurid woodcuts—and his smile deepened.

"Lord Trent, surely you don't need to remind me of it?" Nigel leafed through the sheets. "So," he said lightly. "I am known to have publicly ravished this exotic woman during a drunken orgy, then murdered her lover with my bare hands. The illustrations are excellent, don't you think? Crudely done, but full of vigor."

Lance looked down, his hands clasped white-knuckled on his knees. "For God's sake, don't make light of it, Rivaulx!"

Nigel made no attempt to hide the disdain in his voice. "I do not, sir, I assure you. We meet here not only because it is discreet, but because, after Farnhurst, I may expect to receive the cut direct if I attempt to appear again in society. Vice may be winked at, even admired, but the beau monde generally draws the line at murder. Shall we get down to business?"

"Bets are being laid at White's," Lord Trent said with deceptive casualness, "that Boney will be in Brussels in a month."

"Bets are also being laid that the Duchess of Winsham will announce happy expectations within the same time." Major Wyndham grinned as he dropped back to English, his face transformed by the smile. "I'm not sure which event will take the greater effort: the moving of the *Grande Armée* across France, or the moving of the Duke of Winsham across his wife. In either case, we may expect convulsions and the possible collapse of civilization."

Lance glanced at him, frowning. "Lord Wellington has never been beaten."

The red-blond hair shone like gold as Wyndham turned to him. "Nor has he ever met Napoleon on a field of battle."

Lord Trent cleared his throat, gathering everyone's attention. "Wellington has a ragtag army; at least half are raw recruits. It's damnable that his Peninsular veterans were scattered after Napoleon's defeat last year. Meanwhile the Allies in Belgium must maintain a damned long front to defend the border. If Boney attacks first, he will find them spread too thin. The French might well punch their way right through to the sea. Then Brussels will fall and Europe follow. Defeat now in Belgium could put us back to the beginning of the whole bloody show, where we'll be facing invasion again. And if, God forbid, Wellington is killed, who the devil could take his place to defend England?''

"Could we not consolidate our forces in time if Napoleon attacks?'' It was Betty, a man's diamond pin sparkling on her dress. "What do you think, Nigel?''

Nigel smiled at her and winked. Betty at least must be clear of suspicion. She had never been out of England. "Napoleon is generally considered the greatest general of our age.''

Lance poured out some wine. "I should say that if anyone can win against Bonaparte, it is the Iron Duke.''

Nigel took the proffered glass and played idly with the stem. "Not necessarily, in spite of Wellington's brilliance, if the French have total surprise on their side. Lord Trent is right. For God's sake, Lance, we cannot let patriotism blind us to reality. Let us only hope that the Allies will be ready to move first, while Napoleon is still pinned in Paris.''

"And if they are not?''

Lord Trent stood and went to the fireplace, folding pink hands over his round belly. "Without knowing where and when Boney is about to invade, not even the Iron Duke can predict the outcome this time.'' He turned to face the younger men. "Which is why I have asked for this meeting tonight. We must have better intelligence directly from Paris. Rivaulx, what have you gleaned so far from Donnington's papers?''

Nigel leaned back, apparently casual. "I have learned a great deal, but nothing useful. As we knew before the fiasco at Farnhurst, someone has been leaking serious intelligence. It goes further back than we knew, but it was not Donnington. He was no more than an amateur. Yet I guarantee he was dispatched by a professional assassin.''

Lord Trent did not meet Nigel's eyes. "What about Donnington's mistress?''

"She is not involved. I am certain of that.''

Major Wyndham grinned at Nigel. "And meanwhile?''

Nigel smiled back with a deceptive innocence. "Miss Woodard remains under my protection.''

Lord Trent made a quick gesture, dismissing this as irrelevant. "We must know Napoleon's plans this time. A forewarning if he begins to move might save Europe from another bloodbath. It will require two men, at least. What is your assessment of the danger?" He was looking at Nigel. "Who might discover us?"

"The secret police, of course," Nigel replied. "Fouché has a firm grip on power. We shall be watched, never fear. However, he has never met any of us face-to-face. There is no reason for Wyndham or Lance to be discovered. And Martin is still in Paris. We can use him to set up our networks, as before."

"Then Wyndham may go to Paris immediately. You will brief him on the details, Rivaulx?"

"Of course." Nigel had been afraid that Lord Trent would ask him to go, in spite of what had happened there two years before. The beautiful, dangerous city on the Seine! He did not want to do any of it ever again. He suppressed a shudder.

Lance glanced at Nigel, almost as if he saw it.

Lord Trent continued, speaking directly to Nigel. "Since you are such a devil with codes, Marquess, you are needed in London at least until you have finished with Donnington's papers. Mr. Spencer can join Wyndham in Paris. If later you want to go, too, that's up to you." He smiled suddenly. "Your rank precludes my using any stronger persuasion." His gaze swept over the other men. "I shall trust your own judgment to arrange the operation as you see fit. You are all professionals."

The conversation moved to details. At last Lord Trent and Lance rose to leave. Betty stood up. Nigel watched the other men's eyes instantly move to her. They seemed oddly surprised, almost as if they had forgotten she was there.

Wyndham grinned, breaking the moment. "Ugly business for such delicate ears! But it is all worth it, Betty, when you are hostess."

Betty ushered Trent and Lance to the door as if to show them out, then smiled over her shoulder. Her gaze caught Nigel's. Something in her eyes looked a little like an apology. "My dears, I am glad that I could help tonight, but, alas, my

daughter in Kent expects her confinement, and I have promised to go to her next week. I may be gone from London for
some time. Good luck in Paris.''

"You have a *daughter,* Betty?" asked Wyndham.

Her dark eyes filled with laughter as she turned her attention
to him. "Even whores may have children, sir."

Betty followed Trent and Lance from the room. Nigel
watched the graceful sway of her skirts. She did have a daughter in Kent, of course.

Major Wyndham poured another glass of wine. "Before we
start into the minutiae of how to handle this Paris venture,
Rivaulx, there is something that I'd like to mention—assuming
I come back from France in one piece." He looked at Nigel,
the green eyes narrowed a little. "Do not, I pray, take this
amiss. I was at Farnhurst, as you know. Should you ever tire
of Miss Woodard, you will let me know, won't you?"

Nigel was entirely unprepared for his sudden rush of rage.
He heard Frances as clearly as if she were in the room: *I am
a ruined woman. What earthly use would freedom be to me?*
She wanted him to find her a lover. It was the only thing she
had asked of him. Wyndham was an excellent prospect, trustworthy, kind to women. Nigel had known him for years. Yet
he wanted to take Wyndham by the throat and choke him. He
wanted to break his word to her and turn down the first man
who would give her what she needed. And he felt it with a
passion that shook all of his hard-won complacency.

Nigel forced himself to smile at his friend. "If you can win
her, she's yours, of course. But it's rather up to her. And I
might warn you, when she is ready to leave me, I have promised her a duke."

Wyndham laughed. "And in the meantime she is yours,
which as an honorable man I must respect." He bowed.
"You're a damned lucky dog, Rivaulx. Now, shall we get
down to our unholy business?"

Nigel grinned back. "And give up an evening with Betty?
Come to my house tomorrow, sir. We'll go over everything
you need to know then."

"Very well," said Wyndham. "Meanwhile I must renew my supply of French linen."

"French linen?" He had not meant it to sound so sharp.

His friend looked surprised. "Of course. I shall need to pass for a Frenchman."

Nine

∞

A SMALL MAN, dapper and neat, was working at the harpsi-chord with a tuning fork. Clear morning light streamed in through the arch-topped windows.

"Your servant, ma'am!" He bowed as Frances walked rest-lessly into the music room. "Lord Rivaulx sent me, in case you wanted to play. But I can come back at another time, if it is more convenient."

Nigel had thought that she might want to use the neglected instruments? It was an unexpectedly generous gesture. Surely the room disturbed him?

"No," she said. "By all means, carry on." She went to the table and opened the violin case. The wood gleamed under the tattered catgut. "Can you take care of this, also?"

The little man took the violin from her hands. His face darkened. "Who on earth let this happen? Was this instrument not properly stored?"

"I believe it sat on this table for some years. Is it dam-aged?"

He carefully examined it. "Fortunately, there is no perma-nent harm done. But his lordship is lucky the neck is not twisted. I can replace the strings, of course, and the bow. You play the violin, ma'am?"

"No. Nevertheless, I would like you to restore it, if you would."

She wasn't sure why she asked it. Rivaulx had given no indication that he ever wanted to play again.

The man's fingers lovingly caressed the scroll. "A man's soul went into the building of this. It was made in Milan by Giuseppe Grancino, over a hundred years ago, with all the passion and fire of the Italian heart. It is a crime against humanity that it lies here without being played."

"But a marquess may own what he wishes," she said sharply. "It is not for others to question why a lord does not put his possessions to use."

Frances left the man in the music room, the sound of his tuning fork resonating in her ears, and walked down the stairs. She saw the second stranger in the hallway and stopped just a few steps above him. He looked up, his elbow resting on the newel post, and smiled. Why did she feel a little nervous?

"Miss Woodard? Major Dominic Wyndham, at your service. I was at Farnhurst, a memorable evening. I have been hoping to meet you."

Frances met his gaze without flinching. He was cast in a heroic mold, big-boned, like a Saxon king. Blond hair hung untidily over his collar, as if deliberately flying in the face of convention. An attractive man.

"Have you, sir?" she replied. "Why?"

"To see if you are as lovely up close as you seemed from afar. The answer is yes, of course."

She wouldn't mind, she decided. She wouldn't mind at all if this man wanted her for his mistress. He was young and strong, and beneath the rugged exterior she could sense his essential kindness.

"You are being gallant, Major Wyndham."

"I am just speaking the truth, Miss Woodard."

"My name is Frances," she said.

He stepped back, allowing her to walk down the last few steps. "Then, Frances, I believe I shall have to flirt with you a little."

She looked up at him under her lashes. "That is generally how it begins, Major."

"Might I hope that our meeting is a beginning?"

Her heart was hammering a little. Could it be so easy? Could she escape from Nigel this very day and leave with this blond man? It struck her suddenly what a contrast the two men made. She knew that Major Wyndham was no threat to her, while Nigel seemed to contain depths that spiraled down forever, into dangerous, dark hidden places.

"A beginning of what, sir?"

"Of a day filled with beauty," he said abruptly. "I have come to see Rivaulx. Is he in his study?"

He bowed and walked away down the hallway to knock at the study door. Frances watched him, puzzled. She had let him know she was willing. Why had he suddenly run away? With an odd sense of panic, she turned and went back up the stairs. The music room lay quiet. The man with the tuning fork had gone. Frances took down the odd Russian instrument and plucked at the new strings. They had been tuned to the Western scale. Automatically she began to adjust the pegs.

∽

Nigel looked up as Wyndham entered. He waved him to a chair.

"I have just met your mistress," said the major without preamble.

"And?"

"I think you will have to fight off the Golden Horde to keep her to yourself. If I weren't an old friend, I'd have been tempted to ravish her on your hall table."

Nigel pointedly ignored this and continued working. "Perhaps I simply have a penchant for exotic women."

"Then I hope she is expiating what happened in Paris. By God, Rivaulx, if anyone can supplant memories of Catherine, it is this exquisite from India."

Nigel laid down his quill. "Is my soul so open to the ministrations of my bloody interfering friends? Why the devil do you bring up Katerina? She is dead."

Major Wyndham closed his eyes for a moment. "Since Catherine had been my lover before she was yours, I think I have the right to speak of her."

"So we are to remember Russia?" Nigel couldn't suppress the bite in his voice, though he knew it betrayed him. "Shall we get maudlin and talk of Moscow? Of the Kremlin, the Italianate palaces, the glittering domes and spires and cupolas? Of that holy city of wooden churches, of monasteries—silk canopies over gold-embossed icons—and of brutal whippings in the public squares? A magnificent remnant of feudal Europe mixed with Asian autocracy, where the wares of the East were hawked in the *Kitai Gorod* like the fabulous gifts of the *Arabian Nights,* while the citizens dreamed over their steaming samovars about their endless masquerades and balls. What the hell for? It was all burned to the ground."

"I know that you saw that. I did not, of course."

Deliberately he laid open the wound, before Wyndham did it for him. "What did it matter? St. Petersburg was already the seat of power. Moscow was a voluptuous pleasure palace. Too much of that Oriental splendor was just gilt over wood. It made an unholy enough conflagration—a metaphor, if you like, for the damage I did to myself—nothing is left but ashes. Of course you remember the Bolshoi dancing in Arbat Street?"

The major looked down at his nails. "For God's sake! I might have known you would do this. I'm damned sorry I mentioned Catherine."

Nigel did not flinch. "It was the night I met her. Frost clung to her hair like diamonds on flame. Lord Trent's delegation had finally persuaded Tsar Alexander to plan an attack on Napoleon. Your part was done and you came home to England. Lance and I stayed on. And, yes, Catherine took me for her lover. We were still lovers nineteen months later in Paris, where she died. What of it?"

"Oh, devil take it!" Wyndham thrust one fist into the palm of the other hand. "You have a mind like a bloody machine, Rivaulx. I think I am displaying heroic gallantry not to steal Miss Woodard from under your damned nose!"

A mind like a bloody machine. Nigel wished fervently it

were true. Right now he felt appallingly human, a mess of untidy passions and contradictions. It was hardly Wyndham's fault. He made himself relax and let his voice grow softer. "I'm sorry. You are about to leave for Paris. When you get back, if Frances will have you, I shan't stand in your way. As it happens, I do not wish to supersede Catherine's memory. But let me assure you of one thing: Frances is in no way comparable to Princess Katerina. You would do well to remember that." He stood up and pushed aside the papers that cluttered his desk, clearing a space. "Now, why the devil don't we go over your plans for Paris? Surely that's what you came for?"

Wyndham leaned forward and picked up a partially decoded message. He glanced over it before setting it back down. "If Donnington was not a serious threat, who is?"

Nigel smiled at him. "Probably someone in the room at Betty's last night."

"By God! You have evidence of this?"

"Donnington's papers make it clear that we were being betrayed throughout 1812 and 1813. While we were working to cement the Russian alliance, false perceptions lodged in the Tsar's mind almost lost us his support. Even when Alexander was committed, someone made sure Napoleon was privy to everything we did. After the fall of Moscow, copies of the information we were gathering in Paris got back to the French, which cost us dear at many of the major battles in Europe."

"One of us? Nigel, I can hardly believe it."

"Who else knew both our secrets in Russia and the work that we did in France? I am hoping some stranger has found a way to penetrate our little group. For otherwise, we are left with the ultimate betrayal. It can't be Betty, but if it isn't Lord Trent, or Lance, then it must be you. And you, of course, are left thinking the same about me. Charming, isn't it?"

Wyndham left at last. Nigel had freely given the blond man the benefit of his analysis and experience. There was nothing else he could do to help him. The major would slip into Paris, contact Monsieur Martin, and begin to set up a network to gather information. Lance would join him there later. Nigel closed his eyes for a moment. Damnation! He did not suspect either Lancelot Spencer or Dominic Wyndham of treachery. Betty and Lord Trent were beyond suspicion. Yet someone from those Moscow days had leaked information to the French all along. Dear God, but this was a filthy business!

He stood up and stretched, crossing the room to the window. While he toiled away in this damnable room, it was spring outside. He let his thoughts drift for a moment. Daffodils were blowing yellow in the grass . . . how peaceful and golden Frances had seemed on the roof, as if she dreamed while awake! Even then he had desired her. Would it be simpler just to bed her and ruthlessly let dissolution take its course? Devil take it, his mind was hideously unlike a machine at this moment!

A faint sound reverberated. Nigel strode to the door and wrenched it open. Music sifted through the house. For a moment memory enveloped him. Behind him his mother's portrait gazed down serenely.

The music welled. Nigel listened intently. He had never heard anything like it. Running rapidly in a hard rhythm that caught at the soul, the melody seemed to dart through the notes like a fey wind through grass, part of the whole yet not defining it. The beat was entirely alien, stresses falling in all the wrong places, like a stand of timber crashing down in a whirlwind. Closing his study door behind him, Nigel ran up the stairs.

The triangular instrument vibrated under her fingers, shivering into the soul of the ancient *ragas*. With her back to the door, Frances perched cross-legged on the harpsichord stool, letting the music flow.

The door clicked open behind her. Immediately she clapped her palm hard across the strings.

His voice dropped into the ringing silence. " 'O sing unto the Lord a new song; for he hath done marvelous things.' "

She should have realized that Nigel would be drawn by the

notes. Frances refused to look at him, although she could feel his presence in every pore of her body. She dropped her head over the balalaika and closed her eyes. "I'm sorry. You sent a man to tune the harpsichord for me? It was generous. Thank you. I will not play this if it disturbs you."

His reply was only a moment too late. "You may play anything you wish, of course. Pray, go on."

She heard him sit down, and knew how he would look— unfathomable, impenetrable, armored with cynicism. Yet that moment of hesitation revealed an abyss of disquiet—and that for him to stay now took something of courage. The balalaika did disturb him. Why? Because the tunes did not tinkle from her fingers in pretty Western trills and arpeggios? Because her music was not safe and civilized, like the harpsichord? Or were there darker memories connected to these Russian strings? Did that account for his bravado? *I lived there. I brought it back*.

He had invited her to continue. Was it a test for him—or for her? Trying to close him out, she touched the strings and waited for the feeling of the *raga* to return. As if under their own volition her fingers moved. It was music designed for clarity, for the finding of peace, a melody of the late afternoon. Yet her tension and distress spilled into her playing, a taut echo under the ancient rhythm and running through it like fever. Desperately she called on the music to cure her.

The exotic notes pealed from the strings, noble and measured, vibrating through the room, carrying Frances unwittingly across the world to a place where the far peaks of the Himalayas glittered against a bruised sky, heavy with rain. White cranes, white cranes soared against the black clouds and scattered in the threat of the oncoming storm. The notes ran, scattered, as apparently random as birds. After the last oscillation finally died away, the quiet glittered around her like snow.

He broke the silence at last, almost reverently. "Dear God! ... 'Let the floods clap their hands. Let the hills be joyful together.' I have never heard anything like it."

Frances whirled about. Nigel was stretched out on the chaise longue at the side of the room. He wore clothes he had ridden out in that morning—tailored coat, tan breeches, tall Hessian boots with short blunt spurs. At his neck the high collar of his shirt was secured by the wraps of his cravat, formally tied at the front and stiff with starch. The light from the window outlined his cheekbone and the strong line of his jaw. His eyes were closed, his expression exalted.

Barely understanding her reaction, still vibrating from her own music, Frances set down the balalaika. His presence had contaminated her playing. Instead of clarity she had found only confusion. Why did he stay?

Without thinking, the words spilled out. "It will not help for you to find me a duke. Or buy me an English dress."

He sat up then, suddenly. His dark gaze devoured her. "What?"

If he had been lost in her music, now she had smashed the moment and brought him back. She knew that he recognized that—and with that terrifying suppleness of mind, instantly adjusted to it. Could she never disconcert him or take him off guard?

She leaned forward, plucking the strings one at a time. To English ears they must sound off-key. "At Farnhurst, I met them and saw them, the men who might give me a future. They ran from me like rabbits. Today I met a friend of yours in the hall. Was he one of the guests you had planned for me to meet at your dinner party? A man you thought might offer me protection and take me off your hands? You are wasting your time. Major Wyndham thinks he admires me, but he is afraid to his soul."

Nigel was still gazing at her steadily. "You are English yourself, Frances."

"Am I?" Frances took up the balalaika. "Then what about this?"

She began a fast beat, slapping her hand on the triangular body between notes, the harpsichord resonating beside her tapping foot. In the same discordant rhythm, she began to chant. Setting down the instrument, she slipped from her perch. Still chanting, she began a classical Indian dance: the turned, stamping foot and moving eyes, shaping the story with her hands and each precise, practiced movement. She was enacting a *padam*, a poem on the ancient theme of love. Each gesture represented a specific word or idea, as if poetry flew from her fingertips; even her facial expression had meaning to anyone who could understand. It was precise, measured, not a movement random or idiosyncratic. The dance required total sublimation of the self to the art. Yet she could not lose her awareness of Nigel. His gaze never left her, and—as if he still heard the sound of the balalaika echoing strangely in his ears—she knew he was as caught up in the arousing rhythm as she.

When she stopped, they were both breathing fast.

"How many English ladies can do that? That is why!" she said harshly. "That is what I have been trained to be. Something as foreign as the Cinnamon Isles!"

"Is it? Is that what you are? Dear God, if it were only that simple!"

Her breath would not slow. It rushed, pounding like a wave through her chest. *Let the floods clap their hands?* "What do you mean?"

"This is only the surface, isn't it, Frances? A wall of silver. Or in this case, duplicitous layers of silk veils. Are you so damned impenetrable behind them?"

Like the white cranes before the storm, her distress spilled into disorder. "It is not just a show! I cannot satisfy one of your lords. They do not understand what I am, and I do not know what they are. What on earth does an Englishman expect in a mistress?"

The dark eyes narrowed. She knew he retreated from her, throwing up that barrier of cynicism. It was a moment before he spoke, the passion carefully stripped from his voice. "The customary things, I imagine."

"Yes, exactly! The customary things! I don't know what they are. Can't you see that?"

He closed his eyes. "I can see that your dance transcends anything a duke's mistress normally knows. Why are you so certain it matters?"

"Of course it matters! You have let the music die in this room. Does sensation terrify you so much?"

"What the *devil* do you think you know of what terrifies me?"

"You claim I hide behind layers of silk. What on earth do Englishmen know of sensuality? Look at the clothes that you wear! You are trapped inside rigid layers of fabric as if you were bound up in chains. You cannot move freely. Your skin cannot breathe. In India the body is a sacred temple. It is allowed its natural expression. Even men wear soft robes and let their muscles have liberty."

"You mean," he interrupted as his eyes flew open, "that they don't use starch?"

"They don't fight against nature and her gifts." Infuriated by his retreat into sarcasm, Frances walked up to him and slapped his cheek with the end of her sash. "This is how silk feels, spun by the creatures that make it." She slipped off her *peshwaz* and brushed it over his hands. "This is how cotton feels, taken from the plant and woven into gossamer. England has been envious of these fabrics for centuries, but what is done with them in the hands of your tailors? Seams, stitches, shapes cut so tight that every other man wears a corset."

His fingers closed over her *peshwaz,* trapping it. "Fashion demands a certain silhouette—"

"And the fabric binds like strapping so you can never relax. What is the point of that stiff collar? That tight waist?"

The quirk at the corner of his mouth deepened as she released her hold on the muslin. "In my case, fortunately, it demonstrates that I don't need a corset—due no doubt to all that tiresome exercise each morning." His voice was wry, yet she knew he reined in something much closer to anger. He ran the soft cotton through his hands, rapidly spiraling the cloth into a rope. "Boots and breeches let me sit effectively astride a horse. It is true that my clothes fit like a glove. They are meant to."

The *peshwaz* snaked from his fingers and looped over her head. It slithered down to her waist, where he pulled it tight, making her back bend as she resisted the pressure.

"We Englishmen deliberately use our clothes to restrain the body. To defy nature is part of being civilized. By demanding conformity, fashion conquers the baser instincts."

As she was pulled taut by the cotton she felt her attention—all her senses—intensify. If she lifted her hand, she could touch him. The crispness of his collar, the waves of hair brushing the starched linen, were infinitely fascinating. His masculine scent sprang clean and sharp in her nostrils. Defying his words, a lock of hair had fallen uncontrolled over his forehead. He did not look civilized. His face held the wild, lethal beauty of demons.

"That is nonsense. Not only can civility coexist with sensuality, it can flourish."

Slowly he increased the force. Vainly Frances tried to take a calming breath. The pull of his inexorable strength drew her closer, until she was between his knees. Her mouth went dry.

"Yet without tension," he replied deliberately, "there can be no release."

He let go of the muslin.

If he had not caught her by the wrist, she would have fallen. Instead he pulled her onto the chaise longue beside him. Every part of her reacted, a surge of agitation.

"Is that why you let yourself be imprisoned by all this?" She touched his lapel, the waistcoat under it, his shirt, the starched linen at his throat.

"Is sensuality concerned only with softness, Frances? Is it not heightened by contrast?" He took her hand in his and ran her fingers over his jacket—the high, stiff collar, the cloth-covered buttons, the little gathers at the shoulder. Her hand tingled at the slight roughness of the fabric, heightened by her memory of what lay beneath it. "My coat isn't soft. But then, I'm a man." He moved her hand to the silk of his waistcoat. It slipped under her touch, the raised seams caressing her fingertips, setting fire to the nerves. "Yet this silk is as supple as yours, is it not?"

As she sat enthralled, inflamed, he touched her fingers to his face. The skin over his cheekbone was smooth and firm. She felt the prickle of his sideburn, the slight roughness at his jaw. Exquisite textures, profoundly male. He turned his head to kiss her fingertip. His lips were pliable, sweet to touch. Frances heard herself make a small sound, an intaken breath, deep in her throat. She dropped her head forward and closed her eyes.

He moved her hand to his throat.

All of her awareness concentrated on the sensitive curve under his jaw. His pulse beat hard. Over the strong tendons and muscles, his skin was satin. The hard edge of his cravat and collar jarred suddenly against the backs of her fingers. Closing her hand beneath his own, he helped her pull the knots out of his cravat. As he let go, her palm slipped suddenly from the unyielding starched linen to the pliant skin beneath it. The contrast reverberated. She knew that she trembled, that she couldn't deny the truth, that his skin felt only the finer against the stiff fabric.

"You think Englishmen are trapped in constant tension? Perhaps you are right. But when red lies next to green, or purple next to yellow, the complement in colors makes each more brilliant. So I wear a superfine jacket over a silk waistcoat. I pick the softest fabric I can find for my shirts, only to starch them where they meet the tender skin of my throat. Is it deliberate, do you think? Or only an accident of fashion? But don't tell me that an Englishman's clothes lack sensuality."

She could feel his heart beat. Warmth, life, lay under her hand, infinitely desirable. She wanted to run her fingers under his shirt. As if the memory lived in her fingertips, her body reacted as it had at Farnhurst, when she had marked the skin of his chest in the library. Her breath came uneven, taut, and she couldn't seem to control it.

Frances snatched her hand away from his naked skin. "Your clothes are only a kind of armor."

He smiled, a lazy, assured curve to his lips, though she sensed the intensity beneath. "Why not? Shouldn't we protect our poor vulnerable selves from the world?" He tossed aside his cravat and opened his shirt. A slight trace of moisture glistened on his skin. His dark eyes were still fixed on her face, the lids lowered a little, shadowing his gaze beneath his lashes. He dropped his head back. "When an animal surrenders to its enemies, this is what it offers, the yielding, sensitive gullet. So I protect mine with starch."

She stood up, flooded with confusion. "Yet you offer it to me?" Her voice shook. "Don't you think I am your enemy, Nigel?"

"It doesn't matter." He tossed one booted foot onto the arm of the chaise longue and pulled up the other so that it rested on the upholstered surface. "I am well enough protected." He unbuckled his spurs and pulled them off, holding them up for a moment. "I even wear metal at my heels." The spurs fell to the floor with a clatter. He ran one palm along his boot. "And from knee to toe I am encased like a crab in its shell. Yet I have always liked the feel of fine leather."

He caught her wrist, pulling her once more against him. The smooth supple surface of his boot lay along her thigh. Leather slid sensuously past the thin fabric of her trousers. It was a compelling enough contrast.

"It is all a trap. Your surrender is false, like the tiger who offers his belly and grins at his prey. Yet style, pattern, they bind you like chains. These perfect seams, the buttonholes designed to never be used, the cut of your coat across your shoulders. It is a denial of the body and nothing but a statement of wealth and power."

"It is the tension in the strings that makes music, Frances. So my clothes fit. I pay my tailor a great deal of money to make sure that they do. As a result they don't hide much. Behind the flowing robes of the East, a man may conceal a great deal about himself that I am obliged to shout to the world. As armor, an Englishman's clothing seems oddly ineffective." The pulse beat visibly in his strong throat. "And as I seem to remember, it was you who bound me when I first met you at Farnhurst."

"I regret it," said Frances.

The tension lay between them like a keg of gunpowder, primed and ready for explosion. Frances shook with the force of it. Her heart hammered, as it had pounded the first night of the dry season. Her legs seemed unable to hold her.

His fingers traveled up her arm to her shoulder. All her awareness followed them, as if they traced the spark of a fuse. She was rapt. His touch fired her. His lips parted a little, and she saw him focus on her mouth. Yet he pulled away, breathing hard, and caught her hands in his, before he stood, allowing her slide to the chaise longue in his place.

Frances sat silent as he strode to the harp. *Fashion demands a certain silhouette?* His clothes only enhanced his sheer physical beauty, the wide shoulders and powerful legs—forcefully, blatantly masculine. She knew quite clearly that she coveted it.

"I regret it," she repeated, and knew that she meant it to the depths of her soul.

One rippling chord rang out into the room. The carved frame vibrated as the strings quieted. He spoke into the sudden silence.

"For God's sake, so do I. You are right. I am bound. But it is not my clothes that imprison me." As if he donned control like a garment, he turned to her. "It is my failing, not yours, that nothing can lie between us but disaster. Yet you do not need to fear for your future, Frances."

"Don't I? What English duke would have me?"

He looked down at the harp strings as if considering this. When he glanced up, there seemed to be nothing but humor in his voice. "Any of a dozen, I should think."

She could no longer read him, but she knew what she wanted. She wanted him. She wanted this man, Nigel Arundham, to make her his mistress. It was an appalling humiliation that he did not want her. She tried desperately to match his mood. "But I don't really know what would be expected, do I? How does a London courtesan live?"

He walked restlessly from the harp. "By knowing the value of jewels, by listening to all the latest gossip, by flattering wisely, by understanding French wine, and by opening her legs."

Frances had also learned control. Although she felt numb and confused, and her fingertips still burned with the memory of his skin, she hid her vulnerability behind carefully schooled features. "I can do all of that—"

"Can you?"

"—except perhaps for the wine. We didn't drink French wine in the *zenana*."

His lips still curved, but the dark eyes were fathomless. "I can teach you about wine. The rest, of course, you already know.''

She met his gaze without flinching. "Thank you, Nigel. Since I have no other future than this promised duke, to educate me about wine would be a great kindness.''

Frances caught her *peshwaz* from the couch and walked from the room.

Take us the foxes, the little foxes, that spoil the vines. Dear God! He had wanted—wanted to take her into his arms, there on the couch, wanted to kiss her until she opened to him. He had wanted, with every ounce of his being, to lose himself in her. The need ran wailing in his blood, mocking his defenses. He had conquered it, proved he could resist her, and been left with an empty victory. She would have welcomed him. It would mean nothing to her. Why, dear God, must he think it would mean so much to him?

Nigel touched the harpsichord. The balalaika lay innocently on the polished top. It had been played in the *Kitai Gorod* by a man whose life Nigel knew he might later be obliged to take, a man in French pay. The fellow had sung passionate Russian folk songs, and offered to teach Nigel the words. The lessons had been filled with bawdy laughter. The songs were obscene.

He hung the balalaika back on the wall, feeling it resonate under his hands. Frances had made it into something else. That extraordinary music—music that didn't obey the mathematical rules of the West, music that upset everything he had ever learned about harmony, music that had spoken directly to his soul.

Frances! Nigel ran his fingers down the long neck.

If he closed his eyes, he could see her dancing, grace and passion in every movement. In his blood he could feel her softness and her lips willing to give warmth to his. Trained lips. Lips that understood every nuance of feeling. Yet her eroticism was offered with a stunning purity. She seemed strangely innocent, free of any hint of lasciviousness. How had she been trained, in her harem in India? What had she learned, besides music and art and dancing—and how to tantalize a man to distraction? What were the women like who had trained her?

Women.

A harem consisted only of women. Nigel let the thought sink in. Dear God, it was obvious! Unless she had been bedded by the maharaja himself, Frances might still be a virgin. He had no intention of finding out, but he would hold on to that possibility. It might be the only thing that would give him enough strength to resist her.

He moved back across the room and opened the violin case. The Grancino gleamed softly beneath four lengths of new catgut. He had denied himself so bloody much these last years, and not even realized it. Nigel plucked the E-string. The note resonated, pure and perfect. He tucked the instrument under his chin. His fingers positioned themselves on the cambered fingerboard, intensely familiar—like the body of a lover. He felt the deep vibration of his desire to make music, to pour out his dark agony in some furious liberation of notes, and reached for the bow.

O sing unto the Lord a new song; for he hath done marvelous things.

With a smothered oath, Nigel set the violin back in its case, leaving the music locked up within its graceful curves.

Ten

NIGEL CAME ACROSS Catherine's name five days later. What appeared to be pages from a bad novel lay innocently among Donnington's papers, tossed in among the bills and the treason. Unlike Donnington's own notes, they were in a code so subtle that Nigel had almost missed it. It had taken him five days to break it—the five days since he had nearly kissed Frances in the music room. *Sweet Betty, don't you trust that I myself have the cunning of the dog fox?* He buried his thoughts and concentrated on the code.

At first the results had seemed hardly worth the effort. The papers were routine French reports from 1813, the year Prussia had rejoined the war against Napoleon, the year of the disaster at Dresden—yet finally of Leipzig and Wellington's entry into France. Nigel had smiled a little wryly to himself as he began to interpret them. They covered the period after the appalling retreat from Moscow, when he and Lance and Catherine had lived in Paris, gathering information and sending it back to London. The not-so-innocent novel revealed once again that the French had been better informed than any of them had guessed about British intentions, but none of it was likely to matter now, two years later.

And then, as if they had been waiting like coiled snakes, three sentences leaped from the page: *We have captured a British agent, a Frenchwoman, who has been moving in the*

*most trusted circles. She returned with the Emperor Napoleon
from Russia and has been known here in Paris as Princess
Katerina, widow of Prince Minkinov. Her true name is Catherine de Marbre.*

The quill bent in his hand.

There are several kinds of courage. Nigel thought he had
been tested in most of them. Nothing could have prepared him
for what it would take to keep on decoding, to put the pen
back in the ink, to transcribe the letters, one after another, that
began to tell a story he couldn't bear to know.

When he had first seen her, she had been haloed by frost—
jewels of ice in hair of an unusual deep red, darkened to mahogany in the dancing shadows. She had been wrapped in furs,
the incomparably rich, soft furs of the Russias, silver and sa-
ble. The sleigh ponies had shaken their manes at her, the bells
of their harness jingling in the clear night. Catherine had
slipped her hand from Wyndham's arm, holding out small,
perfect fingers, heavy with rings, and welcomed Nigel to Moscow in her perfect, throaty French—the language of the entire
Russian aristocracy, but in her case the pure tongue of Paris.

Then she had turned to her lover, lifting her hand to his
blond hair, and pulled his face down to hers. In front of Nigel
and Lance, she had kissed Major Wyndham full on the mouth.
Catherine exuded sexuality. Yet she was delicate, and beautiful, with a body as slender as a birch tree. She and Nigel
had first made love an hour after Dominic Wyndham left for
London, and not emerged from the bed for three days.

Nigel forced himself to go on, to keep writing. Every page
summoned nausea. When he had to stop to prepare a new
quill, for a moment he wasn't sure if he could start again. Yet
he made himself sit at his desk, though mind and muscles both
cried out for relief. The pages filled, one after another, and
every page filled him with horror. He didn't notice that the
daylight had faded and night dropped over his London garden,
until a servant came in to light the candles. Nigel signaled to
him.

"My lord?"

Nigel wrote rapidly on a fresh sheet. He folded the paper

and sealed it, pressing his ring into the hot wax. "Have this taken to Lord Trent immediately."

"Very good, my lord."

The servant bowed and left.

It was as if he had spent days and nights in exhaustive combat. As if once again he had ridden without sleep for a week with the Cossacks. As if the fierce cold of Russian snows once again corrupted his bones. Fighting to suppress the tremble in his muscles, Nigel pulled the knife out of his boot and stared at the sharp, wicked blade.

Nigel had given her books. Frances sat cross-legged in the old nursery with the bars on the windows and tried to concentrate on them. *The Young Ladies' Guide to the Making of Wine. The Wine Grapes of France.* For the past five evenings they had eaten dinner together. He had instructed the butler to open several different bottles, showing her how to hold a taste on her tongue and move it over the sensitive buds so she could appreciate the subtlest of differences. It was a strange echo of her training in the *zenana,* transformed into something quite different by his gentle teasing. Since their encounter in the music room he seemed to treat her with an almost reticent kindness and courtesy.

These same dinners had demonstrated a sensitivity to her feelings that she had never expected. If Nigel ate meat, he did not do so in front of her. The kitchen staff must have called on every ounce of ingenuity to prepare meals from grains and vegetables alone—probably after first offering their notice. It was something the Marquess of Rivaulx must have found difficult to explain to his lordly London chef, yet he had done it without asking and without comment. Frances found it disconcerting that Nigel could be so generous.

But as she had learned for her own protection in India, she did her best to avoid any personal contact. It was far safer that way. She sipped the wine without looking at his hands. She remembered the flavors without meeting his eyes. Once he thought the danger was over, Nigel would find her a duke and she would never have to see him again. There was a strange pain in the thought.

For the entire five days she had not gone back to the music room, and apparently neither had he. The encounter there was never mentioned during their light exchanges over the dining table. Nor had he again offered her his naked throat, like a defeated enemy. The image of it haunted her. She looked back at the drawings of grapevines and tried to put Nigel out of her mind.

Without warning, her door banged open. Frances leaped up, the books sliding to the bed. Lancelot Spencer stood in the entry with something close to panic in his wide blue eyes.

"Miss Woodard? Could I prevail upon you to come down?"

"What is it?"

His shoulders hunched a little, as if afraid to receive a blow. "Rivaulx sent a message to Lord Trent. I have come in answer to it." Lance ran both hands over his hair. "It is something quite dreadful. Nigel is in his study, but he won't open his door. Sometimes a man's mistress can reach him when no one else can—"

"Of course," she said. "I'll come at once."

She did not question her own lack of hesitation, or Lance's definition of her status in the house.

Lance ran ahead of her. At the bottom of the stairs he turned into the hallway leading to Nigel's room and stopped dead. Nigel was standing in his study doorway, quietly waiting. He was dressed in tall riding boots, light glinting from his spurs— and he had the look of a man being devoured from within.

"I have been expecting you." Nigel leaned back against the jamb and folded his arms across his chest. He fixed Lance with eyes like black pits. "But why the *devil* have you fetched Miss Woodard? Don't you have any more imagination than that?"

Lance's back was rigid. "You wouldn't open your bloody door!"

"Since when," replied Nigel coldly, "has a peer been obliged to admit any fool that pounds at his study?" His voice changed, softened. "Frances, this doesn't concern you."

Frances felt suspended, lost, yet she knew she was in the presence of tragedy. "No," she said. "Of course not." She turned and walked away, yet she stopped at the base of the stairs. She was shaking too badly to go up.

Lance seemed unable to move. "Lord Trent said you had found something that might affect my upcoming trip to Paris?"

"I hope it does not, for all our sakes, yet I fear that it does. You had better come in."

The angel's face was as white as his collar. "You have discovered something about Catherine?"

Frances leaned her head onto the newel post for a moment, clinging to the polished wood. Nigel still stood at the study door, and Lance was immobile in some kind of agony on the hall rug. Neither of them seemed aware of her.

Nigel glanced away, as if searching for patience. "I am sorry, Lance. I wish there could have been a way to avoid this. Life insists on playing its little jokes, that's all." Frances felt terrified by his control, by this mask of irony. Yet when he looked back at Lance, it was as if Nigel were blind. "What could be more appropriate than that Catherine's last lover should be obliged to decode an account of her death?"

Lance seemed to grow roots. "What happened to her, Rivaulx? I insist that you tell me."

"I don't wish—" Nigel took up his riding crop from the hall table and studied it, the brass top and leather-wrapped wand.

"You must," said Lance. "If I am to leave for Paris tonight, I must know."

Nigel glanced up. "She was tortured. For three days. With a knife. Yet she told them nothing. You don't need to know more—and I would rather not be obliged to repeat the details. I have prepared a report with the relevant information for you and Dominic Wyndham. It's there on my desk. Someone in Paris betrayed her, someone who knew all our plans and movements. That person must still be there. Otherwise I'd never have told you, and I'm damned sorry it was necessary. Now, if you don't mind, I'm going out."

Lance flung out his arms and barred the hall. "Over my dead body!"

"Dear me." Nigel pulled on a pair of gloves. "I am doing my bloody best to avoid histrionics. In spite of your obvious fears for my sanity, I don't intend any act of desperation. I'm going to take out a fast horse, that is all."

Lance stared at him. "Nigel—"

"If you don't stand aside and allow me to leave my own house, I shall knock you down."

It was a voice that might have commanded the Horsemen of the Apocalypse. Lance dropped his arms and walked stiffly past Nigel into the study.

Frances was left standing alone at the base of the stairs. Nigel strode up to her. She was afraid, yet she laid her hand briefly on his sleeve.

"Nigel, I'm so very sorry."

He reacted as if he had been touched by a ghost, and stared at her in silence for a moment. Then he reached out to touch her cheek, fleetingly, with an infinite tenderness, his voice softened by an unexpected compassion. "Don't be, Frances." He took her hand to his lips and kissed it once on the palm. His lips were cold enough to chill her to the heart. "Be sorry, if you like, for poor Catherine. She had skin like silk."

Frances heard Lance leave, perhaps an hour later. Without hesitation, she went into Nigel's study. His papers were stacked neatly. There was no evidence of what he had been through that day. She closed her eyes and took a calming breath. *For three days. With a knife.* There was ash in the grate. As controlled as an automaton, Nigel had burned the account of Catherine's death. Then she noticed the knife sunk in the mantel, as if thrown across the room. It was buried to the hilt.

Frances immediately rang the bell for a servant. She ordered fuel for the fire. She would build a huge blaze. She would make this room as hot as summer in India, and when Nigel came home—if he came home—she would use every skill she possessed to thaw him. It didn't seem relevant that she mistrusted him, or had fought him, or had been groping to understand his strange generosity for these last five days. Even a deadly enemy deserved succor in the face of catastrophe.

It was a long vigil. The clock ticked steadily into the silence. Sounds from the rest of the house had died away. On the sofa at the side of the room Frances sat and waited. The air was warm now. Every once in a while a coal would shift and fall in a tiny shower of sparks. Perhaps Nigel would not come home at all? And if he did, what rights did she think she had to intervene? Frances closed her eyes and sought for certainty.

There was a small click. She glanced up. Two o'clock in the morning. Footsteps in the hall. Not the tread of a man's boots, but the sharp, staccato rap of a woman's heels.

The study door opened.

"Thank God you are here! Lance told me what happened."

"He did not come to you?"

The dark eyes glittered with tears. "No, my dear, this is more than Nigel would share, even with me. He will think he must bear it alone."

Frances gestured to a chair. "Will you wait for him here? I'm not sure—"

Her hand still clasped tightly on the doorknob, Betty shook her head. "I don't care about your scruples, my dear. In the face of this, I only care about Nigel. Can you understand? But I shan't wait. I should have left for Kent hours ago. This isn't something . . . though if I thought I could—oh, damnation!" The shadowed corridor swallowed her, the raven hair and black cloak. Against that darkness Betty's face seemed unnaturally white. "I just want to know this: Why do you think your body is your only asset? You have brains and courage enough. Frances, I know what he will do. And it is vital . . . Oh, dear Lord! You cannot fail him now!"

∽

"Frances?" Nigel was poised in the doorway, pulling off gloves, tossing his whip and hat onto a chair.

Behind her the clock struck four, the darkest hour of the

night. Her senses leaped alert, keenly aware of him. His face seemed carved in some terrible beauty, the remote, dreadful beauty of angels, overlain with exhaustion and a glasslike fragility.

When the chimes died away she spoke quietly, carefully, into the silence. "I am not here to pry or to talk, unless you wish it, but I thought perhaps you would not be able to sleep."

He walked up to her and touched her cheek with one hand. "Frances. Tell me, how do you do it?"

She looked up at him, searching his features. "Do what?"

"Find such calm!" He wrung one hand over his eyes. "I cannot—oh, God! I cannot get rid of it!" Before she could respond, he spun away and went to the fireplace. In one fierce movement he yanked out the knife. "I cannot explain Catherine to someone like you."

"Do you wish to?"

His fist clenched on the handle. "Dear God! What is there to tell? I met her in 1812, early in the year before everything began. She was French, the widow of a member of the old Russian nobility, and still cared passionately for the France she had grown up in. She even held a salon in the French style. All Russia was in love with her."

"She was beautiful?"

He was staring at the blade, as if studying his own distorted reflection in its polished surface. "Oh, God, yes! Lovely! Though with a passion more Russian than French. She had lived there since she was sixteen. She hated Napoleon, and had been of incomparable help to British interests. When the Tsar finally decided to attack France, Catherine moved to Moscow from St. Petersburg. British intelligence officers were being sent there as observers. Lancelot Spencer was among them, and that's when Dominic Wyndham became her lover."

Frances allowed this to sink in without prejudice. "The major I met here?"

"Yes. He knew her for only three weeks, but he has never forgotten her. I arrived a few days before he was due to leave."

"So you took his place. Did the major resent that?"

Nigel tossed the knife onto the mantel. "No. Yet it wasn't

possible to have a casual affair with Catherine.''

There was silence for a moment. Frances spoke softly. ''You fell in love with her, too.''

She had no idea what emotion lay beneath the intense glance that he gave her. It seemed almost derisive. ''In love? I became obsessed. I lived with her until I was ordered to Vilna with Tsar Alexander—two months. For the first time in my life I was tempted to tell duty to go to the devil. Yet Catherine made sure that I left, so my honor would not be compromised.'' It was as if the derision deepened into open mockery. He strode away, taking the candelabra from the mantelpiece with him. The flames guttered, striking gold highlights on his face and hair. ''When the news came that Napoleon had crossed the Nieman River and was on Russian soil, Alexander retreated to Moscow. His Cossacks stayed behind. I spent the next half year with them fighting back the French advance. That's where I began my education.''

There was silence for a moment. What did he mean—his *education*?

''I don't understand.''

Setting down the candles, he turned to face her. The light was behind him. ''You were in India. Of course you can't know what happened in Russia.''

Frances could feel the intensity of his gaze, devouring, intense, and knew he had deliberately put himself in shadow so she could not see his face. Yet his voice was measured, as if he explained something that had happened long ago to someone else.

''Tsar Alexander had only a hundred thousand men to Napoleon's four hundred and twenty. Mother Russia herself was the only weapon he had left. So the Tsar's army retreated east, while the Cossacks torched the countryside—fields of standing grain, stores, villages—anything that might feed French men and horses. The countryside was devastated for more than thirty miles in each direction so the *Grande Armée* would meet nothing but starvation as it advanced.''

''What about the people who lived in those villages?''

''What do you think? They fled, they starved. But as strategy, it was excellent. By the time Napoleon reached Moscow, only a remnant of the *Grande Armée* remained. At last the Russians gave battle at Borodino, which was nothing but a massacre on both sides. After the slaughter they retreated, leaving Moscow open to the enemy. While Napoleon waited for a formal surrender, I rode into the city ahead of him. Most of the people had gone, taking their stores with them, but Catherine was there, waiting for me.''

''She must have been brave.''

''Brave? Catherine feared nothing.'' Nigel glanced at Frances and spoke the next words with a ferocity she couldn't understand. ''It was a reconciliation of matchless passion after our long months apart. But Catherine had decided to be taken by the French. She thought she could do more for the Allied cause by returning to Paris. It was obvious that France was facing defeat in Russia. Not in battle, of course, but in the face of Russian obduracy. Napoleon had counted on finding supplies and succor in Moscow. Instead the Russians set fire to their own holy city. It burned for five days.''

Frances closed her eyes. She could imagine the city, roaring out its last rage in defiance of the invader, and knew there was horror in it. ''You were there.''

''For a month, in the ashes. I helped Catherine prepare her troika. We filled it with dried food and her jewels and gold, hidden in secret compartments. Her seat was made of hay for her ponies. Grain was buried in her cushions. I knew what she was about to face, since I'd helped to create it. It was not possible to ride with the Cossacks and remain simply an impartial observer.''

He paced away, running a hand along the leather backs of his books as if trying to keep some connection with the world of learning and culture. The candles wavered and danced, sending grotesque shadows about the room. ''In October, Napoleon began his retreat back to Paris. Catherine went with him, cradled in furs. Ten days later it began to snow. With the Cossacks I harassed Napoleon's army all the way to the border. I cannot begin to describe those months. The French, the greatest army in the world, starving, freezing, dying in the Russian winter. It was a chaos of suffering. Yet the Cossacks also starved and froze as they took what revenge they could for the rape of Mother Russia.''

Frances wanted to reach out to him, to touch him, to say that she, too, knew there were things in life that couldn't be changed. She also knew that there was more pain in the world than one person could prevent, and that platitudes could not ease it.

Coal settled in the grate with a small crunch.

Nigel knelt and added more fuel to the fire. ''Catherine established herself openly in Paris. Lance and I secretly joined her there. Throughout 1813 we collected information about French plans and set up a network of couriers and informers, headed by a man named Martin. Napoleon's victories evaporated in his hands, and by October we knew he faced defeat. That's when Catherine disappeared. She had gone to meet an informant. I had arranged it.''

''But she was captured?''

His voice was ironic. ''The same day news arrived that my father had died. It made me too important to risk, I suppose, and I was ordered home.''

''You left France, knowing Catherine was missing?''

He glanced up, and this time that lethal self-derision was plain on his features. ''Not willingly, as it happens. Lance hit me over the head and brought me back unconscious. In spite of my orders, I was going after Catherine to find out what the devil had gone wrong, but a message arrived that she had been arrested and killed. Lance didn't want me to throw away my life for no reason, so he stopped me. It was only today that I learned otherwise—that Catherine took three days to die, that she was still alive when I left Paris.''

Frances was filled with terror for him. ''You cannot blame yourself, Nigel.''

''I don't. Yet she suffered to protect us—and we had already gone. She couldn't have told them much. I'd not shared most of my information with her for some months, so her agony was for nothing. Oh, God! I cannot control the images—''

''They are only thoughts. Let them go.''

The poker was in his hand. He brought it down hard across

a side table, smashing the delicate wood to splinters. "For God's sake! In a vain attempt at oblivion I have just ridden my best horse to a standstill! What the devil is left when courage runs out? Shall I drown myself in drink?"

"Come here." Frances willed herself to be calm, to project certainty. "Sit down."

Nigel tossed aside the poker and walked up to the couch. He gazed down at her for a moment. "Go to bed, Frances. I have lived with my thoughts all these years. What the hell's one more night?"

She reached out and took his hand in both of hers. "There is a core in us all that lies deeper than thinking or imagination. It is the only place any of us can find peace."

He dropped to the chaise longue beside her, looking down at her fingers. "Is that where you go? Where you were when I found you on the roof? For God's sake, peace isn't possible for me." He let go of her hand and wrung his palm over his mouth. "For you, perhaps, but the poison in me has sunk to the depths."

"It cannot, because in that place there is nothingness."

"Oblivion?" He gave her a strange half smile.

"Oblivion is a negation of something—it implies pain and loss. There is a place beyond that, a center, empty and full at the same time, where you find the Real and know all the rest is illusion. Christians talk about the grace of God and find it through prayer. India has another language and another path. They are all one. It's easy. Did you think it was hard to find?"

"I think these are only words for the ignorant—a mockery of a philosophy! But for God's sake, take me there, Frances, if you can."

"Then be still. Relax. Close your eyes."

To her amazement he obeyed her, dropping his lids over his bruised gaze. She studied his face. The warm firelight enhanced the beauty of bone, but his skin seemed stretched, too taut around the mouth and at the corners of his eyes. It was only his control that had prevented him erupting in rage or destruction, or seeking obliviousness in drink. Could she help him use that control to find ease, just for an hour?

"Listen to the silence."

He buried his face in his hands. "There is no silence, Frances."

"Hush. Concentrate. Begin with the quiet in the room. *Listen* to it, as you would listen to music. If any thoughts come in, let them go and bring your mind back to the stillness . . . . Listen to the silence."

The clock ticked slowly into the profound quiet. He dropped his hands. There was the faintest release of the white tension about his lips.

She dropped her voice to a whisper. "Now, feel your breath. Let each one sink deeper . . . deeper . . . . Open your body to your breathing. Surrender to it." She relaxed into the rhythm with him, watching the rise and fall of his chest, waiting until it became slow and even. "Each time you breathe out, repeat one word to yourself, like this—*hush*. If a thought or an image intrudes, let it float away. Gently bring your mind back to that one word: *hush . . . hush. . . .* It is very easy."

She saw the meditation slowly come over him. The tension left his body and his hands. The griffin ring seemed to smile at her as his fingers relaxed. She knew the power of the images that wanted his attention, as they wanted hers. She didn't allow the thoughts to linger; all her focus remained on him. When he wavered, Frances was there. In rhythm with his breathing, she softly repeated the mantra, carrying his mind back with hers—*hush . . . hush*—letting the word whisper between her lips.

At last her own concentration seemed to mingle with his, their breath blending, until even the slow beat of the clock seemed to disappear, and there was nothing in the room but purity.

∞

Dull light streamed in the window. The morning had begun with drizzle. Nigel stood with his hands on the bars. He had put her into a room with bars, like a jail. After four years of imprisonment in India it must have been agony for her, yet she hadn't complained or asked for a different room. He turned around and looked at her. Frances lay in deep sleep on the bed, a confusion of honey-gold hair on the pillow.

He had carried her here from his study. He wasn't sure what had happened last night, but somewhere in his core he had found what she had promised, an overflowing well of strength and calm. It changed nothing, removed nothing, left him still with his pain and his dilemmas, but like a wave it had carried him through the worst of the storm and cast him up on a new beach. When he had opened his eyes he had been amazed to find that he had been in that mysterious state for over thirty minutes, and that Frances, exhausted, had fallen asleep with her head on his knee.

For an indefinable eternity, he had stroked the hair back from her forehead, filled with a grief he could not fathom. When she had not stirred he had carried her up through the silent house, laid her on her bed, and covered her with a blanket. Then he had stood at the window watching the dawn creep over London while he thought through everything that had happened. He did not know what was going on. He had no idea why Donnington had died, or who had killed him, or who had given the Marquess of Rivaulx poison at his own orgy. Yet everything had led inexorably to the moment when he had discovered what had happened to Catherine, and known he alone was meant to decipher it.

But no attempt whatsoever had been made against Frances. Nigel's men had uncovered no rumor or hint that she was in danger. This room, these bars, had proved unnecessary. Yet those fears had made him bring her here and take responsibility for her future. Had that been an unpardonable presumption? Did he not owe her the dignity of self-determination now? He had promised, and in the face of what he had decided, what other option was left?

He moved from the window and crossed the room to the bed. Desire for her lived in him now like an ache. How easy it would be to lean down and kiss those curved lips—and after last night, what a travesty to do so! He had not told her the whole truth about Russia, or about Catherine. Instead he had given her a history lesson, safely skirting the personal. There had been that one moment when he had almost forgotten, had almost allowed her to see what he really was. He had not had the courage to face her revulsion.

Nigel paced back to the window and leaned his forehead against the cold iron. If he died pursuing this next adventure, he would never see her again. If he came back, it would be to an empty house. Either way he would have what he wanted. Yet he could not bear to face it.

"Nigel?"

He whirled about. Frances was sitting up, her flower-blue gaze fixed on him.

"You slept," he said lightly, "like a princess surrounded by briars. It is morning."

"I have remembered something. I believe it might be important."

She slipped from the bed, her silk robes rumpled and her braid coming undone. Her grace took away his breath.

He smiled. "And I have decided something. So who will speak first?"

Frances leaned over her washbasin and splashed cold water on her face. "You first. What have you decided?"

"I am going to Paris."

She did not look surprised, though he saw something of dread in the set of her shoulders. She turned to him with drops like dew on her eyelashes as she reached for a towel. "Then you must know this about Catherine: Lord Donnington told me that you had betrayed her."

It was so unexpected that Nigel almost staggered. "What the devil? Donnington? When?"

"The day I met you at Farnhurst. He told me you had betrayed your last lover to her death to save your own skin."

"But no one knew but myself and Wyndham and Lance—and Betty and Lord Trent, of course."

"Lord Trent? Tell me about him."

He was still too surprised to wonder much at her question. "Why? He holds some fat government purse strings, that is all. He is above suspicion. Dear God! A connection between Catherine and Donnington. How the hell could Donnington have known that I arranged the rendezvous that led to her capture?"

She had pulled out the ribbon and begun combing her hair. The long strands fell through her hands like threshed wheat, the highlights of flax and gold fascinating. "This means that someone you have trusted must be a traitor, doesn't it? Will you still go to Paris?"

"Of course. Wyndham is there. Lance left last night. I shall join them immediately."

She set down her comb and began to make a plait. "There will be danger?"

He shrugged. "From the secret police, from the people, from an enemy who undoubtedly expects me. It doesn't matter. Someone betrayed Catherine. Someone betrayed England for years. Donnington makes it obvious those two things are connected. The answers all lie in Paris. I shall offer myself as bait. Perhaps I may draw our traitor out into the open." He smiled at her, vainly trying to offer a reassurance he didn't feel. "Like Absalom and Achitophel, neither of us will be what he appears, and perhaps he will be unmasked before I am."

She tied the ribbon that secured her hair. "And perhaps he will not."

"I shall still go. There is another part to my decision. It concerns you."

"I'm not surprised," said Frances dryly. "You are in the habit of making decisions concerning me."

The ribbon made a small loop over her index finger. He could not take his eyes from it. "I no longer believe you are in danger from Donnington's killer—in fact I don't think you ever were. I hope you will forgive me for imprisoning you here. If you wish, before I go to Paris I will hold that dinner party and you may choose a protector. Or you may stay here while I am gone and entertain whomever you wish. I will leave you some funds. The house is yours. Which would you prefer?"

He paused, watching her, trying to gauge her reaction. Tiny stitches ran down each side of the ribbon. Nigel hardly realized he was holding his breath as if his very life depended on her reply.

Frances walked back to the bed and sat down. As if trapped

forever at the window Nigel stood and watched her. It was a bloody awkward good-bye. The long silence stretched between them. She was gazing at his painting, the white horse that he had loved as a child—the horse that ran free and defied the storm.

At last she looked around and met his gaze. He was horrified to see a glimmer of tears on her lashes. To spare her he looked away, leaning back against the window and closing his eyes. But her voice when she spoke was cool and controlled.

"There is another option, Nigel. It is this: I will come to Paris with you."

Eleven

FRANCES HELD HER breath. He jerked as if struck, and stared at her. "That's impossible!"

She had known she would have to brave his anger over this, or worse: a cutting, scathing repudiation. "Is it? Why?"

His eyes burned. Nigel seemed drunk with fatigue. "I cannot believe—Frances, for God's sake! Paris is a chaos of factions—there is even fear of a renewed Terror!"

"I have ridden alone across India. I have sailed around the Cape of Good Hope. I have faced tigers and monsoon. I am used to loneliness. I don't care about danger. I want this chance at independence. I can surely fool a handful of French aristocrats?"

His hand struck hard against the window frame. "Do you have any idea what you're saying? France has a new aristocracy. Le Duc d'Otrante is a prime example. The revolution made him a duke, though there is no noble blood in his veins. Some would say he has no blood at all, which is why he enjoys shedding that of others. Now he is head of the secret police. Will you beguile him, do you think?"

Her tongue seemed to fill her mouth. "You know him?"

"I have seen him—sharpness, angles, shoulders stooped like a hooded hawk. Pale eyes in a thin, bloodless face, entirely without expression, as if the man behind the gaze were completely soulless. I know what happens in his offices in the Quai Voltaire.''

''No one is without a soul.''

''Would you have said that during the Terror, when the gutters ran red with the blood of his victims, when he reverted to cannon and firing squads because the guillotine was too slow for his tastes? In Lyons a nun was dragged through the streets by his orders and killed with a meat cleaver—she was my mother's cousin. His name is synonymous with fear. It is Joseph Fouché.''

She stood up to face him. Would he know she was lying? That she was terrified to the soles of her slippers? That the thought of the secret police filled her with horror? Yet she had been offered a chance that might change her destiny. Or did she lie to herself? Was she denying her true reason for going to Paris?

Frances kept her voice steady. ''I have been offered a job. It will be very well paid. I have agreed to take it. You will not frighten me away.''

''For God's sake!'' The muscles clenched hard at the corner of his jaw. She knew he was at the end of his resources. ''Offered a job? By whom?''

''Lord Trent. Betty came here last night to explain.''

She received the blast of acerbity she had been dreading. ''*Betty?* Of course, I might have known—a conspiracy among harlots! Will she come, too, so that I might be lord of a harem?''

Frances turned away. Through a blur of tears she stared at the horse, at the painted mane flying silver in the wind. ''Perhaps you should have thought of that, my lord marquess, when you claimed your prize from Lord Donnington. Since then my life has been yours to order as you have seen fit—in your infinite arrogance, you will even find me a duke.''

''I had been led to believe,'' he said caustically, ''that such was your wish.''

''I thought I had no other options. You have deprived me of my own will and freedom. Now will you veto the one chance I might have to recover it?''

She knew his dark eyes bored into her back. Anger still

crackled in his voice. "So what is the plan that Betty and Lord Trent have hatched up? No doubt Lance is privy to it, also? Are you allowed to tell me?"

Frances sat down on the bed, clasping her hands, unable to meet his gaze. "Lord Trent thinks you will achieve the most if you are public and brazen, and can move freely. If you and the others spring upon Paris with silks and spices, you will be welcomed everywhere—gentlemen traders from India, bringing with you proof that you have been there. No one would question it, and doors would open immediately."

To her immense surprise he began to laugh. She glanced up. He seemed filled with genuine mirth, as if she had dreamed his shock and anger. "Proof? You speak French?"

"Not fluently. Lord Trent doesn't think it will be necessary that I pretend to be French."

She waited in quiet agony for his reply. Once again, in spite of the promised payment from Lord Trent, all the choices were his, weren't they? Without his agreement she could not go, could not take this chance at something else, could not prolong the inevitable moment when Nigel gave her to a duke and walked out of her life.

He rubbed both hands over his face as if to wipe away all emotion. "Of course. Even if we are discovered, Fouché will have no interest in you. The Parisians will think your mistakes charming, no doubt."

Frances couldn't bear it. He was going to agree, though he did not want her. She would be in the way, a burden. Yet last night it had seemed impossible to refuse Betty's desperate plea.

"He will go to Paris," Betty had said, "and throw his life away. You must go. You must go with him. If he is forced to be responsible for you, then he will have to keep himself alive, at least. I have spoken with Lord Trent. He has agreed to my idea—and you will be well recompensed, my dear. You won't have to live as a harlot."

Suddenly Frances hated the manipulation of it. This was Nigel's battle, not hers. If he wished to die in Paris, what right did she have to insist that he live? Twice since that first meeting in the library she had tried to offer him compassion. Yet he did not want any kind of intimacy. Now she was forcing his hand by appealing to his gallantry—did he not deserve his own freedom, instead?

She made herself say it. "If you prefer, you may tell Lord Trent you have a better plan."

It was too late. He gazed at her like a drowning man who laughs one last time as the waves close over him. "No. Take this chance, Frances. Who am I to stand in your way? It is an excellent ruse. Lance and Wyndham and I will make very pretty traders."

"You can all pass for Frenchmen?"

"Of course. In fact we had already discussed something similar, as Lord Trent knows. The more outrageous the lie, the less likely it will be questioned. So come to Paris, Frances, by all means. I have only one condition."

The bitterness had crept back. It made this seem a very empty victory. She looked away. "What is that?"

"For your own protection, you will continue to pose publicly as my mistress."

"So nothing changes?"

He had gone to the door. She heard him open it. "This is purely a business proposition. We shall be comrades. Though of course you may make Wyndham your lover if you wish."

"Spring is always my favorite time in Paris."

The dark-haired woman smiled. Her French was rapid and perfect, but the aristocracy of England and Europe all spoke French—a language essential for diplomats and for courtesans, though equally the language of every peasant who milled past the window below them. This was not the most fashionable part of Paris, but it was very discreet.

He grinned back. "He has taken the bait. I have heard from our watchers at the coast. Lord Rivaulx should arrive tomorrow."

Triumph was clear on her features. "Ah! He is a man who never learns his lessons."

"He brings the Indian harlot."

Her shrug was infinitely dismissive. "She will soon be irrelevant—a minor irritant, like a burr in his shoe. But Rivaulx
comes to Paris! That is what counts." She tapped her fan
against her chin. "And meanwhile they have hired a house for
themselves near la Place du Palais Royal. Such charming ef-
frontery!"

"Lancelot Spencer is also living there."

"And so the courtiers await their little king, with all of his
devious plots. Rivaulx thinks he is so very clever. But this
time he will not win. If he is stubborn, he will die, like Donnington." She moved to the center of the room, where a small
table held several china figurines, shepherds and shepherdesses
in pink-and-blue painted clothes, picked out in gilt. Idly she
picked up one of the shepherds and examined it. "Which
would be a shame, Pierre. After all, the marquess is a very
pretty man."

He grinned again. "As pretty as the man who waits next
door, madame?"

The woman deliberately opened her hand. China shattered
on the floor. "These golden fellows are comely enough, but I
prefer my men dark, Pierre. Dark men are so much more challenging."

Leaving the scattered shards of pink and gold, she crossed
the room and opened the door. Pierre followed. The man sitting in the anteroom looked up at them. Beneath his blond
hair, he was white, a sheen of cold sweat on his features.

"Ah, *le petit Anglais*!" She switched to English. "You will
give me a kiss, won't you, my dear?"

In spite of his obvious unease, the reply was also in English.
"Should I?"

The anteroom was dark. Like the flowers known in England
as "yellow flag"—wild spring irises bright against the brown,
damp mosses—his hair gleamed golden in the gloom. He did
not move as the woman bent and kissed him on the mouth.

"You are nervous to betray your friends, *mon cher*? But I
think we must have a little fire."

The blond man remained silent, gazing at her, his lips red
and moist against his white skin. Pierre observed it without
emotion.

She leaned close and whispered in his ear. "The house that seemed so suitable for your little trading venture, the house by la Place du Palais Royal, it does not seem appropriate to me."

His voice was a little blurred between his swollen lips. "How vexing. We went to a great deal of trouble to secure it."

Her coal-black brows lifted a little. "Your venture will have to move to a new house. I have a little place in mind—it might strike you as perfect, indeed."

"No doubt it will. So what shall I call you, *chérie*? Do you have a new name now you are in Paris?"

"Don't be droll," she said. "I am la Belle Dame. What else?"

He laughed. "*La belle dame sans merci?* Well, lovely lady without pity, where is my place in all this?"

The woman caught his chin in her hand and turned him to face her. She switched back to her perfect French. "You men all think you are so very brave. We shall see."

∽

Frances and Nigel had quietly left London, crossed the Channel in a smuggler's boat, then ridden fast and unnoticed through France. For the entire journey he had been polite, but remote. And always, even when curled under a hedge or in the bottom of the boat, they had slept apart.

Their exotic cavalcade—a tidy train of wagons—appeared suddenly in a foggy wood, as if a genie from the *Arabian Nights* had granted a poor fisherman his dream of splendor. Frances saw the conceit of their being traders from India unfold with breathtaking nerve and brilliance, like a magical blossom from scented vapor. Nigel had rifled the warehouses of the East India Company of silk and spices, all the luxuriant wealth of the East, to supply them with goods. For the first time she truly realized the power and wealth at the disposal of a marquess. It was a little disconcerting.

Surrounded by the fog-damp trees, Frances pulled up her chestnut gelding and watched Nigel ride among the wagons, giving orders and inspecting details. Moisture darkened his coat and hair. He was riding the horse she had first seen at Farnhurst, the horse with the strange metallic glitter to its silver-gold dapples. The animal's shining coat melted into the mist. She felt something melt deep in her heart, a yearning, strange and forbidding.

As they entered Paris a ragged crowd of urchins ran screaming after their convoy, gabbling unintelligibly. Nigel called back to them, laughing and joking. Frances knew another moment of disquiet: the French she had learned as a schoolgirl had certain limitations. Nigel, Lance, and Wyndham, of course, spoke the language like natives.

"Why not Lance?" she asked suddenly.

Nigel glanced at her and raised a questioning brow.

"You do not ever suggest that I become his mistress," Frances continued.

"Lancelot Spencer?" He laughed openly. "Lance is a delight of quaint notions. He is keeping himself pure for marriage."

"And you find that risible?"

"No, I find it charming. His betrothed would no doubt agree."

Frances wondered why she felt so surprised. "Lance is engaged?"

"For the last several years. Miss March lives in Surrey. Alas, a series of elderly relatives have prevented the nuptials by dying in the most ill-timed way, one after another, but he will marry her this summer."

"And he loves this Miss March?"

"Enough to stay virginal for her. We are almost there. Ask him, if you like."

Frances looked away. Tall buildings—a confused impression of white plaster walls, iron railings, and steep blue roofs—soared above her head. The cobbled streets rattled under the horses' hooves and the iron-shod wheels. The city smelled of urine and horse sweat, with undertones of damp stone and mosses. Paris, the capital of culture, and now the springboard from which Napoleon would once again conquer Europe, unless someone could stop him.

She smelled the smoke before she saw the ruins. Where the house near la Place du Palais Royal was supposed to be waiting for them lay nothing but ash, still smoldering. A small crowd had gathered, gesticulating and pointing. As Nigel and Frances rode up, the people turned and stared at her Indian trousers and silk veils. Except for his magnificent mount, Nigel had dispensed with any sign of nobility. His jacket did not quite fit across the shoulder; his hair was a little long. The difference was subtle, but absolute. He looked like a prosperous French trader, not an English lord, and as if he had been traveling for a very long time.

Nigel leaped from his horse and engaged the crowd in a discussion that required much waving of arms and Gallic shrugging. After a few moments he returned to Frances. He was barely controlling open laughter.

"It happened very early this morning. It was the cook. He has been dismissed. The butler who hired him has been dismissed. The maids who worked with them have been dismissed. The understairs servants and the stable lads have been dismissed. The gentlemen who rented the house have disappeared. No one has seen them."

He spoke in French, of course. Nigel had introduced himself to these people as Monsieur Anton. From now on, they must all live in character, day in, day out.

There was a rustle from the crowd, then sudden shouts. *"Le voici! Le voici!"*

Frances turned her horse to see Lance riding at a rapid trot down the street toward them.

"Mon Dieu! Monsieur Anton! Vraiment, ceci sont les temps du diable—"

Frances managed to translate to herself as Lance continued to speak rapidly to Nigel in French. "That wretched cook! The bloody man set fire to the kitchen. With the Emperor Napoleon returned to Paris, it's almost impossible to find anywhere to rent. We had to expend a considerable sum of gold to get this house." Lance wrung one hand over the back of his neck, avoiding Nigel's eyes. "But I have found another place . . . There is other news I can't tell you until we get there. The place is not . . . I hope to God you won't mind."

"Mind?" said Nigel. "After that contemptible ship and the long months journeying, I will stay in a pigsty if it has a roof and hot water. Lead on, sir."

Lance glanced about at the curious crowd and turned his horse. Remounting, Nigel followed him, with Frances and their baggage wagons close behind. He had agreed they should be brazen and open. This arrival was about as brazen as it could get. Frances felt a prickle of fear. She straightened her back and rode on. The ragged tail of the crowd followed them.

As they crossed a bridge over the Seine Nigel remonstrated in his easy French, indignantly reminding Lance of the perfidy of landlords. He, Monsieur Anton, was expected to pay to rebuild the burned house? Nonsense! The landlord was responsible for his traitorous cook. Why had no one thought to throw water on the fire? Why had the servants all run away? It was a conspiracy against honest gentlemen. Let the landlord go whistle in the wind for his money!

At last the crowd lost interest. The last few stragglers ebbed away.

Frances followed Nigel and Lance into a quiet street, dozing in the spring sunshine behind a small garden of trees. Fallen blossoms clogged the cobbles. The houses seemed forlorn to Frances, shabby with long neglect. Most of them were obviously unoccupied.

Her gelding jibbed violently. The silver-gold horse had stopped dead in front of her. Nigel turned in his saddle and hissed at Lance. "Is this a joke?"

Before Lance could reply, Nigel put his heels to his mount and cantered down the street. The dappled horse skidded and stopped before a set of double doors with a courtyard beyond.

Nigel turned back to Frances and Lance as they rode up. He was deadly calm, but his voice held both mockery and anger. "For God's sake, Lance! Did you do this deliberately for the good of my immortal soul? Or was it just the whim of the moment?"

"I'm sorry," said Lance, his face set. "There was absolutely nowhere else." He glanced down at his horse's mane. He was very pale. "Paris is packed. It's all I could find at such short notice. For the same reason we got it the last time."

Nigel gazed up at the shuttered windows and peeling plaster. "Yes, of course. The locals believe that it's haunted."

"As soon as we can find something else, we can move."

"Move?" Nigel looked at Lance and laughed. "Why the devil should we move? I can think of nothing more perfect. Life should always offer symmetry, if possible. It's our only defense against chaos. Let's hope to hell a decent cook comes with the place this time, and not a bloody arsonist."

"What have you done?" Frances heard herself speak to Lance as if she had the right to ask. Nigel's composure was terrifying, only the small flare of his nostrils betraying his distress. Lance had become wooden.

Nigel whispered softly in English. "We are in the Rue des Arbres. An enchanting choice, don't you think? This is the very house where Lance and I lived with Catherine in 1813 before she was arrested."

Frances watched Nigel ride in through the wide double doors, and felt the fear pressing on her heart like a great weight.

It was an ancient house, a remnant of the Paris that had disappeared long before the revolution, long before an upstart from Corsica had decided to invade Russia, and long before a princess from Moscow had come to live here in these very rooms around this very courtyard with her English lover.

The noble Lord Rivaulx betrayed his last mistress to her death to save his own skin.

Frances took a long breath, vainly seeking strength and calm.

For three days. With a knife.

Her horse moved restively, nervously mouthing the bit. Frances eased her grip on the reins and rode in after Lance and Nigel.

The locals believe that it's haunted.

∞

Nigel oversaw the disposition of the baggage. A large room downstairs was appropriated to become a showroom for the riches from India. It was done rapidly and efficiently. After all, Nigel and Lance had lived here for almost a year, from that February after the retreat from Moscow, to the October when the news arrived that Nigel had become a marquess and Catherine had been arrested. Frances quietly directed the servants as the spices were stored, so that some logical order was maintained. Lord Trent had suggested not only that she attract customers, but that she run the business so the men were free to pursue their more deadly aims. She had a job to do. There was an odd comfort in it. Or would be, if she had ever run a business before.

"Come," said Nigel in her ear about an hour later. "Enough. The men can finish this. I have ordered a fire lit in a room upstairs, and a pot of tea. Lance is going to have to tell me what he's hiding, and I want you there. For your own safety, you must know what's going on, but you don't need to feel involved."

Frances glanced up. Not involved! If she had not felt she was already involved so deeply with this man, she wouldn't be here! But he looked away, speaking to a servant, and the moment was gone.

The room was damp, with the smell of long-unused spaces. The fire smoked and sputtered in a desultory way, as if reluctant to shed either light or warmth. Frances tried the teapot. The tea was already cold.

"Good God!" Nigel strode to the window and threw wide the shutters. "French servants!"

Lance entered the room and dropped into a chair. He looked exhausted, almost as if he were ill. "Nigel . . ."

"Lance, it's easier to disgorge the devil in one heave." Nigel turned from the window. The dull light behind him exaggerated his menace, for his voice was gentle. "Where is Dominic Wyndham?"

Lance laid his head against the back of his chair. "I could not tell you until we were private. Wyndham hasn't been seen since the night before the fire. The parlor maid claimed he drank a great deal of wine and passed out. All the servants swore he did not leave the house."

Nigel looked away. The light caught his strong profile as he gazed out across Paris. "And the blaze was very early. If he was dead drunk, perhaps he never awoke. In which case Wyndham would appear to have perished in the flames.''

Lance's blue gaze was as wide as the sky. ''There was no sign of a body in the rubble, but we will only know for sure if he doesn't appear.''

''And where were you?''

''Near Montmartre, making contacts. I spent the night in a tavern there. I can produce witnesses, if you like.''

Frances saw Nigel's exasperation and knew it was genuine. ''Oh, for God's sake, Lance! If I believed you a traitor, I would believe you bribed the witnesses. As it happens, I do not.''

''But you discovered that someone from our days in Russia was working secretly against us. It could have been me.''

Nigel strode across the room and attacked the fire with the poker. ''Damnable, isn't it? If Wyndham doesn't appear, that fabulously suspicious arson is going to make him seem the suspect, instead.''

''I don't want to believe it.'' Lance pulled out his snuffbox and stared at the lid.

''Then let's hope to God he shuffles in here soon with a sheepish grin and announces he spent the night in a brothel. But I told him, you see, before he left London, what I had discovered. I also told you and Lord Trent, of course.'' Nigel tossed down the poker and picked up the teapot. He dashed the cold liquid over the smoking coals. ''We shall have to get these damned chimneys cleaned before we can expect a decent blaze.''

Lance coughed at the sudden belch of smoke. ''When I brought news that you were coming to Paris, Wyndham seemed pleased.''

Nigel set down the pot. ''You mean he didn't look like a man about to panic and flee, covering his tracks with a con-flagration? If Wyndham's our traitor, of course he wouldn't have. We are all professionals, used to hiding our true feelings. Yet, dear God, it seems strangely out of character!''

''But how well, really, does any of us know each other?'' Lance was looking at his hands, as if examining his carefully manicured nails.

"I thought I knew Wyndham," said Nigel with a hint of mockery.

Lance glanced up. "I thought I knew you. I thought you would not be able to bear this house. I was terrified of your reaction. But except for your initial annoyance, you insist on acting as if it doesn't bother you. Yet Catherine lay on that very chaise longue, and looked out of that very window. What she and you shared—"

He glanced at Frances and stopped, as white as the plaster.

"Shared what?" Nigel asked in a voice like silk. "What do you think you know, Lance? Don't spare me, I beg of you. Frances knows about Catherine, and if she doesn't want to hear what you have to say, she is free to leave the room."

A knock at the door broke the sudden silence. Nigel glanced up. *"Entrez."*

A servant stepped in and bowed. "Monsieur Anton? You are wanted in the stables. There is a quarrel among the grooms about the horses."

Nigel bowed to Frances and Lance, his face lit with derision. "As I was saying, we live always on the edge of chaos. Quarrels between the servants are never to be tolerated. You will please excuse me?"

⚭

Lance buried his face in his hands. "Oh, dear God! Dear God! Why can't you do something about Rivaulx?" The long-fingered hands clenched over the blond hair. "You're his mistress, for God's sake! Can't you turn him from this dreadful . . . Oh, devil take it! Perhaps—after Farnhurst—you hate him and don't care?"

Frances made her hands relax, hiding her feelings as she had learned. "Dreadful *what*, Mr. Spencer?"

Lance sprang from his chair and rustled about in a satchel he had carried in with him. "I brought these from England. I'm not sure why. I should burn them."

He tossed a handful of papers at Frances. She picked one up. The crude woodcut seemed to show several figures, both men and women. For a moment she couldn't make it out, and then she understood. She looked at the next one: *The Pursuits of a Marquess, or They All Do It*. This time the figures included a donkey.

She glanced up at Lance. "But these are not true."

"Aren't they? How do you know? Do you know where he goes when he's not with you?"

Frances sat down, staring at another sheet. *Lord R*******x and Miss R***r, or the Trials of a Virgin*. Like a crude sacrilege of the sacred temple carvings in India, the writhing figures jeered at her.

"I do not, of course. Nigel says he goes to Betty's, or to some boxing club."

Lance began to gather up the sheets. Fiercely he crumpled them in his hands and tossed them into the grate. "I don't say all the facts are exact—this Miss River, for example—though the story was all over London. But there are secret clubs where such abhorrence is practiced. Rivaulx is reputed a member of most of them. He's hardly received anymore in society."

She felt incredulous. "Because of all this absurdity?"

"Absurdity? For God's sake! Most people would think such corruption unspeakable. Or do you mean you don't believe it? You think he'd be the subject of this slander if he were living like a saint?"

Frances watched the paper sheets as Lance crushed them. "So he eases himself with courtesans or with other men. It is only natural, another expression of *Kama*—pleasure in love."

Lance was staring at her as if she had grown two heads. "*Love?* By God, love is the purest of human emotions! How can you breathe the word in connection with all this filth? Love is what Rivaulx felt for Catherine. If you could have seen them here together—" He dropped to one knee, framed at the grate as if it were an altar, head bowed. "When Catherine died, something broke in Rivaulx. All his friends know it. He has tried to forget her by sinking into dissipation and vice, but it will destroy him."

He struck a spark and set the papers on fire. The room filled with smoke. Lance started coughing.

The air was thick with the stench. Frances went to the window and opened it. *Lord R******x and Miss R***r, or the*

Trials of a Virgin. Then why had he spared her at Farnhurst, even when ravaged by the drug? But there was Lance, who knew Nigel so much better—and had for so much longer—suffering a distress that couldn't be faked.

"I'm sorry," said Lance, choked. "I should not have said anything to you."

"It doesn't matter. It must be hard for you, too." Frances folded her hands. "You also lived here with Catherine."

Lance dragged his fingers over his mouth before he spoke. He gazed away across the room. "She was so perfect, you see, like a pure flame. I remember once how she teased him, laughing at him as he stood in that doorway. She pulled the pins from her hair and let it fall—there at that window. It came to her waist, shining like red fire in the sun. Rivaulx was drawn like a moth. He knelt before her and took her hair in both hands, burying his face in it. He worshiped her."

Frances had a clear vision of Nigel, kneeling like a medieval knight at his lady's feet, his head startlingly dark against her soft red tresses. "Why are you telling me this?"

"So you will understand what is happening to him. This bloody house can only be torture. Yet I think he must face what happened here before he can find peace. If he would admit it or let us mollify it, perhaps it would be easier for him."

"Is that why you rented this place—to force him to a reckoning?"

Smoke still wreathed about the room. "No, no! Truly, nowhere else was available. But now that he's here—"

"You think we should conspire to offer solace? How?"

"Solace? I don't know. You're his mistress. Solace is your profession, isn't it? Where will you sleep? For God's sake, don't take Catherine's chamber. I don't mean to be cruel, Miss Woodard, but I think you must understand."

Frances studied the delicate bones beneath the fall of blond hair. Lance seemed too fragile to be a spy. "I understand that he will not take our interference kindly, Mr. Spencer."

The blue eyes snapped with a sudden fire. "What the devil does that matter? He can never love another woman as he loved Catherine. When the news came that she was arrested, he was like a madman. He would have recklessly sacrificed his life. I wouldn't . . . I couldn't let him do it! That's why he punishes me, for forcing him to go on living without her. I want him to live. I don't mind.''

The door opened. The sudden draft swept away the smoke.

''Dear me,'' Nigel said softly. He was carrying a tray. ''The atmosphere seems positively cloying in here. You have been talking about Catherine, haven't you, Lance? I wish you would not. Did you really think the gods would allow Princess Katerina to settle for hearth and home and children? That may be your dream of Elysium; it was not hers.''

Lance leaped to his feet. ''Neither of us will ever meet anyone like her again in a lifetime, and you know it. Why can't you face it, and at least treat her memory with respect?''

Nigel set down the tray. ''She is dead. And you are engaged to Miss March. I would much rather we didn't spend our time in this house in maudlin absurdities. Would you like tea?''

The angel's face crumpled. ''Damn you, Rivaulx!'' Lance stalked from the room.

''God help me,'' said Nigel, pouring tea into two cups. ''One of these days I shall run out of patience.''

He turned and offered a steaming drink to Frances.

She wanted to strike him. ''Yes, no doubt you will. Because your old friends care about you.''

He set down the cup. ''Care about me! Dear God, if this is caring, pray give me indifference!''

''Lance also loved Catherine, didn't he? Can you not forgive that?''

Nigel turned away and began to pace, his voice controlled, as if he explained something very simple with great patience to a child. ''For Catherine, an ordinary existence was impossible—her passions ran too high. Of course Lance was in love with her, along with every man who met her. That does not give him the right—''

Frances walked up to him and took him by the sleeve, forcing him to turn and face her. ''Lance loves *you*! Why must you throw that back in his face?''

The muscles around his mouth set in anger. ''I would rather have trust.''

She had no idea what he meant. "Have you no compassion for him? For heaven's sake, you mock him at every turn. Does friendship mean nothing to you?"

The rage left his face as if suddenly stripped away, leaving nothing she could reach behind that mask of masculine beauty. He seemed remote as a god. "As it happens, friendship is extremely important to me, but I consider some things private, that is all. Unless there are innocent victims involved, what the hell business is it of his what I do, or what I feel? I do not condemn Lance's moral choices, or stand in judgment on the state of his conscience. I just wish he would extend the same courtesy to me."

His control chilled her to the soul. Frances knew then that Lance was right. Nigel was destroying himself. She asked the next question, knowing it must be said. "But there *are* innocent victims. What about Catherine?"

His reaction was faster than she expected. His lip curled, and his beauty became terrible, like the mask of Kali—goddess of death, demanding human sacrifice. "Why do you think I have come to Paris? Only I know enough to track down Catherine's betrayer. Lord Donnington was right. Only I knew her plans that day. Only I could have delivered her to the torturers. How else could she have been captured?"

He held out his hands. The light from the window outlined their strength, shining red around the long fingers, scattering from the griffin ring. "Shall I admit that these fingers in essence held the blade? God knows, they were practiced enough in annihilation at the time. Don't try to interfere in this, Frances. You don't know what—" He shuddered and turned away. "For God's sake, leave me alone!"

With a roar like a forge, a bird's nest thudded down the chimney, scattering filth and ashes across the floor. It was followed by the bird. Startled into panic, a jackdaw beat about the room, scattering feathers and dirt.

As if a dam had ruptured, Nigel burst out laughing—and the bitter sound of his own voice mocked him. Was everything he touched to fall into chaos? Or was he simply to lose himself in self-pity and the kind of emotional indulgence he abhorred? He dodged the creature's frantic wings and almost struck

Frances. She stood as if frozen, her hands over her hair. Dear God! She knew what it meant to lose someone to a cruel death. And now he had let her come to Paris, and subjected her to this.

He caught her to him as the bird thudded into the ceiling, dislodging cobwebs and dust. "Frances, I'm sorry."

She shook in his arms. Nigel held her tightly until the spasms passed. Over the curves of her hip and waist, silk slid tormentingly under his fingers. How he longed to strip it away, enfold her, bury himself in her—as if there could be a world without dark memories or pain!

The jackdaw launched itself to the window and burst away into the open skies of Paris. Frances looked up at him, blinking back moisture from her long lashes, and smiled.

His longing took fire in his hands, burning back to the heart as if it were a fuse set to gunpowder. Nigel took her face in both palms and kissed her. He put into it everything he felt, his remorse, his desire, his confusion. Her mouth trembled beneath his, moist, pliant, intensely female. The fuse blazed ever closer to the powder. Forcing himself to regain control, he tore away.

Frances dropped to a chair. "How can you be such a hypocrite? You said . . . You said we would merely be colleagues. What on earth was that for?"

He felt stripped, grotesquely vulnerable, but he told her the truth as well as he could. "I'm not sure. Perhaps it was just for all the folly and cruelty of the world."

She glanced up at him, her eyes dilated. "No," she said. "That's not good enough. You don't want me for a mistress. Very well. Then treat me as a comrade. Tell me about Major Wyndham. Do you believe he is the traitor?"

Nigel took a deep breath, calming his heart and his yearning. "Everything points to it, doesn't it? Donnington proved there was a link between Moscow and Paris; whoever betrayed Catherine was also in Russia. If everyone else is eliminated, only Wyndham is left. Our traitor cannot be Lance, because as you guessed, he was in love with Catherine. That he arranged her arrest is inconceivable. He would have betrayed his country and his soul to have saved her."

The question was there in her eyes—*As you would, Nigel? As you were in love with her?* What else was she to think?

She went to the door. "Then, dear Lord, you are a man of very little generosity."

Nigel longed desperately to drag her back, let her hear the truth. He stood silent, his hands at his sides, like a guardsman. Frances left him standing alone in the ruins of the room. *Catherine sat in that very chaise longue, and looked out of that very window.* Nigel gazed at the couch for a long time, his fists clenched and his back rigid. Katerina, princess of Russia, who had ruined Nigel Arundham for any other woman. He had once made love to her there throughout a long, lazy Paris afternoon, while the sun shone golden on her smooth skin and blazed fire in her russet hair. He had hated himself for every caress.

Twelve

∞

FRANCES DID NOT take Catherine's bedroom. Nigel had installed her in a room at the front of the house and taken for himself the bed in the anteroom adjoining it.

"We are supposed to be lovers," he said dryly the next day when she questioned it. "We are newcomers to Paris. Fouché may have installed spies. It would look odd to the servants if I were halfway across the house."

Frances thought of the frail door that separated the two rooms. "What servants?"

It had proved impossible to find someone to clean the chimneys. The jackdaw was a baleful token. That afternoon most of the chambermaids left. The next day they were followed by the kitchen maids who had heard noises in the night. There were evil spirits in the pantry. The cook was white-faced as she brought this information and her own notice.

Nigel received the news casually. As Frances stood at his shoulder he was setting up books and showing her how to run their silk trade.

"Tiresome," he said after the cook left the room, "but not unexpected."

He continued working in silence, his pen scratching across sheets of paper. Frances looked at his bent head, the thick hair curling over his collar, the ink stain on his fingers that would no longer wash off. An ink stain he had acquired decoding secrets. A cultured man, her father would have said, well-read, a penetrating thinker. With an odd sense of dismay, she realized that her father would have liked this difficult marquess. Something moved in her, treacherous and confusing.

"We must do something about staff for the house," she said.

He continued working. "Must we? Enter the inventory like this—"

"The women say they heard clanking and rattles last night, and saw a strange light. They fear ghosts."

He glanced up at her and grinned. It was a warm day, promising a hint of the summer to come. His high-collared shirt hung open at the neck, offering glimpses of shadow and smooth skin at his throat. "And you don't, Frances?"

"What if a mortal hand is behind these apparitions? Didn't the servants flee that first house on la Place du Palais Royal?"

He dropped his head back to the ledger, but his voice was wry. "Only after it burned down."

"So you don't think your unknown enemy works to rid us of the household staff?"

The feathered end of the quill moved gracefully as he wrote. "Have you never managed without servants, Frances? I was raised in a castle with a staff of one hundred and eighteen, yet there is nothing in my life that I cannot do for myself, while you—"

"I was the daughter of a respectable gentleman who kept only six servants, yet I always had a maid. Even on that last trip into the mountains, our guides waited on me like a princess. In the harem, of course, I learned entirely different skills. Do you expect me to cook and clean and sweep chimneys?"

He looked up. "God, no! I expect you to be decorative and utterly useless."

It hurt—for no justifiable reason. "Then why are you showing me how to keep the ledgers?"

"To torment myself, of course."

She had no idea what he meant. He dropped his head back to his work, yet he laid his left hand over hers so their fingers lay touching on the table. She could feel his steady pulse and the warmth of his palm. For the briefest moment Frances stood transfixed, staring at his dark hair and the curve of his shoulder, his concentration and leashed power, before she pulled away her hand.

Lance stalked into the room. "For God's sake, Anton, now the damned grooms have left." Nigel looked up and raised a brow. "They say ghosts tied knots in the horses' manes last night. They ran off in fear for their souls."

"Then we shall have to feed and groom the animals ourselves," Nigel said. "I have already arranged the delivery of meals."

The next morning, as the last footman brought them an inedible breakfast, soot belched down the chimney and into the room.

"With ash on our foreheads we serve penance for past sins." Nigel brushed black specks from his sleeve. "Or at least, I do. Lance is without sin, though equally punished—like Job. Who will buy spices from traders who are covered in soot? Dear God! But this is a bloody awful place. I would give my soul for hot water in the mornings."

Lance glanced up at him. "Don't say such things!"

Mirth shone brightly in Nigel's eyes as he raised his eyebrows at Lance. "Don't you think me already consigned to the devil?"

The footman crossed himself and gave his notice on the spot.

Something rattled, like a clanking of chain. They had housed no servants for two days now, yet there were these small noises in the night. Lance was out, no one else should be in the building. Hair prickled at the back of her neck. Straining to listen, Frances sat up, staring into the darkness. A thump, the house settling and creaking as all old houses do, then silence. She slipped from her bed and went into Nigel's empty room. Every night he left without going to bed. He came back in the mornings drawn and taut, as if living entirely on his nerves. Did he search for Wyndham? Did he sleep at all? Frances didn't know. He shared nothing with her. She had been left with the inventory of the goods they had brought, to finish the ledgers and complete the columns he had begun in his strong black handwriting. It should have been simple, except that every morning the bolts of silks seemed to have moved by themselves in the night.

The house lay in deep slumber, a scarcely breathing darkness. The chain clanked again. Goose bumps rose over her entire body. India had been filled with ghosts. Spirits had watched over the lives of her father's guides. Trees and rocks had sentience of their own. Frances had seen fakirs climb ropes to nowhere, or step barefoot on hot coals. Daily life was a walk hand in hand with the supernatural, but her father had been a scientist. He had shown her the trickery and the superstition that lay behind such beliefs. Frances did not believe in ghosts. Yet in the dark and the silence, her body reacted on its own.

She shook herself and took a dark cloak from Nigel's wardrobe. In the hallway enough moonlight filtered in through the windows to let her find her way downstairs. With the soft, silent tread she had learned in the *zenana*, Frances went into the showroom. It lay in absolute quiet. The gray light had stolen the color from the cloth, but one thin white stripe dissected the room like a sword cut. The door to the courtyard lay cracked open.

Frances went to close it. Nigel must be somewhere out there in Paris, on one of his mysterious midnight excursions, but perhaps Lance had come in. The courtyard lay shadowed and silent. She gazed up at the dark silhouettes of the roofs against the high, drifting clouds. There was a small noise, like a heavy breath. Something moved by the stable—caught eerily from the corner of her eye. Something white. Stark horror grasped her by the throat. She stared into the shadows. A wraith of silver wavered in the blackness. Her breath came back in a rush. A white tail, swishing gently. A horse. Nigel's gilt horse. He had returned.

From the pure relief of it, Frances wrapped herself in the

cloak and crossed quickly to the stable. In a moment Nigel would light a lantern and put his horse away. But he should know that he had carelessly not latched the house door, and it would give her a certain wicked pleasure to tell him of it.

"You are so competent," she said as she opened the stable door. "So why do you neglect the simplest of things?"

She choked. Hands grasped from behind, jerking her off her feet as hard fingers crushed over her mouth. Her head snapped back. As the hand crushed her lips into her teeth, Frances looked up to see the glint of eyes, a shadow of thin hair, the harsh cut of a cheekbone. *A stranger.* Oh, God! Panic beat and flailed. Her heart hammered. Death waited in a garden of oleander. *I had a vision of you being carried away, like a Sabine.* An infinite regret. Would he care at all?

"Let her go, you damned fool!"

Nigel's voice. It was real. The hand dropped away and Frances stumbled forward. A lantern flared. In shades of *grisaille* and gold, Nigel sat casually by a pile of straw, gazing at her. She couldn't read his expression.

Behind her, the man with the thin hair coughed into his hand. "Your pardon, madame."

"This is Monsieur Martin," said Nigel. His voice was clipped. "He is going to solve our household problems and hire us some ostlers."

The man swept her a bow. "Your servant, madame. Most humble regrets if I distressed you."

She stared at him, her hands at her throat, groping for understanding. The man met her gaze with blank disinterest, like a nut with the fruit stunted, a self-contained hardness surrounding a desiccated kernel. She shook herself. *Martin.* Like an echo she heard Nigel's voice—*a network of couriers and informers headed by a man named Martin.* This was one of Nigel's Paris contacts. She tried to make her voice light. "And mine, if I caused alarm. I warn you, monsieur, we cannot get servants. They believe the house inhabited by ghosts."

Martin smiled, a small, cool smile. The soft light flattered his nondescript brown hair and freckled forehead. "Then we must get fresh servants from the country who have heard no such nonsense. I shall arrange everything." He glanced at Nigel, who nodded. Monsieur Martin bowed to Frances and walked out of the stable.

Nigel held a stalk of straw in one hand. He crushed it and tossed it aside. "You were afraid? I am sorry."

Her heart still hammered. It made her voice sharper than she intended. "Monsieur Martin has interesting manners."

"He is a mercenary. He works only for money." Nigel stood up and trimmed the light. "Can't you tell that this place stinks of danger? The house breathes it. It always did. What the devil were you doing creeping around outside after dark?"

"You are right," Frances said. "It was foolish. But I thought you should know that the house door stands open. Did our ghosts do that?"

He stiffened, but it was neither anger nor fear, only shock transmuted to laughter, instantly suppressed. "Oh, damnation! No, of course not. But it doesn't matter, the courtyard gate is locked."

"Then we cannot have intruders?"

He turned, the light casting bizarre shadows across his face. "Only down the chimney. But Monsieur Martin will ensure no more jackdaws."

Frances shivered. "He is not very likable."

"No." Nigel paused as if considering. "Your paths need never cross."

"Then tell him," said Frances, going to the door. "That if he finds any more jackdaws, I should like them. Did you know that I can teach birds to talk? It is the forty-third art."

He grinned then, openly. "Even jackdaws?"

"Why not?"

"The Cardinal of Rheims had a tame jackdaw, a bird of piety and devotion." He had the easy charisma of the story-teller, as if they were transported to an ancient marketplace—in India, in Russia, in a tale from the *Arabian Nights*—and she were his audience, breathlessly waiting. "When one day the archiepiscopal ring was stolen, the cardinal put a curse on the thief. Alas, it was the poor jackdaw who turned up, bald and piteous—he had been unable to resist the allure of the shining. He led the cardinal to the ring, the curse was lifted, and the bird lived out a godly life. But jackdaws can't talk.

At no point does the tale say he was able to beg absolution.''

"If I train the bird, it will resist temptation and not need absolution," she said.

"Will it?" asked Nigel. "We are all tempted by things that shine. Except you."

"You think I don't know temptation?" *I have felt it about you,* she wanted to say. *In the library and the music room and every damnable day since. I feel it now, like a stream of heat flowing from your gaze into my veins. I am burning because of you. Don't you know how you shine? We all covet you— Lance, Betty, me—even Wyndham probably. Don't you know it?* She looked away. "I felt it about the roses one afternoon in the palace: a surge of pure longing. They laid petals in my hand, one of my exercises in touch. I had to concentrate on lovely things of different textures, searching for their essence— carvings of stone or of sandalwood, a jewel or a feather. To pursue the three aims of life, *Artha, Kama* and *Dharma*— wealth, sensual pleasure, and virtue—the senses must first be made aware."

"Is that why you can conjure an opening flower with a gesture?" He moved his fingers like petals unfurling, his eyes on her face, teasing.

"What do you conjure?" she asked.

"In the face of your garden? Nothing but silence. I assure you I am only too aware of the cardinal's curse."

Restraint hung between them for a moment. The flickering light caressed his lean cheek. Gold flashed on his ring as he stepped up to her and touched her lips with his forefinger, smiling with that keen awareness, the laughter in his eyes masking whatever lay beneath. "None of your three aims of life is mine, Frances. There will be no more disturbances in the night. You are quite safe."

She turned and fled, her mouth flaming, back to the lonely bedroom where Nigel never slept. Why on earth had Betty thought that Frances Woodard could do anything to save Nigel? She was a fraud. And she was not safe. The house of secrets. Nigel's secrets. He kept them from her. Why should she resent it?

Only later she realized that he could not have just returned, for she had heard hooves clatter in the courtyard as she closed the door behind her. He had taken the gilt horse and gone out.

By the following day, peace reigned. As if with a snap of the fingers, the house was put to rights, the fires blazed, hot food arrived regularly from the kitchens, the horses were content, as Monsieur Martin took over the running of the household. The men came to breakfast freshly shaved. No more soot blackened the newly polished floors. And curious customers began to arrive at the house on la Rue des Arbres to inspect the silks.

"We have been invited," said Nigel, striding into the showroom a few days later and tossing his gloves onto a chair, "to a hunt. Do you hunt, Frances?"

She glanced up from her ledgers. "What?"

His dark eyes filled with irresistible mischief. "A duke offers us a taste of magnificence, the glorious excess of the *ancien régime,* served up in gold lace and wearing a wig, though also sporting the *tricolore,* of course. We shall pursue the white hart through the forests of romance, and catch nothing but whimsy. Will you come?"

Frances forced herself to match his mood, to avoid noticing his hands or the sudden burn of his eyes when he thought she didn't know that he watched her. She made herself smile. "Is this the duke you have promised who will offer me security?"

"If you like. Though you will meet gentlemen only of a certain age. The young ones are all in the army. This is le Duc de Freinville, a remnant of a racier epoch, aging more or less gracefully."

"Freinville? He was here yesterday, full of compliments and admiration. He bought a great deal of silk—for waistcoats, he said."

Nigel propped himself on a table, carelessly pushing aside bolts of carmine and lavender. "For his mistress, rather. But he is tired of her."

"I thought the royalists had fled Paris. Does a duke support Bonaparte?"

"Paris is full of aristocrats who support Napoleon, and laborers who are secretly royalists. It is part of the delightful confusion of the times. And why not? What is one monarch over another? Freinville supports whoever will allow him his sport. If you do not come, Freinville will pout. Then he will not take me into his confidence and I shan't learn what I need to know."

"Napoleon trusts Freinville with secrets?"

Nigel gazed from the window, light caressing his profile. "Of course not. Napoleon trusts no one. But this duke is a dear friend of the head of the secret police. And if anyone in Paris knows how Catherine was betrayed, it is Fouché."

A finger of ice touched her heart.

There was a shattering explosion. Flakes of paint and plaster rained down from the ceiling. Frances looked up in alarm.

Nigel laughed. "The Emperor is testing his artillery and training new gunners. He has chosen to do it in the heart of Paris—at the Invalides. Don't worry. It means nothing, except that we have very little time left to discover his intentions."

The explosion was followed by another. Frances took a calming breath, but not because of the guns, or because they were here in Paris to spy on Napoleon, or even because Nigel would brave the secret police in his quest to discover who had betrayed Catherine to her death. But because Nigel didn't care if he lived, and no mortal woman could compete with a ghost.

So Frances faced him, his obvious indifference, the fragile camaraderie that lay between them, and smiled. "Then all the more reason to leave town for a day. By all means, let us go hunting."

∞

It was a brilliant spring day. Mounted on her gelding, Frances followed Lance and Nigel through the streets of Paris. Gold lace foamed at Nigel's neck and wrists. Above their riding boots both men wore breeches of silk. Although their hair wasn't powdered, they were a riot of color and rich fabric, a startling echo of the *ancien régime*. Lance's fine elegance was almost lost in it, but Nigel looked magnificent, a dark pirate resplendent in stolen finery on his gilt horse. With her Indian robes hidden under a cloak, Frances rode behind him like a shadow.

She had a sudden vision of Major Wyndham—a man far too big-boned and rugged for such dress. He was no longer mentioned. She had listened silently while Lance and Nigel debated it. It seemed obvious now: Dominic Wyndham had been the traitor, and had deliberately set the suspicious fire in order to cover his flight. Lance still refused to believe it; he thought Wyndham must have died in the flames. She couldn't tell what Nigel believed, or how he felt that a friend had betrayed him. He had answered Lance with a quote about Shadrach, Meshach, and Abednego, who had been saved from the fiery furnace by an angel: *Nor was an hair of their head singed, neither were their coats changed, nor the smell of fire had passed on them.*

They were forced to pull aside to allow a procession to pass, the marchers hysterically waving tricolor *cocardes*. *"Vive l'Empereur! Vive la liberté!"*

While the horses fretted, Nigel and Lance raised their hats, similarly adorned, and joined in the shouts. If they had not, would the mob have pulled them all from their horses and torn them limb from limb?

The Duc de Freinville's château lay about an hour's ride from Paris. Though missing its most openly royalist members, the cream of Parisian society was converging there. Frances heard the baying hounds long before the château came into view. When it did, she held her breath for a moment. Perched on a small rise, an elaborate confection of stone and glass, windows and corbels, it rioted in Gothic fancy, like a castle from a fairy tale.

"Good Lord," Lance said. "How the devil did it escape the mob during the Terror?"

"Probably because the eyes of the patriots were unable to focus on it long enough to see where to set the flames," replied Nigel, grinning. "This promises to be a morning to remember."

On the open expanse in front of the château was a scene from the last century. As if the revolution had never happened, as if Napoleon were not at this moment training his gunners in Paris, the grass was alive with horsemen and women in a wealth of finery, at least half of them in wigs and powder, patches and lace.

"It is time," Nigel said to Frances, "to shed that cloak and dazzle."

She did so. She had agreed to this; Lord Trent was paying her. Sunlight glittered on her veils, on the borders of cranes woven in gold thread, on the procession of tiny embroidered horses and elephants. Small silver bells tinkled as she moved. Frances lifted her chin and rode forward, smiling—the freak from India, in her trousers and short jacket, riding astride on her chestnut gelding while the bells rang in her ears and the sun beat on her silk-clad shoulders. Like the Red Sea before Moses, the crowd parted and the men swept off their hats, then began to converge, in a wave.

She glanced once at Nigel. He gave her a wink, then— carrying Lance with him—he rode away, leaving her to cope with the onslaught alone. He was immediately surrounded by a curious crowd of his own as he began to charm the men and flirt with the women.

Frances was assailed with compliments and questions in rapid French. Faces white with powder, stained carmine lips with a patch at one corner, open admiration. For a moment she felt nothing but panic. There was a painful difference between knowledge and experience. What happened to girls brought up in nunneries? Frances was as unsure as any novice. The irony of it was breathtaking. So she must pretend, that was all. Pretend to a sophistication she didn't really feel. Pretend she was the experienced courtesan of her training. For everything that happened in Paris was reported to Fouché, and if she failed in her charade, she might take Nigel and Lance to destruction with her. This was no more than the kind of occasion she had been trained for, after all. *The following are the things to be done as amusements: In the forenoon, men having dressed themselves should go to gardens on horseback, accompanied by public women. . . .* She began to relax.

"*Enchantée, messieurs,*" she replied, curving her lips beneath her gold nose ring. "*Mais je ne parle pas bien français.*

Pourriez-vous parler plus lentement, s'il vous plaît?''

Nigel had been right. They thought her accent charming. Every man there tried to woo her in exquisitely slow French.

∞

The crowd broke apart as the hounds were brought out. "It is only a farce," said a voice in her ear.

Frances turned to see Nigel grinning at her. He seemed filled with gaiety. "But a deadly one for the stag," she replied.

"No, we are only woven figures in a medieval tapestry. This morning the huntsmen presented Freinville with fresh droppings on white pillows as evidence of the whereabouts of the best animal, although the chosen quarry was caught and caged yesterday. He will be released at the appropriate moment for the embroidered hunters to chase."

"Then there is no danger?"

He controlled his restive gilt horse and smiled down at her. "Only to me, thanks to Betty. But it's a danger I brought with me from England. It isn't easy to be beautiful, is it? It is what we all think we want, to have heads turn at our entrances, to be desired by strangers, to attract fervent admiration because of our physical perfection, but there's a price to pay. Can you manage?"

"I am not beautiful," replied Frances. "It is just grooming, training, an illusion. They think they see something glamorous and exotic. If it weren't for India, they would know I'm quite ordinary."

"Oh, no, Frances, you aren't that!" He spun his horse away and laughed over his shoulder. "There are men here I must talk to. And here is the duke, seeking your company. Promise me you will charm him?" He set his heels to his horse, but she heard him speak one last time, as if to himself for his own amusement. " 'O thou fairest among women, go thy way!' "

Horns echoed. Surrounded by her new admirers, Frances moved her horse forward in the wake of the duke. Soon they were trotting beneath the arched limbs of a beech wood, then cantering, hounds streaking away ahead. The horns shrieked three rapid blasts. A stag burst from the forest and bounded away. The horses leaped into full gallop and streamed after it. Leaning low over the neck of her chestnut, Frances was swept with them, through a brook, up a long rise, in and out of trees. In the hail of splashing at the water, she saw Nigel, teeth bared in a laugh, soar over the brook on his shining horse, and race away at the head of the field.

There was a sudden check at the edge of a lake. The stag had plunged into the shallow water and was trotting through the cattails. The hounds leaped in after it, swimming valiantly. Deliberately, Frances checked her horse and stayed at the back of the crowd.

"In the words of a long-ago Duke of York, 'An hert lyveth lengest of eny beest.' Don't worry. You will not see this valiant stag die."

Frances turned to see Nigel once again sitting beside her. He was breathing hard from the gallop. He dropped his head, hiding the merriment dancing in his eyes, and ran his hand down his horse's damp neck. His lean fingers made a stunning contrast to the froth of gold lace at his wrist. Her heart turned over.

"It will get away?"

He glanced back at her, his cheeks still creased in that devastating smile. "Oh, I think so. The huntsman will call in the hounds, and our stag will disappear into the gold thread at the back of the tapestry, so that he can be chased another day. But no man here wants you to escape. You are a success, Frances! How many propositions have you received so far?"

Frances smiled back, her heart lifting suddenly like a bird set free. It was impossible not to respond to his gaiety—it seemed more precious than gold. "Let me see. Five, no six! Counting the declaration of the Comte de Lecreux."

"Declaration?"

Frances nodded toward an elderly gentleman in bright blue brocade and snow-white wig. He met her glance and bowed deeply from the saddle, hand over heart. "He invites us to accompany him to Napoleon's great military spectacle on the first of June. Le comte offers me his hand—in marriage, no less."

Nigel's mirth burst into open laughter.

Frances frowned at him, teasing. "You think Lecreux won't marry me?"

"Alas, he is already married—for the fifth time, I believe. Five countesses is hard enough on any man, let alone two at once."

"But that would not stop me becoming his concubine," said Frances wickedly. "And partaking forever in these summer amusements. How else can I fulfill my training?"

"I thought you were trained for the bedroom," Nigel replied without blinking.

Frances glanced away, with the inviting turn of the chin she had been taught, unsure why heat burned in her cheeks. "Good heavens! Did you? Public women can do many things. Let me quote: 'In the forenoon, men having dressed themselves should go to gardens on horseback, accompanied by public women. Having done there all the duties of the day, and passed the time in various agreeable amusements, such as the fighting of quails, cocks, and rams, they should return home in the afternoon, bringing with them bunches of flowers.' It says nothing about dalliance, though I suppose that's implied."

She looked back at him under her lashes, unsure of his mood. But he still seemed merely amused.

"We are definitely witness to the fighting of quails, cocks, and rams." Nigel indicated the crowd of men jostling about on their horses as they tried to get the best view of the stag. As Nigel had predicted, the hounds were being called in. Sleek and dripping, shaking off occasional sprays of bright water, they tumbled about on the grass.

"Now we are at the lake, perhaps we may all go swimming." Frances nodded to the stag, then continued to quote: " 'The same applies to bathing in summer in water from which wicked or dangerous animals have previously been taken out.' "

"Oh, no," Nigel replied softly, glancing behind her. His merriment vanished, though the irony remained. "The wicked and dangerous animals have only just arrived."

She followed his gaze and felt her heart contract. As the gaily dressed hunters milled about in a confusion of wit and flirtation, a column of horsemen was bearing down on them from the woods. Brilliant in uniforms of red and gold, bristling with arms, they rapidly deployed around the crowd.

"Who are they?" she asked.

Nigel's eyes narrowed a little. "Polish lancers. The Emperor has sent his soldiers after us."

"Then you lied," said Frances. "There *is* danger."

She willed herself to stay calm, but a trembling began deep in her muscles. As the lancers rode up, sun glancing from their weapons, an officer trotted forward and signaled his men to stop. The soldiers sat in a ring, lances lowered, menacingly surrounding the flock of quails, cocks, and rams. There were men here whose relatives had gone to the guillotine during the Terror, and more whose loyalty lurched uneasily between Bourbon and Bonaparte. In April, aristocrats such as these had been set upon by a mob, their houses burned. But surely Napoleon did not intend death to this ragtag collection of harmless old men?

"What, sir?" cried the duke, pushing his horse forward. "Does the Emperor have need of his loyal subjects?"

A reedy cry wavered up. *"Vive l'Empereur!"* It was instantly taken up on all sides. *"Vive l'Empereur! Vive l'Empereur!"*

"I have an order from His Imperial Majesty," replied the officer, holding out a paper. "You will be recompensed." He signaled his men. "Seize them!"

A group of soldiers rode forward. The Comte de Lecreux jerked an ornamental gold-hilted sword from its scabbard. *"Pour la patrie!"* he cried.

A lady in pink satin screamed.

Frances fought back a wave of terror. *Trampled vines and smashed fountains. Steel blades slashing silk. Blood blossoming in a garden.* The images swarmed into her mind.

"Give me your hand!" It was Nigel's voice, but she could not move. He reached over and grasped her fingers. "Frances! I'm here. It's all right."

She called on her training, the breath control, the hard-won ability to block any emotion, though panic beat like a trapped bird. "Nigel—"

"Hush, *chérie*. They requisition the horses, that is all."

Frances clung to his hand, feeling his confident strength as his pulse beat against hers, and forced herself to focus on the scene. It was true. One after another, the guests were dismounting. In their magnificent finery they stood on the grass while the soldiers gathered up the horses. The Comte de Lecreux thrust his sword back into its sheath and stepped stiffly from his mount. Lance bowed from the waist as he handed over his bay to a lancer. A slip of paper was pressed into his hand.

"A chit for payment." The gilt horse pressed close so that Nigel's knee touched hers. "Though I'm afraid Lance will never see it. Napoleon's treasury is as empty as his hopes for victory. Feeling better?"

There was an immense reassurance in his relaxed, amused voice and commonplace observations—a simple enough gift, yet Frances treasured it. His firm grip felt like a lifeline to sanity. She wanted never to let go. She wet her lips, trying to match his light tone. "The Emperor needs our horses for the war?"

"There are not enough horses or men in France to satisfy his appetites. But I don't believe he'll have mine. There is about to be a diverting little skirmish instead."

With a vivid concentration, his dark gaze was focused on something behind her. Frances looked back and released his hand. An officer approached.

"Your horse, monsieur!" He rode directly up to Nigel and scrutinized his features. "But I have seen you before! Who are you?"

Nigel smiled. "My name is Anton, Captain."

"You have served in the *Grande Armée*?"

"Alas, I have not."

"Then, Monsieur Anton, will you tell me this: Why the devil do I believe that we last met in Russia?"

Frances clenched her hands on the reins. Fear leaped and darted in her blood, barely contained. Russia! Where Nigel had fought these very troops? He had seen this man coming. He could have slipped away. Instead he had stayed to offer her comfort!

The officer fixed Nigel with hostile inquisition. "Are you a loyal Frenchman, sir? Or are you something else? That is a Don horse, is it not?"

Nigel grinned with reckless arrogance. "Indeed. I had it from an *esaul* of the Cossacks."

"And what," asked the officer, leaning forward like a dog scenting pray, "was a loyal Frenchman doing with filthy Cossacks?"

"If you will ride a little aside with me, Captain, I will tell you."

Curious glances were being directed at them. A group of lancers now cut off any possibility of escape.

"Are you not French or are you not loyal?" The officer was obviously searching his memory. "You will answer me here."

Nigel's expression was almost pitying. "Ah, Captain Genet, I think not! Monsieur Fouché would not like to hear that you have been indiscreet."

At the use of his own name, the officer lost his smile. At the mention of Fouché's, he turned white. Nigel disdainfully inclined his head, and he and the officer rode a little apart. Frances edged her horse just close enough to overhear them.

"Do you remember, Captain, a barn close to a river? Russian peasants had used it for butchering hogs. We had rope, our knives, and a captured Cossack. This Don horse was his."

Beads of sweat broke out on the officer's face. He was deathly pale. *"Que diable!"*

"That is right," said Nigel softly. "My name at that time was not Anton. You knew me then as Raoul Pargout. I would rather no one here knew of it."

"My apologies, sir! If I had realized—"

"You will of course allow me my sleek Don horse? And my mistress her chestnut?"

The white-faced officer fell back, signaling the lancers to make way. Nigel nodded to Frances. A few minutes later they were riding away. As soon as they were out of sight of the soldiers, Nigel's silver-gold horse broke into a gallop. Frances stayed at his heels until several miles of woodland lay between them and the Château Freinville. At last Nigel pulled up. He leaped from his mount and strode down to a stream. Ignoring his lace, he knelt and splashed water over his face. Frances scrambled from her chestnut and tied it to a tree.

"That is a Russian horse? How did Captain Genet know?"

Nigel sounded remote, preoccupied. "The Don is a distinctive breed—the shoulder and long legs—the color is found nowhere else but Russia. It's striking, isn't it? Horses with coats like metal. The Cossacks turned Turkmene and Karabakh stallions loose on the steppes with their native mares. There isn't a tougher horse in the world, nor one with more stamina."

She felt breathless, stunned. "Are you mad? You deliberately brought a Russian horse with you to France? How had you really met that officer?"

"In the barn," he said, without looking up. "But I was the Cossack, Raoul Pargout was the man with the knife. It is fortunate that Captain Genet did not remember more clearly who was the prisoner and who the interrogator."

Tears of fear pricked at her eyelids. Why had she thought this sunny, laughing day could last? "Dear God! Won't Genet recall the truth?"

Nigel remained still, crouched at the stream. Sunlight and shadow dappled over the curve of his back and the strong line of his thigh. He held one hand over the water, watching the bright drops run off his fingers. "He might. But Pargout and I were of similar coloring and build, I wore a beard, and it was getting dark. As it happens, Genet did not have long to study either of our features. When the interrogation began he had to go outside."

Frances dropped to the ground, hugging her arms around her knees. "Why?"

"Not stomach enough, I'm afraid." Nigel shook his fingers, looked up at her, and smiled. The gold lace at neck and wrists was daubed with muddy water. He took out his handkerchief and wiped his face. "After an exquisite beating with some imaginative excursions into sadism, Monsieur Pargout threatened to turn his Cossack into a capon. It was rather a cold moment and not one I like to remember."

The hard bark of a tree pressed against her back; the damp

ground was seeping moisture into her robes. She felt tense as a harp string just jerked into tune. She pushed away her panicked thoughts and concentrated on his features. "You withstood it?"

His lip curled. "Don't think it was nobly done, or some great act of courage." He thrust the handkerchief deep into a pocket and stood up, turning away from her to watch the brook, water gurgling over a stone, the small eddies. The long line of his back, waist, and legs was rigid. "Pain is an interesting thing. There is no connection between courage and how one reacts to physical agony. Courage belongs to the mind; it takes a deliberate act of will. Beat a man for a while and his mind is gone. If he is brave then, it is only a kind of animal stubbornness."

"Yet you were stubborn?" Frances stared at him, at his beautiful hands, the fine bones of his face, the body she had marveled at beneath her fingers. *Monsieur Pargout threatened to turn his Cossack into a capon.*

"It was a time I could have done without my bloody senses," he said dryly. "I would have told Pargout anything he wanted to know, even without the promise of castration, but I couldn't seem to make my tongue work any longer. Some deep brute hatred for him made me keep shaking my head, that's all. And then I heard artillery."

"There was a battle nearby?"

He glanced at her and grinned with open bravado. "I believed so, for I was past thinking clearly. It seemed just so bloody insignificant to suffer under his knife, when so many would meet worse from those guns. Somehow the thought gave me the strength to hold on. But the noise was hoofbeats. My Cossack friends burst into the barn. The French fled for their lives. In the confusion, Monsieur Pargout took my Don horse instead of my manhood. It was a mistake."

Frances looked at the horse, standing quietly beneath the tree, white tail swishing at the occasional fly. "Why?"

He laughed. "The Cossacks train their horses." Nigel shrugged out of his jacket and flexed his arms. His shirtsleeves glimmered in the broken light. "Watch this."

He caught up the Don horse he had brought back from

Russia. Beyond the stream was a small clearing. Nigel led his mount onto the open patch of grass, stripped off both saddle and bridle, and turned the horse loose. Frances caught her breath as it galloped away. Nigel whistled. The horse slid to a halt and turned, the dark, intelligent eyes fixed on Nigel's face. He whistled again. In a thunder of hooves the horse galloped straight for him. Nigel stood in its path, smiling. At the last possible moment the horse swerved aside and Nigel vaulted onto its silver-gold back.

Frances stood transfixed. The beautiful animal seemed to read Nigel's mind, stopping, pirouetting, springing back to an instant gallop, or sliding to a halt with no visible signal from the rider. As if they were one creature, his body lithe and strong, Nigel rode, flowing, melding to the horse's movements. Frances watched with pure longing. The embroidered waistcoat, the gold lace, the white shirtsleeves, the horse gleaming gilt in the sunshine. That beauty, that intensity, that ineffable oneness with another creature. It was as if Nigel and the horse gave each other some exquisite gift.

He rode up to her at last, and the horse dropped one foreleg and bent its head in a bow, allowing him to slide off its back.

"How did you do that?" Tears tickled her eyelids. "The horse obeys because he loves you?"

"No," he replied dryly as the animal turned and galloped away again. "He obeys because he knows I love him." Nigel let out a different whistle. The horse leaped, twisting violently and lashing out with its hind feet. "And that's how Pargout lost his seat."

Frances knew nothing but dread. "Then you killed him?"

He walked forward a few steps, holding out his hand. The horse trotted up to him and laid its velvet nose against his palm. Nigel ran one hand down the dappled shoulder. "As it happens, this brave creature did it for me. Pargout broke his neck."

Frances dropped to the ground, covering her face. "You have trained your horse to kill?"

"He is a warhorse. He is trained to do what he must. If Pargout had not died in the fall, the Cossacks would have shot him. Do you think he didn't deserve it?"

She glanced up. Nigel was leaning his forehead into the white mane, one hand spread on the silver-gold withers, the other stroking the horse's face.

"How could you take something so beautiful and use it for such ends?"

He turned and faced her, his hair a dark shadow against the gilt dapples. "Doesn't love always contain something of destruction? Dear God, Frances, didn't India teach you that, at least?"

He picked up the saddle and bridle and led the horse back to the tree.

"I don't know!" she cried. "Don't think I judge you for the death of this Pargout. But you just claimed to be him. What if Captain Genet had known that he'd died?"

Nigel tightened the girth. "I guessed he did not. Fortunately I was right."

"It was a hideous risk to take!"

"Should I have let him recognize me for what I am—a British officer he once helped to torture? Don't worry, Frances. He won't want to investigate. The lancers leave the secret police alone."

"And that's who Pargout was—a member of Fouché's police?"

He laughed. "I have no idea."

It took a moment for the enormity of this to sink in. She looked up, studying the bones of his face, his dark eyes, and knew that she melted with fear, deep in her being. "Dear God! You claim something outrageous that is easily disproved, and use the name of the most dangerous man in Paris. Why? Why must you risk the edge of the blade?"

Sun danced on his hair and dazzled from his gold lace, beautiful, like an avenging dark angel.

He answered with one word. "Bait."

"This is madness! Will this win the war against Napoleon? How will it help Catherine? I cannot understand you!"

His mouth was set. He stared away into the trees. "Understand me? Dear God! There is nothing to understand. *You* are the mystery. Who are you, Frances? I know what you pretend to be, what you appear to be, but I'm damned if I know who you are!''

She stood up and went to her chestnut gelding. "I don't know what you mean."

"No, you don't, do you? You move through your days as if life were a ritual, with that ready escape into the universal. That evening in my study, you even shared something of it with me. Don't think it wasn't the most extraordinary gift, because it was. But what you showed me that night in London was not personal, was it? Any more than a prayer to a god, or a sacrifice in a temple. Your training, your compassion, it is all remote, detached, while you keep yourself safely locked away. You took me to some common human center, but I don't know Frances Woodard. Neither do you, do you? You don't really belong to a foreign culture. I don't believe you know much more of India—the real India—than I do. You are as English as I am, but you have lost yourself with no idea how to find the way back.''

She breathed in the innocent, grassy smells of horseflesh. The chestnut's sleek coat was warm and solid under her hand. Nigel came up behind her. Frances was painfully aware of him, his height, his intensity. She buried her face in the red mane. "So I am all artifice. Why should it matter to you?''

He seemed distant, as if in order to allow an admission of the truth, he dropped a wall between them that could never be breached, yet his voice was tender.

"Because a fox can recognize another one, of course.''

Thirteen

⌒

LANCE ARRIVED AT the house on the Rue des Arbres several hours later, his finery sullied with dirt from the road.

Nigel leaned back in his chair and laughed. "They say exercise is good for the soul, Lance."

The blue eyes locked onto Nigel's face. "But damned hard on the feet. These riding boots are the devil for blisters. Why were you allowed to keep your horses?"

"Let us just say that Captain Genet is an old friend of mine."

Lance grimaced at the muck on his boots. "Dear God! He recognized you from Russia? I was afraid of that. How did you get out of it?"

Nigel grinned. "He now believes that I work for Fouché."

The angel skin paled to alabaster. "*Fouché!* For God's sake! Are you mad?"

Frances calmed her heart and kept quiet. Yet Lance was only echoing her own thoughts. Was Nigel plunging them all into disaster? And was there nothing she could do to change it? She had thought her destiny determined by the blind, inexorable workings of fate—wasn't that how she had seen her life, steeped in Eastern fatalism? She wanted fiercely to break it, to recover her self, the Frances Woodard who had existed before India, before the corruption of knowledge. Yet she had no idea how to find her way back, or if she would have the courage to face what might happen if she did.

Nigel gazed at him thoughtfully. "Mad? Perhaps. It will be interesting to see how he'll react when he finds out."

"I only hope you know what you're doing! I imagine Fouché has some interesting punishments reserved for English spies who misuse his name."

Nigel was still watching Lance. His voice was sweet with irony. "I am an old hand at interesting punishments."

The candles guttered. It was close to midnight. Frances sat back and looked at her columns of figures. She wrung her hand over her eyes. What an odd gift for a man to make to a courtesan! Nigel rejected her training, yet he had taught her accounting. There was a strange allure in it, in the order and certainty of numbers ranked on paper. In spite of his manic schedule, he had taken the time to do this. Why? To give her another tool toward independence, so he would never again have to take responsibility for her?

Frances closed the ledgers and went up to her room. Nigel and Lance were in the anteroom, talking. Unsure, she hesitated at the door.

Nigel was preparing to go out, as usual. A furious concentration lay over his features as he checked his pistols and the knife in his boot, and rapidly exchanged information with Lance. The names of the people and streets meant nothing to her. Lance leaned in the doorway between her room and Nigel's. He was also going out. He wore a close-fitting black cap over his yellow hair.

"You realize," said Lance, "that if Napoleon were dead, it would all be over tomorrow."

Nigel glanced up from checking the powder in his pocket pistol. "Lance, your dewy innocence never fails to amaze me!"

Lance flung himself forward. "How can you speak of it like this? Don't you have any normal emotions? Have you closed out every human feeling? This one man—Napoleon—is the root of all Europe's misery! Who else ordered Catherine's death?''

Nigel became very still, as if struggling for patience. ''I do my best to put up with your solicitous attempts to save my soul, Lance; pray spare me your naive speculations about French politics. Your job, dear sir, is to gather information. Will you please go and do so?''

Flushing scarlet, Lance stalked from the room, brushing by Frances. A glimmer of moisture shone brightly on his lashes.

''Why must you do that?'' she asked.

Nigel thrust the pistol into his pocket. Frances knew he had been aware of her as she stood in the doorway. He was always aware of her. Whenever she came into a room, he seemed to get sharper around the edges, impatient, more dangerous.

''Do what?''

''Treat Lance as if he were some infuriating child?''

He dropped to a chair and strapped on spurs. ''Do I? Frances, our situation here is precarious enough without all these maudlin excursions into the past. The fate of thousands of ordinary people might depend on our success. All this rampant emotion will only get in the way. I want to know who betrayed Catherine because that person is still working against British interests. The rest is irrelevant.''

''Is it? Is the past ever dead? What else makes us? Our mother's dreams and our father's impatience, the enthusiasms of a teacher, our first disappointment. What else are we?''

He leaned back, stretching his long black-clad legs in front of him. ''What were your mother's dreams, Frances?''

Surprised, she went to the dark window. Beyond the glass, Paris lay in deep slumber beneath the steep rooftops. It was raining softly. ''I don't know. Nothing out of the ordinary. Her world was limited by the concerns of our home. She was not a wit or a scholar or a beauty. She was nothing like your mother, of course.''

''My mother? Yes, she was all of those things and a marchioness. She was also a person of grace and wisdom, and her dreams were all for my happiness. But I'm damned if I see where I carry any of them around with me.''

She glanced back at him. "No, for you have negated her, haven't you?"

He was silent for a moment, but he replied without raillery or sarcasm. "If I have, it was not by my choice. Do you think that I like this existence? All this self-denial and coldhearted manipulation? I could happily have spent my days in idleness and dissipation like any other young rake. But my mother always tried to make sure I fulfilled my duty to my country and position, and it seemed to my father that a future marquess should see something of the world. As heir to Rivaulx, it made little sense to become a professional soldier like Wyndham or Lance, but I found I had a gift for some essential work—I could decipher codes. When a man was captured in Margate carrying coded dispatches, Lord Trent asked for my help. I left London within the hour. That was over four years ago. My mother died suddenly while I was gone. After her funeral I went to Portugal and made myself useful to Wellington."

Over four years ago—when he had abandoned the music room at Rivaulx House and never used it again? "So why Russia?"

"When I returned home for Christmas in 1811, Lord Trent asked me if I would go with him to St. Petersburg. I was fluent in French, the court language in Russia. I went right away. Napoleon invaded. One thing led to another. I never saw my father alive again. He died twenty months later."

"You were close to him?"

"Very. He was a remarkable man, gifted in a thousand ways. He and my mother were deeply in love."

"I can't really imagine that. My mother was a dutiful wife, but I don't believe my father ever noticed her much. He was too absorbed in his plants. I never imagined that people of your class—" She broke off and took a calming breath. "I always thought a man like your father would be very cynical about women and sexual experience."

He grinned. It was a genuine, relaxed amusement. "He was cynical in all the right places. It was my father who introduced me to Betty."

"Your *father* took you to a professional courtesan?" She laughed and turned back to the window, the mysterious darkness, and the rain. "That was no doubt wise of him. How old were you?"

"Sixteen." She could hear the answering humor in his voice. "He didn't want me populating his estate with little copies of myself—there were several local ladies willing to give me the chance."

Frances tried to imagine Nigel that young. It was hard to believe he could ever have been innocent or naive. "So you have known Betty for a very long time."

"She is one of the few people alive that I am certain I can trust."

He was telling her the truth. It was a precious, momentary openness. Frances treasured it. "Because she loves you? So does Lance, yet you do not really trust him, do you?"

"I trust his patriotism and his honor. I don't trust his damned emotions. But do you think for one moment that I'm not sorry for it? That I'm not sorry for what Lance is suffering? That I don't desire something quite different?"

Her reflection wavered like a ghost as Frances turned from the window. He smiled with that disarming recognition of his own absurdity, as if his feelings were ridiculous and insignificant. Yet there was something else in his eyes—it reached out and touched her. Warmth spread through her body, passion dissolving erotically into the blood.

"What do you desire?" she asked.

He stood, took up his sword cane, and went to the door. He hesitated for only a moment before he opened it.

"Like every quail, cock, and ram in Paris, I desire you, Frances."

She had no idea if he was serious.

La Belle Dame wound a strand of dark hair around her forefinger. Rain made slow rivulets down her windows, a pit-pat of sound in the candlelit room. "So, Pierre! How is life in the Rue des Arbres?"

He bowed from the waist, the brown hair a little damp. "It is a very well-managed household."

"No doubt." She smiled at the man who lounged at the side of the room. Candlelight glittered in his blond hair. "You see, sir, it all goes like clockwork. You do not need to be concerned."

He leaned his head against the wall and said nothing. His arms were trapped viciously behind him, chained to the window grille.

"The household is settled into a routine," continued Pierre. "Their primary purpose, of course, is to explore the Emperor's plans for the war. Rivaulx already knows more about France's preparations than the war minister himself, but he does not know the one vital fact: exactly when and where the invasion of Belgium will begin."

She laughed. "Because Napoleon himself has not yet decided! Let Rivaulx find out what he will. He will not get the information out of the country."

He bowed his head in acknowledgment. "Meanwhile Rivaulx furiously pursues every clue about Catherine de Marbre's betrayal, while Lancelot Spencer tries to protect him from memories of her."

"I'm sure Rivaulx finds his solicitude insufferable?"

Pierre smiled. "There is a certain lack of domestic harmony—particularly when all clues lead to a blank wall."

"Ah, the incomparable Princess Minkinova! It must be a sorry spectacle to see two men suffer such torment over a dead woman. So what do you think now of Rivaulx, Pierre?"

He told her the truth because he thought she ought to know it. "He frightens me."

Her beautiful eyes narrowed. "What? Surely you don't doubt that I can destroy him?"

"I did not say that. You will win because you hold all the cards and because he has no idea of your existence here. But if I did not know when to be afraid of a man, I would not be of much use to you, madame." He bowed again.

She gazed speculatively at her hands for a moment. The long fingers were laden with rings. "And the whore in the silk veils?"

"They share a suite, but not a bed. Miss Woodard is inundated with invitations from the men she met at the Château

Freinville—to musical evenings, to dances, to rides in the Bois de Boulogne. Rivaulx encourages them.''

She looked slightly annoyed. ''He trains her to spy for him?''

''He tries to avoid her. Meanwhile she is becoming surprisingly proficient managing the silk and spices. She keeps the books.''

The annoyance turned to open laughter. ''Then it is time, Pierre!'' She turned to the man chained at the side of the room. ''Don't you agree, Major Wyndham?''

His voice was thick, but dry humor still glimmered. ''You have it wrong, *ma belle dame:* three men—*three* men suffer torment over a dead woman.''

''Ah, my dear!'' She came up to him and touched his bruised face. ''Are you tired of your beatings? Pierre is not. He enjoys them. Never mind, I intend to replace you, but I shan't kill you. Not yet. When Nigel joins us, he might yet find you useful.'' She ran a knuckle over his cheek. Her ring drew a tiny bead of blood. ''Does it disturb you to hear us talk thus about the fate of your friends? How would you like to live forgotten in the cellar, instead? No one will know you are there. They all think you dead. Won't you do as I ask, and give me your love? I can give you so much pleasure, instead of all this pain.''

Wyndham laughed then, though it obviously hurt his cracked lip.

''Never,'' he said.

Pierre hit him, and enjoyed it.

∞

The first day of June dawned with a petulant echo of March. Above the blue roofs of Paris the sky glowered and threatened rain. It was early when the Comte de Lecreux arrived in a carriage with four bay horses to escort Frances, Nigel, and Lance from the house on the Rue des Arbres. In their most elaborate finery, they were carried past the deserted homes of the royalists in the Faubourg St. Germain, up the Rue de Varenne, past the Invalides. Troops lined the streets in an attempt to keep them open to traffic, but near the École Militaire they had to abandon the carriage. A crush of notables carried them along in the crowd to the open space known as the Champ de Mars, where His Imperial Majesty the Emperor Napoleon was about to hold a great military spectacle, and thus thumb his nose at the rest of Europe, who had outlawed him in vain.

Frances clung to Nigel's arm as they followed Lecreux to their seats. She sat between the old count and Nigel while Lance took a seat a few rows back. Nigel was protecting her, as he had at Farnhurst. The conceit that she was his mistress had saved her horse at the hunt. It had also enabled her to turn down the offers she'd received ever since. She did not want to be concubine to any of those cultured, elderly Frenchmen. Which left her no future at all.

"The last one of these," Nigel said teasingly in her ear, "was held in honor of the Allied victory last year, with Wellington in attendance. The Iron Duke was faintly embarrassed. He hates pomp and ceremony. Napoleon, alas, adores it—a sorry hint of his vulgar beginnings!"

She glanced into his face. "You were here?"

"Briefly. I was with the Cossacks and disguised as one of them. We were hanging our laundry from the trees and grazing our horses in the parks. Then I returned with them to London for the Victory Celebrations so we could scandalize the Prince Regent. A few months later I went to Vienna, but you might say the fashion for Cossack trousers is partly my doing." He winked. "Now you will no doubt see something to rival the Sun King."

Nigel seemed filled with gaiety and a lighthearted gallantry, his wit softened, the hard edges gone. Frances forced herself to look away from his dark eyes, warm with mirth, before she should be tempted to ask for some of that warmth for herself.

The open space running down to the Seine was packed with thousands of Parisians. The river had become a solid mass of boats filled with more spectators. A huge wooden stand, draped in red fabric and banners, with two tricolor flags, stood at the south end of the Champ de Mars. The imperial throne sat at its center on a raised platform. Throngs of guests filled the stands, and behind them stood thousands of officers and troops in their brilliant uniforms.

Frances was deafened by the roar of cannon, several hundred guns firing salutes. The sun climbed in the sky, still veiled by clouds. The air felt heavy. The old count began to mop at his face. Another salvo rocked the stands, guns from the nearby Invalides and from as far as Montmartre.

"The Emperor comes," whispered Nigel. "Prepare to be diverted!"

Frances followed his gaze to the procession that was now marching across the Pont d'Iéna. Accompanied by the muffled thump of drums, a wave of sparkling steel rolled across the bridge. She had a confused impression of color and flash that resolved into shining horses, marching soldiers, and a score of magnificent carriages.

"The Red Lancers of the Imperial Guard. Following them come the leading dignitaries of Paris, and behind all those coats of arms and golden eagles, surrounded by the marshals of France, is the Emperor's state carriage."

She leaned forward. "Which are the marshals?"

"The men with the prettiest decorations, of course."

Nigel's humor was infectious. Frances laughed. "And the state carriage?"

"You can't mistake it. It's the one with the mirrors."

The procession crawled its way toward them, and at last she clearly saw Napoleon's carriage. The mirrored panels brilliantly reflected the scene, a myriad of colors beneath the gold-encrusted imperial arms. Huge white plumes nodded on the heads of eight horses harnessed together.

"You think I shall be impressed by all this spectacle?" she whispered. "Good heavens! I am impervious to splendor. In India the maharaja wore such plumes on his head."

Yet Frances felt oddly disappointed at her first glimpse of the man who had devastated Europe. Napoleon was dwarfed by the tall Frenchmen around him. Draped in rich ermine and velvet, gold chains and huge medals, he was a vision of extravagance. His round paunch strained his gilt buttons. White plumes nodded grotesquely on his velvet-draped hat.

"Good God! His coronation robes. It would seem," said

Nigel, "that, like your maharaja, Napoleon has a veritable crown of feathers—not quite the thing to reassure Paris that he bows to a new constitution!"

Frances tore her eyes away from Nigel's face. She knew she craved his body, but she hadn't expected this—to *like* him so much! Confused, she glanced over the crowd—a riot of robes, jewels, medals, and ribbons, all enriched by military glitter. The Duc de Freinville and others she had met at his hunt shone in their *ancien régime* finery. Yet one man stood out among the dignitaries. In a simple blue uniform with silver braid, he was smiling faintly—a smile not of amusement, but of calculation, or satisfaction perhaps. The man's cold, pale eyes were slightly narrowed, but his attention was clearly focused on Nigel.

Lecreux leaned close, and whispered. "Those are not eyes we would wish to notice your friend, madame."

Frances looked between them in alarm. "Who is it?"

"Joseph Fouché," said the count. "Le Duc d'Otrante." He lifted her fingers to his crepe mouth. "He is head of the secret police."

She looked back to make sure. This time the man in the blue uniform met her gaze. Graying reddish hair, pale eyes, a face entirely without soul. His thin lips widened, just a little, and he gave her a small nod. Her blood ran cold.

Nigel gave no sign of having noticed. He had glanced away over his shoulder.

Frances tried to calm her breathing. "Nigel!"

But his gaiety was gone also. "Devil take it!" he said in her ear. "Where the hell is Lance? Dammit!"

He slipped from his seat. Frances caught him by the sleeve. "Nigel!"

His eyes were alight with urgency. "Stay with Lecreux, Frances."

Nigel thrust away into the crowd.

The bloodless face still watched from the opposite side of the stands. With a quick excuse to the startled count, Frances plunged into the throng after Nigel.

Instantly she was lost. In the press of people no one seemed to notice her. Voices were shouting, *"Vive l'Empereur!"* Martial music resounded from the field, followed by the raised voice of some official making speeches. Desperately pushing through the crowd, Frances tried to follow the direction she thought Nigel had taken, but there were hundreds of thousands of spectators jammed together. A wave of agitation swept through them, and all other sound was drowned by a great roar from the mass of soldiers, cheering Napoleon.

Frances fought her way past the throng until she found herself among some of the carriages waiting for the officials. Nigel was nowhere to be seen. She leaned back on the corner of a building and cursed her own stupidity. She was lost. She didn't even know how to find Lecreux. She would wait here until it was over. Perhaps the count would come this way searching for his carriage?

∞

"Well, my dear," said a voice in her ear. "Your lover seems to have abandoned you. Won't you look more kindly on my suit now?"

She looked up into the face of the Duc de Freinville. Oh, Lord! At this very moment Nigel might be walking into some kind of trap! But she must not let anyone, least of all this French duke, a friend to Fouché, know that she was upset. Hating the necessity for it, Frances called on her training yet again and began to flirt.

"Are you not already married, monseigneur?"

"What if I am, madame?"

"You openly admit the existence of your mistresses to your wife? What kind of manners are those, pray?"

"French ones, madame." The duke took an elegant pinch of snuff. "More honest than the English, certainly, who keep their mistresses secret even when they have no wife."

"Your grace is familiar with English manners?"

Freinville sneezed. "The English swarmed over Paris a few months ago, before they fled with their tails between their legs at the Emperor's return. I can think of at least one English lord who openly ignored the charms of Parisian society, yet secretly kept a mistress near the Rue St. Sulpice and went there in disguise. No Frenchman would treat his mistress with such a lack of respect.''

Frances forced herself to appear light and teasing. "How do you know of this? Did you spy on this Englishman?''

"Servants talk." He gave her a thin smile. "It has always paid in Paris to keep one's ears open."

Perhaps this mattered. Perhaps it was something she should report to Nigel. Forcing herself to pay attention, Frances asked, "Near St. Sulpice? Where, pray? I'm sure you cannot tell me her exact location."

"I assure you I am perfectly correct. I can direct you to the house and give you both his name and that of his mistress."

The lady's name and address meant nothing, but Frances memorized it automatically. "What a tale!" she said gaily. "How can I believe you? You malign some innocent Englishman. If I ask you his name, it will no doubt be someone who does not exist."

The duke grinned as if to be in possession of this gossip secured his own place in the world, and told her. Her breath froze. She covered her confusion by rearranging her veils. In the midst of this crowd of Frenchmen, the words seemed outlandish, a ludicrous impossibility.

"I would swear the tale on my life, madame. His name was Donnington.''

There was no way to escape Freinville without raising suspicion. Frantic, desperate, Frances allowed him to help her into his carriage. They swept across the Seine toward the Tuileries, and Napoleon's grand reception that evening. Where was Nigel? She must get him this information. For whatever Donnington had kept in his secret rooms in the Latin Quarter, it wasn't a mistress!

The royal palace blazed. Thousands of candles, enough to keep all the poor of Paris in light for a year, sparkled in mirrors and crystal chandeliers. The throng filled every space. Making an excuse to visit the powder room, Frances broke away from Freinville and headed away from the milling guests. At last she found a deserted chamber where perhaps she could open a window. She wanted to be alone, to feel the cool night air on her face. But she was not alone. There were hushed voices somewhere nearby. Frances turned from the window, her blood chilled. These were voices she knew, and they hissed together in deadly enmity.

She moved silently through the shadowed room. At the end was a small antechamber. Two men were silhouetted in the light of a single candle. The flame glanced off a blond head to be swallowed in the dark hair of the other, gilt and shadows. Menace stalked in the room like a tiger.

His voice thick with intensity, Nigel swore. "I want your oath on it! Devil take it, Lance! Now, before your Maker, you will swear this one thing to me! Or shall I wring your bloody intransigent neck instead?"

Blue angel eyes stared blindly into the taller man's face. "You foiled me this afternoon. You block me now. Who benefits? Surely not England!"

Nigel took Lance by the shoulders. "*England!* What about France?"

The reply carried heartbreak and something of venom. "I do not work for France, Rivaulx! Do you?"

"You know what I work for. Swear to me there will not be another attempt! Now!"

His face white, Lance dropped suddenly to a chair, his head in his hands. "Very well. On my soul, I swear it. For your sake. Yet I pray my oath is not a betrayal!"

Nigel's voice dropped. Frances could barely make out his words, though they carried the bite of his wrath. "King Louis has fled. The Jacobins wait in the wings to unleash the Terror again. If the Emperor had a convenient attack of apoplexy tomorrow, who the *hell* do you think would control France? Fouché?"

"I don't know," Lance whispered. "You seem eager enough to involve him! How long do you think it will be before he hears that you claim to be a dead man, and working for him?"

Frances closed her eyes and sank to a sofa. All this long day, intrigue and danger had hummed about her, as they had been her daily companions in the *zenana*. And now she could no longer find any escape she could trust.

"*Do I interrupt?*" asked another voice.

On the soft carpet she had not heard the footsteps. Her eyes flew open. A stoop-shouldered man towered over her, his shadow dancing grotesquely on the wall. Bland, pale eyes gazed at Nigel and Lance from a bloodless face. Joseph Fouché, head of the secret police, soft as a cat, had discovered them. How much had he overheard?

She looked frantically from the cold, smooth face with the tiny smile to Nigel's profile. Nigel seemed to be burning with icy fury, barely contained. To cover the moment, Frances made herself rise and bow over folded hands as if it were merely a social occasion. Fouché bowed in return, took her fingers, and kissed them. His lips touched light and cold, like a damp fog.

Nigel interrupted. From some hidden depths he had found a place where this disaster was only ridiculous, an occasion for wit. "Only a lovers' quarrel, my lord duke. I thought my friend too familiar with my mistress. I misunderstood." He gave Lance a smile and held out his hand. As if in a daze, Lance shook it. "You will fetch the lady's carriage, *mon ami*? We must take her home."

His features barely under control, Lance bowed briefly to Fouché and left the room. Nigel turned to Frances. "Come, *chérie,* forgive me?"

Confused, Frances went up to him. He held out both hands. Fouché's cold voice echoed behind her.

"You do not have much warmth for your lover, madame?"

Nigel grinned, pulled her into his arms, and kissed her. She wanted to struggle, to cry out. It was hungry, possessive, the commanding kiss of a ruthless man, without subtlety. Her knees buckled so that only the strength of his arm supported her. Yet ineffable sweetness flooded her tongue. She felt his fingers slide down from her waist to cradle her buttocks, firing excitement. In an odd rage, Frances opened her mouth and suckled his lower lip. Nigel caught hers in his teeth and nibbled. Heat raced through her blood. Was this only playacting? For desire flamed between them and roared to the heavens.

When he released her, Fouché had gone.

"What the devil are you doing here?" asked Nigel, a little

breathless, setting her away as if nothing had happened. "Why didn't Lecreux take you home?"

Frances ignored the question and pressed her fingers to her mouth. She was shaking. "Was that for Fouché?"

She could not read his expression, but irony was clear in his voice. "What do you think?" He wrung a hand over his face, then to her immense surprise smiled with genuine warmth. "Thank you for not exposing my story. I think we were convincing enough, but for God's sake, let us get out while we can! The inexpressibly dewy Lance will have found a carriage."

"Wait," said Frances, her lips still singing with his kiss and her blood thundering symphonies. She took a deep breath. It was all playacting for him, but for her—who had been trained to act this role—what was it for her? *We were convincing enough?* Dear God! Dear God!

Her breathing steadied as she concentrated her mind, burying her distress. "We cannot go straight home. I have something to tell you."

∾

They rode to St. Sulpice under a strain so intense that Frances wanted to scream. The men were barely speaking—a few hissed words while Nigel told Lance what Frances had learned, then silence. Lance seemed as brittle as glass. *On my soul, I swear it!* Had he tried to stop Nigel from involvement with Fouché? Or had Lance uncovered something about Nigel that was unforgivable, and been forced to swear secrecy? *I do not work for France, Rivaulx! Do you?*

Yet in the end Nigel's voice became almost gentle. "Lance, you do not need to come. You know what we might find."

"I know." Lance's face seemed bruised. "But in spite of what just passed between us, you will not keep me away."

A few streets from Donnington's secret apartment, they left the carriage and continued on foot. Nigel reached for Frances's hand and held it, leading her through the dark streets. Am I led, she wondered, as a lamb to slaughter?

∞

Dust lay thickly in the dark room. As they stepped inside, it rose in a haze. Lance coughed. He was still pale. Nigel released Frances and set his lantern on the mantel. The yellow light washed over boxes and trunks, the lids open and overflowing with papers.

"Well," Nigel said softly, turning and facing the others. "As we surmised, no one entertained a mistress here. We would seem to have a night's work ahead of us."

Frances looked at him, at the cool competence, the control. Could nothing break this man? "Where do we begin?"

Nigel stripped off his jacket and hung it by the door. "We begin by looking for the obvious—anything concerning Catherine. Shall we start?"

The long, cool hours of the night slipped away. Lance seemed stretched to the breaking point. Frances could not read Nigel at all; an unyielding, self-contained reserve shuttered his features. His white shirt flickered golden and ocher in the lamplight; his brilliant court waistcoat was embroidered with red flowers that looked like flames. The devil dressed in celestial raiment—fallen angel mocking his Maker. Had that flaming kiss been designed to mock her? She looked away, hiding her agony, and concentrated on sorting the papers.

The sky began to lighten, an infinitesimal change from true darkness. Frances stood, stretched her cramped limbs, then crossed to the window. Faint shapes began to emerge in the dark street, as if seen briefly from the corner of the eye, shapes that if looked at directly might disappear. For a moment she thought she saw two figures, a denser black in the shadows of a doorway opposite, but when she looked again they were gone. Perhaps, tired to the bone, she had imagined them?

"*I have it.* Oh, dear God! I have it."

Frances turned. Lance stood clutching a sheaf of papers. Staring at Nigel, he had gone deathly white.

Nigel calmly took the papers from him and carried them to the lantern. As Lance watched him, frozen in some kind of horror, Nigel began to laugh. It was a genuine mirth that shattered the overworked atmosphere.

"You bloody bastard!" cried Lance. "You bloody, bloody bastard!"

"What is it?" asked Frances. Fear beat about her like a trapped bird.

"What we have here is treason," Nigel replied lightly. "An accomplice of Donnington's sent some very indiscreet messages to the French."

Her heart hammered. "Who? Are they signed in any way?"

He met her eyes with open hilarity. "Indeed! With a heraldic crest. It gives me the most delightful frisson of familiarity. It needs only the addition of color to be unmistakable: *griffin rampant argent langued gules*—a rearing silver griffin with a red tongue."

Frances sat down and buried her head in her hands. "The arms of Rivaulx?"

"You bloody bastard!" shouted Lance. "If this had been discovered before the war was over, you would have been hanged."

Nigel grinned at him. "You have to admit it shows a splendid sense of humor!"

"And this?" Lance held out another sheet he was holding. "What the devil does this show?"

Nigel took it and glanced swiftly at the writing. He stood silent for a moment before looking up. A derisive, deadly lightness colored his voice. "Why, that I wrote the message betraying Catherine, of course. It does look exactly like my handwriting, doesn't it? What else did you expect?" The subtle tones darkened as he began to quote Shakespeare. " 'Is not this a lamentable thing, that of the skin of an innocent lamb should be made parchment? That parchment, being scribbled o'er, should undo man?' "

Lance moved so quickly that Frances barely had time to duck out of his way.

"Damn you, Rivaulx! Did you think to find it first and destroy it? Is this why you suggested I might stay behind? By God! *No one* else knew where she was going that night—not even I! Of course anyone could have used the Rivaulx crest, but only *you* could have written that: the message that betrayed her! You won't bloody well get the chance to try to talk your way out of this!''

Frances saw a flash of steel as Lance vaulted over a chest. Nigel spun back. He had earlier set his sword cane down near the door. His pistols were in his coat pockets, hanging out of reach across the room. Lance threw himself bodily at the taller man and they crashed together to the floor.

Frances screamed. "Nigel! He has a knife!"

But Nigel had somehow wrenched away and regained his feet. Leaping another chest, he backed up to the wall. "Lance, for God's sake!"

"If no one else will avenge Catherine, by God, I will!" Moving the knife to his left hand, Lance stalked up to Nigel. Dark eyes locked onto blue. Nigel did not move as Lance struck him hard across the face with his open right hand. "You will give me satisfaction, my lord marquess?"

The livid mark of fingers began to flood crimson on Nigel's cheek, but he smiled. "I don't think it particularly politic to fight a duel, Lance. We are *guests* in an enemy capital. Fouché frowns on dueling as wasteful, as does Wellington, of course."

Lance tossed the blade back to his right hand. "In that case, I shall have to kill you here."

With the raised knife he struck once, hard and accurate, for the heart.

Nigel ducked and rolled, and came up grasping his own knife from his boot. " 'Then is sin struck down like an ox, and iniquity's throat cut like a calf?' "

Lance stared at him, sweat staining the ivory-yellow hair at his forehead, and grinned. "So you do have a knife. I thought you would."

Nigel continued to quote gently, faintly mocking. " 'He shall have the skins of our enemies, to make dog's-leather of.' "

Lance smashed a side table to splinters against the wall and grabbed a wooden leg to use as a club. Nigel rolled away just before the heavy wood cracked into his skull, but Lance's knife struck his right arm, slashing the white lawn, leaving a trail of blood.

Frances had watched English officers fencing in India, before she and her father had left on that last trip to the hills. It had been beautiful to watch, graceful, controlled, a dance at once deadly and lovely—an art of discipline and strange decorum. This was none of those things. Shrinking into the window embrasure, she began to shake, nauseous, horrified. Death swaggered crudely.

Nigel shifted his blade to his left hand. His right arm hung useless, bleeding freely. Lance closed again, striking, kicking like a demon, using the advantage of the chair leg to batter at his opponent. They struggled, sweating, grunting. Papers scattered and were shredded. Furniture broke. Trunks overturned. Like snarling, fighting mongrels, the men fell to the floor, straining together, rolling amid the wreckage, locked in a deadly embrace. Filth and dust covered their white shirts, black boots, hands and faces. Then Lance was on top. He straddled Nigel's hips, panting hard, the angel's face an agony of grief and fury. He had Nigel's wounded arm pinned beneath the table leg and a booted foot across the other wrist.

Nigel gazed up at him with a strange lack of emotion. "It's the only thing—the only thing I can't give you, Lance."

Lance's features convulsed beneath their mask of tears. Frances thought suddenly of an Indian painting she had once seen of lovers, the physical union, the ecstasy so blissful it looked like pain.

"I hate you!" Lance almost choked on the words. He raised his knife. His hand arced above the blond hair. With the entire force of his body he drove the blade toward Nigel's heart.

Fourteen

❧

STEEL SCREECHED AGAINST steel. Nigel had twisted, freed his wounded arm, and tossed his knife into his right hand. His bloodied arm moved in a blur of speed. His blade blocked the blow. As Lance's knife spun away Nigel slashed his toe into the other man's left elbow, crushing the nerve so that, with a strangled cry, he dropped the club. Lance threw himself aside, trying to reach his knife. Nigel instantly went after him. They scrabbled among the wreckage, kicking, twisting, using anything that could injure—a knee, an elbow, a booted foot. Lance was also a deadly fighter, taught in a hard school.

Lance reached his blade and turned, crouched, ready to spring. Deliberately Nigel dodged to one side. Following him, Lance stumbled against the broken side table. In the instant he lost balance, Nigel caught him by the wrist. He smashed Lance's hand against the wall, and without compunction kneed him in the groin. With a choked cry, Lance dropped his knife and curled into a ball, sobbing.

Nigel's breath came hard and ragged, beating loudly in his ears. "You know that I did not betray her, Lance. This is madness."

"Then who did?" Lance stared up at him through a film of dirt and moisture. "Who the bloody hell did?"

"I don't know. Dear God, I don't know! But I know this: All these papers are fake. This was a trap."

Gasping, still clutching at his groin, Lance stared at him. "A trap?"

"Just another diabolical twist of the screw, that is all. Can't you see the pattern in all this? However stained my hands, I did not betray Catherine and you know it. You are making a bloody fool of yourself."

Lance stood up, grimacing. "I have wanted nothing, from the beginning, but your respect. Can't you at least allow me that?"

Nigel leaned back. He was smeared with dirt and blood. His breath rasped, ragged, in his throat. *What the hell had this just done to Frances?* "Oh, for God's sake, take care of your own sensibilities for a while! Go home, Lance."

Collecting hat and coat, Lance stumbled from the room.

She had turned away. She seemed infinitely vulnerable, the curve of her shoulder and waist fragile—a symbol of everything lovely and graceful, of everything that deserved protection from violence. Nigel felt helpless to make amends, helpless to reach her.

He spoke at last, with nothing but stark honesty. "I wish you had not been forced to witness that."

"Leave me alone," Frances said.

Blood trickled down his arm, making strange patterns on the back of his hand. "Since the day we met, I have had nothing to offer you but apologies. I'm sorry, Frances. I'm sorry for all of it—for the whole bloody mess. Can you not . . . Oh, devil take it!"

She turned and faced him, with a courage that seemed desperate. "You have driven Lance to the edge of madness! Why? Why must you do it?"

He no longer had the energy to conceal his bitterness. "You don't think Lance has a hand in his own fate?"

Her breath, too, was uncontrolled. The silk rose and fell violently over her breasts. "Oh, dear God! You are all the same. Devastation lives in your pocket and Death crouches on your shoulder. I can't bear it!"

There was agony in her voice. Nigel forced himself to face her revulsion and the depths of his own shame. Yet quite desperately he wanted her to understand. "I *had* to learn to fight, Frances."

"But in a personal quarrel, I thought there were rules—things no gentleman would do to another."

For a moment he wondered if he could offer excuses, but he felt stripped of duplicity. "There aren't any rules. The Cossacks taught me that. I am not proud of it. War isn't a parlor game."

She did not answer. Nigel looked up and saw the tears streaming openly down her face. Avoiding his eyes, she turned away. He longed to go to her. He wanted to take her in his arms and offer comfort. The absurdity of the thought was staggering.

Longing to reach her, he told her the truth. "I cannot eliminate the blood lust that is in the world. I cannot right all wrongs, or save nations from destruction. I have searched for the right path to the best of my ability, but sometimes every path leads to disaster. I have tried to do good, even when evil was the result. I did not want to be trained for carnage, but dear God, you must have seen that it doesn't control me. I did not want to fight him, but if I had desired Lance dead, he would have died."

Her face was mottled with crying, her eyes a startling blue, like periwinkles. "I know. That is what terrifies me."

Why must it be so painful? He *liked* her. He respected her. And to the depths of his soul, he desired her. Did those three things amount to something more than he could crush, more than he could control? Nigel dropped to sit on a trunk. He was vaguely aware that his arm ached, though the bleeding had stopped. It was a superficial cut. He had pretended it was worse only to fool Lance. "My *control*? For God's sake! I don't understand."

"You are all intellect, aren't you? You are dead to the senses. Only your damned devious plans enthrall you. You say war isn't a parlor game. What about love? Is love a parlor game?"

He knew she was talking about Lance, that she upbraided him for what she saw as his cruel treatment of a man who loved him, but a new idea struck him with the force of a knife blade. It was so obvious he wanted to laugh, or break things. He remembered her lips beneath his, hot and urgent, as for a moment in spite of Fouché he had lost control. *What about love?*

As if it were trivial, merely superficial banter, Nigel kept his voice light. "Like most parlor games, love has three parts."

Disdain poisoned her voice. "You mock me, and my training? Three parts?"

Nigel grinned. It was that or weep. "Of course. Liking. Respect. And desire."

Lance stumbled down the steps and into the street. He leaned back on the iron grille at the doorway and stared up at the white faces of the opposite houses. God help him! Was he mad? He had just tried to kill the only man more important to him even than England, the only man who could best him in hand-to-hand combat, the only man that he loved. The only woman he loved was already dead. He had never held it against Rivaulx that Catherine had loved him. What woman would not? Even Betty let her sun rise and set on Nigel Arundham, though she had known so many men over the years. How could Rivaulx so carelessly spurn all the love he was offered?

And what of Miss March, his innocent, brown-haired fiancée? She embodied England in all its purity and wholesomeness. For he loved, fervently and without question, the England into which he had been born—the green fields and snug cottages; fields of ripe wheat dappled with ox-eye daisies; larks rising. He had clung fiercely to the idea of it for all these years. Let Napoleon once be defeated, and he could claim Miss March and offer her his purity in exchange for hers. Yet in truth it was love for Rivaulx that kept him pure. A vain hope, perhaps, that if he proved it could be done—if he proved that a man could retain his virtue and his ideal of chastity— he could somehow save Nigel Arundham from destruction.

Lance walked away down the silent streets. The sound of

carriage wheels arrested him as he turned into the Boulevard
St. Michel. He strolled on, deliberately staggering a little, like
a drunk. The coach stopped beside him. Lance glanced up
casually, hiding his alertness. With a snap, the window came
down. A white hand dropped from it, heavy with rings, a
woman's hand, pale in the pearly dawn light. Soft fingers
touched his face.

"*Chéri,* you are bruised! What *have* you been doing?"
Stunned, Lance looked up at the lovely face smiling down at
him from the carriage—a white oval glimmering faintly in its
frame of black hair. "Ah, *mon cher*! Do not look so very
surprised to see me."

"Oh, God." He could barely breathe. Blood seemed to be
hammering in his ears. "I don't understand! How are you
here?"

"In Paris?" She laughed. "The usual way: by carriage.
What do you think? That I have wings?"

Shock left him barely coherent. "No, no! Does Rivaulx
know?"

"My dear, how could he? I am known here only as la Belle
Dame. Come, give me your hand and I will explain everything."

As if mesmerized, Lance held up his hand. She opened the
door, put her palm into his, and helped him into the carriage.

"Yes," she said softly. "Though he broke my heart, I love
him still. As you do, sweet Lancelot. Don't be upset. I have
always known that you loved him. But he cannot return it. His
heart is dead. He mourns, does he not, for Princess Katerina
of Russia? I think it is only we two who can save him."

In a clatter of hooves, the carriage bowled away.

It was a week of strange silences. Nigel was gone every day
and most nights. Frances feared he was driving himself to the
brink of collapse. Yet something of humor and gallantry was
always offered to her—like a rare gift—in their brief encoun-
ters. She couldn't fight or refuse it, so she buried her fear and
returned it with humor of her own. He did not want a mistress.

He did not want her. She only hoped she could maintain this uneasy courtesy until he took her back to England and found her a duke.

Frances also saw Lance only briefly, in passing, as he, too, disappeared into the labyrinth of streets and the arcane world of secrets. Lance seemed subdued, contrite. Since the fight he had been an attentive comrade, as if offering some unspoken apology to Nigel and hoping to win back his esteem. Nigel was courteous, even gentle, with the man who had so recently tried to kill him. Frances couldn't understand it.

Paris waited in an odd anticipation. Since the Champ de Mars, most of the customers who came to buy silk and spices seemed to be looking nervously over their shoulders, as if aware of impending cataclysm. Others were too bright, shining with false gaiety, as if desperate for one last chance at indulgence. Their nervous energy vibrated in the Rue des Arbres, and left Frances struggling to maintain her equilibrium. Beneath it all ran fear—fear for Nigel, wantonly devouring his own strength, living on the knife edge of exhaustion. Frances was always afraid now. She had tried meditation, but her thoughts spiraled out of control, shattering her peace. When she did her breathing exercises, she would hear his subtle voice, tinged with an irony she couldn't begin to comprehend: *I am an old hand at interesting punishments.* She had nothing left, and nowhere to go where she could escape.

He returned one morning with the dawn, stark with fatigue. Unable to sleep, Frances watched the sunrise mist over the sleeping city. Catherine had once stood here and let down her red hair for him, then left him bereft. Turning blindly from the window, Frances collided with a wet cloak. Chilled hands caught and steadied, though warmth seemed to flash over her. Nigel met her eyes and grinned, yet he was tired, tired.

"I have been trying to avoid this," he said. "The sudden fire and the heart leaping. After what happened in Donnington's rooms, it's unforgivable, isn't it? I'm sorry."

He dropped his hands and turned. Lance stood in the doorway. His moist hair was darkened to umber. Once again Frances noticed that new edge to him, as if blissful contentment warred with dreadful disquiet.

Nigel strode away from her, speaking to Lance over his shoulder. "We have action at last! Napoleon has sealed the frontiers and stopped all traffic from Paris. He will move within the week. If we only knew exactly where he planned to cross his Rubicon, our mission here would be done."

Frances made herself say it, though she did not want to. "And Catherine's betrayal?"

"All we know is that Catherine died. I'm not sure we shall ever know why." Nigel began going over some papers—household accounts left by Monsieur Martin, nothing of importance, but his voice betrayed the depths of his frustration.

Lance glanced at Nigel with his heart in his eyes. "Perhaps this evidence from Donnington is wrong, and there is no link between Catherine and all the treachery since Russia?" There was definitely something new in Lance's voice, something tragic, painful.

"No, we are being watched and every move reported to someone. What else accounts for those false papers signed with my crest? Why else should every clue about Catherine's death lead to a blank wall? We are being deliberately blocked, as if we were toys tossed about by a petulant child. There is an unknown player in this game, someone with an undeniably charming sense of humor."

Frances spoke without thinking. "You think it is Major Wyndham? That he is alive? That he plots against you?"

His dark eyes met hers for a moment. Passion burned in them. A passion of sorrow or of hunger? She wasn't sure, but it sent a renewed flush through her veins. "I don't know. But whoever it is, perhaps he will slip before we do. If not, I shall have to force the game a little more, that is all."

Without looking again at Frances, Nigel walked from the room.

She went to the window. Nigel strode across the courtyard and swung onto his Don horse. Something melted in her to watch him. The animal's coat gleamed, the tail a flag of silver. Who was their enemy in Paris? Freinville? Lecreux? She prayed that it wasn't Dominic Wyndham, that Nigel was not being betrayed by an old friend. Yet if it was not, that left only the bloodless Fouché. Was that who was waiting, plotting, ready to pounce? If so, they had no chance at all—three helpless strangers against the entire police power of France and the secrets of the Quai Voltaire.

∞

The next week passed in the same desperate haze. Nigel returned only to catch an hour here or there of heavy, drugged sleep, before having a servant wake him to go out again. Lance, too, was gone most of the time, but he came in one morning just as Nigel left. Frances saw them exchange a few hissed words in the hall, before Lance marched into the room where Frances was working and threw down his gloves.

Lance spoke without preamble. "Do you *want* to see him die?"

She was surprised into bluntness. "I don't know what you mean."

"You aren't his lover, are you? For God's sake, why not?"

It took courage to stay calm. She wanted to scream and rail at him, pound her fists. His golden hair had fallen forward over his white face. He looked at her with the eyes of an angel.

Frances took a deep breath. "No, I am not Nigel's mistress. Nothing of the kind happened between us at Farnhurst, or since then in London or here." *Nothing of the kind?* She could still taste his kisses and feel his hands on her skin. "I am here only because I can help sort the silks, because I know the names of the spices. Because I can keep these books and help maintain the illusion that we are here only for trade. That is all."

"But you are a professional courtesan. Go to his bed, for God's sake! He is exhausting himself, killing himself!" Lance closed his eyes in genuine distress. "Dear God, all of our lives depend on his judgment. With no other solace, this house is driving him insane."

"But I cannot—" Fighting back tears, Frances stared at Lance. "His grief is for Catherine. I cannot replace her."

Lance dropped his golden head on his hand, pressing his knuckles into his eyes. "Bloody hell! I'm not talking about love. You saw those scandal sheets. He needs a woman for sex, that's all. Give him that release, at least! Perhaps then he would sleep. Perhaps then he won't drag us all to destruction. Do you hate him too much to do it?"

The words almost choked her. "No, I don't hate him."

Lance looked down at her, the blue eyes rimmed in red. She knew what he was about to say, and she knew that she could not bear it. "Then I beg you, Miss Woodard! I beg you! Give him what he needs, or we shall all die!"

Nigel put the Don horse into a canter as soon as he was free of the city. Green trees arched over his head. Green fields stretched away on each side of the road. He passed an occasional village, and was forced to slow down to avoid scattering geese and chickens. He noticed none of it. He had no particular destination, but he wanted to be free of Paris. He wanted to think.

The traffic in messages from the Tuileries to the war ministry had increased markedly in the last few days. Any day now Napoleon would probably leave Paris. Nigel had already sent Wellington a preliminary warning that French attack was imminent. All he needed to know was where they planned to cross the Belgian border, and Napoleon's plans could be foiled. But it would all come to a head too soon, when he was no closer to knowing why Donnington was dead, why Catherine was dead, and who had been betraying Britain ever since Russia. On that score, failure stared him starkly in the face.

Since his unknown enemy obviously knew he was a spy, why didn't the man move now, before he and Lance found out any more? Was it because he cared nothing for Europe or for the outcome of the war, but only wished to bring destruction to Nigel personally? *Why?* Dear God, Nigel had not thought there was anyone alive who could hate him that much!

The Don horse shook its head as he allowed it to wander from the road and take a path through a wood. Nigel was

barely surprised an hour later to find himself in the little clearing by the stream where he had told Frances about Raoul Pargout. He slid from the horse and set it free to graze. Then he
dropped to the ground and leaned his back against a tree.

Images of Frances swarmed into his mind. Dear God, but
she was brave! Did she know it? For she moved through her
days fighting her fear—of chaos, of violence, of cruelty—with
a breathtaking courage. He was trying so hard to keep her a
stranger, not to allow her close enough to find out what he
really was, yet he wanted, so desperately, to offer her reassurance, to see her laugh, though he could not bear the tenuous
friendship that had resulted. Nigel dropped his head in his
hands, his fingers clenched over his eyes.

*Behold thou art fair, my love; behold thou art fair; thou
hast doves' eyes.*

Why the hell had he allowed her to come, allowed this crazy
scheme of Betty's to go forward?

*Set me as a seal upon thine heart, as a seal upon thine arm,
for love is as strong as death.*

The little brook gurgled and sang over its stone bed. His
heavy lids slipped over his bruised eyes, shutting out the sun.

∽

La Belle Dame was alone, waiting for him. Lance stepped into
her chamber and leaned back against the door. "Are you
sure?" he said.

"*Chéri?* Will she do it?"

"I don't know. I don't know. Are you sure this is the right
thing for him?"

She brushed back a strand of dark hair, and smiled. "My
dear, I know that it is. Who knows Rivaulx better than I? Who
loves him better? Ah, that I could only let him know that I
am here! But my heart is not strong enough yet. But you, you
will heal it."

He made a broken gesture. "I cannot bear it that you should
be reduced to living like this." He waved his hand around the
modest room. "You should be in a palace!"

"Come, my dear. Come here. Your presence makes it a palace for me."

Like a man drugged, Lance crossed the room and knelt beside her. She lifted his head by the chin and ran one ringed hand over his blond hair.

"Kiss me." Her voice was throaty.

He shook his head, but she pressed her mouth to his, moving her hands over his jacket. At last, with a small bite to his lower lip, she released him. Lance said nothing, his eyes filled with tears.

"Stand."

Lance stood before her, head bowed, as she released the buttons at his waist and folded down the flap at the front of his breeches. Her clever mouth soon followed. Lance groaned, his hands in her dark hair. Yet he wept. He didn't know if they were tears of bliss or of bitter remorse. His carefully tended memory of the brown-haired Miss March in Surrey had faded away, but Rivaulx was always there. And in spite of everything la Belle Dame had explained, this still seemed very like a betrayal.

∞

In another part of Paris, Joseph Fouché indulgently watched his wife across their dinner table. He knew perfectly well that the world thought him a monster. They did not see him, like this, in the bosom of his family, or understand the things great men must endure. But he was a model husband. Gabrielle spoke quietly to the servant who came in, then made a little face. She knew he did not like to be disturbed at home, but a courier had arrived, insisting it was urgent. Setting down his napkin, Fouché rose and received the man in his private study.

The message was simple.

"Ask Captain Genet of the Lancers about the man in the Rue des Arbres who calls himself Monsieur Anton."

∞

By the time Nigel returned to the Rue des Arbres, it was close to midnight. Lance was out. Except for the servant who let him in and took his coat and hat, the rest of the household seemed asleep. Nigel spent a few moments going over some papers that Lance had left for him, then he ran up the stairs to the little suite he shared with Frances. So that he would not wake her in the room beyond, he opened the door to his antechamber softly.

It had changed.

Nigel stood in the doorway and narrowed his eyes. Only one candle burned, but as if in a crystal cave, light danced and glittered on every wall. The flame wavered in myriad scintillating, ever-reflecting surfaces of glass, repeating and repeating to infinity. She had filled his room with mirrors. Smoke trailed, burning incense, heady and sweet, sandalwood and spices. White silk covered his bed. Red flowers lay massed at the head of it. And a tub of steaming water waited on the rug.

She was not asleep. Ivory silk over ivory skin, gold glinting in her nostril, a veil thin as cobweb over her hair, Frances sat cross-legged on the bed, her eyes pools of blue as she gazed at him steadily. He didn't know what he saw there, except an intense concentration. Somewhere in the house behind him, the servant who must have just brought the water closed a door. It echoed dully.

Nigel stepped into the chamber. *"What is this?"*

"You are tired," said Frances. "You should take a bath."

With the trained grace of the *Ganika,* she rose and left the room.

Nigel was too exhausted to question it, this strange gift she had made him. He bathed, gazing up at the piquant sparkle of the tiny, infinitely multiplied flame. The hot water soothed. The scents offered subtle solace. There was nothing to hear but deep night and silence. A relaxation as profound as death.

The candle flame flickered, almost burned away.

At last Nigel splashed from the cooling water. A million naked men dazzled in the mirrors. He felt suspended, bemused, looking at them. Dampness sheened over his muscles, drops of water like jewels on his skin. He rubbed himself dry.

Then a million doors opened and a million images of Frances, ivory silk over ivory skin, came into the room. She was carrying something, a small jar. Nigel turned to her, utterly naked. The hair prickled at the back of his neck, and his cock stirred, betraying him.

∞

Frances saw his arousal and the moment of stark dismay in his gaze, before he laughed, covering his emotions. Her heart skittered. Fear peeled the strength from her limbs. She lowered her eyes and took a calming breath. She could not retreat now! Not when she had spent the day preparing the room. She had woven sacred herbs and flowers into garlands. She had pounded together cardamom and citrus peel. She had draped the bed in white silk, worthy of the citizen. She had gathered mirrors from all over the house. Only the cages with trained parrots were missing.

He did not move or cover himself. Glorious, naked, like a wary stallion he gazed at her, his eyes black against his candlelit skin, his sex a little darker than the rest, and his hair black.

"What the devil is that?"

She set down the pot she was carrying. Her educated hands didn't shake, though her nerves quailed. "Cream with sandalwood and musk, saffron and aloes."

The bite in his voice was veiled with an odd courtesy. "May I ask what it is for?"

She tried to make her answer merely teasing, light, so he would not suspect. "Massage. The forty-fourth of the sixty-four arts. I am very well trained. Lie down—it will feel good."

Nigel sat on the silk bed and wearily put both hands over his face. "Dear God! Why?"

"Why not? We are all dependent on your strength. You have not taken enough rest for weeks. Don't your muscles ache?"

"Like those of the traveler stretched on the bed of Procrustes." His voice was dry.

"But this time neither your money nor your life is at stake."
The trembling ran deep inside. Heat and cold pricked up her
spine. She wanted to gasp, to let her breath shatter, but her
voice remained calm, the trained voice of the courtesan. "I
offer you merely the domestic arts of the citizen—this one
comes between teaching birds to talk and the art of sign language."

Nigel laughed, a little unsteadily. "Do you think I have the
strength left now to refuse? God, I am tired! Do your worst,
if you insist."

He stretched out on the bed, his face buried in his crossed
arms, his back to her. Frances lit a new candle. He lay like a
dark prince, long and lean, sculptured in the flickering light.
Controlling her breathing, she poured a little scented cream
onto her hands and touched his shoulders. Her fingers slipped
over mitered muscle, lingering in the crease of his spine. Beautiful, like the carved flank of an Ashokan lion.

It seemed to shiver into her soul, the beauty of touching
him.

Frances closed her eyes, struggling for calm. She felt heavy
and hot. Yet his sinews relaxed under her palms. The small
dimples at his waist swirled beneath her fingers. The firm,
tender curve of his buttocks shaped into her palm. She pressed
and rubbed, attuned to every nuance of texture—where he was
smooth and where fuzzed with dark hair, the firmness of muscle, the resilience of skin.

And she was burning, burning, her own limbs languid, as
tension built in an agony, and the sweet, heavy song of desire
fired fiercely in her heart. He turned his head, settling into the
white silk, and sighed. She concentrated, relaxing her mind,
removing her self as if it were only an exercise in the *zenana*.
*I am trained for this. It is only ritual. It is only another of the
arts*. Before she should lose courage, she shrugged off her
loose robe.

The scented air of the room caressed her. Spirals of incense
shivered in the little currents caused by her movements. She
trembled like a harp string as her thumbs slid past the secret
places of his body. Shutting out all thoughts, she stroked her
fingernails firmly over his smooth buttocks, then pressed, hard

enough to mark him. *Utpalapattraka. The lotus leaf.*

He stiffened, a sharp inhalation, skin rough with sudden gooseflesh. Before he could move, Frances straddled him, holding him down on the bed, her thighs across his. He bucked violently beneath her. His buttocks thrust as he twisted, turned over, and grabbed her wrists. His erection throbbed against her belly, hard and imperious, but his eyes were like the sky of a moonless night—wide, empty, and black.

"Frances, dear God! Don't do this!"

She smiled, breathing in his breath, leaning between their clenched hands. Her nipples, puckering, brushed his chest. "I have already done it," she murmured against his lips, and pressed her mouth over his.

He kissed back. He dropped her hands and cradled her face as he kissed her again, devouring, his mouth hot and hungry. She was flooded, inundated, shaken to the soul by the force of it, surging into her blood. All the kisses she had learned roared together into one overwhelming sensation. She tried to wrestle with him, play the kissing game—all the little bites and suckles—but he tore her away and lifted her by the waist. The muscles stood stark on his arms as he held her over him, helpless.

His mouth was swollen, his nostrils flared—sensual demon, prince of darkness, man of the devil's own beauty. Her plait had come loose, her hair skeined gold across her back. The mirrors embellished them, infinite pairs of lovers, bruised with passion.

"I cannot . . ." He closed his lids for a moment, covering the hot black depths, then opened them and gazed straight into her eyes. "God help me, I cannot refuse this, Frances. I beg you, stop now!"

Stop now? She grasped the little pot and poured cream over his chest and belly. "It isn't right that we should," she said fiercely. "This is the sacred rite of Radha and Krishna. I am a professional, a courtesan. Denial is senseless."

Cream spread, streaming off his flat nipples, running down to his navel, filling the air with sandalwood. With a single flex of muscle, Nigel swung her to one side. Skin slid over skin, slick with musk and milk. She was trapped beneath him against the white silk. Grasping her hips, pressing her into his body, he kissed her again.

"Frances, dear God, I'm on fire for you! Damn you!"

Give him what he needs, or we shall all die! Afraid to hesitate, she grasped a garland of flowers and threw it over his head. Surprised, he reared back. A lover in red petals, a warrior prince, god of creation and destruction. Scarlet, vivid in the candlelight, carmine splashed into the mirrors as if the whole room were splattered with blood.

Hot, confused, she spread herself beneath him. Petals rained down on her. "I am a public woman. It means nothing else. Take your pleasure, Nigel. Come, I am willing!"

He gave a groan like a sob and rubbed his hands over her slippery belly, up to her breasts, wiping away the shredding red flowers. "*Willing?* Every harlot is willing. Is that what you offer—a path to oblivion? Damn you! Damn you!"

He took her by the waist, rolling beneath her so she straddled him, intimately close. Scent burst and soaked about them. He secured a hank of her long hair with one hand, holding it firmly behind her back, forcing her to arch her spine. As she put her hands back onto his raised thighs to steady herself, her naked breasts thrust forward, multiplied in the mirrors into images as opulent as erotic temple carvings.

His free hand slid up her body, brushing between her breasts as if he no longer had the will to control it. He cupped her jaw, his palm enclosing her stretched throat, and stroked below her ear in a spot so sensitive she ached with the pleasure. In the mirrors, a million hands stroked a million naked women, blurred with yearning.

Slowly, slowly, his fingers slid down her body, brushing gently over her breasts, lingering at her waist, rubbing sure and certain down her thighs. She sat helpless, her back bent like a bow, open to him, defenseless. His caress ran over her flank, up the curve of her ribs as if her body was a miracle to him. Held by her hair, she was stretched like a string, ringing in his hands with a wild, confused music. Then his palm cupped her breast, his thumb rubbing over the raised peak, and she gasped. Sensation spiked, a sweet arrow of lust running into her belly.

He teased mercilessly at her nipple, ringing the music higher and wilder, uncontrolled. She swallowed, frantic she might melt, dissolve. His arousal thrust hard beneath her, impatient and certain. This was no longer an idea learned from a painting. It wasn't an exercise. This was real.

Grasping a handful of flowers, he stroked down over her flank and stomach as if to follow the mad feelings he was creating in her. Helplessly, she opened her thighs wide. Petals caressed softly, over and over, like tiny fingers, exploring her tender, quivering flesh. She was shaking above him now, panting, as at last his thumb—slick with cream—touched the piercing heart of her excitement. His fingers slid over moistness, then slipped inside. He would not know. There would be no blood. She had used her body as no English girl ever should, riding astride, moving in the energetic dances and in yoga. And in case that had not been enough, the *praudha* in the *zenana* had checked to be sure.

Determined, desperate, Frances wrenched her hair from his hand, then dropped forward and closed her mouth over his. As he began to kiss her she bit hard. He swore, but she sank her fingers in his hair and bit him again on the neck.

"*Kapatadyuta*—the trick," she said, seizing his lower lip in her teeth. Then she released it and licked at his mouth, before biting harder. "*Jihvayuddha*—the fight of tongues."

He swore again, then laughed wildly, his erection leaping with it, and slid his hands to her hips. He pulled her body forward over his chest, her knees sliding on the silk sheets. His strength was inexorable. As his tongue nuzzled and swirled on her breasts, she was rubbed intimately over his throbbing, raised rim. He held her there for a moment while she choked back the wild cries that welled in her throat. Then he slid himself beneath her, scattering petals, and groaned as he fastened his mouth where his thumb had been. She heard her own breath, shattering in a wild rhythm as the pleasure rippled from his tongue, terrifying in intensity, making her swollen and hot.

Panic welled, uncontrolled. She wrenched away. He rolled with her, pinning her to the sheets, his hands in her hair, his dark eyes burning. The red flowers crushed between them.

"Shall I take you, Frances, very slowly? Explore the hot, sweet depths of you? I am mad for you. Yet, though it kill me, I will stop—even now—if you say so."

"No," she said desperately. "No. I am a harlot, and I want you."

The bitterness in his laugh threatened to break her heart. "Then I cannot help myself. For God knows, I want you."

Rolling her, he again held her above him. She looked down, stung to the core by his beauty. Then slowly he began to impale her, lowering her onto his erect shaft, and his eyes closed. Her prince of darkness, possessing her. She was stretched open helplessly, distended, completely filled, one flesh. But wildfire blossomed from their joining, too intense, frightening.

It hurt. There would be no blood, but it hurt. Falling forward, Frances bit his shoulder—in alarm, in passion, she didn't know. He pulled back and thrust again, his hands on her hips, rocking her in time with his movements. The pain became fused with unbearable heat. The rhythm seized her, shattering her control. Her fingernails raked over his skin, unconstrained, any pattern lost. She bit harder, until he cursed and laughed. He thrust deeper, flooding her with hot fire, fierce, wild, clamoring. He would destroy her!

The king of the Panchalas killed the courtesan Madhavasena by his excess.

In agonized confusion, she pressed her mouth onto his, biting at his lips until they were swollen and bruised, her fingers locked in his hair, wrestling with him. If he tried to offer tenderness or subtlety again, she would deny him. She knew more than enough to force him to his release. Yet fiery pleasure pulsed, shivering, profound, as he stroked in and out. She gasped for breath. In the mirrors a million women gasped with her.

The smoke wavered in the heavy air, the scent overwhelming. Oleander and a garden in bloom. Glass reflected an illusion of scintillating tile. Red flowers splashed carmine, a sacrifice. And her own reflection, dazed, wide-eyed, mocked from every wall in the room. *But I love him! I love him! I don't want to be his whore!*

She didn't know when it had happened. There had been no sudden fall. It had come upon her slowly, and just as slowly and thoroughly it had been threatening to break her heart. But she had not seen it. She had not seen it until now, when it was too late. Frances forced herself beyond the sudden rush of regret, beyond feeling. She had compelled him, against his will. She was a concubine, all artifice, without soul—how else could she go through with this?

She wrenched her mind away, negating the overwhelming feelings and the fear, locking her soul into that secret, inner haven where she could always be safe. But her senses went dead, robbed of delight, as her trained hands and bereft body drove him into a frenzy. At last he shuddered, blind in his ecstasy, and Frances knew herself lost, unable to share in his passion, unable to respond—condemned to the wasteland, alone and desolate.

Fifteen

NIGEL AWOKE TO blackness. Frances slept softly beside him in the dark. He listened to her steady breathing. The scent of sandalwood filled his nostrils. *I have gathered my myrrh with my spice; I have eaten my honeycomb with my honey. O beloved.*

Ignoring his instant arousal, he swung from the bed and went to the window. The shutters opened quietly on the pale wash of dawn. Smoke from morning fires was beginning to wreathe about the rooftops. Wrapping himself in a robe, Nigel stepped into the hallway and tugged the bellpull. A few minutes later a sleepy-eyed servant brought him a pail of hot water.

Frances slept as if drugged, her hair drifted about her, curled on her side with her hands folded together against her breasts. Nigel wet a cloth in the hot water and began to wash her, soothing away the sticky, scented reminders of the night. He did it fully aroused, burning, but he would not wake her. She stirred and moaned a little as he tenderly dried her breasts and her slender legs. Then he covered her with a clean sheet and began to tidy the room, sweeping up the crushed flowers and the ash of the incense, before he bathed himself and dressed. As he moved, myriad reflections moved with him—like the infinitely reflecting images that had amplified his passion all night. He had a sudden empty desire to smash them—smash every treacherous, mocking mirror, to indulge in a deluge of broken glass in a vain expiation of shame—but that would wake her.

He had taken her again and again. She had driven him into a kind of madness. He had tried to soften his urgency, determined to carry her with him, longing to see her ecstasy match his. Yet she had not been there with him. She had held back, denying him her ultimate surrender, as a harlot does. The pain was bitter. It meant nothing to her, as she had said. She was a courtesan, offering her professional arts, that was all. Even in his rapture he had known her remoteness—as if she moved in a trance—hands, mouth, making motions while her soul stayed away, somewhere safe. Somewhere safe from *him*!

Nigel took a seat by the window and dropped his head into his hands.

"Are you angry?" Her voice sounded bruised.

He looked up. Her lips were dark against her pale skin. "Angry? No. Should I be?"

Frances sat up. Honey hair slid over her breasts. She looked down at her hands. "I don't know what to say."

The desire to make love to her again hurt. "What do you usually say to a man you have ravished?" He was relieved that it sounded only faintly amused.

"Ravished?"

He gave her a wry smile. "Seduced, then. Yes, I was willing enough, after all, wasn't I?"

Her saw her hesitate. She looked unexpectedly vulnerable. "It is what I have been trained for. If you are a chef and you see a starving man, you cook him a meal."

"What if food is not what he craves?"

"You seemed hungry enough."

"Perhaps I was." He laughed, surprised at his own bitterness. "I haven't slept so well in years."

She looked down. He had no idea what she was thinking. "Good. That's what Lance said would happen."

It exploded from him. "*Lance!* Dear God! What the *hell* does this have to do with him?"

Frances hugged her arms over her breasts. She felt bruised, sore. She felt like weeping. Nigel stared down at her with that burning, hot fire in his eyes. He *was* angry now. In two strides he was at the bed.

She took a calming breath. "He showed me some broadsheets about you—what you liked to do in London. He thought that you needed such relief. He was right, wasn't he?"

His sarcasm hissed. "Right? About what? About my sordid past? About my degraded tastes? That I cannot live without a whore? Good God!"

She kept her voice level, not looking at him. "I did not think it was all true, but I did think you needed release."

"Then you have it exactly wrong, Frances. I have lived without a woman in my bed for twenty months. Twenty bloody months! It ought to have been my choice to change if I wished it. Certainly not Lance's, for God's sake! But before that—"

Before that lay Catherine. It hung unspoken between them.

Nigel moved away from her, collecting gloves and hat. He did not look up and meet her eyes. "I will tell you this much: that I used to be rake; that carnal indulgence once defined my life."

Frances climbed from the bed, catching up her robe. "I could not satisfy you? You wish to watch women and donkeys? Take men to your bed?"

"Donkeys!" He glanced up then, his mouth twisted in irony. "There is little I have not done, but donkeys and other men were never quite to my taste. Women have provided all the sensual indulgence I ever desired. At one time it was a great deal. But, dear God, if I *have* denied the senses, I embraced them thoroughly enough last night!"

She was more afraid now than she had been when Donnington died, when she saw Fouché watching Nigel, when she had been captured and taken to the *zenana*. This was a different fear, deeper, closer to the heart. "Then what happens now?"

"What happens now is that I have work I must do before we go back to England. But after last night, I don't have the strength to resist you. You have won. I will set you up as my mistress. Why not? Your training and my corruption! You will be generously compensated. I have never left any woman in want—except Catherine.''

Turning on his heel, he strode from the room.

Frances stumbled through the day. Her mind refused to function. She couldn't meditate. *When a man, from the beginning to the end of the congress, thinks all the time that he is enjoying another one whom he loves, it is called the "congress of transferred love."*

There were not many customers, so she sat at her small desk in the showroom and tried to go over the inventory. There was not much left. If this dreadful suspense lasted much longer, they would run out of fabric and their cover story at the same time. She ran her fingertips over some cream silk lying next to her chair. Warm from the sun streaming in at the window, it was rich and smooth. It reminded her wantonly of a man's skin, hot with desire—powerful, beautiful, flooding her senses.

She had melted to touch him. Shouldn't everything have followed from that? Throughout the night he had pursued his exquisite passion again and again. But each time as he reached his culmination he had left her behind—growing numb as she gave him his pleasure. She was cold, like the harlot she had been trained to be. It was an agony to her. It had been agony to see the rapture on his face and know none of her own. It was agony to know that she had made the greatest mistake of her life. *The practice of* Kama *with public women is neither enjoined nor prohibited. The object is pleasure only.* Frances had achieved her goal. She had given him pleasure. But at what cost? Dear God! At what cost?

Hooves clattered in the courtyard. Frances rose and glanced outside. The cream silk slid from her hands. Horses, at least twenty. The glitter of weapons. A troop of Polish lancers trotted in through the archway. At their head rode Captain Genet, who had recognized Nigel's Don horse at the hunt. In the lancers' wake came a closed carriage, shuttered against the sun. It halted, the door opened, and a long, thin form emerged. The man stood for a moment, looking about, the brilliant light washing over his angular face and reddish hair. Languid, emotionless, he studied the house and the ramshackle stable block, his dark clothes a marked contrast to the lancers' brilliant uniforms.

Frantic, Frances sought for solutions. Her private grief and confusion meant nothing compared with this! It was up to her to create something plausible, cope with disaster, send him away. For Joseph Fouché, head of the secret police, had come to visit the house at the Rue des Arbres, and brought Captain Genet and his soldiers with him.

With no clear idea of what she should say, Frances opened the front door. Fouché bowed to her, a caustic smile curving his thin lips, just as Nigel and Lance rode fast into the courtyard. Captain Genet's gaze fixed on Nigel's face with open hostility. He drew his sword and signaled his men. Lance's bay reared. The soldiers slammed the heavy oak gates shut across the opening. Lance turned stark white as he struggled to control his mount.

But Nigel laughed, and the Don horse dropped a foreleg in a deep bow to the thin man waiting by the carriage. Sleek dapples rippled on the coat of silver and gold, the mark of a horse from the steppes. Nigel slipped to the ground. The gilt horse stood at his shoulder and blew softly through its nostrils.

"Monsieur Anton?" Fouché, still with that tiny inscrutable smile, spoke softly to Nigel. "An admirable beast! Russian, is he not? Where did you find such an animal?"

Nigel bowed deeply and smiled back. Frances saw with confusion that his amusement seemed genuine. "Let us discuss it. Shall we go inside and take wine?"

There was silence for a moment. Then Fouché shrugged and bowed assent.

Frances stepped aside as Nigel led Fouché and Lance into the house, then she followed the men to the upstairs parlor, her legs trembling. Nigel must have known this might happen. But how could he talk his way out of it this time, how could he escape, with Captain Genet and his lancers waiting in the courtyard below? Had all these weeks of exhaustion finally caught up with him? Had the fatal error of judgment just happened? Or did Nigel want to die, as Lance had feared? And after last night, did he not care if she and Lance died with him?

Fouché took a chair and set his cane on the table beside it. Lance walked stiffly to the window, an angel on judgment day, stern, disapproving, pale. Nigel crossed to the dresser at the side of the room and poured wine.

"Now, my lord duke," he said gently, handing each of them a glass. "I do not believe you came here to discuss horses?"

"I am by nature sanguine, Monsieur Anton, but it is not usually considered wise to play games with me." Fouché took a considered sip of his wine, like a connoisseur, savoring the moment. "I received a message suggesting I visit you. You were not in my service in Russia. Why, I wonder, did you tell Captain Genet that you were? Pray, what is your real purpose in Paris at this delicate moment in her affairs?"

"At this particular moment?" Nigel settled more comfortably into his chair and grinned. "I'm not sure. Perhaps it should be to climb from that window to escape over the rooftops? I must admit it seems a trifle melodramatic, but would it be wise? You must see, my lord duke, that I am bound to ask myself the question."

"To escape from me is impossible, monsieur." Fouché held up his glass to the light. It shone red, like blood. "Raoul Pargout was indeed once in my service. He died, did he not, at your hand? Do you plan assassination again, Monsieur Anton? Is the wine poisoned?"

"I hope not." Nigel raised his own glass in salute, then swallowed a deep draft. "Why would I offer harm to a guest when I am about to make him a proposition?"

Fouché leaned forward with ill-concealed intensity. "And does this proposition come from you, or from the English government? *What business brings you to Paris, Lord Rivaulx?*"

"Trade," said Nigel calmly.

"An English marquess rarely stoops to trade."

Nigel frankly met the gaze of the most dangerous man in Paris. "My trade is in secrets. As you have guessed, my lord duke, I am here to spy for England."

Lance stalked away across the room to stand at one end,

head bowed, his white teeth biting at his lip. Frances pressed her hands together. Had Nigel decided this in some wild, self-destructive moment of despair? And had she contributed to it, amidst the scent and the mirrors? Had she unwittingly impelled them all to destruction?

Fouché grinned, the bloodless grin of a snake. "You have discovered that the Emperor Napoleon left Paris at three this morning. But unless you know his exact destination, the simple fact that Napoleon rides north isn't of much use to Wellington." He set down his wineglass. "So what do you suggest, Lord Rivaulx?"

"I suggest we are in a position to do business together. You know the Emperor's plans, do you not?"

"I do."

"And there is something else I would like to know."

"Name it."

"Catherine de Marbre. Why was she killed?"

Fouché's expression did not change, but his hands moved nervously. "What will you trade me for the information?"

"Guns."

It was said so baldly that Frances wasn't sure she had heard him correctly.

Fouché's fingers touched the corner of his mouth. "A nice touch, Lord Rivaulx. One I appreciate. English rifles?"

"They are in the stable."

"But I have the soldiers. I may take the rifles at my leisure and have you shot as a spy."

Nigel met the unemotional gaze calmly. "I am prepared for it, of course."

Fouché stood up. "Let me see the guns."

Nigel bowed and led him from the room. Lance hurried after them. Frances felt paralyzed with fear. Why should Napoleon's chief of police let any of them escape this with their lives? Yet she made herself stand, and followed the men downstairs. The lancers still stood at attention in the courtyard. Fouché and Nigel disappeared into the stable.

"Did you know about these rifles?" Frances asked Lance.

Lance looked blankly at her. "Of course. You brought them from England yourself, hidden in the bolts of silk. That's why

Rivaulx got rid of the servants, so he could unload the guns in secret.''

It buffeted her like a strong wind. "*Nigel* got rid of the servants?''

Lance ran one hand over his hair. "He frightened them off, clanking chains and such nonsense, then moved the guns and hid them in the straw. Monsieur Martin helped him.''

That night she had found the door ajar. The bolts of silk that had been moved. Had Nigel planned to supply Fouché with rifles all along? Wasn't this treason? Whatever his reasons, it stank of intrigue, of poisonous hidden motives. The man to whom she had given her body only last night, knowing nothing of this. She began to shake.

Fouché emerged from the stable with Nigel at his shoulder. He ordered Captain Genet and his men to load the rifles into the closed carriage. Several minutes later the great gates were pulled open and the lancers swung onto their horses. Fouché hesitated for a moment at the steps of his carriage.

"Lord Rivaulx?''

Nigel bowed. "My lord duke?''

"Napoleon will cross into Belgium over the bridge at Charleroi in three days. He will drive between Wellington and Blücher, thus splitting the English forces from the Prussians. That Don horse will get you to Brussels in plenty of time to warn your Iron Duke. I will send you safe passes to leave Paris tonight.''

"And the lady—Catherine de Marbre?''

Fouché stepped into the carriage and slammed the door. "You did not have enough rifles for that.''

With a clatter of hooves, the soldiers and their master rattled away.

Nigel cursed softly under his breath. Frances had turned to walk back to the house, her back rigid. The crisis had come too soon. *Charleroi*—he must act on this now, without knowing why Catherine had died. Worse, he must act on this now, without time to explain anything to Frances.

Lance was glaring at him. "So this is what the rifles were for—to be used against our own men."

Nigel forced his attention to Lance. "British muskets have been pouring into France. These few cases of rifles will make no difference. In any case, they will not reach the French army. Fouché only wants them as a contingency, a sop to his pride. It makes him feel more clever than Napoleon. It was just a gesture. He has no desire to fall out with England."

"Yet his loyalty is to France!"

"His loyalty is to himself. Fouché has served Napoleon faithfully, but he has also been plotting with England for years. Whoever wins this little conflict in Belgium, Fouché intends to land on the winning side. Now it is up to us to make sure the winner is Wellington."

The open blue gaze seemed guileless, yet once again Nigel sensed that shadow of disquiet. Something had haunted Lance ever since the disasters of the first of June, the Champ de Mars. It was the night Nigel had kissed Frances in front of Fouché, the night he had fought Lance for his life. It wasn't surprising that Lance was upset, but this seemed more than that. What had happened that Nigel didn't know?

Lance glanced away, narrowing his eyes against the sun. "I wish you might have taken me a little more into your confidence."

In pure exasperation, Nigel grinned. "Really? I have been thinking the very same about you." There was no time for any personal issue. He looked at the Don horse, now quietly nuzzling its hay, a horse with enough stamina to handle the long ride to Belgium. Nothing else could be allowed to matter now. Tens of thousands of lives might depend on him. If Lance had problems, he must sort them out for himself.

He glanced back at Lance. "Pray, have Monsieur Martin dismiss all the staff—use any excuse that you like. We must close down the house, then go into Paris and take care of our contacts. No one must question why."

"And Miss Woodard? You have plans for her, I assume?"

Nothing else could be allowed to matter now—not even Frances? "Now, thanks to you, I owe her something more than just courtesy. Yes, I have plans for her."

Lance blushed, the wash of color tingeing his pallor. "I gave her advice, that is all."

"Next time, keep your bloody advice to yourself."

"I was only concerned for you."

His grin turned into derisive laughter. "For me? What about her? For God's sake, go and be useful somewhere. Any more sentimentality, and I shall do you an injury."

∽

Nigel found Frances in the upstairs parlor, silhouetted at the window. As he came in she turned and faced him, the silk rustling about her as she moved.

"What now?" she asked.

He made himself keep to the impersonal. "I shall leave for Brussels tonight and Lance will take a message to the coast. Forewarned about Charleroi, Wellington cannot fail. I have arranged for you to be taken back to England."

"Have you?" There was a frightening hint of sarcasm in it.

"I hope you will wait for me in London, Frances." He gave her a wry smile. "There is unfinished business between us."

She dropped suddenly to a chair and put her hands over her face. "Oh, no," she said. "There is nothing between us now that need concern you."

Nigel was unprepared for his sudden rush of anger. "I have offered to make you my mistress. Isn't that what you want? When it is over, you will have sufficient in jewels and gifts to retire to any refuge you choose. Or are you more ambitious than that? Is a marquess's bed not good enough? Of course, I did promise you a duke—by the time I return, do you intend to have found one?"

Frances dropped her hands. Her lip curled. "Ambitious? Good God! No, I am very sensible of the generosity of your offer, Lord Rivaulx. I am sure you will keep any mistress in adequate style. But I cannot abide your company. I cannot live with a man whose every thought is duplicitous. Why did you let me feel fear over losing the servants? Let me think that an enemy stalked us in the night? How do you think I felt when

Fouché rode into the courtyard? Couldn't you have told me about the guns? You love it all, don't you? The trickery, the intrigue. Do you really think I would agree to spend one more hour with you, if I had any choice in the matter?"

"How could I have told you? Dear God, I myself didn't know until the last minute if it was going to work."

She stood up, her control gone, her eyes blazing. "Can't you understand? I want simplicity. I want straightforwardness. I want to live in a world without scheming and plots. I don't want you, Lord Rivaulx!"

Sunlight gleamed on the gold in her nostril, maddening. Nigel felt his fists clench. "*Simplicity!* Is that what happened last night? I don't know which of us is the greater fool. Damnation! I had to get this information by any means possible. The future of Europe might depend on my taking it to Wellington now."

She turned her face away, the veil caressing her cheek. "You had it planned—didn't you?—from the beginning: that someone would notice the Russian horse and suspect you. Fouché was the only source for what you wanted, whatever the risk, however foul the encounter. That's why you told Captain Genet those lies, why you put yourself in Fouché's way, even kissing me in front of him. So who sent the message that brought Fouché here?"

In spite of what she obviously felt, he told her the truth. "I did. When I discovered Napoleon had left Paris, I had to force events."

Her veil glittered. "Yet Fouché defied you in the end. As does your enemy. We leave Paris without knowing who plots against you, or who betrayed Catherine."

"It doesn't matter. All that counts now is Napoleon's defeat."

It wasn't true. Yet it was impossible to escape this duty, whatever it cost, even if it cost him Frances. After all, what the hell was really left between them now?

She looked up at him with clear defiance. "Dear God, how you have let us all suffer these past weeks."

It was best to end it. His rage was genuine enough, and his humiliation. His body had betrayed him into her hands, and cynically she had used it. Nigel knew well how to wound, how to put derision into his voice. Yet he heard the finality of his words with intense pain.

"Did you think you would be left to starve in Paris? Then suffer no longer, Frances. Return to London and do what you will. Whatever Lord Trent pays you, I will double it—that should be enough to set you up in your own establishment. Find your own damned duke. I have arranged your safe journey to England. Go and pack. When Lance gets back we must all be ready to leave. I don't expect that we shall ever need to speak privately again."

Frances left him. Before she should break down, before all of her hard-won control deserted her. She thought she would carry the image of him in his rage to the grave, an image to meld with that of him swept away by his passion—the tension, the intensity, the vibrant male power. Had she told him the truth? She was afraid of him. Afraid of his brilliance and his mastery. Afraid of his beauty and his courage. Afraid of the power he could wield over her. But that subtlety was also fascinating. Perhaps in the end Catherine had gone willingly to her torment, for with Nigel Arundham death was the only possible escape.

It seemed incredible that the farce they had lived in the Rue des Arbres was over. As Frances packed, the staff stripped the house of everything personal. The remaining bales of silk were bundled into wagons, the furniture draped in dust sheets. The servants were paid off. Monsieur Martin disappeared. By dusk, Frances stood alone in an empty shell.

Deep silence fell as shadows crept across the courtyard. Nigel was working in the stable, currying the Don horse, waiting for Lance to return with the passports. At any minute a carriage would arrive for her. She would get into it alone and be taken to the coast. She would board a boat for England and live out her days as a harlot. As if nothing had changed and nothing had happened since she had first met him at Farnhurst and marked his chest.

∞

She heard the clatter of hooves and the creak of iron-shod wheels as a carriage rolled into the courtyard. Footsteps sounded on the stairs. Nigel strode into the room, pulling on gloves, the dark hair falling wildly over his forehead. He looked at her like a man starving. "Frances! I wish—"

She longed to find any excuse to touch him. There was none, of course. It left audible bitterness in her voice. "Don't, Nigel! There is nothing new. God speed to Belgium!"

"Oh, bloody hell! Lance is here with your carriage and the passports."

He paced impatiently to the window and gazed up at the evening star rising over the roofs of Paris, as if that cold, dead world was all he wanted from life. Frances waited, knowing he had more to say, and stunned if he—the articulate Marquess of Rivaulx—couldn't find the words.

A door banged below, resounding in the empty house. Nigel turned as boots rapped on the stairs. Frances could not take her eyes from his face. Might this be her last glimpse of him? The last time she would feel the force of his feral beauty? He would greet Lance, collect his papers, then sweep away on his Don horse—out of her life. As a last act of munificence, would he as casually sacrifice his own, as Betty had feared? She didn't know if she could bear it.

Frances heard the door open behind her, but she could not take her eyes from Nigel. Like dregs draining from a wine-glass, the color fled his skin. He became white, as white as his collar and shirt, leaving only a bright red spot burning high on each cheekbone. The dark eyes and hair were as startling as a wound in contrast.

"What?" he said, staring at the door. "What have you brought me this time, Gabriel?" His lip curled as he began to quote Coleridge, almost like a chant. " 'Her lips were red, her looks were free, her locks were yellow as gold: her skin was white as leprosy, the nightmare Life-in-Death was she, who thicks man's blood with cold.' " Then he smiled, the empty smile of a man in deep shock. "Of all the persons I might

have expected to see tonight, I did not expect you, sweetheart.''

Frances turned. Lance stood in the doorway, his yellow
head tipped back, his skin damp with an almost unearthly pallor. He met Nigel's gaze with an odd mix of defiance and
sorrow, like a child who has broken something.

Beside him, her gloved fingertips resting lightly on his
sleeve, stood a woman. As Nigel spoke she walked into the
room and stopped before him.

''*Pas jaune,* Nigel,'' she said with the pure accent of Paris.
Not yellow.

She dropped back the hood of her cloak and revealed hair
the color of midnight.

Frances had never seen her before.

Sixteen

NIGEL SPOKE DIRECTLY to Lance, looking straight past the slender figure with the midnight hair, his voice like a lash. "And you wished that I might have taken you a little more into *my* confidence? What a lovely turn of mind!"

Lance tilted his chin a little higher, as if pinned in the doorway. "I thought—" He broke off and wrung his hand over his face. "I couldn't, Nigel, I couldn't—"

Was Nigel on the edge of losing control? Frances saw it with fear, but not for herself or the others, only for him. He seemed almost blind, throwing up words in a wall of defense as he refused to acknowledge the woman at his elbow. "If you have something you wish to articulate, Lance, just say it. I doubt seriously if any of the thoughts now rambling about in your infinitely inventive brain will give me the vapors."

His eyes burning in his face, Lance said nothing, though he turned his face aside.

The dark-haired woman touched Nigel's sleeve. "Ah, *mon cher*! Don't! Don't! It is not Lance's fault. I cannot bear this. I cannot bear what we have done."

Nigel turned to her at last, his ferocity undimmed. "No, my dear. Nor I. But what creatures we are for dramatic entrances, aren't we? And exits?"

Dropping as if struck, the woman took a chair. The candlelight was swallowed in her black hair. She was lovely. Her skin was fine and clear, delicate as a china figurine's, with a high, bright blush to her cheeks and lips. Her dark eyes swam with moisture.

Slowly she pulled off her gloves. Then she looked up at Nigel with that sparkling, black diamond gaze. "Forgive me, my love. Forgive me this one thing. I wouldn't let Lance tell you. I had to do it myself, and I hadn't the nerve for—oh, so long! I know it was wicked, but you can't know how I have longed—" She held out her naked hand. Rings trembled, sparking fire, as she caught his fingers. "Ah, come! Come, Nigel! Forgive me, or I shall die."

With his other hand, Nigel reached for the black curl at her ear, a lover's caress. "I liked it better red, *chérie*."

Turning her face, she pressed her lips to the inside of his wrist. "It is only dye. It washes out."

He stood still for a moment, allowing her to kiss his hand. At last she took it in both of hers and rubbed the back against her temple. She was weeping openly now.

Nigel looked over her bent head at Lance, frozen in the doorway, biting his lip. "How long, Lance? How long have you known?"

Lance swallowed. He was watching the woman's tears dropping freely onto her rich skirt. "Since the night after the Champ de Mars, the first of June—"

Frances knew Nigel would offer no mercy. She was right.

"—when you thought the world would be a better place without me? Perhaps it would have been more appropriate if you had succeeded." Nigel looked back at the dark-haired woman and pulled away his hand. She dropped her face in both palms, leaning into his thigh, sobbing against his coat.

Frances knew who she was. There was no one else it could be. The knowledge blossomed with a scintillating inevitability, as if this were the only possible outcome. Who else could move Nigel so deeply, or send him into such obvious shock? Who else had he once loved enough to die for?

I liked it better red. Her hair had been a flame. *It came to her waist, shining like red fire in the sun.* The name resounded in her head like a tocsin: *Catherine, Catherine, Catherine.*

∞

Nigel fought for equilibrium. Catherine was not dead. *Catherine was not dead!* She was as beautiful as he remembered. Irritatingly, he wondered about something completely unimportant: *Had the red been dyed, too? What was her natural color, for God's sake?* Her shoulders shook against his thigh, flooding him with memories. *Why? Why?* Had all his torment been for nothing? *For three days, with a knife*—it had never happened! Was none of it true, then? And worse! *Had he been chasing a chimera all this time?*

He moved her hands and turned her face up to his, making his voice gentle. "What happened, Katerina?"

She smiled through her tears—a clear, inviting smile, devoid of guile, begging his trust. "I went to the rendezvous that day as we had discussed. The police were waiting for me. They had received a message. They said you had sent it. I could not believe them, Nigel! But you left Paris. It broke my heart. How could you have gone away? How could you have abandoned me like that?"

"Lance has not told you?"

Nigel heard the dry humor in it. In spite of what he suspected, he was repelled by his own flippancy. He was painfully aware of Frances, standing like a statue at the side of the room. Dear God, if only he could have sent her away before this! His thoughts were running rapidly now, diving into the enormity of it, searching for what it really meant and coming up with the only possible answer. It filled him with fury. But he could not be distracted, not for a moment—even if Frances should misunderstand, even if she should forever despise him. If fate decreed that he be dogged by absurdity, then so be it.

"Catherine, how could he have known?" Lance's agony was clear in his voice. "We thought they had killed you."

"And why not, Katerina?" asked Nigel. "Why didn't they?"

A charming blush stained her cheeks. Her eyes became brilliant. "Bonaparte himself interceded for my life and sent me safely from France. I went back to Russia. You cannot blame me for that. But I should never have doubted you. Wyndham was the traitor, wasn't he?''

Nigel saw the truth clearly. He concentrated on forcing himself to accept this new reality. "But Wyndham has disappeared, and you are in Paris again—to wreak what mayhem you may?''

Catherine stiffened and glanced down, the smallest betrayal, before her eyes once again met his. "How can you? How can you be so cruel! I have loved you. I have loved you for all these years.''

"Then why?'' he asked quietly. "Why have you now taken Lance into your bed?''

⚭

Frances folded onto a chair. The hard back bit into her spine. The wooden arms callously enclosed her. Lost in the void, she put up both hands and pulled her veil over her face—from pure cowardice, because courage abandoned her, because pride forbade that Nigel should see that she was flayed to the bone and could no longer hold back tears.

Why have you now taken Lance into your bed?

Lance jerked as if struck. "Dear God! What the devil do you want, Rivaulx? Do you think the usual rules should apply to Catherine? It was *you* who said they could not! Dear God! Dear God! It is *you* she loves! Yet you will make her pay. You will make her crawl, begging to you? She wouldn't humble herself like this to any other man!''

"Would she not?'' Nigel asked softly. "Then Princess Katerina did not humble herself when she took Bonaparte for her lover on the retreat from Moscow?''

Lance paled. Frances saw his mouth move, but he said nothing aloud.

Catherine stood up and grasped Nigel's arms. "Are you jealous—of Napoleon? That little man? Don't be! Be glad that he saved me for you.''

Nigel seemed relaxed, infinitely casual, as he allowed her hands to sink into his jacket. "And Lance? I am right, am I not?''

"Does it matter?" said Lance dully. "There is only one great love in a lifetime, isn't there? The kind that is yours and Catherine's. I shan't stand in the way of it."

Frances longed to leave, but the chair held her imprisoned as her heart skittered and leaped.

Catherine reached up and took Nigel's face in both palms. "Lance loves you as I do. He understands."

Nigel gently removed her hands, but his irony was undimmed. "What a lovely proposition—a *ménage à trois*?"

Frances barely heard Lance stride across the room to her. He took her by the hands and dragged her out of her chair. The veil fell back and she met his eyes. Lance seemed frantic, an angel fallen, facing doom. "Miss Woodard! Frances! Don't you see? Rivaulx feels trapped because of us! For God's sake, you are nothing to him, and I am nothing in this. Come with me! Let him and Catherine be together. There is nothing else, nothing else we can do for him now."

"By God, what a noble sacrifice!" Nigel's voice vibrated clear and cold. "Leave Frances bloody well out of this, Lance! Haven't you interfered enough? What the *hell* do you think you understand? You send Frances to my bed as if it is nothing, but you wallow in sentiment over Catherine. What the devil do you think you are playing at?"

"So this Indian-trained harlot warmed your bed?" Catherine had dropped back to her seat. She smiled up at Nigel, a smile offering depths of sophisticated tolerance. "Why not? We are not children. But how can you claim to be jealous of me? I am not jealous of you. We have both sinned. It changes nothing. Give me your loyalty again, my love." She leaned forward, intensely seductive. "Come with me now and we shall carve empires."

"I do not claim jealousy," Nigel replied flatly. "I claim nothing. This whole absurd, nasty little melodrama was not of my making. And in case everyone else has forgotten, I have not: Lance and I have urgent duties to England. The future of Europe hangs in the balance. Don't you think that is a little more important than all this bloody inappropriate emotion?"

As if brushing them all aside, Nigel strode toward the door, but Catherine ran to block him, catching at his sleeve. "No,

Nigel. Not yet. Tell me now! I must know before you leave.''

He stopped and stared down at her, his voice sweet with sarcasm. "Apart from everything else, we had a bargain. You have broken it."

Lance started forward, but Catherine raised a hand, stopping him. "Nigel is right, *mon cher*. You don't understand. Go down to the others. Tell Pierre to do as I asked." As Lance hesitated Catherine calmly went to him and pulled him into her arms. The lids dropped over the angel blue eyes as she kissed him passionately on the mouth. "Go," she said. "It is all right."

Without another glance at Nigel or Frances, Lance left the room.

Catherine closed the door and leaned back against it. "Will you kill me in order to fulfill your precious duty, Nigel? For I shall not step aside. Tell me this: Do you deny that you love me?"

He looked down into her upturned face as if faintly amused. "I deny that I have *ever* loved you. After all, you have hated me since we met, that night in Arbat Street, and I would not do your bidding."

The atmosphere changed, shifted—as if with the echo of the thunder ball the heavens would open and bring the deluge. With a fierce movement Frances brushed away her tears, swallowing the burning pain in her throat, the taste of ashes in her mouth.

Catherine reached up once again and traced his lip with her finger. "But you cannot deny passion! We can have it all back, beloved, and the world with it. If I can forgive you, can't you forgive me?" Her hand slipped behind his head and she pulled his mouth down to hers.

In one movement, Nigel broke free. Every word bit clear and cold. "Oh, no, sweetheart. Times change. Whatever price you want this time for a kiss from me, I'm not prepared to pay it."

A flush of angry red turned Catherine's cheeks scarlet. Her lips opened in a snarl. "Then be damned!"

∽

Nigel stalked back to the window. He didn't know how far he could trust himself, but he was sure it was too late—that it had been too late when Lance and Catherine first arrived. Why had he not seen this? He had failed, utterly! The one thing he had not allowed for had happened: *Catherine lived.* It explained everything—the gaps, the times and places that couldn't be reconciled, the impossibility of doubting the others. What had he said to Wyndham? *Who else knew both our secrets in Russia and the work that we did in France? I am hoping some stranger has found a way to penetrate our little group.* It was not a stranger. It was one of them. Catherine.

One glance into the courtyard confirmed what he suspected. Even if he weren't responsible for Frances, he could not have escaped. Several men, armed, were entering the house. Except for the small knife in his boot, he was unarmed. His pistols and sword were strapped to the saddle of the Don horse. And Frances—Frances was in mortal danger because of him.

"I shall not get to Wellington, shall I?" he asked quietly. "Even if I were to break your lovely neck, my dear Catherine, my vital information will stay here in Paris. Yet it is not to be a *ménage à trois,* after all. There are to be four of us— including Napoleon."

"How did you guess?" said Catherine.

There was a pistol in her hand. She held it steady, pointed directly at Frances, the one life—as Catherine knew perfectly well—that he would not risk.

He dropped to the sofa and spread his arms along the back, careful to show nothing but a careless, ironic humor. "Because there is no one else, my dear. All this time I have let myself be driven to distraction by facts that refused to make sense. We were betrayed in Moscow; we were betrayed in Paris. It could have been any one of us. But no one could have delivered you to Fouché, unless you informed him yourself. Did you plant all those papers in Donnington's rooms? The evidence of his treachery and then mine, that delicious account of your own torture and death? Is that why poor Donnington had to die? Were you a double agent from the beginning?"

She laughed, but she did not look away from Frances. The pistol did not waver. "I work for no one but Napoleon, Nigel.

Yes, the great man I first met many years ago in Paris, and took for my lover again after Moscow burned. He is the genius of our age, the man who brings us the future.''

Frances sat pinned in her chair, her wide blue eyes locked on Catherine's face. She seemed very calm, yet Nigel knew her terror—he could feel it in his bones. Whatever the outcome of this, he was damned if he would let that brave soul die for his folly!

"And is the Emperor a good lover?" he asked dryly.

Catherine gave him a seductive glance, under her lashes. "Better than Wyndham, not as good as you. Wyndham was my agent in England. He poisoned you."

It hurt. "So you killed him, too, Katerina?"

She shrugged. "He is dead. I have a proposition for you."

"I am to be allowed choices?"

Her eyes stayed fixed on Frances. The pistol remained steady. "The world is being remade. This Wellington—what is he? The sepoy general! He will be forgotten, his name wiped out. But Napoleon Bonaparte straddles our age like a colossus."

He kept his voice light, tipping back his head, as if the threat to Frances meant nothing. "Yet I believe the original in Rhodes collapsed under its own weight. Don't waste your breath, Katerina. I shall not come to your side in this."

There was noise on the stair. "I will give you a week to change your mind."

"How very generous! You will not dispatch me here and now?"

Catherine lowered the pistol and went to the door. "Your mind is too good to waste. That is the truth. Napoleon knows it. Fouché knows it. When the Allied armies are crushed and England destroyed, you will see the sense of making your contribution without all these outdated loyalties. You will come to our side, Nigel, because there will not be any other."

Nigel carefully judged the distance and the timing—could he reach his knife before Catherine reacted? Frances might well die first!

He shrugged. "So I will not ride to Belgium? I trust Lance will take care of my Don horse?"

The door had opened.

"Why should I take your horse?" asked Lance. "Because you won't forgive Catherine? You won't swallow that bloody pride and admit that you love her?"

The pistol still lay ready in Catherine's hand. Nigel wondered briefly quite how little Lance knew. "No, Lance, sadly I will not."

Lance strode up to him. "Why not? Why not?"

Nigel met the blue gaze with absolute sincerity. "For the sake of England, if for nothing else. Catherine betrayed us, Lance, in Moscow and Paris. You heard her admit that Napoleon was her lover. She has plotted all this. She has killed Dominic Wyndham."

But Lance spun away. "Wyndham! He was a bloody traitor! Catherine has done only what she has had to do."

"Ah, Lance! I always knew you had execrable morals, but I hoped that you honored your friends. What about pretty Miss March? You have a choice: Catherine or everything you have ever loved. Which is it to be?"

Lance dropped his head against the wall. His eyes closed. "You don't understand! I don't matter. You are the only man with the gifts to change history. Yet you betrayed Catherine and your country—for what? Passion? I could understand that. Yet she offers you redemption now. Chivalry alone demands you accept it. Why do you refuse her? Is it Frances, after all? Is Frances a greater passion? Are you in love with her?"

Frances sat motionless, an easy target in her chair. Catherine still held the pistol in her hand. Her fingers tightened very slightly on the grip. Nigel forced into his voice all the coldness he could muster. "Dear God! Why the devil should I give a damn about either of them. One woman is much the same as another in the dark."

Catherine laughed.

Lance flushed deep red. "Then stay here and rot! And yes, I will take the Don horse, for I doubt that you give a damn about him either!"

There were five men, charmingly arrayed with weapons, now waiting in the doorway. Lance thrust between them. His footsteps ran rapidly down the stairs. Catherine picked up her

gloves and slapped Nigel once across the face before she followed him.

The men advanced. They were all grinning. Even with his
knife and his nasty skills, Nigel knew that he had no chance
at all. So what sheer perversity made him fight them anyway,
one against five, and let it be proved?

∞

Something rustled. Someone was bathing his jaw with cold
water. Nigel reached up with unerring instinct and grasped.
The wrist was slender, fine-boned, a woman's. He opened his
eyes.

"You are only bruised," Frances said. "Remarkably, your
face is untouched. Catherine must have told them you were
not to be too seriously harmed."

She leaned over him, pressing the cool, damp cloth to his
jaw once again. Dear God, she was beautiful! There must be
a lamp lit somewhere, for light rimmed her hair like a halo.
She had not been harmed! Thank God! Thank God!

Nigel moved his lips carefully. His teeth were all there,
though he was a little sore under the jaw and every breath
burned like a brand. "How considerate of her! Frances, I'm
sorry."

He wanted to press his mouth to hers and drink her like
wine, instead he could only mumble more empty apologies.

"Oh, I'm sorry, too," she said. "Three of those men had
to carry the other two out of the room."

Everything seemed to be working, though movement was
excruciating. There was a certain skill involved in beating a
man to inflict maximum pain without doing him permanent
damage. Catherine's henchmen had been very skilled. "They
have left now?"

"The house seems to be empty, but I can't be sure. We are
locked in the kitchen in the cellar. There are no windows, only
a high grating above the shelves over there. It's just that the
stone walls are so ancient, of course, but it feels as if this
room is hewn out of solid rock."

"Equally impregnable, I'm sure," he said with a grin.

"Equally impregnable." Frances smiled back.

Did she have infinite forbearance, his damsel of the dulcimer? Yet it wasn't personal, was it? Only a universal compassion.

He had been dumped on a long kitchen table. A cloth had been folded beneath his head. Frances must have done that. Someone else had removed his coat, none too gently, guessing from the state of his shirt. Perhaps one of them thought he had money or messages concealed in the seams? *Bloody fool!* No, that was him, wasn't it? He had been stupid, incompetent, a grotesque fool to the end. He glanced about at the room, as secure as a medieval dungeon.

It was far too late now for heroics, so with gratitude Nigel lay where he was and allowed Frances to minister to him. The stone arches of the vaulted ceiling stretched over his head. Red light danced and wavered. The room was warm, so there must be a fire, though the yellow glow of the lamp was closer. Frances moved quietly. He heard the clink of her basin and the rustle of her robes. Her voice sounded disembodied, softly echoing in the stone spaces. "Why didn't you admit what Catherine was really like?"

Nigel closed his eyes and savored it. "Those words soothe like the balm of Gilead—'behold, they come from Gilead with their camels bearing spicery and balm and myrrh.' I don't deserve your faith. Thank you, Frances."

"My *faith*? If you had made one mistake, she would have killed me."

"Can you forgive what I had to say? If I had not, I think she might have fired. I am glad you saw through her. 'Babylon is suddenly fallen and destroyed: howl for her.' It has been bloody exhausting maintaining that Catherine was a saint."

He didn't know if she accepted the apology. She sounded distant, cool. "Why did you?"

"Because of Lance. It seemed cruel to shatter his ideals. How shortsighted that was! Of course, I thought she was dead, so it didn't matter."

There was the sharp sound of water rushing from a pump, and the creak of the handle as Frances worked it. "Has Lance been a traitor all along?"

"He is barely aware that he is a traitor now. Lance hates Napoleon. At the Champ de Mars he tried to assassinate him."

She drew in a sharp breath before she came back to him, her slippers soft on the stone floor. "Lance tried to kill Napoleon?"

In the lamplight her skin was golden, as if lit from within. Luminous Frances! Nigel grinned, vaguely aware that he must look like the village idiot to her. "His chivalrous instincts convinced him the Emperor must die. I stopped him. Napoleon's demise would do nothing but plunge France into a bloodbath."

He saw her recoil—it was yet another thing he hadn't told her, another example of his damned duplicity. "So that was what you made him swear never to do again? Oh, God! Now it makes sense."

Could he make her understand? "Lance has always been so bloody vulnerable to his romantic impulses. Sometimes it's been like trying to carry Sir Galahad away from the Holy Grail. Yet amid all that insufferable sanctity there is something very fine in him. He felt such a fierce, pure passion for his ideals! Grotesquely, he thinks women generally incapable of evil. But when you try to take moral responsibility for another person, I suppose it never works."

She peeled up his shirt and laid the cool cloth over his bruised ribs. "And that's what you tried to do for him—take moral responsibility?"

Nigel watched her face, knowing the cloth would come away bloody, but Frances did not flinch.

"Not exactly. I doubt if I could have changed his mind, but I didn't want Catherine to do it either. She can have . . . cruel tastes. I didn't want her besmirching his integrity, or corrupting him in her bed. It was bloody presumptuous of me, but so much decency is destroyed by war. Couldn't Lance at least return to Miss March with his ideals intact?"

Frances wrung out the cloth, then wiped carefully at the abrasions on his chest. "Catherine wanted Lance as a lover?"

"Oh, yes. Precisely because he believed in chastity. She thought he looked like an angel and that his seduction would be an affront to God. It revolted me. After the retreat from

Moscow, when we were all together in this house, I made her swear she would not do it.''

The soft, precise touch of her hands on his body stopped. ''And her price?''

''She agreed to leave him alone if I stayed faithful to her instead. She only wanted him as a diversion—to break and toss aside. It seemed little enough to save him if I could. As it turned out, I should have let Lance defend his own honor.''

''Yet he loves you. Isn't there hope for him in that?''

''Now I have at last proved that his idol has feet of clay? Dear God, I've been trying for years, but he isn't likely to forgive me in a hurry. Besides, Catherine has him enthralled, like Circe. She told me once that at least three men had taken their own lives because of her. She was proud of it. It will amuse her to destroy him.''

He looked up at the pure line of her jaw. She dipped the cloth in her basin calmly, but she could not hide the tension in her voice. ''Yet you and she were lovers for so long!''

He felt savage, full of rage. How deep was her abhorrence? For he owed her the truth now, whatever the risk. ''Lance was my reason at first. Later, it became something quite different. As for Catherine, I was a unique kind of challenge—another disciple of the devil, already wedded to sensation. It became in the end a fierce battle of wills. I was as caught in it as she was. There were times when she would exact some small retaliation, and because of Lance—'' Nigel closed his eyes, hiding his distress with a practiced gloss of irony, yet the savagery was there like a tiger in the dark. ''Catherine was my lover because I wished it. For God's sake, don't think it was any noble sacrifice!''

∞

Frances walked blindly back to the sink, almost dropping the basin so that it clattered against the stone. *In love? I became obsessed. For the first time in my life I was tempted to tell duty to go to the devil.* And she had thought to offer him her trained sensuality—this man who had explored the depths of carnality with a woman as devious as he! He was so sure of his own strength and his own corruption. Had Catherine broken him in the end, after all?

"Surely Lance must realize it's vital to get your information to Wellington?"

She heard Nigel sit up, and knew he winced. "I doubt it. Catherine has obviously convinced him that I intend to betray England. He was suspicious enough of my dealings with Fouché—machinations far too subtle for his artless worldview. By the time he realizes he is wrong, it will be too late."

There was a stool by the pump. Frances sank onto it and leaned her head against the cold stone of the sink. She had no more courage. "And Wyndham? What was his role?"

"Wyndham knew perfectly well what she was—except for the key issue: that she betrayed us to France all along. Catherine must have arranged the fire and killed him. Wyndham was never a traitor. He was my friend."

Could he, even now, have faith in friendship? Light danced over the stone walls, glancing off copper pans and rows of earthenware. Frances had never been into this cavernous kitchen before. She had taken the meals for granted, appearing as if by magic on the table upstairs. "Then who killed Donnington?"

"Catherine's agent, I imagine. I don't know his identity."

"And Fouché—can you trust him?"

"I trust the information about Charleroi. Yet the secret police knew that Catherine was alive all along, and Fouché deliberately chose not to tell me." There was a hard intaken breath. "Damnation!"

Frances glanced up. Nigel had swung his legs off the table and was leaning back against it, one hand pressed to his side. His shirt hung about him, stained with blood and dirt. "Did they break a rib?" she asked.

He shook his head and grinned. "More whimsical than that. It's nothing I don't deserve, but I won't be much use for a while."

Frances looked away. She knew what the men had done. She had seen it—that vicious blow where he was most vulnerable. "Once I thought people were simple, some heroes, some villains—the way Dutch children believe Saint Nicholas judges them good or naughty, then gives the gifts they deserve.''

He laughed, though it made him gasp with pain. ''It's a fine line between the sheep and the goats, isn't it? And a cruel belief that makes rich children good, and poor children wicked. Nothing about this bloody war has been simple. Napoleon is not entirely wrong. England's motives are not entirely pure. But if we want peace for Europe, this time we must win decisively.''

She felt a strong anguish, a longing for that innocent world of childhood, however unfair it might be. ''Then what are we left with?''

''Our own souls, I suppose, and whether we act from kindness or cruelty. Yet whatever our motives, we can never be sure of the final outcome. Only the line soldier clearly knows his duty. Men with real power must constantly juggle compromise and expediency. Sometimes it is necessary to deal with men as foul as Fouché, though it leaves a permanent stain on the soul. There is always a price to pay. What do we do if even the right path is cruel? What if our ideals lead us inexorably to war, the single greatest crime against mankind? Wellington has been known to break down after a battle and weep, but there is no better general.''

Frances met his gaze, dark depths filled with subtleties and complexity. He was as beautiful and as unreachable as a night sky. Yet he did not seem defeated. With a small shock she realized that he was talking to her completely openly for perhaps the first time.

''Can Wellington vanquish Napoleon without knowing about Charleroi?''

Nigel grinned and the shadows seemed to flee. ''I hope the Iron Duke *will* know. I sent him the message hours ago.''

Frances sat stunned for a moment. ''What? I don't understand.''

''I have a long-established courier network, Frances. That is how I've been sending information to Belgium all along. Monsieur Martin has been my contact. I got rid of our servants not only to hide the guns, but also to have an excuse to get

Martin into the house. This message about Charleroi is so vital I knew I must also go myself, but I never quite trusted Fouché's willingness to let me leave Paris. Of course, now I know what he was hiding from me—Catherine.''

Though her instincts warned her away, at some deeper level she longed to understand him. "If you never loved Catherine, why did you come to Paris?"

He was now walking purposefully around the room, looking up at the high iron grating, testing the doors. He limped a little, a wounded jungle animal on the prowl.

"Because of what happened at Farnhurst. Because someone we trusted was working against Britain. Because I believed those accounts in poor Donnington's papers about how Catherine died.'' He stopped, idly picking up a bowl and setting it down again. "I would not wish what I read there on any living soul.''

Frances remembered him, stark with distress—*I'm going to take out a fast horse, that is all*. "Yes, I can see that.''

Nigel took up a candle, lighting it at the fire. He walked restlessly to another door at the end of the kitchen. After working the handle a few times, he wrenched it open. Frances stood up in surprise as he spoke to her over his shoulder, his voice still wry. "Whatever I felt about Catherine, I would have tried to rescue her from the Quai Voltaire. That is the one thing I have found hard to forgive Lance—that he intervened and got me out of Paris. Of course, he had no idea he was playing directly into her hands.''

Frances tried to imagine that world and the relationships it had engendered. She had always thought that working together as spies would bring people closer together. It had not. Instead the constant atmosphere of secrecy and mistrust had poisoned them all. As it had this time?

His voice was muffled now. With a sudden hint of amusement, he spoke again. "Do you realize there is a pantry and a linen closet in here? The door was not locked, just stuck a little.''

"Is there a way out?''

She walked quickly across the room, only to almost bump

into him as he came back into the kitchen, grinning.

"No," he said. "Something better. There are multitudes of feather pillows and bolsters. Certainly enough linen to make us a bed."

Seventeen

∞

SHE STEPPED BACK, but he caught her by the hand. "The world must wag on without us for a while, Frances, so this is all that remains—the subject we have not yet touched upon: you and me."

"There is nothing to say," she replied, pulling away.

Nigel let her go and leaned one shoulder against the jamb. "I think there is a great deal to say. But I am also aware of being very hungry, and there is food in that pantry. Can we make ourselves a meal, do you think?"

Frances followed him as he turned and disappeared. There was a tiny corridor. On the left a door opened into a space lined with marble shelves. There was a strong smell of onions. He thrust the candle into her hand. "You'd be amazed at my hidden talents. I can fix a very passable rabbit over a campfire."

Frances moved the candle to give him light as Nigel began rummaging about. "The last time I saw you eat rabbit was at Farnhurst the day you were poisoned. Is there rabbit?"

"No, only oatmeal. Like the poor woman of Zarephath, 'I have not a cake, but a handful of meal in a barrel.' Ah, we also have potatoes and onions and plenty of garlic."

"*Allium sativum,*" said Frances.

He straightened, clutching some vegetables. "I suspected

your knowledge about plants was entirely useless. Can you cook an onion?''

''I don't think so.''

''I thought cooking was one of the sixty-four arts?''

She hesitated. ''Yes, but—''

He raised a brow, the candlelight dancing over the planes of his face. There was something dangerous in his expression. ''You learned a great deal of pretty theory, and never learned how to cook onions? Bring some meal. We shall eat like kings upon potato soup and unleavened bread.''

Frances filled a bowl with oatmeal and carried it back to the kitchen. Nigel had rolled up his torn sleeves and was washing his hands at the sink.

She felt apologetic, almost guilty. Every woman knew the rudiments of plain cooking—except her! ''I went to India too soon to learn anything useful, and everything there was done by servants.''

Nigel set the onions on a chopping block and attacked them with a knife. ''Though you are an expert on spices and can no doubt determine every ingredient in a curry once it is prepared. See if you can find some oil.''

She let him direct her, stirring the chopped onion and garlic with the oil in a pan, adding potatoes, water, and salt. Nigel sprinkled in dried chervil and tarragon from some hanging bunches of herbs in the pantry. Then he took the oatmeal and kneaded it together with a little oil and water to make flat cakes that he set to brown on a griddle.

''That smells wonderful,'' said Frances, surprised.

'' 'And they called the name thereof Manna, and it was like coriander seed, white, and the taste of it was like wafers made with honey.' Or so is any food to a man starving in a desert. Though the making of these was taught me by a Highlander named Grant.'' He piled the oatcakes in a basket with a clean cloth, then turned and held one out to her.

Frances nibbled at the edge. It was hot, nutty. ''Thank you. It's good.''

A light menace stirred in his eyes. Like the sheen on a moonlit pond, silver and black, humor danced with danger—

the mischief of a god, not a child. "And what will you give me in exchange?"

The cake broke in her fingers. "What do you mean?"

He seemed invincible. No longer lame, but undamaged and deadly. "Tell me, Frances: How many ways are there to kiss a man?"

The soup bubbled, rattling the lid of the pot. Her little cake crumbled to the floor. She felt petrified where she stood.

He stepped closer. "At Farnhurst we agreed that Englishmen do not know how to kiss. Very well, I will teach you to cook. You will teach me to kiss."

"Now?"

"Now, Frances."

"Because I am a harlot?"

"If that is all you offer!" He caught her to him. "Tell me!"

"There are three kinds to begin with: *nimittaka, sphuritaka, ghattitaka.*"

His mouth was only inches from her own. "Explain them."

"*Nimittaka* is just a nominal kiss. The girl—" She swallowed hard.

"Go on!"

"The girl touches her lover's mouth, but does not herself do anything."

His breath scalded her cheek as he touched his mouth lightly to the corner of hers. "And the next?"

"*Sphuritaka* is the throbbing kiss." The length of his body pressed against her, lithe and lovely. "She wishes to touch his lip, as it is pressed into her mouth, and moves her lower lip only."

His lips touched hers again, a little deeper. "And the next?"

"*Ghattitaka*—she closes her eyes and covers his with her hands, then she touches her lover's lip with her tongue."

"Like this?" he said, lifting her hands.

It was sweet, like honey wafers in the desert. As she held him blind he teased her lips, tempting softly until she moaned and opened her mouth to him. *Ghattitaka*—a lover's tongue to the tender lip. Yet he led her deeper and deeper, forcing her to follow, until her knees buckled. Dropping her fingers from his face, she clung to him, kissing, kissing. Tears stung, hurting her throat, as her mouth swelled and her blood caught fire.

"And what comes after that?" he asked at last against her lips, still savage, without mercy.

"Don't!" She begged, knowing she had no right to ask.

He held her by both wrists and made her step back. "Why not? Because all your sixty-four arts are just an elaborate construction of theory, Frances, like your cooking?"

He forced her back inexorably. She stumbled as her legs hit a low bench, and she sat down. Still gripping her hands, he knelt before her so their eyes were level.

"You will tell me, Frances. What mercy do you expect from me, when you showed me none? Was it all just rote learning—your scent and your flowers—your mirrors that drowned me, as if in a delirium I made love to a thousand women—your bites and your kisses—the devastating things that you did to my body? Was it just heroism? Had any man ever known you?" His anger darted like lightning, rending from seething black clouds. "For God's sake, tell me: *Were you a virgin?*"

She turned her head aside, trying to escape that devouring gaze. "You are the rake. What do you think?"

His lip curled in fury. "How the devil would I know? Even in the days of my worst excesses, virgins were never my style. Dammit to hell! Didn't Lance think to ask before he sent you to my bed?"

She bit her lip, determined not to weep. "You will kill him?"

He stood up, towering over her like an avenging angel, dark with derision. "*Lance?* For God's sake, why? It is painfully obvious that Catherine put him up to it, to give herself yet another weapon against me. And it worked. Dear God, it worked. If I should kill anyone for this, it is Katerina of Russia. Tell me the truth, Frances!"

"Does it matter?" she asked through the betraying tears. "Does it matter? It was wrong, wrong. I wish I had not!"

∞

Nigel knew himself transfixed. It was as if something broke, deep in his heart. The anger died away like a fire robbed of air, leaving nothing but ash. He dropped onto the bench as her tears came, holding her while she sobbed into his torn shirt. He had taken a virgin, without mercy or gentleness—and in his heart of hearts he had suspected it from the beginning. He had known, and ignored the knowledge.

She had been an English schoolgirl, brutally orphaned by bandits and alone among strangers. She had been told and shown things that would shock the most dissolute roué, violating her innocence. She had been taught the sensual wisdom of the ages, but she had not known it in herself, with her body—until she sacrificed herself for him. She had been afraid. As she captured him with flowers she had been afraid. No wonder she had been left behind, unable to respond. Dear God! Dear God! Had Catherine known how exquisite a revenge this would be?

When he spoke again, offering her a handkerchief, he let the words fall slowly, infinitely gentle in the face of his own despair. For surely now it was too late?

"Come," he said. "You are right. It doesn't matter a tinker's damn. Let's have soup."

∞

Frances lay in her nest of pillows watching the silver-pink dawn barred across the ceiling. Nigel slept in a similar pile on the opposite side of the stove. The bedding and clean linen he had shown her, in that second little room off the pantry corridor, included aprons and tablecloths and a stack of white shirts. He had taken off the bloodied remains of his own shirt and burned them. At times in the night he had groaned aloud, and once he had shouted something, fast and unintelligible, without waking. Only Frances lay awake through the long night hours and waited for a morning that seemed destined never to come.

She felt as alone as she ever had in her life. It had been such a long journey—lost at sea with the wind wailing—cold wind blowing through her thin cloak, the darkness howling about her, salt spume towering—and no land in sight. Was there no berth for her? No safe harbor? Was she to be tossed

on this black sea forever, until the cold waves took her and
made coral from her bones?

*I don't know Frances Woodard. Neither do you, do you?
You have lost yourself with no idea how to find the way back.*

What was she? What had she ever been? An ordinary English child, not particularly pretty, all bones and angles, like
a foal. She had played by herself in an infinite meadow of tall
grasses and buttercups, weaving fanciful tales. Prince Charming. Romeo. Mr. Edward Merton, with his laughing eyes, who
had come to stay in the village one summer. He had smiled
at her—shy, just fourteen—in church, until she had imagined
a complete three-tiered fancy, but he had gone away with Miss
Wright and married her. At seventeen, Michael Penshaw, who
had told her she was pretty and tried to kiss her, except that
she giggled when his earnest blond mustache tickled her lip.
The young officers in India, where she had danced away a
season before that fatal trip into the mountains.

She had never questioned—never questioned her fate. When
they came back to England for her official London Season,
she would fall in love. In snow-white innocence she would go
to the altar with a sensible young man approved by her father.
With her eyes closed she would accept her duty to her husband, and bear his children.

Now she knew how *not* to bear children. Her innocence had
been stripped away. No sensible young man would ever want
her. She was ruined. Yet she could not even be a successful
courtesan. Nothing was left. Nothing. She had tried for so
long, so hard, to be brave. But she had fallen in love, and he
was not Prince Charming, or Romeo, or an affable young officer, but a man full of brilliance and duplicity. Oh, dear God!
Why must it hurt so much?

Frances pushed back the covers and sat up. She crossed her
legs and closed her eyes, inviting the steady breath, listening
for the silence. Instead the images crowded in, like monkeys
pouring off a temple roof, screaming. She curled back into the
pillows and pulled a comforter over her head.

☙

"Breakfast," said Nigel.

He had heated water. They had each washed and dressed, Nigel waiting in the pantry while Frances bathed. He was no longer limping. How absurd that he should offer to honor her modesty, and yet she had been grateful. He had made little jokes about it, as if she were an old comrade, as if he didn't know that he had been fooled, as if nothing need lie between them but humor.

They had found dried mint for tea, and Nigel made porridge. Frances gazed at the smooth mass of cereal in her bowl and bit her lip. Steam came off in little curls. "How long do you think Catherine will keep us here?"

He leaned back in his chair, pushing away his empty bowl, and laughed. "You are suppressing visions of fresh eggs and crusty rolls? Eat your gruel, madam, and be grateful! Catherine won't abandon us indefinitely. I am a burr under her saddle, a stone in her shoe. I always was. She will have to peck at it."

Frances dutifully took a mouthful. It was salty and flavorful. She ate another and almost scalded her tongue. "Penitence and sacrifice? Porridge and hair shirts? Actually, the oatmeal is not so bad. Was she the same to you? Didn't Catherine love you?"

"Oh, no," he said softly, grinning. "Love is only her name for power and manipulation. Katerina was my saddle and my boot, and buckled tightly enough to kill."

"Yet you didn't die?"

"I'm not sure. What do you think?"

She gathered the crockery and carried it to the sink. "I think if you had never come to Farnhurst, I would be mistress to a nice elderly gentleman right now, with a library. And I'd have had cream with my breakfast."

He took a clean cloth and began to dry the dishes. "Alas, Frances. Are you sure you want cream? The last time we had cream—"

She blushed, suddenly and without warning, because she couldn't help it. Nothing could have surprised her more. "And lunch?"

"We could have a little skirlie."

She went to the stove and poured hot water on mint leaves in a pot. "*Skirlie?* What's that?"

"What Mr. Grant called his mealie pudding—another famous Scots dish—oatmeal and onions steamed in a basin."

"And dinner?"

Dishes rattled as he set them on the dresser. "We could have stoved potatoes, with a handful of fine oatmeal sprinkled on top, but alas, we ate all the potatoes last night. How about trout fried in oatmeal, without the trout?"

Frances burst out laughing. If there was the edge of hysteria to it, she didn't care. "And did this Mr. Grant teach you that also? Who is this man that he has such a familiarity with oats? An ostler?"

"Hardly," said Nigel. He grinned, accepted a cup of hot mint tea, and sat down at the table. "Major Colquhoun Grant is a perfect Highland gentleman and head of Wellington's intelligence, though no doubt he can turn his hand to groom a horse when he desires. There's not much he can't do. Among his other gifts, he makes an unbeatable Atholl Brose."

"What's Atholl Brose?"

"Oatmeal, whisky, and water, with a little touch of honey."

She came back to the table, with her own cup in hand. "Well, we're lacking only the whisky and honey. Can't we make it without them?"

His eyes were impenetrable, watching her intently. "I was thinking," he said slowly, "of making love, instead."

Her heart leaped like a doe startled into flight. She set her tea on the table, refusing to flee, though the dish rattled against the wood. "Do you want to know more of my training? I assure you we've barely scratched the surface."

He caught her wrist and pulled her between his legs. "Don't!" he said fiercely. "Don't offer me your damned training. What the hell does it mean? Give me yourself, Frances!"

"I can't! I don't know how!"

"Then let me teach you something else about kissing."

She stood between his knees as he ran both hands up her body. "There is nothing I don't know, Nigel."

He grinned at her. "Will you wager me on that?"

"Wager you? What with?"

"With your virtue, foolish maiden. Tell me more about kisses, Frances."

She met his eyes, accepting the challenge, gathering her courage, though her soul felt bleak as a winter wind. "Very well. The authors describe four other kinds of kisses: straight, bent, turned, pressed."

"It's as damned cerebral as breaking a code! There is more between lovers than skill or knowledge, Frances. Won't you allow surprise, or fun, or ingenuity?"

"I'm not sure what you mean. How could I be surprised?"

His grin widened. "Now, that is a challenge, if I ever heard one! So you think you know all about kisses?"

He pushed his fingers under her silk top, sliding it up from her waist, touching the naked swell of her breasts. Slowly he rolled aside the fabric, cupping his hands over her, brushing past the nipples. He did it again with the ball of his thumb, over and over, until her nipples stood out hard, pinioned between the thumb and forefinger of each hand. Frances dropped her head back. Sensations pulsed, throbbing through her belly, pooling between her legs.

"Now, Frances, did you learn this one?"

He filled his mouth with tea. He held it there for a moment while his eyes laughed into hers. She felt a stab of trepidation. What on earth did he intend? As if he answered her question, he swallowed and instantly covered her nipple with his hot mouth. Melting heat pulsed, blazed. Frances gasped, sinking her fingers into his hair. "Nigel!"

He suckled, his tongue burning and liquid, while she moaned and swayed against him, helpless in the grip of this erotic fire. Her nipple stood out, aching, fiery, as he took another scalding sip, only to fasten his heated lips to the other. Faint with desire, Frances cried out, holding his head to her breast, his hair silk under her fingers.

"Oh, don't, don't! I can't bear it!"

He let go. Kissing lightly at each hard nipple, he opened his hands and released her. "You can bear it, Frances. I bore it when you seduced me. It's only pleasure, freely given."

Like a peeled willow, she fell forward against him as he

stood up. In a single movement, he lifted her into his arms. Tenderly he feathered small kisses over her cheek.

"Frances, let's make love, for God's sake!"

She wrapped her legs around his waist, clinging to him, and nodded.

His mouth, still hot and sweet with mint tea, pressed against hers as he lay her back on the table, scattering teacups. Their clothes fell away in a tangle. Nigel kissed her and suckled her. He trailed his heated tongue down her belly and into the curls of her sex until she was moist and flaming. He forced her to accept it, holding her legs apart. It was exquisite. Exquisite and terrifying. Frantic, Frances twisted beneath him so that he moved to kiss her again on the mouth, his tongue sweet with mint and musk.

As he lifted her again, throbbing against her, she wrapped her legs about him, opening to him. Opening to the sweet, yielding pressure, as standing, he lowered her onto his shaft— exquisite, exquisite. She thought she must shatter from pleasure. Shatter and be destroyed. The whisper stalked among the oleanders, stirring the vines, corrupting the air of the garden. In a frenzy of fear she called on her training, working her muscles, desperate to wrest command and shield her vulnerability.

He whispered, his breath hot in her ear. "Frances! Don't fight me! Let it happen, sweetheart!"

Yet she moved strongly, stroking him with long sure strokes, so that he groaned and began to thrust, laying her back on the table. Sweat glazed his forehead—his eyes sharp and black, fired with ecstasy. He was angelic to her, beautiful as Shiva, the bold lines of his throat taut and lovely—but the terror struck deeper, freezing and numbing her, so that the pleasure died and she could no longer feel him.

He stopped, poised, stark with desire as he stared down at her. "Frances! Be with me! Be with me! For God's sake, don't let us use one another like whores!"

Blindly she shook her head, barely hearing him, closing him from her soul as she opened her body. She reached down deliberately. Her palm brushed his buttocks. Her fingers slid on their shared moisture. She cupped him, stroked and pressed, knowing he could not resist. He moaned, tightening in her hand, struggling to deny her. But at last he shuddered, throbbing under her fingers.

"Dear God!" he roared. "Dear God!"

Frances turned her head aside on the hard wooden table, and burst into tears.

∽

He had known combat less devastating. Nigel carried her to their makeshift bed and held her for a long time, her head cradled on his shoulder. Her throat must be bruised from crying. He wished he could shed bleak tears with her, as Wellington wept after a battle. He let his fingers drift through her hair, the hair that a man could get lost in, and wondered if any worse degradation was left.

"Nigel, I'm sorry," she said at last, her voice faint, the words whistling like wind in a reed.

"Hush. It's all right. It doesn't matter. Tell me, Frances. What happened in India?"

"It's nothing," she said.

She sat up. Her honey hair fell about her still-swollen breasts. His beautiful, unreachable damsel of the dulcimer. The curve of her thigh brushed against his. Desire stirred instantly, with its own relentless demand, making him rigid. He ignored it.

"No," he said slowly, watching his fingers spread over her spine. "It isn't nothing."

"I am a coward, that is all." She tried to grin at him, a smile breaking through like a weak winter sun. "It is only the sharp rustle among the vines and the long silence that followed."

"Tell me about it, Frances."

She twisted, resting her weight on one hand, as she reached out to him with the other. Tentatively she touched his shaft, her thumb flicking deliciously over the rim. "Did I bring you pleasure, Nigel?"

"Ah, yes," he said lightly, while his mind filled with bitter words, and he cursed himself for a brute and a fool. She was afraid. She was touching him as if forced to some terrifying duty.

Gently he pushed away her hand. In an agony of frustration, Nigel held her in his arms until she slept.

∽

Frances woke, huddled in linens. She was hungry. She seemed to be wearing a large linen shirt, and the room was cool. Had the fire gone out?

She stumbled to her feet. She was a little sore. "Nigel?"

He did not answer.

Coming fully awake, she looked around the kitchen. The stone spaces were empty, the iron and copper hanging dumb on the walls. Oddly, a pair of candles flickered brightly on the table, though late-afternoon sunlight still streamed in the high grating. Drawn like a moth, Frances walked to the flames. Beside the candles, pinned to the table with a knife, lay a blank page torn from a book. A round drop of red wax was spilled at the bottom beneath several lines of vigorous black script.

I am sorry I had to put the fire out. Soot I must accept, but smoke and flames might have made me feel a little too close to judgment day. I may deserve roasting, but duty requires that I postpone it just a little longer.

When you light the fire again with these candles, you should first remove the sack which is hanging in the chimney.

You were wrong about Saint Nicholas. He makes no judgments. He gives us gifts because we are children.

I must know that my little bird flew where I sent it.

I shall be back for you. Don't be afraid.

The wax was indented in a blurred pattern, almost like a tiny rose. Frances knew what it was without looking any closer—a griffin, impressed from his ring. He had gone. He must take his vital message about Charleroi, his little bird, to Wellington. There were more important things in his life than a harlot from India. There always had been, ever since Farnhurst.

Frances went to the stove. Hanging just above the open grate was a sooty bag. She thought perhaps it had once held grain for horses. With the knife she cut it down and peered up the chimney. The long black tunnel stretched away to a tiny round blue circle, as far as heaven. He had climbed up there? She knew she could never do it, whether the house burned down around her or the cellar filled with floodwater. She could never force herself up that fearful tunnel.

She opened the bag. There was another inside it, a clean flour sack. She pushed her hair out of the way and opened that, too. Instantly she was enveloped in the nutty smell of yeast. There were rolls: crusty, white, fresh rolls. There were two long loaves of bread, still slightly warm. Beneath them, she found fruit—apples, strawberries, gooseberries—and salads, nuts, and cheeses. In a daze she set it all on the table. Beneath the fruit were several little pots and bottles, and a basket with a lid. She opened the pots: jam, clotted cream, honey. The bottles: milk, cider, wine. Almost frantic, she tore the lid off the basket. Eggs. A dozen bright brown eggs, some with freckles.

Frances sat down and stared at them, at this sudden cornucopia—manna from heaven. Slowly she ate a strawberry dipped in thick cream. *A strawberry should let us know that sweetness is most satisfying with undertones of tartness. Cream alone is enough to display that.* She spread a little soft cheese on some bread. The bread broke crisply, soft and fragrant inside. It almost stuck in her throat as she choked back tears. The paper drifted on the table. She picked it up and laid the wax against her cheek for a moment, knowing it was foolish. *Griffin rampant argent langued gules—a rearing silver griffin with a red tongue.*

On the other side of the page was a printed recipe. The print was a little worn and faded, but it was quite clear:

OATMEAL PUDDING

Pour a quart of boiling water over a pint of the best fine oatmeal; let it soak all night; next day beat two eggs, and mix in a little salt; butter a basin that will just hold it; cover it tight with a floured cloth, and boil it an hour and a half. Eat it with cold butter and salt. When cold, slice and toast it, and eat it as oatcake buttered.

Beneath the printing he had written in his strong black hand:

Now you have eggs.

Eighteen

⚭

NIGEL REACHED THE roof, panting hard. In spite of the tablecloth he had tied over his head, soot had filtered into every possible orifice, eyes, ears, nose. At one point the chimney had narrowed just enough to make panic clutch tightly at his throat. Yet he had wriggled free and pulled himself to the top, where he had broken away the screens and rolled to freedom. There were still places that ached from the beating, but at least he was no longer limping.

Nigel untied the bundle from his waist, the towel, clean shirt, and cravat stuffed in a pillowcase hauled up beneath him. He found rainwater in a gutter and washed his face and hands before changing clothes. His breeches and boots were beyond repair. They would have to do as they were.

He wriggled to the edge of the roof and looked over. Armed men waited in the courtyard and deserted street. Catherine was far too thorough to leave him unguarded, even if she happily left him to starve. And that of course was the first order of business, whether Belgium fell to Napoleon and empires toppled like a tower of cards, Frances must have food. She had slept like Snow White in her coffin, like one dead. It filled him with anguish.

Nigel climbed over the ridge cap and slid down to the roof of the next house. From there he leaped to a balcony. The open window gave onto a stair. A few minutes later he was in the street and had money in his hand. It had been in his pocket, the coins hidden inside a block of sealing wax. Quite openly he sauntered through the market, buying rope and whatever delicacies he thought Frances would like.

The climb back took a little more nerve. If the guards looked up from the street, they would see him, spread-eagled on the face of the building with the sack tied over his shoulder. But no one looked up; no shots rang out to disturb the sleepy afternoon. A drainpipe helped him over the gutter and eaves. Soot rattled as he lowered the sack down the chimney on the rope. He had first kissed every one of the pots and bottles, like a fool.

Nigel was aching now. If he had tried this the day before, he would not have had the strength for the climb. So he owed the delay to Catherine. Of course, he owed her something else. For neither could he have made love to Frances again, and once again proved to himself that she didn't care.

He left the Rue des Arbres over the rooftops, and slid silently into the small courtyard where Monsieur Martin had his rooms. Was he home? Had the message to Wellington been sent? Nigel ran lightly up the stairs and rapped at the door.

It opened. A face peered out, surprise obvious on the nondescript features.

"Martin," Nigel said. "Thank God. The message has gone?"

"Yesterday. Why are you still in Paris? Come in!"

"No, I must ride north immediately. But Miss Woodard is imprisoned in the Rue des Arbres. It's well guarded, but for God's sake we must get her out of there and to England."

A brilliant light exploded in his brain and shattered into rainbow jewels before everything went black.

Frances set the food in the pantry, then she ran her fingers along the shelf of cookbooks. He would come back for her. When? Not today, certainly. But she would wait. She would not rail against this new prison. He must come back for her soon. She would practice her yoga and her meditation. She would wait.

The next day passed. She ate strawberries and cream and made herself a salad.

The following morning she cooked an egg. She ate it with butter and bread. It was Thursday. They had been locked in here on Monday. Frances had made a mark for each morning since then. If he did not come back, she would run out of food. Then the only choice left would be that hideous chimney. She couldn't face it.

On Saturday she woke to the sound of rain. Frances sat cross-legged on the pile of bolsters and thought about it. Had he abandoned her here? He had been gone for almost a week. Did he not know what this prison would do to her? Even if he had gone to Belgium, wouldn't he be back by now?

She rose and began to pace. If she ever escaped from this cellar, there was only one premise that mattered now: she must be free. *She must be free!* Lord Trent would pay her. Somehow she had to make it enough. Whatever penury she endured, there must be open skies and a place without walls, or she would go mad. She could never, never be any man's mistress.

She ate the last of the bread and fruit, leaving only a little butter, two eggs, and the tub of finely ground oats. With a laughter close to hysteria, she looked at the recipe for oatmeal pudding. She would make it for dinner. Tomorrow, if he did not return, she must climb up the chimney. Frances knew she couldn't find the will or the strength. Had she finally run out of courage? She put her head in her hands and tried desperately to find oblivion.

∽

He stared into blackness. It was stifling, airless. He was bound hand and foot, trussed like a roast chicken in some kind of cupboard. A filthy rag was tied over his eyes. He had no way to keep track of time. He slept or woke apparently at random. Occasionally he was aware of the glare of a lamp through the blindfold while food was thrust at him, then a chamber pot. Since his hands were chained behind his back and iron cuffs cut into his wrists, these humble functions were done for him as if he were an infant. So his captors knew better than to release him, even for an instant.

Nigel bore it because there was no other choice. It wasn't the humiliation or the treachery that made black fury boil in him. He was furious that he was helpless, and rabid over Frances. Images tormented. Frances! Had she been left in that damned cellar to starve? Yet if he allowed himself this all-consuming rage, he would go mad. The irony of the fate that had dogged him for the last four years came forcibly home now. He had tried to lock himself away, taking refuge in reason and cold columns of symbols, decoding mysteries, cracking codes. He had fled sensation, even music. Frances had dragged him back to the world of the senses, but now his enemies had put him in a black prison, with nothing but his thoughts.

He wanted to create a barrier of logic against what was happening, to build mental cat's cradles, a net of rational analysis, to keep his mind busy. But there was another path. Not to deny sensation, but to surrender to the darkness, dive into it, through it, and find that quiet center. Calling on the tattered shreds of his self-control, Nigel recalled the night in London, the night Frances had saved his very sanity, the night he had surrendered intellect to something more profound.

Hush. Concentrate. Begin with the quiet in the room. Listen to it, as you would listen to music. If any thoughts come in, let them go and bring your mind back to the stillness.... Listen to the silence.

Music. Why had he denied it? Because his mother, who had loved music, had not waited for him to come home before she died? Because in Russia a man had played indecent songs on a balalaika? Because he would no longer let his hands despoil a violin? Like an echo, a wild rhythm ran through his mind, like trees falling. Had he been afraid to open his soul to its power? His mind filled with melody. Soaring, thrilling, the great music of the masters. He let the notes pass, symphonies dancing on the wind from the world's end, and opened his mind to the fathomless quiet that lay beyond.

Hush. Hush. His breathing became deep and even. At last even thoughts of Frances floated away.

∞

There was a dull rumble, like thunder. Nigel braced himself, though the chains bit. Sometimes, he thought wryly, it would be better not to be known as a ferocious fighter, then perhaps his captors might have left him an opening. The wall behind him reverberated. Rapid footsteps. The sound of the door handle. Light shone dull red through the blindfold.

"Hear that?" said the familiar voice.

The boom of cannon resounded somewhere close. "What day is it?" he asked.

"Sunday, the eighteenth. That's the guns at the Invalides. Napoleon has triumphed. The English and Prussians are crushed. Your cause is lost, my lord. Time to move."

There was another rumble of cannon fire, and the sound of cheering. So the news was true. Bile rose in his throat. At every step of the game, Catherine had won.

"Why, for God's sake?" asked Nigel. "Why the hell have I been kept here?"

"Orders."

"Devil take it! Whose orders?"

But it was obvious. Who else would sit so carefully on the fence until he knew the outcome of this battle in Belgium? Who would have welcomed back the Bourbons, but now would curry favor with Napoleon to secure his own future? Who else was the very epitome of double-dealing? Of course. And that's whose orders had kept him locked in this cupboard—not Catherine's. In these slippery times, didn't everyone work for everyone else?

The man chuckled. It was not a pleasant sound. "You're chained like a bloody corpse on a gibbet! Don't lose your temper, my lord. Better think about saving your breath."

A suffocating blanket was bound over his head. He was lifted bodily by at least two men and carried outside. In spite of the blanket and the darkness, he could feel the fresh air on his hands and hear the crash of the victory cannon bright and clear, no longer muffled by walls. The cheering was unmistakable now. He was dumped into some kind of cart and covered with heavy sacks. Nigel suspected they were bags of oatmeal, but he was too exhausted to laugh. The cart rocked into motion. Above the hoofbeats and the creaking wheels, he listened to the roar and excitement of a city celebrating victory. Wellington was defeated. Nigel had failed. In this, in everything, he had failed. Moreover, to his enemies he had just become disposable—and Frances totally irrelevant. Would they kill her?

The streets became quiet. The cart stopped. He was pulled from the sacks and carried into a building. Apart from his captors' grunting and thumping, the hush was as profound as death. They carried him down a staircase. His wrapped head cracked into a wall and his elbow scraped viciously against stone. Nigel swore creatively, but no one answered. He heard the sound of a lock and a door opening. He was dropped, sickeningly, to roll across a hard floor. With his hands and legs still in chains, he had no way of protecting his head as he fell, but Nigel heard the sharp tinkle of metal striking stone, then the solid thud of the door closing. In every language he knew, he let the full range of his inventiveness fly.

There was the rustle of silk and a dry voice. "What does that mean?"

He stopped with a string of execration half-formed on his lips.

"Oh, God," he said. Rolling onto his left shoulder, with his head still muffled in the blanket, he found himself laughing, weak with relief. "Just curses, Frances. Curses to shame the sun into sinking before its appointed hour; blasphemies to make the devil blush; the swearing of sailors pressed into the navy; the ranting of fishwives in childbirth. But the sound of your voice washes everything clean. Are you all right?"

"Saint Nicholas came in June this year." Her voice was cool, almost grave. "I must have been very good. And I have learned to cook eggs."

They had returned him to the Rue des Arbres.

Brightness flooded over him as she pulled away the blanket

and untied the blindfold. He blinked up at her. Golden Frances! She had a key in her hand.

"Thank God!" He tried to focus on her as she knelt and began unlocking padlocks. "The sound of those chains falling is more soothing to my soul than a mother's voice to a babe, or a whore's offer to take a sailor around the world for sixpence. Thank you, Frances."

He sat up and tried to rub his arms, closing his eyes against the explosive pains in the unused muscles.

"You have a beard," she said. "Very dark and forbidding. You look like a brigand."

"Or a Cossack? Did they leave you alone here?"

"Yes." She unlocked the chains on his legs. "You would seem to be in need of a bath. I shall heat water."

There was a large copper tub in the corner. Nigel sat on the floor in the circle of unlocked chains and watched her. She pumped vigorously at the sink, filling pans and setting them on the stove. He didn't have the strength to help her, so he let her do it while his heart craved her grace. Slowly he flexed his indignant limbs.

She came back to the table and sat on the edge of it. "What happened?"

He laughed, dismayed that his bitterness should show. "I was left in a cupboard—Fouché's idea, I think, not Catherine's. Martin must be working for him. I was betrayed. England was betrayed. Napoleon has won."

"Is that what those guns mean?"

"The city goes mad with rejoicing, yes." He managed to get to his feet, aware that he stank, aware that he must look like a madman. "We can't always win! It's nothing a hot bath cannot cure."

Frances met his eyes and smiled, almost shyly. "And a hot meal? Hoping I would have company, I made oatmeal pudding."

∞

Three hours later he was bathed and dressed again. He had shaved with a boning knife honed to a lethal edge, and donned another fresh shirt from the store. He would rather have pick-led his breeches than put them on again dirty, so he wore them into the tub and washed them. He had hung them to dry above the stove. Now they smelled strongly of smoke, but at least he no longer reeked of that cupboard.

He sat down opposite Frances and ate the oatmeal pudding. It was dreadful. He watched her putting her spoon into the gelatinous mass and forcing herself to swallow it. The long lines of her throat filled him with longing. Frances! How did he tell her what he felt?

"Frances, if we get out of this—"

She glanced away, up at the high grating. "Don't, Nigel."

"Don't what? Don't say that I'm grateful, or that I'm sorry that I have failed? And yet that I have one bright light left in my life—"

"Don't!"

A rustle of wings. He looked up. A jackdaw sat in the grat-ing, its silvery cape glistening against the black feathers. The round black eye was fixed on Frances.

"I have been feeding it, so I might teach it to talk," she said.

"Did it work?"

The bird sidestepped and opened its beak to emit a raucous squawk—*ak, ak.*

"Oh, yes," she said. "Birds are very simple, without com-plexity. It can already say its name." She grinned at him. "Don't you hear it? It says 'Jack.' "

Noise in the hallway. Several footsteps. A rattling at the door. The jackdaw squawked again loudly and left. In an ag-ony of frustration, Nigel forced himself to adjust, to thrust away what was happening with Frances. He had duties. He had placed her in danger. Nothing must distract him from that.

Frances watched him do it. Put on that clear, detached attitude as if he donned a coat. She knew it was necessary, but it terrified her. He had barely risen to his feet when the door opened. Catherine was wearing blue. A large blue feather draped around her cheek and her perfect chin, framing her wide black eyes.

"Nigel? You look pale!"

He crossed his arms and laughed at her. "I am but a sadder and a wiser man."

"You do not complain?"

"Oh, yes. But you are the cause of my complaint, Katerina, so I have had to wait for you. For God's sake, come in, and bring your henchmen along. I promise not to attack them again."

Lance stood sheepishly at her shoulder. The five burly men came in behind him, and following them—his features wiped clean of expression—Monsieur Martin. Frances glanced quickly at Nigel. If he was surprised, he hid it well.

"Good heavens," he said. "The gymnasiarch is female. What a lovely gaggle of athletic young men! Or is this polyandry—like a hen with her own flock of cockerels?"

Catherine flushed angrily. "Do not, please, try to be clever, Nigel. England is defeated. You have lost. Would you like the details? Napoleon crossed into Belgium at Charleroi on Thursday as planned. Totally unprepared, Wellington and the Prussians were caught strung out across the countryside—"

"You make the Allied armies sound like washing, Katerina."

Her teeth bared in a sneer. "Yes, and like clothes shredded in the wind, they are scattered and destroyed. On Friday the Emperor annihilated the entire Prussian army at Ligny, while his marshals defeated the English at some crossroads called Quatre Bras. The Allied armies are shattered. Wellington is dead. Paris is delirious. The Emperor will return in triumph. You have only one option left now, Nigel: join us."

"And if I don't?"

"For God's sake, Rivaulx." Lance started forward. "We can never go back to England after this. But there's another future here, in France."

"You turn coat more easily than I expected, Lance."

Lance flushed deeply. His agony was obvious. "No, I still love England. But she has no more business in Europe. Napoleon's victory was inevitable. Catherine is the only one of us who saw that. Unless we want this bloodshed to continue forever, we must make the Emperor secure on his throne.''

"Then thank goodness,'' said Nigel, "that you didn't succeed at the Champ de Mars.''

Catherine's sneer softened into a smile. "England is a backwater for a man of your talents—dear God, but you are wasted there! Join us, Nigel. The Emperor will make you master of Europe.''

Nigel grinned at her. "Can I be a king, too, like his brothers?''

Catherine did not seem to realize he was joking. "I don't see why not.''

"A crown *and* a coronet!'' Nigel said with perfect irony. "May I quote from Monsieur Fouché: 'Let Napoleon win one or two battles, he will finally lose the big one.' You are entirely wrong about your beloved Emperor, *chérie*. Even with England defeated, Napoleon won't return to Paris in the flower of his success. He must subdue the Russians next, then the armies of the rest of Europe. But in the end he won't triumph because France won't stand for it. The man she raised as liberator has turned tyrant. That is what Fouché has seen and you have not: Frenchmen have had enough.''

"Fouché!'' she hissed. "That monster of deception! So is this your fatal flaw? Like him, you know no loyalty, only expediency? Or is it pride that makes you refuse to bow to a greater man? Give your loyalty to Napoleon, Nigel. He will win. Good Lord, the Tsar will fold like a reed. Without the control of the strong we have only chaos. The Emperor needs men with your gifts. He has the greatness of mind to see what you are worth.''

Nigel seemed perfectly calm, as if he pondered some fine point of argument over port. "Expediency? For God's sake, loyalty to a great man sounds so grand and simple, doesn't it? But how many times has that pure ideal taken a people down the path to bloodshed and destruction? No thinking man can be blindly loyal. And no thinking man makes choices without recognizing that they are often between lesser evils. I am not an admirer of Fouché's, and I recognize the good that was once in Napoleon. If I thought you cared for his old ideals of liberty, I could forgive your treachery, but all you care about is tyranny, the strong crushing the weak. I can never join you, Katerina.''

There were tears in her eyes. "I will kill you!"

Nigel seemed indifferent. "Kill me if you wish. For God's sake, I've been bloody useless up to now. No one will miss me.''

Catherine's eyes glittered insanely. "You think I am bluffing?''

As if in a nightmare, Frances watched Catherine raise her pistol. She pointed the barrel directly at Nigel's chest.

Frances wanted to shout. Instead she bit her lip, unable to tear her eyes from his face.

Yet his voice stayed casual, even a little amused. "I think you should go back to Russia, *chérie*. This game is too deep for you.''

Catherine's face contorted. "Why can't you be faithful to me? That is all I ask! I *shall* kill you!''

Frances saw the fatigue in him. Would he make a fatal error of judgment now? He must know with absolute clarity how near he was to death.

Nigel shrugged and casually moved aside. "If you like. But I do wish you would tell me something first. What is Monsieur Martin's role in all this? I thought he worked for me.''

"Did you?" Catherine laughed in triumph. "Once he did. But he has been true only to me for many years, Nigel. My loyal Pierre.''

The edge of sarcasm darkened his voice. "Did you know that he kept me chained in a cupboard for five days?''

Catherine glanced at Pierre Martin, standing quietly to one side. "What?" It was obvious she had not known. "On whose orders? On whose orders was this done?''

Nigel kept moving, still casual. With a flash of insight Frances knew he was buying time to make sure she was nowhere close to the line of fire. From where he stood now, he might even have a chance to drop behind the copper tub. If Catherine fired and missed, there would be one split second before she could shoot again. Could he disarm her? Yet the five men hulked at the side of the room. Frances had no idea if Nigel

could influence Lance. The angel's face seemed frozen, like
the paint on a fresco.

Nigel spoke. "Isn't it obvious, Katerina? Did you think
Monsieur Martin has only two masters, you and me? Alas, he
has a third master—the man who really rules Paris—the man
who will come out on top however the wind blows. Control
of events has slipped through your hands. Martin is just a
mercenary, without loyalty. Didn't you know that? A handy
little lapdog for everyone."

Martin's eyes narrowed. "You don't know what—"

Catherine swung the pistol and fired. Eyes fixed in surprise,
Martin fell. His brown head dropped back as he rolled to the
floor. It was a shock like a blow. Frances did not scream, but
her breath shattered. She couldn't control it. She sat rigid,
trying to block the flood of panic and pain.

Nigel jerked, and bitterness stained his voice at last. "I
see," he said. "But it wasn't necessary. I never thought you
were bluffing."

"Bring the body," Catherine said to the henchmen. She
paused at the door and fixed Nigel with her dark eyes. "You
have two days, *mon cher*. Two days to change your mind.
Then I want your oath—on your honor—to serve the new
France at my side."

His lip curled. He looked dangerous, but he did not move.
"And in your bed?"

Catherine smiled with seductive force. "But of course."

She turned and left. The men hefted Martin's body and
shuffled through the door. Lance stood as if stunned. Nigel
walked up to him and grasped his sleeve.

"Lance, for God's sake! You see now what she is!"

Lance looked him in the face. "I see now what *you* are—
what everybody is. What the hell difference does it make
which side we are on?"

Would Nigel strike him, shake him? Lance was a trained
killer also, he had not had his legs and arms chained for five
days, and the five men were still within reach.

Nigel dropped his hand. "Disillusionment with the world is
lovely, and Catherine's abilities in bed are legendary, of

course. Are they enough to abandon everything else and race to the devil with open arms?''

"I don't know,'' said Lance baldly. "You did.''

Nigel seemed merely weary, as if he'd had enough. "Then wallow in whatever sentiment you like, but will you promise me one thing?''

Lance was flushed, his eyes very bright. "What?''

"Safety for Frances.''

Lance glanced at her once and nodded. Frances wanted to intervene, to say that she didn't care about her own safety, but the look in Nigel's eyes stopped her.

"Swear it, Lance.''

The angel's face looked back into his with utter contempt. "Happily. On my honor I swear no harm will come to her. Unlike you, I believe in chivalry to women.''

The door clanged shut behind him.

Nigel stood helpless, watching Frances. She was sitting at the table with her cold oatmeal pudding in front of her. Her breathing was rapid and shallow. So this, too, *this, too,* was part of Catherine's diabolical plan. She had never cared if innocent bystanders were hurt. He limped to Frances and touched her shoulder.

"No,'' she said, flinching. "Don't! Leave me alone!''

He dropped to the bench beside her. "Frances, it's all right. You will be safe. I trust Lance in that much, at least. It's over.''

With the frantic eyes of a wild creature she turned to him. "No! It will never be over—all the cruelty, all the hatred. All these layers of intrigue, they're so natural to you, aren't they? Is everyone you deal with rotten to the core? Is no one too foul to use? Even Fouché? Even Catherine? Can't they defeat you yet? Who poisoned you? Who killed Donnington? Why did she kill Martin?''

"Does it matter?''

"Matter? No, nothing matters anymore! Except that I cannot bear it.''

Nigel stared helplessly at his hands. His wrists were still raw from the manacles. If he could have bought her freedom with his life, he would have done it gladly. She was a captive here only because of him. And it had all been for nothing, all her bravery, all the intrigue that made her despise him. Napoleon had won. Wellington, with his dry wit, was dead. The Allied cause was lost. Poor Lance was lost. Frances was lost. And it mattered. Dear God, how it mattered!

"Oh, damnation!" he said.

Nigel reached for her, enfolding her in his embrace. She struggled for a moment like a trapped bird, but she let him hold her. Warm, soft curves filled his arms. He ached with tenderness. Again and again he stroked her hair back from her forehead and over her ear, his longing and despair an abyss of darkness in his heart.

When her breathing became deep and even, Nigel tucked his arm under her knees and lifted her, her head heavy on his shoulder. In spite of his protesting muscles, he carried her to the mound of bolsters. Gently he set her among the feather pillows and lay down beside her. With Frances still nestled in his arms, from pure exhaustion he slept at last.

Frances woke, the shreds of her dream slipping away—the wraiths of the *zenana,* the sparkling tile and the never-ending fountains. As she had done there, she slept in a pile of pillows—a faint echo of horror. She would never be free of it, would she? Even if she lived alone on a moor, with the wide-open sky and the wind blowing from the edge of time, she would never be free.

She turned over. Nigel was deeply asleep beside her. His dark eyebrows winged over his closed lids, the planes of his face as pure as a Renaissance painting. A curl of intensity moved in her, somewhere deep inside. Her gaze wandered down his throat and over his chest where his shirt gaped open. His hands lay abandoned, the fingers curled a little—male elegance and power melded together, infinitely fascinating. Yet that glamour brought terror with it, making her heart beat faster as desire warred with fear. He was beautiful. As Shiva was beautiful—Shiva, god of both creation and devastation. In his most terrifying aspect he danced with the drum of destruction in his hands. Yet Shiva was also the seed of life, the phallus.

She wanted to wake him with *ragadipana*, the inflaming kiss. Instead she slipped from their bed and began to heat water for porridge.

A slight sound made her look around. He was awake. Propped on his elbow with his head on one palm, he watched her. What she saw in his eyes sent a rapid flush of heat through her limbs. Frances leaned against the table for support to hide the trembling of her legs.

"It's time for breakfast," she said. "Would you like croissants?"

He lay back, flinging his arms wide. "Too buttery, don't you think? How about syllabub?"

Frances laughed, weak and giddy, like a virgin. Was it because this urgent heat was making her a fool, or because he spared her—and for that did she feel relief or disappointment? "And then will you go up the chimney?"

"Where to?"

The disdain in his voice sobered her instantly. She had been so sure that he would leave, though she dreaded it. "But you must escape while there is time!"

The dark eyes smiled at the high grating, focused on nothing. "What for? There is nothing more I can do for England's cause, and they will be watching the rooftops now."

"But Catherine will kill you!"

She saw the dimples deepen in his cheeks. "Possibly, though I have other plans. Meanwhile you and I have today, tonight, and tomorrow morning, unless Catherine plans my execution at dawn. For those hours I want only one thing, Frances."

Her heart pounded. She had long ago given up any attempt to control it. "What is that?"

Nigel stared at the ceiling. "To be here with you."

She sat down suddenly. "Well, I don't have any choice in it. Betty told me when I first met her that you needed a friend—"

He whipped around, startling her into silence. "A friend? Dear God! What the hell made her say that?"

"Perhaps she thought you didn't have any. Lance hasn't proved very loyal, has he?"

He stood up. "Frances, is this something else they taught you in India, to probe a sore with a needle?" Crossing to the stove, he poured warm water into a basin and splashed it over his face and hair. "Thanks to this bloody war, I have lost too damned many friends. As for Lance, it depends a great deal on your definition of friendship." He rubbed his head vigorously with a towel, his shirt stretching across his shoulders. "Lance was a colleague. If not for our work, I don't suppose we should ever have exchanged more than pleasantries. What the devil do we have in common? Yet I would have offered him friendship if he could have taken it. Sadly his passions get in the way. It would be simpler if he weren't jealous."

She couldn't hide her surprise. "Jealous?"

"Of course. Jealousy the one emotion the recipient can't do anything about. While he claimed to offer me his love, Lance has always been discontented, envious, begrudging. At every turn he has accepted the worst possible interpretation of my behavior and motives. That's not the kind of trust I want in a friend. You didn't believe those scandal sheets. Why should he? Because it salved his troubled soul to think in sexual virtue at least he was superior?"

Frances noticed the compliment, made so lightly in passing—*the kind of trust I want in a friend.* She didn't want it, did she? "So why did you try to save him from Catherine?"

He lowered the towel and turned to look at her. "For a whim, I suppose. Dear God, whatever I have tried with Lance has been an explosively splendid failure, hasn't it?"

Frances met his eyes without flinching. "Why do you try to make me, too, believe the worst? It was not a whim to want to prevent what has happened to him now!"

He gave her a wry grin. "Perhaps I didn't try hard enough.

I should have taken him to my bed instead. It's what he really wanted.''

"It would not have cured it."

The grin became derisive. Turning his back, he wrenched off his shirt and laved water over his chest. His breeches hung from his slender hips, revealing the strong curve of his loins. "No, sex doesn't solve much, does it? Alas, I could never quite bring myself to do it—a marked failure of altruism."

"And Martin?"

"He must have been working for Catherine for a very long time, yet he was also a trustworthy messenger for me—perhaps just because it maintained his cover. He had dealings with Fouché, but then everyone has dealings with Fouché. Certainly he betrayed my trust, but he was hardly a friend."

Frances stood up and went to the stove. She busied herself with the porridge so she would not have to look at him, glorious, half-naked. "Then who was?"

Silken muscles rippled in his back as he dried himself. "Dominic Wyndham, of course."

Major Wyndham of the Saxon face—who had also been working for Catherine? Was there no one who could stay loyal to Nigel? It hurt too deeply. Betty had asked her to offer friendship to this frightening man, and she couldn't do it either. She couldn't even offer him passion. All she wanted was her freedom, to decide her own future, to never hear a door lock behind her again, to forget that Shiva had both aspects: creator and destroyer.

The porridge was sticking, burning on the bottom of the pan. "Major Wyndham? But Catherine said—"

Nigel shrugged into yet another clean shirt from the store. "That he was the hand behind the mayhem at Farnhurst? He was certainly the only one of our players I know to have been there, but I don't believe he played Judas." The protective edge of irony was there, as if the treachery of his closest friends were merely a prank of the gods. "Since he is dead, it can't hurt to have faith that he was indeed a true friend."

Frances carried the oatmeal to the table. "So Betty was right. Have you no friends left?"

Nigel strode to the dresser and picked up two bowls. "Only

traitors, it would seem.'' The clear mockery was back in his voice. "I have wondered, of course, if the flaw isn't mine.''

The pan crashed from her hands, spilling porridge in a gelatinous flood. Filled with distress, Frances turned to him. Her eyes burned. A mountain choked her throat. She had wanted to close him out, but something flared in her, out of control. She had never known the bitter wound of betrayal, yet she had no friend in the world.

"Their treachery isn't your fault! It says nothing about your worth, or about what you deserve. So many men have died because of the war. What is your flaw, Nigel? That your friends were fighting men?''

"Oh, no,'' he said softly. "That I am.''

With a broken gesture she sank to the floor.

He came to her instantly and lifted her, holding her close in his arms, rubbing her back. "Frances. Don't, beloved. You aren't alone.''

"What does it have to do with me?''

"Didn't it occur to Betty that you might need a friend, too?''

"I had a friend in the *zenana*.'' She rubbed fiercely at the welling tears. "She looked like a gazelle, as graceful as moonlight. I don't believe she was much more than twelve. Sometimes she would kiss me, just for comfort, as a child does. Once when I was most afraid, she told me about a boy she loved. She thought he would come for her and carry her away. We would talk of it, weave tales of her freedom and the life she would live with her lover—as free as the white cranes that flew over the mountains. One night she went into the gardens, just to be alone, to dream about him. It was the last day of rain before the dry winds came, destroying the garden, shredding the flowers. But she never knew that. Her lover had come. They were both strangled that night by the guards.''

Nigel sat down on the bench, still holding her. He was acutely aware of her legs across his knees and the soft rise and fall of her breasts. The honey hair and the curve of her cheek lay under his careful palm. *It is only the sharp rustle among the vines and the long silence that followed.* Was this it? Or was there more, something worse that she hadn't yet told him—as he shrank from telling the ultimate truth to her?

At last she looked up at him and tried to smile.

Tenderly he kissed her lips. "We both know about loss. So let us be friends, Frances."

Nineteen

∽

IT WAS A surprisingly gentle day. Nigel cleaned up the spilled breakfast and made more, without burning it. He teased Frances and she joked back. They talked about music and books, about the exotic places they had seen—in Russia, in India—and about trivial, ordinary things from childhood. They had never spoken together like this, as friends. Yet his desire for her was more ardent than ever. It burned in him, stirring his blood, exciting his body, every time he met her eyes or watched the graceful flow of her garments.

So he was careful, allowing her the courtesy of humor and never coming too close. How strange that they had not spent such simple time together before, for now—if he misjudged—he might indeed die the next day, like Martin. Deliberately he refused to think about the remaining pieces of the puzzle. What could it matter now? Instead he only wanted to understand the puzzle that was Frances—more infinitely fascinating than all the world's intrigue.

"So it would seem," she said at last, after they had exchanged some stories of misadventure in high places—in Moscow, in Calcutta, in London—"that all of civilization is just a muddle."

He laughed. "Perhaps that's why I like mathematics. It's the only endeavor that offers certainty. Equations are extremely refreshing after dealing with people. Human affairs are usually just chaos and confusion."

"Including personal ones," she said dryly.

Nigel grinned. "Especially personal ones."

It was getting late. Bars of red sunlight marked the ceiling like a woodpecker's breast. Nigel was lying on the bolsters, slowly flexing muscles that were still sore. As a boy he had lain like this under an open sky as birds thrilled into the heavens—unimaginable now to have such leisure, or such peace. Frances moved restlessly about the kitchen, idly touching the shiny coppers and picking up spoons only to set them down again. He was as aware of her as he was of his own aching body.

"What was it like before you met Catherine?"

He glanced at her under his lashes, and smiled. "With women, you mean? Very pleasant. It's great fun to be a libertine in London."

"And you were a libertine?"

Her ear curved delicately, like the heart of an iris. "Oh, yes. But I hope you will believe that I was never careless or vicious. I was principally in demand among married ladies, after all."

"You make it sound as if you were some kind of male *Ganika*."

He found himself matching the wry acumen in her voice. There was, simply, delight in him at her lack of prudery. "Except that I didn't get paid."

She was busy with some detail of her dress, smoothing the embroidered end of her sash. "And you kept mistresses, as well?"

"Of course. Sometimes more than one."

Frances glanced up, her eyes filled suddenly with mischief. "Two ladies in the same bed?"

He grinned at her wickedly. "Why only two? But it gets . . . complicated, shall we say? Unfortunately, even though I have two of everything else, the most vital part comes in the singular."

She covered her mouth with her veil, but her eyes sparkled. "You refer, of course, to the heart."

"No. The tongue," he said, trying to keep a perfectly straight face. "I was careful not to involve hearts if I could help it."

Frances burst out laughing and dropped the veil. "That's the only thing they didn't teach us in the *zenana*!"

Her laughter warmed his blood. "What, about tongues?"

"Oh, no!" she said gaily. "We learned all about tongues—I thought you had already noticed that."

"I did." Then the question slid out, because he truly longed to know. "What else did you learn?"

This time she grinned openly. "In addition to teaching birds to talk and decorating chariots with flowers? Well, let me see: that a man may be made like a hare, or a bull, or a stallion—"

"Which am I?"

She blushed, just a little, and sat down at the table. "Oh, a stallion, certainly!"

Nigel wanted her so much that it hurt. "And what else?"

"That there are more ways to copulate than stars in the sky. We learned about blows, and sighs—"

"And areas of the body receptive to scratching?"

Her lids veiled her eyes, but the corners of her mouth were like those of a child given sweets. "And there were pictures."

"Pictures?"

"Paintings, drawings. I was horrified at first, but once I had overcome my initial reaction, I realized my shock was totally misplaced. They were very beautiful. We English aren't very comfortable with bodies, are we? As a child I never saw a man whose clothes didn't cover him from toe to chin—or a woman, for that matter. I wouldn't even bathe without a shift, lest I see myself." She stroked back her hair with her hand, the hand that bent and moved like a bird's wing, and giggled. "If I hadn't watched my father roll up his sleeves once in India, I wouldn't even have known that men have hair on their arms!"

"Or in more interesting places!"

She assumed a mock innocence, teasing. With her elbows on the table, she laced her fingers together and peeked between them. "*Are* there more interesting places?"

He rolled over on one side, propping his head on his hand.

His very soul craved her. "Oh, I think so, don't you? Though I love your arms."

Frances held them out. The delicate bones at the wrists shone beneath her skin. "My arms?"

So he risked it, knowing she might refuse him, knowing that it might only complicate things further, but unable any longer to deny himself. "And your waist, and your hips, and those little dimples in your bottom. Frances, let me make love to you."

☙

If she hadn't known that he might die in the morning, she would have said no. In spite of her own craving, she knew it was a mistake, that he would try to enthrall her in sensation, entrap her with passion, so that she would never be able to leave, to fly free—so that he could keep her as his mistress.

His gaze was fixed on her. Black, fired with longing. In spite of her misgivings, her blood answered in a powerful surge, demanding resolution. Simple honesty made her stand and walk to him. He lay completely still, as if turned to stone, but his nostrils flared and his eyes glittered like moonlit water. With hot humility, she dropped her veil and stepped out of her slippers. As her blood burned with a strange echo of shame, she pulled out the knot, so her embroidered sash uncurled like a snake and slithered to the floor.

His breath caught, then rushed back, ragged. He did not move a muscle.

One by one her robes fell to make a small pile about her feet, the silk whispering over her burning thighs. Her toes were buried in fabric. A border of little horses cavorted over silken hillocks; embroidered stars flew down a muslin Milky Way. So not even her hair would cover her, she did not untie her braid. As the last garment fell she was completely naked to him.

Her heart beat hard, making her breathless. The warmth from the stove touched her breasts and licked over her belly, but her soul had already melted.

In a single lithe movement Nigel stood up, breathing a little

fast. A faint flush dyed his cheekbones. Frances met his hot
gaze, feeling the echo throb deep within, a blazing heaviness,
pooling in her. With his dark eyes locked on hers, he shrugged
out of his jacket and tossed it aside. Cravat, waistcoat, and
shirt followed, falling to the floor as he bared himself. He bent
to take off his boots and stockings, the muscles of his back
flexing—like a hare leaping, a bull pawing, a stallion pacing—
an animal grace and strength that she craved as if starving.

His eyes met hers again as he unbuttoned his breeches and
kicked them away. His arousal thrust hard against the thin
fabric of his smallclothes. Ripping apart the tapes at the back,
he pulled off the fine muslin underwear. It fell to the floor.
With his hands relaxed at his sides, he stepped forward, naked
as a god striding from the sea, and bent his head to hers.

Fleetingly his lips touched her mouth as he whispered, "Are
you sure?"

She slipped her arms around him, liquid strength under her
palms, and pulled him close. "I am sure, Nigel." If that was
a lie, what she said next was the truth, for her body flamed
with it. "I want you."

" 'My love, thou art too dear for my possessing—' "

He caught her face in both hands, his penis pulsating between them as he began to kiss her, deeply, thoroughly,
searching for any shred of reticence, and merciless in his quest.
Frances clung to him, letting him burn away her doubts. Oh,
yes, she wanted him! Desperately she held on to his strength
while her knees trembled like windblown reeds.

Nigel felt it, her shaking, her openness. His excitement quick-
ened, urgent and compelling, and he swelled against her. He
wanted her, now, wrapped about him. But he was not a boy.
He would take his time. They had all night.

With her mouth still captive, he lifted her. She wrapped one
leg about his waist, her breasts crushed against him, and broke
the kiss. Her lips touched his ear.

"*Vrikshadhirudhaka,* climbing a tree," she said with a broken laugh.

He closed his mouth over hers, silencing her, before he bent and laid her on the bolsters. He knelt for a moment gazing down at her. She stared back, her eyes shining. She was beauty itself to him. Beauty he hungered for. He reached out a hand and laid it on her burning skin. He would worship her slowly, from her toes to her hair.

The smooth curves slipped under his palm, the delectable female swells from thigh to waist, hip to shoulder. Over and over he traced the line of her flank and the hollows of her throat. He rubbed the soles of her feet until she whimpered, small sounds of desire. He traced the arch of her breasts, savoring the valleys beneath them. He stroked the honey-gold hair from her forehead and temple. Surely she could not retreat from him now, or shut him out? He wanted with every fiber of his being to win her absolutely and irrevocably, to feel her possess him as he longed to possess her.

He, too, had been educated in a school of sensuality. He had spent his youth learning how to pleasure a woman, all those little places that made her soften and yield, the touch that made her moan as if wounded. He ran his fingers over her breasts, teasing and retreating until she became frantic for more, then he tugged at her nipples. She was gasping now, mewling like a kitten, helpless and open to him. A flame burned under her skin, heating his palm. Her nipples were hard and dark, like raspberries. He stroked and suckled, pinching just a little with fingers or teeth, while his arousal beat and leaped, pulsating with pleasure.

Dear God, she felt good—like silk, like a woman. Need for her permeated him, a sweet agony of tension. His cock thrust hard, urgently. Deliberately he held back, holding himself on a knife edge of suspense and hot agitation, letting his hands and mouth show her how he felt.

Dear God, how he loved her! He loved her more than life. He loved her more than his own soul. If the devil would trade him that for her happiness, he would give it.

She moaned. Her lids fluttered. A fine film of moisture sheened on her skin. He slid his fingers to her soft thighs and the hot slickness that awaited him there. As he touched her she caught his cock in her hand and tantalized him. Shattering sensations shot through him. He heard a groan, and realized in the next moment that he had groaned. He bent and kissed her deeply, control shredding.

"Tell me you want me, Frances."

"I want you," she murmured, her eyes black as night.

"How? Tell me how."

She moved him to touch her, the soft curls, her hot sex firing the dark heart of his ardor. Her moisture met his, beaded on the sensitive tip. "Desperately. Achingly."

He rubbed his shaft against her silky flesh, a long stroke, letting the head throb. "Like this?"

"Yes, yes." She grasped his shoulders, gulping, and opened her legs wide for him. "Deeply."

She moved intimately, caressing him, inviting him, like a kiss.

It was a sensation that courted screaming, wild in intensity. Nigel groaned, mad for her. He sank himself to the hilt. He was enveloped in fiery heat. Hot wet silk. Helplessly he moved in her—helplessly, as the waves seducing the sands of the millennia, helplessly obeying the importunate intent of his seeking male body. Timeless. Ecstatic.

She moved with him, rocking her hips to meet his, sucking him as the beach sucks at the sea. Her nails scraped his skin. Her nipples thrust against his chest. An endless eternity, a perfection of pleasure. Until at last, desire beaded on her skin as his madness reached its peak, bringing him to the cataclysm of the final release.

A rapture.

He closed his eyes, throwing back his head as he thrust deeply. She was with him. She wanted him. They would share this ecstasy.

Like a lead ball tearing into flesh, she cried out. "No, no, no! I cannot bear it! I cannot bear it!"

And tore her hips down, away from him.

Too late, too late, he tried to hold back. On the edge of insanity, in his delirium he didn't know when he had lost her. He couldn't have lost her! Shuddering, his climax over-whelmed him. Frances stiffened, her hands clinging to the stark muscles of his arms, as his powerful contractions shook them both.

But all the pleasure he had built in her, all the ecstatic tension that should have exploded in rapture, welled into her eyes. She burst into violent weeping.

"Nigel, I'm sorry. I'm sorry. I'm sorry."

Still caught inside her, Nigel touched his lips to her eyelids and cheeks, trying to kiss away the tears. "Frances, beloved, don't cry! Please, please, don't cry!"

Shaken by sobs, she was ravaged, desolate.

His heart shattered within him.

He pulled out, not knowing if he should hold her, how to offer comfort. But she turned to him, burying her face in his shoulder. Tentatively he put his arm about her and stroked her hair.

"What is it?" he said.

"I don't know." Her eyes were black with distress. "I don't know. As you moved in me I wanted to give you my soul, the pleasure was so intense. It built and built, until I thought I would die of it. Then—oh, God!—I was numb. I couldn't feel you. I couldn't find any pleasure, only the terror of death and the void waiting."

He groped for the right words. "Frances. The climax is known as *la petite mort,* the little death, but you won't die, my love. There is nothing to be afraid of. If you were left behind, it's my fault."

"No, it's not your fault," she said. "I cannot be your mistress, Nigel. I cannot bear it. I don't want—" She rolled away from him, clutching her discarded silk robes to her breasts. "I'm sorry! I'm sorry! What would the *praudha* think of me now?"

The curve of her shoulder and back was an agony of beauty to him, the fragile, delicate woman's bones and the white skin. He sat up, knowing he was becoming erect again, despising himself for the insensitive autonomy of male desire. He didn't know how to reach her, but he knew that she groped for any escape from the enormity of her distress.

"Frances, these things happen. Dear God, it's happened to

me once or twice, though it's different for a man—he can't perform at all.''

She wiped her eyes and smiled with a breathtaking courage. ''Aren't men always potent? You are already—''

He followed her gaze and grinned. ''If we ignore it, it'll go away.''

She grinned back. ''They worship it in India. People bring flowers and milk to the temples to adorn the sacred phallus, an aspect of Shiva.''

''Worship it?'' He thought he might choke. ''It's just my body.''

She touched him, running a finger tentatively over the slick head and down the shaft. An exquisite pleasure throbbed in response. ''The skin is so velvety, like a horse's nose.''

He gasped back laughter. ''Frances! If you do that much longer, I can't answer for the consequences.''

She pulled her hand away, dismissive, a deceptive lightness in her voice. ''It's that power, isn't it? Shiva's power. The power of creation. As if it had a mind of its own, determined on conquest. You would think I could respond to it with some of my own.''

So much lay between them that he had no idea where to begin. And over it all lay the reality of tomorrow. A man could forget the sky was falling while he was making love. But now, like a bloody inconvenient visitor, it thrust into his thoughts: he might die tomorrow. He could not make her any promises. He could not even be certain that he could protect her. He had no idea how to mend what had happened. So why the hell had he been arrogant enough to think she might forget both the past and the future, as he had forgotten, in the madness of sex?

He groped for the words. ''Sex is something we have to learn, Frances—and not from books or paintings. It's a matter of feeling, not knowledge. What did you think? That as a virgin, you would come to rapture the first time? Or even the second, or the third? Some women take a long time to learn how to climax. Why do you think it should be instant for you?''

She stood up, her legs pale in the dying light. ''Alas, I must have been born under a contrary star. I was so sure that those pictures in the harem were enough guidebook for anyone. But in spite of all those lessons, it's not something I have a knack for.''

"Oh, I don't know," he said. "What the devil was all that stuff about climbing trees?"

"The kinds of embrace." Frances wrapped herself in her robe. He could see that she still needed escape. "When a woman places her foot on the man's and wraps her other leg about him, while sighing and cooing, it's called climbing a tree." She tied her sash. "If she clings to him like a vine and makes the sound *sut sut,* it is *jataveshtitaka,* the twining of a creeper.''

Their eyes met. The realization blossomed in her like a flower unfolding, the sheer absurdity of it in English.

"Really?" he said dryly. *"Sut sut?"*

She laughed. In the next instant she was clutching at her robe as she doubled over, her breath ragged and shattered. "There are correct sounds for each move," she gasped. "Eight kinds of crying. But I forgot! I sighed, but I forgot to *coo!"*

He fed her laughter deliberately, assuming astonishment. "You must think about the correct *sounds?"*

Still gasping, she drew in great shuddering breaths between phrases as she tried to control her hilarity. "But it also says— passion overrides the rules—spontaneous—as irregular as dreams. It's compared—to a horse.''

"Oh, my God!" He felt quite desperate. "Who the hell is the horse? The one being ridden?''

"No, no. The act itself, the congress—it's supposed to be like a horse bolting, blind to all obstacles—that's how it is for you, isn't it?''

Dear God, he had never considered it before, let alone tried to find words. How the hell did he climax? Thinking about it was enough to take care of his arousal. He reached up a hand and caught her fingers. She dropped down beside him, her laughter with its sharp edge of distress fading away.

"I don't know . . . perhaps it's like the meditation you taught me. Removing yourself and letting the process take

over. Believe it or not, I learned something of that with Raoul
Pargout—there is a place in your head with the least pain. If
you look for it, you can go there. There is also a place in your
mind with the most intense sexual pleasure.''

''In your *mind*?''

''You must put yourself there, that's the only way I can
describe it. If I thought about it too much, I doubt I could do
it at all.'' He grinned and indicated his dying erection. ''You
must surrender to it, put your mind in the place with the most
delectation, and let go.''

''But I can't,'' said Frances. ''I can't let go.''

He wrapped the sheet around her and pulled her into his
arms. ''You can have whatever your heart desires, but now
we must sleep. If we're lucky, it'll be a long day tomorrow.''

''Lucky?''

''There is luck,'' he said gently, ''in everything.''

She lay down beside him and let him kiss her once, lightly,
on the lips. When at last she fell asleep, Nigel stared at the
dark ceiling and thought briefly, and with deadly irony, that
if he did not survive, he would take the ruins of this with him
to the grave. And if he did survive? Then he would fight this
battle for her. Whatever effort it took, whatever sacrifice it
demanded, he would find the path to peace for Frances, or
destroy himself in the attempt.

Frances woke to bright sunlight and the nutty smell of oatmeal.
Nigel was already up. She heard him moving before she even
opened her eyes. So he spared her. After the disaster of last
night, he would not try again. She sat up and hugged her arms
about her breasts. Perhaps she was not made like other women.
Perhaps something dreadful was wrong with her. The *Kama
Sutra* taught that sexual rapture was mutual, to be shared, and
a worthy goal in itself. Passion should move the lovers past
their training and their understanding and into the sacred ecstasy. Yet she had disgraced herself. It was not Nigel's fault.
Until the very end he had brought her exquisite sensations.
She could have fainted with pleasure. So why had she gone

cold, as if ice water had congealed in her veins?

She had accused him of duplicity, but she was all artifice, shallow, without soul, like a painted doll. That she longed to be different was as painful as a burn. What had she offered to this fascinating man but deceit and denial, after all? She didn't know how to meet his eyes. Yet he eased it for her, offering her a small joke, so she could get out of their makeshift bed and join him for breakfast. And then he offered her another, so she could slip into camaraderie, and not be forced to admit her deficiencies.

The bowls had barely been put away when there was the sound of hooves, echoing down through the high iron grating.

"Ah," said Nigel. "The execution is to be later than dawn, but not much later. Now, Frances, what do you think: should I save my miserable hide for Bonaparte's service, or sacrifice it nobly for England?"

"If Catherine flays you first, you would have that option," said Frances. "Otherwise, I would rather the whole man was preserved, just to spite her."

He laughed. "I'm not sure I'll have the choice!"

She grinned back. "In that case, what the devil would I do with your hide?"

"Tan it, of course—unless Catherine plans to do that, too."

Footsteps sounded in the hallway. Bolts thudded back, the lock squealed. Brutally Frances repressed the sharp edge of hysteria. "And make purses to jingle coins in?"

"Don't be afraid, Frances," said Nigel, kissing her quickly. "Go and sit at the table and stay there, whatever happens. Promise me!"

She wanted to shout at him, shake him! But she read the fear in his eyes. It was for her, not himself. Unless she obeyed, she would distract him, maybe endanger him. So she groped for the calming breath and sat down.

"I promise," she said steadily. "It is not my quarrel."

And almost choked on the words.

∞

Nigel knew he could trust her. Thank God for that! The door opened with a clang to reveal Catherine and her henchmen.

They were all armed. Lance was nowhere to be seen. Nigel registered this with an unspoken curse. Damnation! Whatever Catherine planned, Lance would have been a check on her wilder impulses. After all, they were still in the early stages of their affair. If she went too far, she might yet turn him against her. But without Lance, there was no limit to what she might do.

"So what is this?" he said instantly. "Surely not the rack and the whip, Katerina? Or, no, I see you have your nice little pistol and blade."

"Do you deliberately goad me?" She gestured with the pistol.

It was hard to judge her mood, though at one time he had thought himself a connoisseur of Katerina's moods. "I merely let you know I won't join you."

Her brows drew together. "I can persuade you."

"Can you? Surely not with the knife? I might whisper our secrets into a hole in the ground, like Midas, and let the wind tell the world."

"That you have ass's ears? You will not *whisper* it!" Catherine caught the eyes of her men. "Bind him."

Alas, he had carelessly left out some stiff rope, slightly sooty! Resistance was so futile that Nigel actively cooperated. They thrust him into a chair, viciously strapping his arms behind him and binding his ankles to the chair legs.

Wrenching the last knots into place, the men looked at Catherine. Nigel had the distinct impression that they were disappointed he hadn't given them an excuse to damage him. With a nod of the head, Catherine dismissed them. There was a moment's hesitation from one, but obviously Nigel was helpless. The man left the room behind the others and closed the door.

"Do they work for money or are they all fanatics?" Nigel was intensely aware of Frances. She sat like a statue, her eyes fixed on him. "Or do they risk their immortal souls for a kind glance from you?"

"I am kind, am I not?" Catherine was lovely, as Deianira had been lovely when she gifted Hercules with a poisoned shirt. "After all, I left you your whore."

"I have wondered why."

Her eyes glittered. "So you would remember the delights of life, of course, and want to live. I hear you have been celibate for a long time, like a monk—an idea so quaint it delights me. When you robbed me of my heart, did I rob you of your manhood?"

"I wasn't aware that hearts were involved, Katerina."

The glitter intensified. "Yet it amuses me to think that they were. How did you get such a scurrilous reputation over the last two years when you were so pure? Lance tells me that you are the butt of every scandal sheet in London, a rake of unmentionable vices. What a trial for a man of your genius, to be bayed at by curs."

"Every dog has a master. But in this case, I imagine, the mongrels yapped to the tune of a mistress. Did you write all that slander by yourself? I might have guessed the donkeys were your touch."

Catherine laughed. "So it pained you to be known as a sink of depravity. Did it hurt just as much to read of my pain under the knife?"

His wrists hurt as he moved them. "As much as you could possibly have planned. More, probably."

"Why?" she said. "If I had read the same about you, I would have rejoiced."

"And therein lies the difference between us."

Nigel would never know where Katerina had learned to love cruelty, to find amusement in suffering. Once he had been naive enough to think he could help her, to uncover some trauma that had planted this rot in a woman so lovely. He had found nothing but a deep love for herself, twisted by a canker of sadism that ate at her soul. Perhaps, after Russia, he had thought he deserved nothing else, even as he had wanted with an absurd idealism to protect Lance.

She flicked her thumb on the pistol and a thin wicked blade sprang from the barrel. "You are a sentimental bastard, aren't you? Beneath all that bravado is the heart of a weakling."

"Very probably," he agreed. "Certainly I heartily dislike torture. Another difference between us, I suppose."

Her nostrils flared. "Which would you dislike most? The

blade on yourself, or on this pretty little creature from India?''

He laughed. ''Ask yourself. My answer is what yours would be.''

''Hah!'' she said, triumphantly meeting his eyes. ''You love no one and nothing but your own hide! You would let me cut this harlot to ribbons and find yourself a new one without looking back!''

It is always good strategy to tell the truth as far as you can. Nigel met her eyes and grinned. ''Only you were irreplaceable. Your skills are unique, Katerina.''

''Very well,'' Catherine said, smiling. ''Then come back to me. What have you decided? Will you take life, or will you beg me for mercy before you die?''

Lance stared at the Don horse. The wise dark eyes looked back beneath the fringe of silver forelock. With the other mounts, he had brought Nigel's horse from the Rue des Arbres and stabled it here at Catherine's place. Otherwise, with all the servants gone, the animals would have starved, locked in their stalls.

''Do you love him?'' Lance asked.

The horse distended its nostrils and blew softly. Lance rubbed his hand over the gilt face, where the dark skin showed blue at the nose. The Don horse dropped its head and nuzzled its feed bin.

''Damn him! He despises me, of course.''

As he said the words he felt a pang like a stab wound. Oh, God! Oh, God! He had never really been a good spy. He could fight. He could ride. He could be brave. He could discover secrets. But he couldn't see the great patterns of events as Nigel could. From the time they first met, Rivaulx had dazzled him with those leaps of reasoning and insight, that stunning brain that could turn to codes or to intrigue with equal felicity. Nigel had always covered for him, saved his reputation, smoothed over his deficiencies. So why couldn't he have lived up to his potential and proved worthy of Lance's admiration? He was a peer. He had wealth and status. He had extraordinary gifts. Why had he deliberately dissipated his talents in vice?

Though now, thanks to Catherine, Lance knew something of the fatal attraction of women. What would he do, if Catherine succeeded and brought Nigel back with her? But worse, what would he do if she didn't?

A boy darted into the stable yard. "Monsieur!"

"What?" said Lance irritably.

"News, sir!" The boy thrust a packet into his hand.

Lance tore it open. "Oh, my God!" he said aloud.

He grasped a bridle from a peg. Without delaying for a saddle, he swung onto the Don horse and thundered into the streets of Paris.

Will you take life, or will you beg me for mercy before you die?

Frances knew nothing but terror. Nigel was tied to a chair, helpless. As if the thunder ball rolled, she wanted the heavens to open and drown the world as a protest. Dear God, why had Nigel joked about being flayed? Did he expect it? Had he been trying to prepare her? She looked about wildly for a weapon. The copper pans hung in their rows on the walls, the poker sat by the range. As far away as the moon, when Catherine had a pistol and knew how to use it.

If the *Ganika* made some foolish gesture, she would die to no avail, and force Nigel to witness it. That was why he had made her promise. She must give him whatever strength she could by her calmness. The longing for action ached, but sometimes it took more courage to do nothing. Action now was only a cowardly guarantee of finding her own way out first. Yet how could she sit still at this table where he had given her oatmeal, and charmed her with courtesy, and delivered kisses witty with mint tea? Frances closed her eyes and sought the frozen breath, but she could not close out their voices.

Catherine's dropped like a stone into the silence. "Death or Napoleon, Nigel. It is not so hard, is it?"

"Let me see," he said gently. "Dying is easy, of course."

"Do you wish for it?"

"Do you think to do me a favor, Katerina?"

She snapped at him in frustration. "But what if between living and dying is pain? Is that all that will move you? Must it be the knife?"

Nigel's voice seemed liquid with sarcasm. "But Katerina! Why do you hesitate? You love the knife!"

Frances opened her eyes, her breath control shattered. Bile rose in her throat. Catherine stood over Nigel. She held the thin blade that had sprung from the pistol barrel at his throat, then slid it down his jacket. The buttons bounced to the floor and rolled like a children's game. The knife cut deeper, slicing his shirt. Catherine touched his naked chest with her free hand.

"You are a beautiful man," she said hoarsely. "Why won't you choose life?"

He shook his head. Light danced in the creases around his mouth as he smiled.

Catherine pressed the tip of the blade into his skin. Beads of blood leaped to the surface like a string of red beads.

Something snapped in her mind. Rage crackled in her like lightning, blinding in intensity. Grabbing her chair, with the sturdy seat as both shield and weapon, Frances charged at Catherine. As she ran she heard shouting—something wild and high-pitched, like a madwoman. Thunder broke, deafening. She was choking. Everything went white. Frances collapsed, the blood roaring in her ears—*had her own voice shouted defiance?*—as everything erupted into chaos. Far away she heard crashing. She was falling, falling, the hard floor bruising her knees and palms. White was everywhere, in clouds. Vaguely, she was aware that the door had burst open and Nigel's chair had fallen sideways. But everything was white, and she couldn't seem to move any longer.

Frances had no idea what had happened, but, somehow, Nigel was there, lifting her. She opened her eyes. He seemed very far away, and misty. He must be looking at her through a veil. He smiled at her once through the gauzy silk, then glanced over his shoulder. Puzzled, Frances followed his gaze.

A blond angel was struggling with a dark woman. "Catherine, it's over! It's bloody over. There's more news from

Belgium. Wellington was not killed at Quatre Bras. Catherine, for God's sake, come away!''

The dark woman fought him, screaming back and flailing with her fists. ''No! No! I won't believe it!''

''It's true!'' White dust drifted down on them, blurring both gilt and black to dull gray. ''There was another battle on Sunday. Wellington regrouped on better ground. The British stood firm in the rain and the mud by some village called Waterloo, and the French tore themselves to shreds. The *Grande Armée* is annihilated. Even the Imperial Guard shattered and ran. Napoleon is utterly defeated. It's finished.''

''I don't believe you!'' cried the dark woman. ''The Emperor will rally!''

''Napoleon has abandoned his army, as in Egypt, and Russia, and Leipzig. He fled the battlefield. The news will be all over Paris in two hours.''

''Then I am lost.'' The dark woman sank to the floor, clinging to the angel's coat. ''I am lost.''

''Come,'' the angel said. ''I have horses outside. We can escape to Russia. Catherine, don't give up!''

''What does it matter?'' she said. ''Why should you care?''

He lifted the dark woman by the shoulders. ''I have sacrificed everything for you. I am ruined. You have made me into a traitor. Let me get you to safety. Come away!''

Nigel swung Frances into his arms. The bolsters sighed as he set her softly on them. She looked up at him, as beautiful as an archangel. Beneath a layer of white dust, he smiled once, then turned away. The other angel, the fair one, still had the dark woman clinging to one arm. Frances tried to focus on their faces as Nigel walked up to them.

''You have triumphed,'' said the blond angel. He had released the dark woman. She leaned against the door, like a discarded rag doll, sobbing quietly. He had the woman's gun now. He pointed the barrel at Nigel's bleeding chest.

''Frances is hurt,'' said Nigel.

''Aren't you used to hurting women? I'm taking your Don horse.'' The words sounded choked, but the gun was steady. ''I must get Catherine away before the Allied troops block our route. I don't care if she was on the wrong side—if Napoleon corrupted her. She needs my help.''

Nigel stopped, opening his hands wide as if to show he was unarmed. ''Always the gallant impulse, Lance? Save the lady and damn the rest? What the devil has your chivalry ever offered Frances?''

The blond angel cocked the pistol. ''What the hell has yours?'' His voice broke and skittered. ''Anyway, Frances is a courtesan; it's not the same. Will you stop us leaving? I am within reach.'' He lowered the barrel, his blue eyes locked on Nigel's face. ''One move, and you could disarm me and have us at your mercy.''

Nigel stood motionless, ignoring the gun. ''You have never understood. I don't want revenge.''

''Then I shall get Catherine to Russia.''

Nigel smiled at him. Frances watched. It seemed so clear, a smile of open generosity. ''Go where you will, Lance. Life is an oyster, they say, fit for cracking. Find pearls, if you can.''

The blond angel reached for Nigel's shoulder. His eyes glittered like water droplets on blue tile. Lifting his head, he pressed his lips to Nigel's mouth and kissed him.

Frances closed her eyes. Somewhere a door had slammed shut, and she was alone under layers of fine gauze, fine enough for an Indian princess.

Twenty

SOMETHING COLD AND damp touched her face. She tried to brush it away. The cool moisture was insistent, dribbling down her neck and into her ears. Concentrating, she felt the gauze veils part a little. Frances opened her eyes.

Nigel was sitting by her, bathing her face. There was blood on the cloth.

"Am I shot?" she asked.

His hand caressed her cheek, smoothing away wetness. "You have been knocked on the head, my brave *Ganika*. Catherine's bullet hit the ceiling and dislodged some plaster. We were all covered in dust. You were in the way of a rather large chunk."

The veils were shredding now, like cobwebs in a breeze. "Catherine tried to shoot me?"

He nodded. "I spoiled her aim."

Frances tried to sit up. Percussion instruments started up in her head. "But you were tied to a chair."

The dry humor was strong in his voice. "It was kind of Catherine to do as I wanted."

"You *wanted* to be tied up?"

He put an arm about her, encircling her so that her head lay on his shoulder. The drums and cymbals faded a little. "It allowed Catherine to get rid of the henchmen. I had no chance against all of them."

Frances savored his strong heartbeat. She tried to calm the noise in her head by following its steady rhythm. "Where are they now?"

"They ran as soon as Lance arrived with the news of Waterloo. No doubt they will fade back into the stews of Paris whence they came."

Frances vaguely remembered the flash of a blade between Nigel's fingers just before the shot, before his empty chair had crashed over as he leaped out of it. "So you had it all planned, the convenient rope, the goading. You had your knife ready."

"Catherine had a loaded pistol. I just had to get her to come close enough, before I could use my knife to get free and disarm her, that was all."

She looked up at the wry lines about his mouth. "Oh, God. I am a fool!"

Long fingers were caressing her hair, smoothing it back from her forehead.

"No, Frances, never that! Lance turning up as he did was an interesting development, of course. As it turned out, rather convenient. But you were very brave. Do you have any idea how brave you were?"

She felt sleepy and stupid. "Why did you let Lance escape? You could have overpowered him. You could have killed them both."

"Yes."

"Instead you let him take your Don horse. Why?"

"There has been enough killing."

"You let him kiss you."

The wry humor deepened. "It took a certain amount of self-control, but why not? It did me no harm, and I owed him something for his impeccable timing."

Frances closed her eyes, and welcomed the darkness.

∽

A storm was shaking the ship. It tossed her high with each wave. The white horse raced with her across wide-open moors, up to the snowcapped peaks. White cranes soared against bruised, purple clouds, the skies of monsoon, but the rain smelled hot. The white clouds were dust, but they smelled of smoke. It must be the dry season. She was a dry, white petal, whipped away in the hot desert wind.

"Frances, for God's sake, wake up!"

She opened her eyes. Nigel was shaking her. "What?" she said.

"Smoke!" He dragged her to her feet. "Catherine must have sent men to set fire to the house. There must be faggots piled up in the corridor. By the time the door burns through, the whole building will be an inferno."

She was instantly awake, though her head still ached. The smell was unmistakable now. There was a roar like falling water in the corridor. Smoke curled around the edge of the door. They were blocked, trapped by fire.

"We must get out," he said. He kissed her forehead. "Don't be afraid. Sit here."

He led her to the table, then dragged their bedding to the door. He flung buckets of water from the sink over the bolsters and pillows and stuffed them around the cracks. Then he took up the rope and some clean cloths that he wet at the sink.

"Tie this over your head," he said, handing her a tablecloth. The roar was getting louder.

"How can we get out?"

He tied the rope about her waist and shoulders in a kind of harness. His eyes were fierce, yet there was that indefinable spark of mischief there, designed to give her courage. "As the jackdaw got in, of course."

The chimney! The bolsters at the door were steaming, drying, beginning to char. The paint on the heavy wood door had begun to blister. If it all burst into flames, wouldn't the heat roar up the chimney and roast them alive?

Nigel led her to the grate and climbed up. "Come up here and wait." He kissed her quickly. "I will pull you up after me."

The narrow black tunnel stretched away to infinity. The calming breath had deserted her. Her heart was pounding, throbbing with the pain in her head. "Nigel, I can't! I can't do it!"

He took her shoulders. "Frances! You must! There are

handholds for the chimney sweeps. I will help you.''

She shook her head, shrinking into herself, surrendering to the pain. ''I can't, Nigel. I am afraid!''

He grasped her chin and lifted her face. ''Frances, look at me!'' His black eyes shone with intensity. ''What the hell difference does fear make? None. It's just an emotion. Climb up here onto the grate and wait. Then for God's sake, do it afraid.''

In the next moment he had disappeared, the end of the long rope in one hand. Frances waited. She listened to the sound of Nigel's boots as they scraped on the bricks, the rattle of soot as it broke free and fell about her. She would die. She was more afraid of the chimney than of death. Her training had deserted her, her training and her courage. She could not be brave any longer. She would untie the rope harness and hide in the pantry.

His voice called down to her. ''Don't you dare! Submit to me, Frances. Don't think. Relax. Trust me. I will pull you up.''

Trust me. The man of schemes. The man of secrets. How could she trust him? Yet she put up her arms as she felt the tug on the rope, and grasped it in both hands above her head. Cloth clung to her face. Smoke smelled hot. Something crackled. Then she was spiraling up, spinning as she tried to get purchase on the black walls, her feet flailing in darkness. It was suffocating. Tears racked her. The harsh black walls grabbed at her like hands. Inexorably she was dragged upward, until a hard edge struck her arms, and Nigel dragged her onto the roof.

He pulled away the tablecloth. He was streaked in soot, mired like a sweep.

''You see,'' he said. A wet cloth gently wiped her face and hands. ''It was easy.''

''Weren't you afraid?'' she asked, shaking. ''It was so narrow!''

He was busy with the rope. ''I was terrified. I abhor tight spaces.'' He glanced at her and grinned. ''But if I'd let you see my fear, we'd both have died. Come, before the roof burns and falls away beneath us.''

He tied the rope to the chimney and lowered her to a balcony. She did not look down. From there he leaped to another house and, using the rope once again, helped her to climb across after him. She kept her eyes fixed on his face, until at last he helped her down to the ground and stood with her in the Rue des Arbres in front of the house.

Smoke poured from the door and windows. Glass cracked, wood burst into flame, and in a sudden bright orange flash the house roared.

Grasping Frances by the arm, Nigel dragged her away from the inferno. "Let the damned place burn."

Like a storm bursting over Paris, the news of Waterloo must be spreading consternation, panic, and—for the royalists—rejoicing. More than ten years of warfare were over. Like a pyre to the dead, the house in the Rue des Arbres clamored to the heavens in a sheet of flame. So every place he had lived with Catherine was destroyed. Nigel felt heartily glad of it.

Frances sat on the mounting block at the corner of the street where he had dragged her. A mob of citizens raced by, shouting, carrying buckets. She seemed oblivious to them. Beneath streaks of soot, she was pale. The gash on her forehead marred the smooth skin and honey hairline. He wanted to touch her, but didn't.

"There are moors at Rivaulx," he said. "And a sky that defies the gods to measure it. You will be safe there forever."

She turned to him, shielding her face from the sun. "Don't ask me!" An eloquent betrayal, she covered her eyes with her hand. "Don't! I can never live with you, Nigel. I cannot!"

"Why not?"

"Must you know? Must you drive me? Compel me, even now? I told you: I am afraid!"

It exploded from him, uncontrolled, with nothing to hide his distress. "Afraid of *me*?"

So she knew. She had seen him fight Lance, she had seen him, in a different way, fight Fouché, and Genet, and Catherine. Black as Hades, the abyss yawned. She despised him, his deceit and his intrigue, as she abhorred the violence that dyed his hands. He had imprisoned her, forced her, cajoled her. Even to save her life. She was afraid of him.

"Don't think you can offer me a future." She dropped her hand. Her skin was alabaster, the gash bright vermilion. Her eyes were a brilliant blue in contrast, cobalt on sapphire. "It is my fault, not yours. I shall never be free of it."

It's just an emotion. "Tell me why, Frances. You must tell me!"

She shook her head. "What does it matter now?"

Nigel grasped her shoulders and turned her to face him. "Tell me, Frances. What the hell is it?"

She closed her eyes. "When the maharaja died, we all knew there would be a fight for his throne. Although he had young sons, there were nephews who felt more ready to rule. Soldiers broke into the harem. They killed his wives and babies. The concubines were butchered, too, in case one was carrying his child. It was a massacre, steel ripping silk, horrific red blossoms flowering suddenly in a garden, screaming women."

His blood ran cold. *Women who couldn't possibly resist.*

"How could you forgive it?" he said, looking at his hands. "No wonder you are afraid. How did you escape?"

"I hid in the tunnel under the courtyard, where they used to roll the thunder ball. I thought I would die there. But I survived. I took a horse left by the gate. It probably hadn't occurred to the soldiers that a courtesan could ride."

"Frances—"

She whirled on him. "Don't you understand? It was always there, like an undertone: beneath the beauty and the brilliance, the sickening scent of violence and coercion. It will always be with me. I don't trust my own kind. I am afraid of thunder which brings no rain. I am afraid of the door that slams shut and won't open. I am afraid of a world where someone would set fire to a house with people in it."

"I can protect you," he said.

"No, no! You cannot! My courage has run out. What is left? I have nothing to offer. I am an empty shell. You think you can heal me with passion, but you cannot. I can never escape the past. Neither can I face the future. I must be free!"

It took control not to push her, to allow her the courtesy of detachment. It took a damned heavy dose of nobility not to use what had just happened. She had overcome her fear in the chimney, thanks to him. She owed him her life. No, no, for God's sake. She had given him her virginity. She owed him nothing. "What future do you want?"

"I shall have money when Lord Trent pays me. I have learned about business." She looked at the house, collapsing now, the roof crashing into the room where she had hung the mirrors, the walls buckling about the tables where she had sold silks and spices. "I know about plants. If I can find a place in the country, I think I could start a trade in herbs."

Nigel felt helpless. There was a taste in his mouth like ash. He knew it was grief. "I have given you a house."

She turned to him, eyes wide as the sky. "What?"

"Before we came to Paris, I had my man of business take care of it, in case I didn't return." He had to swallow hard. This was not how he had imagined giving her his gift. "Your parents' house—where you grew up. I bought it. It's yours."

"But my father sold the house to finance our voyage to India."

"The new owner had no objection to selling." Or at least he had not objected to the price offered—the power of naked wealth and determination, the advantage of being a marquess. Damnation, how empty it was now!

She sounded formal, reserved. "I don't know what to say. I shall recompense you, of course, over the years."

Something snapped in him, like a hawser giving way, recoiling with fatal force. "For God's sake, I owe you that, at least. It's a gift! Take the damned house!"

She dropped her head and was silent. Nigel forced himself to unclench his fists, knowing that he had made a wreck of this, of everything, but unable to stop himself now. "Frances, I love you. I want us to be together. For God's sake, I wanted to ask you to marry me."

"Marriage? Are you insane? Never! I cannot!" Her voice was muffled suddenly by her hands.

"Are there sins that can never be expiated?" he asked bitterly. "What is mine? The faults that led me to Catherine? Arrogance? Cruelty?"

"You are not cruel!"

He heard his own fist hit the wall beside him. Pain exploded in his knuckles. Like a ship recoiling from its broken rope, he yawed wildly, out of control, as the words spilled. "I didn't think so, until Russia. It was a training in cruelty. It wasn't like the exercises at Gentleman Jackson's or the smart maneuvers of the parade ground. War isn't fair, or gentlemanly, or honorable. The Cossacks couldn't afford such luxury. I couldn't be with them and not fight as they fought. The first man that I killed with my own hands had green eyes. He was about seventeen. It was his life or mine, but, by God, it was cruel!"

He paused for a moment, but there was no going back now. As the memories surfaced, his voice grew rough with loathing.

"As Napoleon's army retreated from Moscow stragglers dropped behind, the wounded, the weak—some of them women. There was no food or shelter, just a wilderness of snow. I found a girl from Provence, abandoned at the side of the road. She was with child and wounded in the leg. She begged me to shoot her. I tried to help. I swore I would take her with us. It was impossible, of course. We were starving ourselves and she couldn't ride. My vain attempt at mercy endangered the lives of twenty men, and there would be thousands more left by Napoleon to die in the snow. The Cossacks killed her that night while I slept. They killed all the stragglers we found. I told myself it was merciful. It *was* merciful. But in December the French wounded who had been left behind in Vilna were butchered like sheep. I could do nothing to prevent it. By then I might even have thought it was right. I don't know."

She sat in silence, her shoulders rigid. There was no going back now. He had told her. He had told her. She had experienced it; he had been forced to perpetuate it: the slaughter of the helpless, the unforgivable sin.

Her voice dropped into the silence. "This is what drove you to Catherine?"

"What else do you think I deserved? How could she soil me any more than I was already soiled? How could Fouché, who butchered the helpless in Lyons? How could Martin, who

worked only for money? How could any of it? I sweated and
slaved for my country. I tried only to save Lance. Dear God,
you have seen the vain results of that! Catherine is like a
vampire. Her kiss corrupts. You should be afraid of me, Frances. I am afraid of myself.''

Hooves clattered. He glanced over his shoulder. A tall man
swung down from his horse. Nigel swallowed his shock and
was barely aware at first that there was joy in it. So it ended
here. The world had arrived to drag him back to his duty, with
no time for weakness or emotion, no time for explanation or
forgiveness. Yet she, of all people, who knew what it meant,
how could she possibly forgive?

''You do have more than one future.'' He forced control
into his voice. ''If the loneliness of what you think you want
appalls you, Dominic Wyndham will give you a home.''

The rugged face was bruised, a half-healed cut over one
eye. The swollen mouth crumpled into a craggy smile as he
strode up to Nigel and took him by both shoulders. ''Thank
God!'' Wyndham said. ''When I saw the damned fire, I
thought she had killed you.''

''You only *thought*?'' Rent in half, drowning in anguish,
Nigel felt the joy at last. *Wyndham was alive*. He forced himself to adjust, and grinned. ''You damned renegade! Catherine
told us she had killed you.''

The most obvious effect of a blow on the head was a need to
sleep a great deal. Frances wanted to stay awake, to think, but
she slept most of the way from Paris to Calais. The boat ride
passed, on calm summer seas, in a blur. Major Wyndham had
brought her to England. She had not seen Nigel since that last
day in the Rue des Arbres, when he had told her what he had
done in Russia—and then lit up with joy when Wyndham
arrived.

*''You damned renegade! Catherine told us she had killed
you.''*

''Almost,'' Wyndham had said. ''But in the end she only
kept me captive.''

The men had faced each other, Nigel staring at Wyndham, grinning defiantly, like a man about to go to the gallows gladly. "Damned careless of you!"

"I wasn't expecting," Wyndham had replied dryly, "to meet Catherine. She bribed the servants at the house on la Place du Palais Royal, and sent me up some kind of drugged wine, I believe. When she came into my room, dressed as a bloody maid, I was already paralyzed. Next thing I knew I was her prisoner, and she was telling me you were in the Rue des Arbres. Pierre Martin beat me a few times. Then I was left in a cellar."

"So how the devil did you escape?"

Wyndham had grinned, grotesque with bruises. "Someone sent a man to release me. Fouché, I imagine. She was in constant communication with him, as was Martin, who must have told him about me. Lance hadn't known I was there."

Nigel had laughed. "Fouché will want favors from Britain now, but if Napoleon had really triumphed, we might all have died—like Martin, who knew too much. Poor fool. It is possible to serve too many masters. Catherine killed him."

"I can't pretend to be sorry. I grew to dislike him intensely. They enjoyed boasting of their successes. You know he killed Donnington?"

Nigel had not seemed entirely surprised. "So Martin was at Farnhurst?"

"Disguised as one of the French chefs, apparently. The bloody bastard. He poisoned a rabbit and made sure that you ate it."

Nigel had begun to laugh in a wild, helpless paroxysm. "*Rabbit*—so that's how it was done! I might have known that particular fall from grace was Catherine's idea."

"Since I have that information, it is also possible," Wyndham had said, "that I am lying to you. I was at Farnhurst. Perhaps I am the villain and Martin a convenient scapegoat. Can you be sure?"

Nigel had touched the other man's shoulder, briefly. "I am sure, you damned rogue. Catherine had no other reason to kill Martin but to stop him talking. Obviously she had Donnington killed for the same reason. She had planted false papers on him—though he was also a traitor in his own right—and she wanted me to suspect you. She wanted me to believe all my friends capable of treachery. She was wrong. I have never doubted you. I just thought you were dead.''

Beneath the bruises and the rugged smile, Wyndham's pain had shone clear for a moment. ''She had me beaten often enough. Not because I wouldn't tell her anything, but because I didn't love her.''

Nigel had looked away for a moment. ''An interesting philosophy of love!''

''And there is something else.'' Wyndham had glanced awkwardly at Frances. ''She had heard of your reputation, Miss Woodard. Catherine sent Donnington to find you in Dover. You were bait, you see, for Rivaulx.''

''Was she?'' Nigel had said without meeting her eyes. ''It doesn't matter. Now, if you'll excuse me, I have to go and save Europe from Fouché.''

After a few rapid instructions, he had taken Wyndham's horse and ridden away. Frances had not seen Nigel again.

If the loneliness of what you think you want appalls you, Dominic Wyndham will give you a home.

He had taken her in charge, gently and with courtesy. Wyndham had bought her a wardrobe of English dresses, and a maid to dress her hair. If she was to go back to Essex and establish a business, she could not arrive looking like a concubine from India. No doubt it was Nigel's idea. The corsets were constricting, the sleeves too tight. Her hair felt heavy and awkward on top of her head. Frances had capitulated to all of it without complaint. She had wanted to give Nigel the love that would heal him, and found she could not. He had tried to offer love to her, and she could not take it. What was left but to set him free? Yet she would remember forever that feral grin and his bloodied knuckles as he greeted his old friend. For the rest, she didn't care. She cared only that she had seen Nigel for the last time with black despair in his heart. Like

the scandal sheets that had dogged him, even she had been
part of Catherine's plot. And in that Catherine had succeeded.

∞

In the Green Man in Dover, where she had first met Donnington, Frances fell ill. Weak and feverish, she lay in bed.
Wyndham hired a competent woman to nurse her, and visited
her formally once a day. He didn't flirt or try to court her. He
never once spoke of Nigel, working for peace, dealing with
Napoleon's abdication, preparing for the arrival of the Allied
troops. But she heard rumors. The maidservants talked of nothing but the great battle that had been fought at Waterloo, and
of the confusion and debauchery in Paris.

"The Marquess of Rivaulx?" One of the girls giggled in
her hearing. "I saw him once—handsome as the devil—and
he gave me the eye, I can tell you." She tossed her head.
"They say his whore in Paris taught him wicked love secrets
from the East."

"Then he'd not be content with a plain English thing like
you!" said the other maid, elbowing her fellow in the ribs.
"Bet he's got a new one now."

Did he have a new one now? Had he taken her cynically
and coldly as he had taken Catherine, because he thought he
deserved nothing better? Frances turned her head into the pillow and hated herself.

It was two weeks after midsummer when she could travel
again. Dominic Wyndham made no complaint. With the same
cool courtesy he escorted her north, riding beside her hired
carriage. His bruises had faded. He looked rugged, attractive,
and unhappy.

The neat fields and hop gardens of Kent spread out in a
quilt of green: jade and lime, emerald and viridian, in the burst
and soar of high summer.

"Maidstone," said Wyndham as they stopped to change
horses. "Betty Palmer's home is near here."

Frances was surprised out of her reverie. "Betty's home?"

"She came from a village close by. Her daughter lives there
now. Would you like to see the baby?"

As soon as fresh horses were put to, Frances found herself
being bowled along a leafy lane out of Maidstone and away
from London. The village was small and neat. The houses
clustered around an ancient church. As the carriage pulled up,
Frances leaned from the window. Like the entrance to a bee-
hive the open space in front of the church was a throng of
activity. People boiled from the church gate and into the
square. Children and dogs darted about in the crowd. The hum
of laughter and good spirits was pierced only by a high-pitched
wail as a young woman came out of the church clutching a
bundle. The bundle wailed again. A baby had just been bap-
tized.

Behind the mother a beautiful woman laughed up into the
face of a dark-haired man. Tall and slender, the sun soaking
into his dark head, he leaned down and kissed her: Betty Palmer and Nigel.

Frances thought her heart must stop. She wanted to leave.
Nigel couldn't have seen her. But Dominic Wyndham opened
the door. When she hesitated, his green gaze followed hers.
As the major saw Nigel he stiffened perceptibly, but then he
smiled up at Frances and held out his hand.

Frances shook her head. Nigel had moved into the crowd.
Along one side of the square, tables were stacked with pastries
and fresh bread. A whole sheep was being roasted over an
open fire. A barrel of ale, rolled from the inn, was filling glass
after glass with potent liquid. She knew with certainty that
Nigel had done it, had provided a feast for the entire village,
to celebrate the christening of Betty's first grandchild. So affairs were settled in Paris. He had come home.

The crowd parted to allow the arrival of a small troop of
musicians, local men obviously, who made a hobby of playing
the fiddle and pipe. With jocularity they were hoisted onto the
steps of the small cross that must have dominated the center
of the square since the Middle Ages. The ale tankards in their
hands were set down without ceremony on the weathered stone
arms. Couples began to form in a clear space, as in a squeal
of strings the musicians began to tune up.

A dog bounded onto the steps and leaped at one of the
fiddlers. To shrieks of laughter, it fastened its teeth in the

man's sleeve. Obviously more than a little tipsy, the musician tried to shake it off. The dog hung, the man toppled and, with a good-natured shout, tumbled down the steps. He stood up a few moments later without the dog, which shot off through the crowd pursued by shouts. The man smiled as if he had just completed a circus act, but he held up his left hand, cradled in his right.

"Broke my damned finger! Sorry folks! No fiddling!"

A collective groan echoed about the square.

Frances watched in amazement as Nigel stepped from the crowd. "See to your hand, Tom Smith. We'll still have dancing. With your permission?"

"For God's sake," said Wyndham. "I knew he was mad."

Was it mad for a marquess to play dances for villagers? Nigel took Tom's violin. With no apparent hesitation he tucked it beneath his chin. Moments later the square echoed to a series of lilting country dances, the notes soaring like the song of a skylark. Frances sat frozen, watching him. Major Wyndham stalked away to stand, arms folded, against a tree.

The square echoed with laughter. The fiddles called and flitted, bouncing merriment, spreading joy, until the dancers began to flag and a large man with a smile like a breakwater started to carve the roast sheep. Frances could not watch any longer. Why had Wyndham brought her here? She wanted only to get to London, to see Lord Trent, to retire to Essex. She shrank back into the corner of the carriage and closed her eyes.

∽

Nigel had seen the carriage arrive, and he knew the rugged face of the escort. Frances should have been settled into her house in Essex by now. What was she doing here with Wyndham? The obvious answer drowned him in pain. He refused to allow it. The gift Frances had made him deserved a better response than petty jealousy. Would she acknowledge it? Or would she ridicule him if he told her how he believed she had gifted him? Of all the kinds of courage he once thought he possessed, she had shown him one more. It was the courage that enabled him now to pick up Tom's violin and make joyful music.

The dancing over, he was swallowed by the crowd. They pressed him with ale and with honest country food, a far cry from the last feast he had provided, with devilry, at Farnhurst. He shook them off, gently, at last. Dominic Wyndham met him several strides before he reached the carriage, out of her earshot.

"She has been ill," he said. "We were delayed. It is not what you think."

"It would be all right if it were," replied Nigel, "if that were her will. The illness, was it serious?"

Wyndham shook his head. "You and I haven't talked," he went on, "since Paris. We should have talked more. I thought I knew Catherine. As her captive I learned more about her than I ever wished. God knows what it did to you to stay with her as you did, but the results must have been ugly."

"Catherine was a vampire. I was bitten."

"So she taught you to devour souls? Does that explain what you have done to Frances Woodard?"

"You said she was ill! How?"

Wyndham's voice held the bite of anger. "It was of the spirit, not the body, I think. She ran a fever and was a little delirious at times. Sometimes she talked without knowing it. If you would be kind enough to meet me, after I have taken her safely to Essex, I would like to avenge her. Swords or pistols, it doesn't matter."

The shock was so absolute that Nigel almost laughed. Instead he collected his wits and forced all of his attention to his friend.

"Dear God, does everyone want to fight me over the women they think I have destroyed? You believe I abandoned her?"

"I think you used her without conscience. Dammit all! When I saw her at Farnhurst I thought she was——" He paused and took a breath. "I know better now. Devil take it, Nigel! I don't care what your reasons may have been. I don't care if it saved Europe, but what happened at Farnhurst, what has happened since . . . I'm damned if I can let it go." Wyndham glanced away, his jaw set. "However, before I attempt to kill a friend, I'd like to be sure I am right."

The merrymakers were milling about with their tankards and plates. "At Farnhurst I used her, though not in the way that you mean. We became lovers in Paris. I asked her to marry me. She refused."

Wyndham snorted. "I don't believe you."

Nigel shrugged. "As you say, she is not like other women. She saw what I am and despised it."

"Bloody hell! She turned down marriage to a marquess? I will only believe this if you ask her again. Now!"

"Or you will call me out?"

Wyndham's face was stiff. "I am well aware that you might kill me. Nevertheless, unless you make amends to her now, I will do it."

The absurdity of it threatened to overwhelm him. Ask her to marry him again? It was what he wanted, with his heart and soul. But not quite like this. Yet he thrust past Wyndham and opened the carriage door. Frances was curled on the seat with her head on her arms. Nigel climbed in and sat down beside her. Very gently he touched her hair, smoothing the silk from her face, and without thinking, quoted softly from the Song of Solomon.

" 'Thy plants are an orchard of pomegranates, with pleasant fruits, camphire with spikenard. Spikenard and saffron. Calamus and cinnamon, with all trees of frankincense—' "

Her eyes opened. "Nigel?"

"Wyndham tells me you've been ill. Are you better?"

Honey-gold strands slipped from their pins over the fine pink mark where she had been scarred, over the perfect cheekbones and delicate ears. He wanted to kiss her.

"I was only . . . It was the accumulated stress, I think. I wasn't really ill. I just had to rest. Major Wyndham has been very kind."

"He is kind. You are still determined on Essex and a garden of herbs?"

A fleeting worry crossed her face. "You said the house—"

"It is yours. You are content?"

"Yes, of course. I must be free, don't you see?" Tears

welled suddenly. She swept them away. "I must, Nigel!"

"Then you still will not marry me?"

"Don't! You think I'm being noble? Or that there is anything about you that repels me? Oh, God, if only it were that simple! No, no! If I could share my life with any man it would be you, Nigel, but I cannot."

He forgot Wyndham. He forgot everything but the distress on her face. "Oh, God, Frances. I love you with all my heart and soul. Must I beg you?"

She put up her hands, the hands that moved like the wind through grass. "Look at me! I am a freak. I wear a gold stud in my nose. In spite of these dresses and this corset and my hair like a bird's nest, I cannot be other than what I am. What kind of marchioness would a harlot make?"

"Do you think any of that matters a damn to me? I love you." He took her fingers as if he could make her see that he meant it. "I love you. I want you to marry me."

The tears welled, reddening her nose as she looked at him. She was infinitely desirable. "I cannot, Nigel. I cannot." He knew from her eyes that she meant it, that it was absolute, not a whim, nothing open to persuasion. "It is not because I don't love you, but because I do."

For a moment he sat in silence. Her words sank like a stone in a deep well. No possible response was left. Yet there was one more thing he must do. "Very well. I won't torment you about it. But before I leave—Frances, there is news about Lance." She stared at him in alarm, as if reading his feelings. "I'm sorry. He is dead."

The English dress made her look younger. It settled delicately over her curves. "I'm so sorry!"

"Catherine died, too. He wrote me a letter, explaining it in his poor, foolish way. They took poison. He couldn't live with her. He couldn't live with himself. With Napoleon defeated, Russia held nothing for Katerina, so after miles of bitterness and recrimination they ended it. I visited Miss March and told her, but not the truth. She wept a little, but she never really knew him."

"You told her Lance died a hero?"

"You think I should have done otherwise?"

Frances shook her head. "No, no. It was kinder." She looked down. "What we think is true doesn't always need to be told, does it? If it is not kind, or necessary. Thank you for telling me. Now everything has come to a close."

There was really nothing left to say. No words to express the longing in his heart. If she had been lovely in her Indian robes, she was lovely now in the soft blue dress. " 'Then be thou like a roe or a young hart upon the mountains of Bether.' Take your freedom, Frances."

He climbed from the carriage before he should change his mind, before he began to cajole or beg or bully.

Dominic Wyndham stared at him blindly. Nigel took him by the elbow and dragged him out of earshot.

"You heard?" asked Nigel. "Get her away. Take her to Essex. And if you want to fight a duel with me, go ahead. I await assassination, for I'm damned if I'll fight you."

"I'm sorry," said Wyndham. "She loves you? I had no idea. How can you let her go?"

"Because I love her, you bloody fool," said Nigel. "Now, for God's sake, take her away."

Twenty-one

⟋⟍

FRANCES SPENT TWO days in London. Lord Trent gave her a draft for the money she had earned. He also backed a small loan for her so she could begin her business more easily. She would not be part of the beau monde, but she would have independence and dignity, which meant far more.

Wyndham did not take her into Essex. Frances thanked him for his care, but she insisted on continuing her journey alone in a hired post chaise. When she arrived at the house, she was glad.

Bright sunshine beat down through a canopy of trees, glittering across the orchard and paddock. Light ricocheted from the duck pond to the far meander of the Pinney Brook. Brightness scattered across whitewashed bricks, two bow windows, a red tile roof, the fresh green paint on the door. The house where Frances had grown up was neat and snug and glowing in the sunshine. She climbed from the chaise and stepped into the hallway.

The red and black floor tiles were just as she remembered. White doors led to rooms echoing with the voices of her parents. Beyond those panels was her father's old study, where he had laid out his plants to the despair of the housemaids. Upstairs in the southeast corner, while the sun rang through the day, her mother had liked to sit with vases of roses, English roses, scenting the air. At the back of the house were the

buttery and washrooms, and the stairs to the cellar where occasionally a small child had been taken to breathe in the scents
of dry brick and dust as she helped her father pick wine. Yet
it had taken a marquess to teach her the real differences in
Burgundies and Chablis.

Between that innocence and that knowledge lay India.

A large package lay in the hallway, addressed in a strong,
black hand. His writing. Her heart skipped a beat, crazily.
Frances tore away the wrapping. Storm-tossed trees, a wild
moor, and a white horse galloping forever to freedom. Nigel
had sent her his painting.

There was a note, sealed with his crest. Her fingers shook
as she opened it. *Defy the storm, my love,* he had written. *Do
not be afraid. These clouds never break. They are only paint—
and the rain they threaten is not real.*

Frances sank onto her mother's old chair in the hallway and,
to the amazement of the housekeeper, laid her head on her
arms and sobbed.

"Very well," said Betty. "You had better account for it."

Nigel glanced up at her. Candlelight flickered over the familiar London parlor. The faint tinkle of music and laughter
drifted in from the rest of the house, but he was thinking of a
village near Maidstone and a christening. "What?"

Betty frowned. "What it is, my dear? Something has happened, hasn't it? Beyond the encounter with Catherine, beyond
the failure with Lance. If I didn't know better, I'd think—"

The soft light flattered her. The baby, Betty's grandson, had
exactly her mouth when he smiled. Nigel was the child's godfather. He had thought it a small enough courtesy, until Betty's
daughter had laid her son in his arms in that village church—
milky charm, wailing at the indignity of the holy water, then
smiling suddenly at a stranger. Nigel had stared, stunned, into
those round blue eyes while his heart lurched. *To have a child!*
The simplest of revelations. An heir for Rivaulx. Would his
first child look like the late marchioness, with her dark, French
beauty, or—?

Betty couldn't hide her obvious concern. "Can you trust in loyalty, or in love, after all the betrayals, after Lance?"

"Poor Lance. It was too hard for him. I am sorry I couldn't save him, but his own failings destroyed him in the end—he could never understand that Frances offered purity, and Catherine corruption."

"Ah, my dear. And Pierre Martin, your nasty mercenary?"

"There's a strange irony about Monsieur Martin. I learned of it only recently: he did send the message."

She studied him as if she were trying to fathom a great mystery. "The message?"

"My message to Wellington about Charleroi. It would have reached Brussels in time, but for an officious Allied officer who delayed it the critical twenty-four hours. As it turns out, Napoleon was defeated anyway, but though Martin was more cruel than I knew, I'm oddly glad that he honored his commitment to me in that, at least."

"Then has it happened, at last, my dear?"

Nigel stretched his fingers. Candlelight glanced off his griffin ring, his touch of gold, never removed, as Frances could never remove hers. Each of them tied, bound, to the past that had made them. Yet he was free now to make music. In the room with the arch-topped windows, he filled Rivaulx House every day with the passion of Giuseppe Grancino. It amazed him.

"My delectable Betty, *you* sent her to Paris. It was your damned idea. What the devil did you think would happen?"

"That you would have to survive, to take care of her. I also thought she would offer comfort, perhaps, a protection against memories of Catherine."

"Which as it turned out," said Nigel wryly, "was a particularly piquant idea."

There was a little gray in her dark hair. It suited her. Honest and wise, Betty glanced away. "Why were you poisoned at Farnhurst?"

"For a diversion, a red herring, so I wouldn't be able to prevent Donnington's murder—and as a punishment, of course. Frances was meant to be part of it. You realize that you played directly into Catherine's plans by encouraging her to stay with me?'' He lay back on the couch and began to laugh. In his mind he could hear music like a forest falling, the stresses in all the wrong places.

"My dear, if only any of us could have seen that at the time! I suppose Catherine thought she could use Frances as a weapon. What better than threats to a woman to coerce you!"

"Especially a woman I had taken to my bed. Catherine hoped I would rape Frances at Farnhurst. Later she used Lance to convince Frances to seduce me, which fell out just as Catherine planned. It was a remarkable seduction. I was bloody helpless."

"My dear man! If the poison had made you . . . Catherine knew your honor, of course."

"And hated it. No, it was even deeper than that. Catherine thought that a woman like Frances would drive me mad. She was right. Like a callow youth, the fearsome marquess was enraptured, beaten to his knees in Aphrodite's storm, lost in the darkest reaches of his own heart: 'a savage place! as holy and enchanted as e'er beneath a wailing moon was haunted by woman wailing for her demon-lover!' Of course, she didn't know what Frances would prove to be. Yes, Betty, it has happened."

She took his hand. Nigel lifted her fingers to his lips and kissed the knuckles, honoring her friendship. Betty clasped his fingers for a moment, returning the pressure, then let go. "Nigel, should I be happy for you?"

He grinned. "Of course. I am in love. Forever, as it happens. Do you really think I intend to do nothing about it?"

There was a rustle in the grass and a soft snort. Frances was instantly awake. The sky arched away in the shell blue of high summer, pierced by spiraling larks. She had fallen asleep watching them. She was lying on her back in the center of the lower meadow, where in the confusion of Nigel's sudden purchase, the hay had not been cut. She had left it to grow tall and wild, and make seed.

The blue dome of sky was fringed with the nodding heads

of cocksfoot and fescue, a rampart of green-gold grass stems. Bending among them, the merry faces of ox-eye daisies—the moon daisy, marguerite—showed off their fringe of white petals about the butter-yellow heart. The larks were mere specks in the blue, but liquid notes spilled down, coating the meadow with music, while chaffinch and yellowhammer sat quiet in the hedgerow.

She was in Essex at her old home. She had been here for weeks.

She had hung Nigel's painting in her bedroom. Every day she gazed at it, as if the dumb canvas could tell her a truth about him that she had been too blind to see. Instead she saw a truth about herself. She could run a business; she was strong; she could face her fears. Nigel had given all of it to her, freely: he had gifted her with her *self*—an Englishwoman.

This was her true identity, embellished by experience, but still English.

Faces smiled at her in the village. They remembered her as a little girl. They remembered her parents. In spite of the gold stud, the villagers accepted her without judgment. Yet as she walked in the lanes where she had played as a child, with an aching heart she sought for *his* face, and the wild humor.

The tame English fields, with their simple, ordinary rhythms, had taught her what she needed to know. Yet she longed for the great reaches of India where white cranes beat their way to the snow-crowned Himalayas—for a white horse racing away into a storm. And more clearly she longed for a man.

For she was a woman very desperately in love.

His name resounded with her heartbeat. Nigel, Nigel, Nigel. She was possessed by it. She loved him. She wanted him. Only the sky seemed open enough, yet it did not quiet her thinking or assuage her regrets. How could she have known she would love him? How known that the failings that stood in their way would be hers, not his? But she wouldn't burden him. She had been right to set him free. Yet she would carry her loss to the grave—*Nigel, Marquess of Rivaulx*. Her one true love. *What could not be changed must be endured*.

But did she still believe it? She had learned something else from Nigel: nothing had to be endured without a fight. How could you tell what could not be changed unless you tried? What if she went to London to find him? Her heart hammered at the thought. Tomorrow? What if she went to him tomorrow? Planning it, she lost herself in the vast sky over the meadows, with the sun beating on her new bonnet, her neck naked without her veil, and called on the calming breath.

Far away a faint breeze stirred the leaves of the oaks. Another snort, like a dragon breathing fire, made her sit up, flakes of grass falling from her hair to her skirts. Hooves thundered away across the field. Dropping her bonnet on the ground, Frances scrambled to her feet. The horse ran, mane and tail streaming, the coat of silver and gold striking fire in the sunlight. Without saddle or bridle, for pure joy he leaped and cavorted, flashing a challenge to the high sun and the bright day. If a horse could laugh, he laughed. Her heart leaped, making her pulse race, dizzy.

A whistle pierced the heavy summer air, scattering the humble buzz of bees. The horse skidded to a stop, turned, and bowed to one knee.

"I am here," said a voice behind her. "Will you send me away?"

Her heart ringing like an anvil, Frances turned. Nigel was leaning against the trunk of one of her oak trees. He wore no jacket or waistcoat, just white shirt, breeches, elegant boots. His arms were full of color: yellow, white, green.

"Your Don horse?" she said, feeling foolish, knowing her agitation showed in her face and her erratic breathing, with no veil to hide it. *He had come to her!*

The sunlight slipped over Nigel like honey, gilding his hair and the slightly crooked line of his nose, scattering in the gorgeous eyelashes. Frances sank to the grass—to the innocent earth of small jewellike beetles and the oblivious lives of tiny creatures—and grasped the strings of her bonnet, dazed with a wild rush of happiness. *He had come to her!* Nigel stepped

up to her and dropped his burden of flowers. Ox-eye daisies
tumbled in a heap.

"Lance sent him back. A groom brought him across France
and delivered him to Rivaulx House."

"Was there a message?" She glanced up at him, her heart
beating crazily.

"Only one line—'He belongs where his heart is.' "

"Ah, poor Lance! But I am glad your horse is returned to
you. From the borders of Russia—"

"Frances, are you happy here?"

She looked down at the sun-dappled grass. "I have had time
to think. I have realized how little I know of life. I thought I
was caught between two cultures, but I am not. I am English.
I haven't really understood what I learned in India. You said
my philosophy was shallow. You were right. It was just a
glimpse of a splendid richness distorted by my own narrow
preconceptions. There are centuries of learning and culture behind the sacred texts. What could I understand of them?"

His shadow fell across the grass as he moved. "You learned
about compassion. English morality is often just rigid and ster-
ile—merely prudery—a vice not a virtue."

"But it was presumptuous to claim I knew anything of
Kama. I cannot unmake what has happened, but everything I
thought I knew has been a very pale reflection of the truth."

He stood in silence. She could feel the intensity of his gaze,
as she had felt it all those months ago in a library, where he
had tried to protect her and been foiled by her stubbornness.
"No," he said. "You have known fear. It was real enough."

"I have thought," she said, the words spilling as if suddenly
released, "of what you told me about the Cossacks, of the
retreat from Moscow. Did you think I feared *you* because of
that? Because when you fought Lance, I knew you had learned
how to kill?"

The horse had begun to graze, every once in a while lifting
its lovely, intelligent head to look at them. Nigel sat down on
the flattened grass beside her. "Frances, it doesn't matter."

"But it does matter. Because we left it there, in the Rue
des Arbres, hanging like the sword of Damocles, able to fell
either of us—without warning—with a stroke. I did not want

you to think I judged you or was afraid of you because of what you had done. I would not leave you with that."

He took a daisy and slit the stem with his fingernail. "But to usurp God's place? It is not for us to judge life and death."

"Not usually, no. But could you have stopped the Cossacks? Fed and clothed and nursed the whole world? Those poor French had no hope but a fast release from the cold and suffering, rather than a slow one. Yet that isn't how life is usually, is it? I think I had forgotten until I came back here. Or perhaps it began in that village near Maidstone."

She caught a fleeting change in his expression. "The christening?"

"Ordinary people with ordinary problems and ordinary joys, marrying in happiness, loving their children, being kind to their neighbors. That is how most people live—in India or here. I had forgotten it, you see. I had just forgotten."

"I am a godfather." He grinned. "Dear Lord, Frances, I wish you could have seen that baby smile."

"I have been visiting the babies in the village. Every one is a new hope, isn't it? A new beginning, innocent of despair. I want to begin again."

"But it is not how I have lived. You know what I am, what I have done."

She watched his supple fingers working among the flowers, and with a flush of heat remembered those hands on her naked skin. "Because only you had the strength to do it. If people like you didn't risk yourselves, all those ordinary lives could not go on. Someone must deal with the Napoleons and the Fouchés and the Catherines, or they will steal the world and remake it in their image. Not everyone is strong enough, or skilled enough, to do it. In the end, Lance was not. You were."

A wry awareness crept into his voice. "Neither of us can deny it had a price."

"If I criticized your duplicity, I'm sorry. In Paris you worked only to save lives and had the brilliance to do it without violence. You even saved Napoleon's life, because you understood something bigger than personal revenge. I'm sorry that I couldn't say all that in the Rue des Arbres, or later when you told me about Lance. Thank you for coming here and letting me say it now.''

He reached out and unwrapped her fingers from the bonnet strings. His hands held hers, strong, confident. ''Perhaps, in my horror over the snows, I had forgotten the summers. But human hands make violins as well as rifles. Human hearts hold more kindness than cruelty. Betty has always believed that.''

''It's what freedom is, knowing that. So are we both free now, Nigel?''

He released her fingers. ''I couldn't have done it without you.''

''Me? You helped win peace for Europe, that is what frees you.''

He smiled. ''No, Frances. My love for you is what frees me.''

It hit hard, making her breathe fast. How hard to love a man with your entire heart and soul, to want him so badly.

''But in spite of this English meadow and this silly bonnet, I am a professional courtesan. That hasn't changed. I am ruined rather thoroughly, aren't I?''

The small flare at the nostril betrayed him—that masculine power and certainty—that determination to win the game at all costs, yet his eyes betrayed something quite different. He laughed. ''Very well.'' He stood up, his arms filled with daisies. ''If you are nothing but a *Ganika,* I would buy your services.''

Something moved in her, treacherous and hot. ''Now?''

He grinned. ''There are only two kinds of time: now and not now. This is now. It is all we have to tie together the past and the future, the turning point. I love you. I want you. You are a courtesan. Lie down.''

Her heart pounded in its own ragged rhythm. ''If you wish my services, you must pay me.''

He tore off his shirt, so the sun poured over naked flesh, and took up more daisies. ''Your flowers were red, mine are gold. They are coin enough.'' Like gold and silver coins, flowers rained into her lap, witty and innocent. ''Give me your hands.''

Frances held out both arms, bare beneath the short puffed

sleeves of her dress. He caught up more flowers. He had laced them together into a long chain by inserting each flower head through a small slit in another's stem. The white petals furled against his skin, yellow pollen gilding his arms.

Nigel took her hands and bound them together with his rope of daisies. Shaking with longing, she lay back on the grass. He pulled her arms above her head and wove the flower chain into the tall grass stems, binding her in place.

"It is forbidden to break them," he said, smiling.

Her heart hammered, completely out of control. The sun warmed her legs as he pushed up her skirt and ran his hands down her legs. He took each foot in turn, pulling off her shoe, rubbing deliciously at her instep. Slowly he dragged off her stockings. The flower stems prickled as he bound them about each ankle and gently tied her legs apart. A pulse beat hot and erratic, deep inside, weakening her.

"I cannot—" she began.

He kissed her. "Hush, sweetheart. I have paid. All the responsibility is mine."

She was helpless, opening her mouth to him, kissing him back. Wild, insistent throbbing answered like drums in the night, washing alarm through her blood. He soothed it, sure and gentle, touching her arms and her neck, the sweet, delicious places that still left her a cocoon of safety, dissolving the fears.

"I love you," he said softly. "You are safe. No, no. Don't move. Relax."

Spread-eagled beneath him, she must give herself into his care or break the flowers. He took a stray daisy and stroked the petals over her cheek and down her neck, following it with kisses.

"I love you," he said. "You are innocent."

She closed her eyes against tears and bright sunlight.

His mouth moved on her. Warmth spread slowly over her breasts and belly. Her muslin dress was being tugged softly away, tantalizing her skin as it slithered, catching at the nipple, gliding over her waist.

"I love you," he said. "You are beautiful."

He kept kissing her as he unlaced the tight English corset.

Kisses dropped lightly on the swell of her breasts, on her shoulder, on her brow. He pulled away her shift. She lay helpless, exposed under the vast blue sky.

"I love you." His voice held a deep gurgle of joy. "You are naked."

She tried to move her arms, but the ropes of daisies held her. He stroked softly over her belly, letting his fingers linger on the curls of her sex.

"It is the tension in the strings that makes music, Frances." He had said that before, in London. "You are only the instrument. Lie still, be played. Perhaps it will be a new melody."

With the wisdom of his musician's fingers, he caressed her flank, a harmony of pleasure, notes sliding through the scale. Petals feathered at her wrists and ankles. She grew taut, while the ropes of daisy stems prickled. His mouth moved on her. She heard the rustle of his clothes, fabric tearing as he undressed himself with one hand. Then the heat of his skin against hers. Smooth. Wicked. Knowledgeable. Like a harp string she resonated as his kisses moved over her. Tension grew, heavy and hot. He flicked over her thighs with a flower, as he had done once before with red petals. She felt herself blushing, a fiery, fierce heat, as he dropped them onto her.

His voice held a smile of delight. " 'Behold thou art fair, my beloved, yea, pleasant: also our bed is green.' "

"Let me touch you," she whispered.

"Ah, no, no. Relax. You are safe. Welcome the pleasure. This is for you. Take it." He lay down beside her and kissed her ear. " 'He should dispel her fears, in some lonely place, and there he should embrace and kiss her . . . making an exchange of flowers.' "

She turned her head, breathing in his scent and the softness of his hair. "That is from the *Kama Sutra*!"

"I have read it," he said, dry humor in his voice. "A traveler's translation, in London. But apart from the charm of the setting and the language, I didn't learn anything new. Now, hush. Whatever happens now, it's not your fault. You are a courtesan. I have paid with gold. Lie still and just feel."

The breath was stripped from her body as his mouth touched again. Hot sun beat on her closed lids. She lay pinned to the

ground in the nest of soft muslins made by her dress and
petticoats. In ripples, the pleasure spread as the bright sun
danced, hot and red, and his tongue touched. The rustle of
grasses and the lark's high singing faded behind a bass of rapid
breathing, his, hers, she didn't know. She was gasping, raggedly sucking in air, her control scattered as the beat ran ever
faster.

His hands wandered over her thighs, teasing them further
and further apart, his thumb brushing gently at the soft hair
between them.

"What do they call it?" he asked. "This woman's flower?"

"*Yoni,*" she said, aching with desire.

His fingers stroked, over and over. "And may I suckle there,
at this lotus *yoni*?"

Her blush was furious, but she had melted now. Melted like
wax in the sun. "Yes. Yes, if you like."

"Oh, yes," he said with the laugh bubbling. "I like."

Hot, clever, his tongue kissed her, suckling at the swollen
nub, swirling in ecstatic patterns. She gasped and cried out,
pierced with pleasure. At last his mouth moved back to hers,
musk and salt, and she felt his shaft against her—hard, slick
velvet—answering the hunger of her own moisture.

"Yes," she breathed. "Yes."

Deliberately—slowly—he entered her. She felt herself
yielding, inch by inch, as waves of sensation flowed out from
their joining. She could trust him. She could trust him, in spite
of his beauty. He was a man of compassion and a man of
humor. Of the two faces of Shiva, destruction and creation,
creation was the stronger. She could trust him. She loved him.

Deep inside, he held still for a moment before he moved
again: rocking and deep, carrying her with him. Frances tore
her mouth from his. Her lips brushed his salt skin, moaning,
reveling in the feel of him, hot and proud in the sunshine. She
loved him. She wanted to make him a child.

He sucked hard at her nipple as he thrust into her again.
She grasped for his arms. Scattering petals, the chains of flowers ripped apart.

"That was forbidden," he said, his voice warm and throaty.
"Now you must take the consequences."

She laughed, wrapping her legs and arms about his body in unalloyed gladness, pulling herself into him, closer, ever closer. His back was lean and hard, smooth under her fingers. They thrust together, a ringing harmony. She rocked, rubbing herself on him, seeking pleasure, seeking that place of joy—no longer overwhelming, but deeply satisfying—an intensity of feeling to pursue single-mindedly. She loved him.

He moved just a little, a small change of angle. She cried out—and her cry shattered into fragments.

The pulse started somewhere deep inside, mounting, thundering. His words echoed in the rush of sensation. *This is for you. Take it.* Then words fled, thoughts disappeared in a concentration of ecstasy. Open, helpless, she knew oblivion as the uncontrolled intensity of pleasure convulsed and convulsed.

He laughed aloud. Frances opened her eyes. Sunshine haloed his hair and his demon's face, glazed with bright moisture. In the dazzle of the summer day, he was exultant, laughing in pure joy. She had never seen him like this—as he must have been before Russia, when he was simply a sensualist. No, never simple, even in his joy. And this was joy. He shone with it, joy in her pleasure, and her heart melted.

Sweet relaxation spread through her limbs, but he held himself inside her, hard and impudent.

"Nigel, was that it? The little death?"

"Yours," he said. "Not mine."

Small pulses rippled from him, deep inside. *Delightful. Delightful. Delightful.* A rhythm of nonsense and happiness, tender and triumphant. Then he moved in her, and she gasped aloud.

"Hush!" he said, kissing her. "You are about to die again, and this time I shall die with you."

He dressed her with the same care he had used to undress her. As she sat among the crushed flowers, weak-kneed and satiated, Frances watched the easy way he shrugged into his shirt, his lean flanks as he pulled on his breeches, the sheer animal beauty of his body.

"Were you afraid, Nigel?" she asked.

"Oh, yes. Until you gave me back my music."

She was puzzled. "Your music? At the christening?"

"Long before that. I knew it in the dark, in a cupboard. I just had to wait until the christening for an instrument." Sun dazzled from his hair. "What have we been afraid of? Of cruelty, of death? But to be afraid of death is to be afraid of life. They are two sides of one coin. I will not let you deny me, Frances."

She knew herself totally vulnerable. "I cannot, after what has just happened. I shall live with you, be your mistress, if you want it."

He held out a hand, helping her to her feet. Far away across the meadow, the Don horse lifted its head and nickered softly. "Then you still deny me, for that is not what I want."

She picked up her bonnet, dangling it from the strings. "What do you want?"

"Say that you love me."

"You don't have to ask. I love you."

"Then you cannot be my mistress. I want us equal. I want us friends. I want us to be lovers, as equals, as friends. I want it forever and every day. I want to be there for you when you need me. I want you there for me when I need you. I want children. Your children. I want to see if they look like you." He grinned. "I also want to play with your *yoni* whenever we both like. There is only one way to achieve it. We shall marry."

Something treacherous moved in her. "This isn't fair."

"*Fair?* I will use every weapon I possess to convince you. When I was chained in that cupboard, I was faced with myself as I had not been in years. Over and over again I sought that place you had showed me—that essential core. At last it gave me the peace to look at myself. I thought I was self-aware. I was not. I was only well defended against living. As I sat in the dark I began to realize that much of what I had taken for courage had been cowardice. You showed me that when you seduced me with mirrors. To refuse sex was cowardice. To refuse music was cowardice. Denial and control aren't the answer to the world's confusion. Why was I afraid to love? Because it cannot be mastered by logic? Until I met you, I was as conquered by fear as you were.''

''It was natural enough,'' Frances said, ''after Catherine.''

He smoothed a stray wisp of hair from her cheek. ''Natural? Yes. I almost allowed her to win. You asked once what is left when courage runs out. The answer is love. Love is our only defense against chaos. But love takes a blind leap of faith. It means risk. Let us take that risk, dulcimer damsel, together. I love you, Frances. You love me.''

''Too much to marry you! I am a harlot. You are a marquess.''

He grinned, an open defenseless grin she had rarely seen. ''Many a peer has married a strumpet, and the world wags on. But that is not what you are. *Artha, Kama,* and *Dharma*—wealth, sensual pleasure, and virtue, you told me—the three aims of life, necessary to attain the sacred. You are the opposite of a harlot. Whether you know it or not, you are the guardian of *Kama*. I shall happily provide the prosperity, and we shall find virtue together. Your father was a respectable country gentleman. Lord Trent will give you away. Dominic Wyndham will be our best man. Betty will applaud discreetly from the sidelines.''

''I wear gold in my nostril,'' she said, touching it.

He took her hand and kissed the palm. ''So? You will be a marchioness. Fashion will follow, not lead, you.''

''But the gossip, the innuendo—''

His eyes laughed at her over her fingers. ''Do you think they will say that the vilest rake in London has found satiety at last with his exotic concubine, and was besotted enough to marry her?''

''Something like that.''

His lips moved to her wrist. ''But it will never be said aloud, or in your hearing. No one in society knows who you are. Certainly anyone who saw you at Farnhurst will never admit it, especially to his wife.'' He pulled back her sleeve and kissed her shoulder. ''As for those who do know? They will be bottle green with envy. They will suppose we spend our days in bliss and our nights in mysteries of erotic indulgence. Let them think it. Let them imagine whatever they like, as long as it is ardent, creative, and ecstatic.'' He pulled her into his embrace. ''After all, it will be true.''

She looked up at him. She loved every line of his face. ''Nigel, is passion enough? Will it sustain us?''

He kissed her, lightly. ''Does passion create love? If that were true, Katerina and I could have loved each other. No, beloved, it's love that creates passion. And true lovers are friends, also. That is what we both felt today. And it will only get better.''

She was giddy in his arms. ''How do you know?''

''My mother told me—and besides, with your training, how could it be otherwise? I want to learn all the rest of it, all the sixty-four arts.'' He grinned. ''We shall never run out of positions, and they all have the most splendid names.''

The Don horse, silver and gold under the dappled trees, was blurred. Her cheeks were wet. All the fear and tension of the last years seemed to be seeping away with the tears.

Nigel held her encircled. His voice was soft against her hair. ''It's all right. You love me. You will marry me. We shall have children. I will delight in you forever.''

Children. Nigel's children. With her entire soul she wanted it. In a blaze of certainty Frances saw a different future unfold—one she had never allowed herself to imagine, glistening, iridescent. To go through life hand in hand with this man, with his brilliance and his passion and his essential core of kindness. To be his friend and his lover. To lay the gifts of her training in his hands, for him alone, and accept the gift of his love in return. To make music. A future of joy and self-determination rather than endurance. They didn't need the world, or social approval, though she knew Nigel's charisma would bring society and the world to his feet. But it didn't matter. Either way, it didn't matter. They had won through to something higher and truer than that.

He saw her answer in her eyes, and kissed her again.

''You have my heart. You will be my wife. You will be free forever.''

''I will marry you.'' She put her hand firmly in his.

"Gladly. If you will accept my love for yours, and find your own freedom in mine."

"There are moors at Rivaulx," he said, smiling, "and a sky that defies the gods to measure it. 'Rise up, my love, my fair one, and come away.' "

Author's Note

∞

The *Kama Sutra* is an ancient work of philosophy, complex, and rich. It accepts human sexuality as a natural, even sacred, part of life. All errors in my portrayal of its teachings are entirely the fault of Frances, a naive Englishwoman of her day. As far as I know, it was first translated into English by Sir Richard Burton in 1883, but we may imagine some earlier traveler secretly circulated his own version in Regency England. If so, surely someone of Nigel's reputation could have secured a copy?

The harem I describe is entirely my own invention, not intended to represent any of the magnificent palaces of India, or any particular area or culture. However, I did not invent the thunder ball or the goldfish with rings in their noses—both existed. And I pored over a great many beautiful and inspiring ancient paintings of harem life.

As for Nigel's poisoning, apparently belladonna is not toxic to rabbits, though it lingers in their flesh—an obscure way to poison, but effective!

The recipe for oatmeal pudding dates from 1816, and is genuine.

Wellington's intelligence network—headed by Colquhoun (pronounced *Co-HOON*) Grant—placed agents in Paris who did indeed discover that Napoleon would invade Belgium at Charleroi. Sadly the messenger was delayed by a Hanoverian officer, Major General Dörnberg, and did not arrive in Brussels in time. Thus the French troops swept across the border unopposed and claimed the first battles—at Ligny and Quatre Bras on Friday, June 16—as victories. Ironically Paris was celebrating this triumph on the very day of Napoleon's final defeat on Sunday at Waterloo.

Fouché, who came to power in France during the Terror, was indeed chief of the secret police. He did plot with England while working for Napoleon. In fact, he was so wedded to intrigue, he would probably have plotted with anyone. By the way, Nigel quotes him accurately.

And the twenty thousand pounds? This enormous sum was once lost by a gentleman—his name was George Harley Drummond—in a single night's gaming. It happened at White's Club. The winner was Beau Brummell.

What happens to Dominic Wyndham? You can find out in my next book from Berkley, *Flowers Under Ice*.

I love to hear from readers. You may reach me at P.O. Box 197, Ridgway, CO 81432-0197. A self-addressed, stamped envelope is much appreciated if you would like a reply.

Linda Francis Lee

__BLUE WALTZ 0-515-11791-9/$5.99

They say the Widow Braxton wears the gowns of a century past...she
invites servants to parties...they say she is mad. Stephen St. James
has heard rumors about his new neighbor. However, she is no
wizened old woman—but an exquisite young beauty. But before he
can make her his own, he must free the secret that binds her heart...

__EMERALD RAIN 0-515-11979-2/$5.99

*"Written with rare power and compassion...a deeply compel-
ling story of love, pain, and forgiveness."*—Mary Jo Putney

Ellie and Nicholas were on opposite sides of the battle that threatened
to rob Ellie of her home. However, all that mattered was the powerful
attraction that drew them together. But selling the property would un-
earth a family scandal of twenty years past...and threatens to tear the
young lovers apart.

__CRIMSON LACE 0-515-12187-8/$5.99

High society in New York, 1896—the story of a disgraced woman returning home and discovering a renewed hope for love...